Mary Nickson has three children and having lived in Yorkshire for many years, she now lives in Perthshire, Scotland. She is also the author of *The Venetian House* and her website address is www.marynickson.co.uk

Also by

FICTION
(Writing as Mary Nickson)
The Venetian House

(Writing as Mary Sheepshanks)
A Price for Everything
Facing the Music
Picking up the Pieces
Off-Balance

NON FICTION
The Bird of My Loving – a personal response
to loss and grief

POETRY
Patterns in the Dark
Thinning Grapes
Kingfisher Days
Dancing Blues to Skylarks

Secrets and Shadows

Mary Nickson

arrow books

Published by Arrow Books 2008

2 4 6 8 10 9 7 5 3 1

First published in Great Britain in 2006 by
Century
Random House, 20 Vauxhall Bridge Road,
London SW1V 2SA

www.rbooks.co.uk

Addresses for companies within The Random House Group Limited can be found at:
www.randomhouse.co.uk/offices.htm

The Random House Group Limited Reg. No. 954009

A CIP catalogue record for this book
is available from the British Library

ISBN 9780099466338

The Random House Group Limited supports The Forest Stewardship
Council (FSC), the leading international forest certification organisation. All our
titles that are printed on Greenpeace approved FSC certified paper carry the FSC logo.
Our paper procurement policy can be found at
www.rbooks.co.uk/environment

Typeset by SX Composing DTP, Rayleigh, Essex
Printed and bound in Great Britain by
CPI Bookmarque Ltd, Croydon, CR0 4TD

To my grandchildren:
Arabella, James and Geordie,
Hermione, William and Freddie,
Octavia and Charles
with great love and gratitude for their friendship
and shared laughter

Acknowledgements

My thanks go to all those who have generously helped me with information and encouragement during the writing of this book, especially Steve Blaylock, Belinda Cox, Hilary Johnson, Nicolas and Diana McAndrew, David Nickson, David and Squibbs Noble, Marshall Roscoe, Alice Sheepshanks, Susannah Tamworth and Stephen Wade.

Special appreciation to my agents Sara Fisher and Sarah Molloy and my editors Kate Elton and Georgina Hawtrey-Woore. Thank you for having faith in me.

Part One

Luciana

Chapter One

If she lay with her eyes half-closed, Luciana discovered she became invisible – invisible that is to all except the child. She was uncomfortably aware that the child not only observed her, but was in no way fooled by her. But she doesn't know I'm in disguise, thought Luciana. None of them know that.

Carlos would have known, and she sent him a venomous message. You should not have left me, she told him. It was always understood that you would look after me. Always. You have reneged on our agreement, and I do not even know where you are.

There were new arrivals at the hotel. The small plane that flew them from the larger island had arrived earlier, sliding along the strip of tarmac that served St Matt's for a runway, as casually as a duck skids along the surface of water, though pilots had to be careful there were no goats lying on the airstrip. The drive up to the Old Sugar Plantation took ages because the road was rough in places, the better stretches suddenly coming to such an abrupt end that speeding was foolhardy, but anyway the taxi drivers who plied their trade between the airport and the island's hotels usually drove their battered cars with the animation of a funeral cortège. Urgency was not a state of mind with which the population of St Matt's was familiar.

The Old Sugar Plantation sprawled on the side of the densely wooded volcano, which was really all the island consisted of, so that from the air it looked like a green pimple on the face of the Caribbean ocean. Stella and Mike Burrows had bought the place in a seedy condition, but were in the process of turning it into one of smartest small hotels in the West Indies . . . or rather Stella was. Since she had more than enough drive for two, Mike saw no reason to exert himself. He came in for enough criticism from his wife whatever he did, so it suited him better to be berated for indolence than to be yelled at for making mistakes.

Luciana could hear Stella doing her welcoming routine now. Stella's voice was sweet and sour like a Chinese meal – especially when she caught Mike having one of his little siestas. She liked to insist that she treated all her guests as if they were personal friends, though she was more successful at doing this with the titled or famous than with those who she did not consider added to the tone of the place.

'Come and have a lovely refreshing drink. I'm sure you both need it. Your first drinks are on the house,' cooed Stella, leaving no doubt that the next ones would be on the bill, and through the nose as well.

Luciana watched through half-closed eyes. She could tell from the sugar content of Stella's voice that the new arrivals were highly prized, as she herself had once been, though she knew that she had become a sad disappointment, insisting on dining at a table for one and resisting all efforts to draw her into a group. Still, she supposed Stella prized her name on the guest list.

'Patsy and Colin will be thrilled to see you – such a sweet couple, we're loving having them here,' said Stella to the new arrivals.

This was a lie. Luciana had heard Sir Colin Fowler, the young, prosperous but already slightly fleshy-looking husband in question, complaining about everything it was possible to complain about, and a good deal more besides.

4

Luciana imagined that his charm factor was not as enlivening as the weight of his wallet: his pretty, pouting American wife looked bored out of her mind for much of the time, and they had committed the ultimate tiresomeness in Stella's eyes – they had brought a child with them. Luciana guessed Stella had no more liking for children than she had herself. *Not suitable for the very young or the infirm*, the hotel brochure stated firmly, on no very obvious grounds as regards the safety of the terrain, but certainly reflecting the owners' preference.

Accommodation for guests was in wooden bungalows scattered about the luscious gardens, and painted in primary colours to resemble the shacks of the local villages. The resemblance ended with the colour. In the villages whole families lived in one room, but at the hotel each bungalow contained a luxury bathroom and double bedroom where the decor smacked more of Sloane Square than the Lesser Antilles. It was all very tasteful, and every day fresh flowers were put on the glass and wicker dressing tables: a sprig from one of the brilliant bougainvillaeas that rioted everywhere, a spray of plumbago, perhaps, or a single, floating hibiscus flower. Mattie and Hazel who cleaned the rooms made beautiful confections with a joyful disregard for colour scheme.

'I expect you'd like to see your rooms,' said Stella. 'We've put you near Colin and Patsy. They've gone down to the beach in our courtesy minibus but they'll be back soon . . . Mike, have you asked Sam to collect John and Delia's luggage?' Stella was a great one for instant Christian names. *The delightful relaxed atmosphere of a private house-party* read another quote from the brochure, which Stella had written herself. Mike was on to his second frozen daiquiri, and his eyes had settled on Delia's thrusting bosom.

'Mike? The luggage . . . dearest,' Stella jogged him.

Luciana let the heat sink into her bones as she lay on a sun-bed by the pool. When Stella and the new arrivals had gone, she flopped into the blue water and swam slowly up and down, watched only by the child, whose gaze was as inscrutable and unblinking as a lizard's. What am I doing here, thought Luciana, among these people who mean nothing to me. Oh, Carlos! Where are you? Come back to me!

Chocky, chocky, chocky, sang a pearly-eyed thrasher from the frangipani tree. *Chocky, chocky.* Later there would be a different species of thrasher clustered round the bar, whose eyes would not be pearly, but glazed by rum punch.

Soon guests who had been away for the day started to drift back. There was much loud laughter and kissing as the Fowlers returned and greeted their friends.

'*Darling!* Heaven to get here! What a blissful place!'

'Honey, it's just so good to see you both! Thank goodness you've arrived! We've been just pining to see you. Most of the other folk here are real boring and geriatric. There's a crazy old Italian contessa – who's rumoured to be fabulously rich but is just so disagreeable it's not true – and some naff types from England – no kindred spirits at all.' Their loud confident voices showed a complete disregard for anyone else's presence.

'Where is Marnie-Jane?' asked Delia. 'We heard you'd had to bring her?'

Patsy pulled a face. 'Would you credit it? We'd planned for her to be in the States with her father but he's on his second honeymoon so he ratted on the arrangement. Luckily with so many staff about we don't have to bother about her too much.'

Luciana and the child were both listening, but both were invisible; Luciana because of her closed eyes, and the child because she was hidden under a bush. Humming-birds darted to and fro, black for a moment and then brilliantly green as they caught the light. A donkey rivalled the braying round the pool. *Chocky, chocky*, sang the thrasher, and the trade wind set the palm trees clattering and rustling. It was very hot. Presently both Luciana and the child slipped away – but no one noticed either of them go.

They were in fact headed in the same direction, though the child, Marnie, followed her own mysterious route, slipping from bush to bush and avoiding the main paths. They both went down below the tennis courts, through the fruit plantation, where mango, papaya and soursup trees were carefully cultivated to give guests the illusion that the hotel provided all the delicious breakfast fruit, though in fact much of it was imported from markets in Florida. Wonderful ice-cream, made from the huge, prickly soursup fruits – sometimes weighing as much as six pounds each – was one of the specialities of the hotel. At the bottom of the plantation, glamour stopped abruptly. A ramshackle gate made of sticks and bits of old wire led to rubbish heaps and piggeries, both of which smelt terrible. Luciana was making for the rough path that led down to the sea, though it was a long walk and most people went to the beach by car or by the free minibus, which the hotel provided every half hour. Marnie had a meeting with Kenneth, the pig-man. He could carry a bucket of swill on his head and never spill a drop, and he had other talents too, which she was learning from him.

Cattle egrets tiptoed among the rotting rubbish, their freshly laundered surplices faintly sinister against the filth, like well-to-do priests in a slum area. The volcano was shrouded in cloud: it would probably rain later.

Luciana walked along the dusty track until she came to the viewpoint above the beach. She stood on a rocky outcrop and looked down. Far out beyond the reef the ocean was navy blue and great rollers frothed and plumed, white against the sky. Where smaller waves broke along the reef, vivid colours, from emerald and turquoise to orange, flashed a contrast to the patches of black shadow, as if a rainbow had been smashed to pieces on the coral. It made perfect camouflage for the huge, colourful parrotfish, which nosed secretly among the pools. You had to watch for a long time before you could pick them out, but most people didn't bother to look, programmed only, Luciana considered, to move between the bar and the stretch of beach where the hotel had its private umbrellas and deck chairs.

But I am alone, she thought, and it doesn't make any difference whether I am here by myself, or surrounded by people. I am always alone now.

Pelicans were diving for their evening meal, the waddling ungainliness of their on-shore deportment transformed to extraordinary speed and grace as they hit the water with the accuracy of guided missiles, angling their hinged wings to steer them exactly to the fish of their choice. Goats bleating in the distance and the occasional crowing of a cock were the only noises to be heard above the hiss of the sea, but memories rang angry bells in Luciana's head. She gazed down, feeling her hair blowing in the wind. All her life, her beauty had been so much a part of her that she had always taken its effect for granted – and it had certainly always had an effect. It was like having royal blood – it made a difference to the way people treated you. She had never felt the anxiety to please that is the lot of plainer women. Even in her present, strange disguise she did not doubt the echo of her beauty's potency. The invisibility conferred by old age would have amused her if she could have shared the joke with Carlos, and a spurt of anger at his defection left her feeling weak and breathless so that it seemed as if the sun no longer warmed her but consumed her. She turned away from the sea and started to walk painfully back along the track, each step an effort.

She saw Marnie in the clearing near the pigpen, and this time it was Luciana who observed.

The child was absorbed in some strange ritual, circling round a pile of stones – stamping, dipping and swaying as though taking part in a ceremonial dance. With her was Kenneth, the pig-man. We have something in common, thought Luciana: we are all three outcasts – I, because the only person I care about has abandoned me; Marnie, because the people who should care about her don't, and Kenneth because he is a freak.

Presently the child ceased her rhythmic movement and saw Luciana. She stopped and stared at her, like a wild animal scenting the air for hostility; weighing up potential danger. Then, slowly, she came over to her.

'I shouldn't go talk to my mom today if I was you,' she said conversationally. It was the first time they had addressed each other.

'I wasn't going to,' said Luciana.

'She's in a grump today,' said the child. 'Oh, brother! Is she in a grump!' And she rolled her eyes, as one well used to the unaccountable grumpiness of grown-ups, but none the less affected by it. They fell into step together.

'You don't like my mom, do you?' asked the child.

'I hardly know her,' said Luciana indifferently, 'so I have no reason to dislike her.'

'But all the same I figure you don't like her,' said the child. 'I can tell by the way you screw your eyes up when you see her coming. Like this,' and she lowered her own lids, leaving a slit open so that she could continue walking without tripping up. 'You don't like her, do you?' she persisted.

'Not much,' said Luciana, not given to sparing the feelings of others, but amused and intrigued in spite of herself.

'Nor I don't like her either. Sometimes I think I hate her. I used to love her but I don't love her any more. Do you hate a lot of people?'

Luciana considered. 'Not many,' she said, discovering something surprising. 'I used to be a great hater, but I can't be bothered now. It's too tiring.'

Marnie threw her a pitying look. 'I like hating. It makes me feel hot inside, like eating chillies. It's feeling kinda hollow that scares me. When I feel hollow I'm feared I might disappear and no one would know. Kenneth knows a lot about hating. You should ask him if you've lost the knack.'

They walked through the orchard, leaving the rubbish tip to the sanctimonious egrets. Tiny quail doves skittered along in front of them. The skinny child with her pale face and straight hair bore no resemblance to her blonde curvaceous mother and Luciana was irritated to feel a certain comradeship with her. I must not get involved, she thought. She only wished to nurse her own grievance and pick around its scab, so that it had no chance to heal. She certainly didn't want to bother with anyone else's emotions, let alone this rather waifish child's.

Nevertheless, as they came back into the garden and met Mattie and Hazel who'd been putting fresh towels in the bungalows, she felt an unwelcome sympathy for Marnie when Mattie said: 'Oh, Mar-nie-Jane! Your ma been yellin' for you. She sure is mad at you! You better come 'long now else she give you big trouble!'

Mattie and Hazel loved Marnie, but they also loved drama, and they swept her off with them, moving as gracefully as a pair of gazelles. The people of St Matt's were mostly tall and elegant; even Kenneth, balancing his pig pails, became beautiful when he walked – provided of course that you couldn't see his face.

Luciana returned to her bungalow. This was the hour

for most of the hotel's female guests to settle down to serious efforts at beautifying themselves before the evening's socialising began, so there were few people about. Soon a terrible screaming could be heard. Sir Colin and Lady Fowler, the 'sweet couple' so prized by Stella, occupied the nearest bungalow to Luciana's and it was not the first time she had heard the piercing wails of the child, though whether they were due to rage or misery, fear or simply temper, as her mother claimed, she had no way of knowing. Her own pain seemed more interesting. Other guests had complained of the screaming, but Stella, who was not going to risk upsetting a baronet, had only enquired with false solicitude if Marnie was unwell and needed medical attention.

'She's just playing up,' pretty Patsy had shrugged. 'I don't intend to have my vacation wrecked because we've had to bring her along with us. She's a spoilt brat who's been indulged by her father. I'll go sort her out right now.'

Luciana lay on her bed. She opened a book but decided to enjoy a session of self-pity instead.

When it was time to go over to the main building for dinner she walked slowly along the path that wound through the garden towards the big house. The paths, which were all made of raised flat stepping-stones to keep the elegantly shod feet of guests dry when heavy rain came down, were lit at intervals by low-standing fluorescent lamps, which attracted toads by the score. Every evening, as soon as dusk fell and the lights were switched on, the toads appeared as if by magic, shambling purposefully towards the lamp of their choice – like elderly gentlemen crossing St James's Street for dinner at their club, Luciana thought. Later they could be seen squatting motionless, waiting to be served with a succulent fly – no doubt as enjoyable to them as a glass of vintage port.

The wailing had ceased, but as Luciana passed the neighbouring bungalow she could hear muffled sobbing, as though the child was weeping under the bedclothes, and this stifled sound was infinitely more distressing than the louder screams had been.

All was darkness. Luciana contemplated going to investigate the cause of such despair. After hesitating for a moment she tried the handle of the door, but it was locked. When she rattled it, she thought she heard a gasp from inside and the sobbing stopped abruptly to be followed by a complete, unnatural silence as though someone were holding their breath. 'Marnie?' called Luciana softly. 'Marnie, are you in there?' There was no reply.

Luciana gave herself a bracing little mental shake and thought better of her impulse to investigate. She was not used to having her heart rent – only broken – and as she turned away she found the sensation as persistent and uncomfortable as indigestion. She walked firmly on towards the main building; towards cocktails and glitter and a four-course dinner, though the echo of the child's misery remained in her head in the most disconcerting fashion. She found herself stopping and straining her ears to listen long after it would have been possible to hear any but the loudest sound.

Old memories stirred in Luciana of a child long ago who had also been terrified of the dark, but she thrust such intrusions aside, and, like the toads, headed resolutely for bright lights and the enticement of food.

Chapter Two

During the day, at the Old Sugar Plantation, a bar operated by the pool, serving delicious light snacks and salads as well as drinks, but in the evenings exotic cocktails were served in the Great Room, which Stella had furnished with beautiful antique colonial furniture. On the walls there was an impressive display of buy-your-own-ancestor type portraits in heavy gilt frames, their expressionless faces disfigured by cracked varnish. If anyone exclaimed on a likeness to herself or Mike, Stella felt she had arrived. She fluttered from guest to guest in a vivid blue silk jumpsuit, her dark hair tossing about her shoulders. There were those who wondered if Stella's ancestry was a little more mixed than the bogus Anglo-Saxon family portraits suggested; she had her hair expensively straightened and took care to let it be known that she'd been educated at an exclusive English school. There was talk of well-heeled relations who had lived for generations in Gloucestershire but also of a raven-haired beauty of a Portuguese grandmother – which explained her own dramatic dark colouring.

Sometimes there would be live entertainment before or after dinner: a calypso singer, a steel band, or the brilliantly energetic carnival dancers, parading in their grotesque masks as animals and birds, jesters or demons; giving displays of stilt-walking in the traditional clown-like role of 'Moko Jumbie', or limbo-dancing to the accompaniment of drums. The strange-looking Kenneth

– who belonged to the troupe once he had finished his daytime job – would be suitably smeared with dirt and sticky molasses and become completely unrecognisable in the role of the mischievous demon Jab-Jab, with horned mask and twisted, coiled wire tail. He was a brilliantly acrobatic dancer, but Stella had recently banned him from performing at the hotel because some guests found his explicit, sexual interpretation of the 'Jab Molassi' extremely disturbing and the malicious twirling of his metal tail was genuinely dangerous. This ruling of Stella's supplied an added grudge – along with many others – for Kenneth to nurture against the hotel proprietors, who gave him such vital employment by day.

Luciana had seen the dancers running through the hotel grounds after a performance, peering in at the windows of some of the bungalows. Coming across them unexpectedly in the dark had been like meeting the nightmare cast out of one of the cruel fantasies of Hieronymus Bosch – a painting come to life.

There were already several people at the bar when Luciana arrived. Stella was talking to a couple from Purley; 'Not quite our sort – a bit suburban, but kind and genuine if you take a little trouble with them,' Stella had explained to the new arrivals a few hours before, lest it be thought that the couple from Purley really were personal friends of hers, though Mike found the Purley husband, 'Call-me-Reg', very congenial and extremely free with his cash when it came to standing his host drinks. His wife had just returned from an excursion to another island where she had found a shop full of genuine batik hangings and was generous with information – to anyone rash enough to listen – about the process of printing batik. Tonight she had decided to waylay Luciana.

'Poor old thing, she must be lonely,' she had said to Reg, as she dressed in the cotton-jersey caftan she had bought from a mail order catalogue. 'Let's try to jolly her up a bit and ask her to sit with us tonight.'

Luciana, who had no taste for being jollied up, walked straight past when the invitation was issued, and had the satisfaction of hearing the Purley woman say: 'Perhaps she's deaf? Now that would explain a lot about her! I had meant to show her my purchases, but I think I'll leave it. We don't want to have to shout at her all through dinner, do we?'

Luciana settled herself on the sofa at the far end of the room with the book of crossword puzzles she liked to do during meals, which Stella considered to be the height of bad manners. She had tried to hint – tactfully of course – that she didn't encourage guests to bring books into the dining room but Luciana at her most autocratic had informed her that she didn't require encouragement or need permission. If she wanted to do the crossword during dinner, then that was what she intended to do. Sam hurried over to her with her usual drink. It was a mystery to Stella why all the staff cherished Luciana in a special way – it certainly wasn't because she threw her money about, thought Stella crossly.

Soon the new arrivals and the sweet couple came in and took the bar over, so that everyone else felt out of place, their clothes not right, their accents wrong – gatecrashers, the lot of them – except the lady-from-Purley who stood her ground. She could tell you a thing or two about the so-called upper classes, and not very creditable things at that! Oh yes. Back at home, she was an avid reader of the glossy magazines about stage and society celebrities. She pinned Stella against the wall and instructed her about the right temperature for wax before the first application on a multi-coloured batik design. Mike and Reg, into their third round of drinks, were happily oblivious of the little drama being played out in front of them, but Luciana watched with malicious pleasure.

Sir Colin had chosen this rather public moment to celebrate a private occasion: the first anniversary of his wedding to Patsy. He clasped a diamond pendant round her pretty neck. The stones were very large and sparkled and flashed arrestingly against Patsy's newly acquired suntan. Stella gave her a nervous look; she had no reason to mistrust any of her staff, but St Matt's was a poor island and she always put up a notice asking guests to leave any valuables in the office safe.

The gatecrashers were all immediately 'in' again: Patsy required audience participation. She ran from group to group with artless little cries of pleasure, occasionally covering the glittering bauble with her hand, so that its impact would strike afresh when she exposed it again. She even undulated over to Luciana, but Luciana heard Marnie's cries ringing in her ears and would not be beguiled.

Colin was the sweetest husband she'd ever had – Patsy it seemed spoke from experience; he was a dear, dear, darling man, and she just adored him. All the other guests were caught up in her rosy glow; everyone ordered extra bottles of wine for dinner when they moved out to the candle-lit tables on the terrace, and there was much festive raising of glasses to Colin and Patsy.

Rain came in the night, beating on the roofs of the bungalows with a fury that could have launched the Ark. There were flashes of lightning and shattering cracks of thunder overhead. Patsy clutched Colin in well-simulated terror with highly satisfactory results. Neither of them gave a thought to Marnie, lying rigid next door, the dread of her mother's anger if she called out being even greater than her fear of the thunder. Curiously enough, Luciana, who had never been afraid of any kind of storm, did think of her – but she thrust the thought aside.

The couple from Purley never heard a thing; Reg because rum had left him insensible, and his wife because she was using earplugs as a defence against her husband's snoring.

Next day the mist had lifted from the volcano, and though there were dark clouds out to sea, overhead the sky was miraculously blue again. Stella announced that the weekly beach barbecue could go ahead as usual. Anyone not wanting to go should notify the staff in the office. In the hotel kitchen, there was much packing up of insulated picnic boxes containing chicken legs and steak, and a strong whiff of kerosene, used for lighting the barbecues, mingled with smells of rum and coconut milk and fruit for planter's punches. It took time to get everyone into the minibuses, the effort of remembering sun-cream, hats and cameras being more than most hotel guests could manage without several false starts.

'I wonder,' said Stella, approaching Luciana with her sweetest smile, 'if you would be an absolute angel?' Not receiving any encouragement, she continued undaunted: 'It's just that as I gather you're not going down to the beach today, Patsy and Colin would be so grateful if you could keep an eye on their little girl so that they can have a bit of time to themselves? Patsy thinks Marnie-Jane's a weeny bit off-colour today and it could be too hot for her by the sea. I thought you might be glad of the company,' lied Stella, 'but please say if it would be a bore.'

'I never let anyone become a bore to me,' said Luciana – but she surprised herself and Stella by adding, 'Marnie-Jane can come and eat her lunch with me if she likes.'

She settled herself in a shady spot, revelling in the departure of the rest of the guests, and opened her book, though thoughts of vengeance for the wrong Carlos had done her proved more absorbing. She watched Marnie going off for her rendezvous with Kenneth. It was an odd alliance, she thought, but there was no doubt that a bond had formed between the American child and the West Indian man with his ashen curls and misshapen face, whose albino condition had robbed his skin of its natural colour so that he looked as though he had emerged, after long darkness, from under a stone.

Marnie did not appear till lunchtime, when she arrived in the bar and clambered up on to a high stool next to Luciana.

'I've come to keep you company,' she announced. 'Can I have a Coke?'

'You can have anything you like as far as I'm concerned.' answered Luciana with a slight shrug.

'Then can I have a virgin pina colada *and* a Coke?'

Luciana ordered them, plus Campari for herself, making it clear that the child's drinks were to be put on her parents' bill.

'Didn't you wanna go down to the beach?' asked Marnie.

'No,' said Luciana. 'I like to feel I have this place all to myself.'

'Except for me?'

'Except for you.'

'But I'd have liked to go,' said Marnie wistfully. 'I wanted to make a huge sandcastle – a palace – and dress it with shells. I wanted to see the pelicans and I wanted to lie on my stomach and watch the hermit crabs digging and scuttling. I wish I could dig a little hole, real quick, like they can, fold myself into it and disappear so nobody could find me. I planned to try my new flippers in the sea. Flippers aren't the same in the pool, you know, but my mom said she thought I might throw up, and oh brother, does she get mad if I throw up!'

'And are you going to throw up?' asked Luciana, watching Marnie take alternate swigs of Coke and pina colada through a straw.

'Nope,' said the child with conviction. 'Drinks don't make me throw up. It's people make me sick, but my mom says I get the pain in my stomach on purpose to annoy her. She says I sure as daybreak do get up her nose when I'm sickly. Do you think people can make you sickly?'

'Oh yes, I most certainly do,' said Luciana. 'I think people can make one very ill indeed.'

'Could . . . could someone make you sick even if they weren't there?'

'People who aren't there make one more ill than anything,' said Luciana, but she wasn't really addressing the child.

'My daddy isn't here and that's what makes me sick.' Marnie sucked first at her sticky mixture of pineapple and coconut and then made her Coke go satisfyingly bubbly by blowing into the glass down her straw. 'I never had a pain when I was with my dad, but now he's gotten a new wife and Mom says he won't want me hanging out at his place and getting in the way any more.'

They sat side by side in a curiously companionable silence, until Sam suggested that they might order their lunch.

'Tell me about when you were little,' said Marnie and Luciana did, transporting them both to a different reality. To the child it was like opening a window on to a strange new country, but to Luciana it was like looking down the wrong end of a telescope, and what she perceived was very clear but a long way off – in fact the further into the distance she looked, the more vivid the details became.

It was a surprise to them both to find that the staff were clearing away round them and to realise that lunch was long over and everyone else had drifted away. Neither of them had the faintest idea what they'd eaten.

'Do you think,' asked Marnie as they got up to go, 'do you think you could make someone sick on purpose? D'you think you could make someone *die*?'

'Oh, I should think so,' said Luciana, who was not one to think of the possible consequences of her words.

They separated then by unspoken consent to go their different ways, and neither was aware of the effect they'd had upon the other.

The next day at lunchtime, Marnie arrived beside Luciana again, and Luciana found herself unexpectedly pleased. Over the following days it became something of a habit – one that suited everyone concerned – and on the few occasions when the child did not appear, Luciana was conscious of a twinge of disappointment.

On the days when Luciana decided to go down to the beach Sam, or one of his staff, would always hurry to bring her a drink – a coconut cooler, perhaps, or a frozen daiquiri – and would move a sun-bed and beach-umbrella to some place of her choice, as far away from all the other guests as possible. Marnie would be drawn to her side as though by a magnet. Sometimes they would talk, sometimes they wouldn't – it didn't seem to matter. Sometimes Marnie would consult her about the design for her latest sandcastle. The old lady seemed to know a great deal about castles and had some interesting ideas about their design and construction. Sometimes they would walk barefoot down the beach together, deep in conversation, sloshing along on the edge of the turquoise ocean, while the waves sneezed gently over the hard, shell-pink sand.

It was not until just before dinner one evening that the trouble started. The wailing of the child would no longer have attracted much interest, but on this particular evening it was the hysterical shrieking of her mother that riveted the attention of those in nearby bungalows, and soon anyone in the vicinity of the office could hear the raised voice of Sir Colin and the saccharine tones of Stella in a rising crescendo of contrapuntal agitation. The lady-from-Purley, rightly sensing drama and wishing to investigate as soon as possible, applied her evening make-up too hurriedly, leaving little streaks of unblended honey-bronze foundation on her face, which gave her a surprisingly tigerish appearance.

By the time most people had assembled for drinks, news of misfortune had spread, with varying degrees of accuracy. The usual sunny smiles of the staff were missing, and their faces wore the shuttered look of empty houses. They did not meet each other's eyes, let alone those of the guests, and an uncomfortable feeling of mistrust made the preprandial chatter curiously forced and staccato. Only Luciana, arriving at her normal time and making for her usual seat, seemed oblivious of the atmosphere.

Stella skimmed over to her and perched on the arm of the sofa. 'I was wondering if I could have a little word with you?' she asked. Luciana said nothing. Stella went on bravely: 'I expect you've heard about our dilemma? We're sure it can only have been mislaid and will turn up any moment – but poor Patsy has lost that lovely pendant Colin gave her for their wedding anniversary. Of course we've pointed out how foolish it was of her not to have put it in the safe, but you know how easy it is to lose things in one's room. Naturally she's frightfully upset – it's obviously of great sentimental value.'

If Luciana thought that it would not be all that easy to lose such a socking great jewel in a comparatively small room, she did not say so.

'The thing is,' said Stella, 'that I wondered if you might be able to help us?'

'In what way?'

'Well,' Stella traced a pattern on the back of the sofa with a scarlet tipped finger, 'well, it's just that you were here all day yesterday while everyone else was on the beach . . . so we, that is Mike and I, just wondered if you might have noticed anything?'

'Like a large diamond pendant, just lying about?'

Stella laughed mirthlessly.

'Well, not the pendant exactly, but anything *unusual*. Your bungalow being next door to Colin and Patsy's, that is . . .' Her voice frayed into uncertainty.

'I didn't go next door and steal it, if that's what you're suggesting,' said Luciana, consciously enjoying herself. Stella's laugh chinked like ice-cubes in a well-chilled glass.

'Oh, you're so naughty! Of course that's not what I meant! But I'm afraid it's no joking matter. We are going to have to call in the police if it isn't found, and you know what unpleasantness that can cause.'

Luciana privately thought that the sight of any of the hotel guests being put through intensive questioning by the St Matt's police would be a delightful spectacle, and one she would not miss for anything.

'Anyway,' said Stella, flitting off her perch, 'if you remember seeing anything – or anyone – out of the ordinary I know you'll pop and find me.' It was clear that Luciana, as usual, was not prepared to be accommodating, and Stella was torn between her wish to placate the sweet couple and fear of the terrible effect that suspicion would have on her staff, not to mention the reputation of the hotel.

Had Mary, Queen of Scots, straight from the original illustration in *Our Island Story*, suddenly materialised in such an unlikely setting, she could not have made a more affecting entrance than Patsy, wearing a simple black dress, unadorned by jewellery, her face bearing traces of tears which had luckily left no unbecoming redness round the eyes. Delia, who clearly felt that her friend's loss entitled her to an also-starring role in the drama was supporting her. A pall of tragedy hung over the candle-lit tables. The lady-from-Purley loved it all. Hadn't she said only the other night that no good would come of such blatant display? She thought that the hand-carved wooden bangles that clattered up and down her own freckled arms were far more suitable and she kept up a cheery flow of chat to Reg – which was quite a feat, as they had long ago exhausted all topics of mutual interest.

There was no sign of the missing jewel next day. The grounds had been searched exhaustively and Colin and Patsy's bungalow turned upside down and inside out. The staff had been questioned into a state of sullen silence. Enquiries amongst other hotels on the island, which Stella hoped might have brought similar occurrences to light – thus pointing to an outside job – had proved fruitless. The hotel guests suspected the staff, and the staff suspected the hotel guests. Luciana wondered about the members of the dancing troupe.

The only people who derived any enjoyment from the situation were Luciana and the local police force. The lady-from-Purley had found the latter's questioning most offensive. She had never experienced anything so humiliating in her life, and when the news got round that everyone's passports were being held, her indignation knew no bounds. Reg would have a word to say to their travel agent, not to mention writing to their MP, when they eventually got home.

Marnie spent more and more of her time at the piggeries, all the grown-ups except Luciana being too preoccupied to pay her any attention. Certainly her mother had no moment to spare for her.

Patsy was in a quandary. She had discovered that the diamond heart was insured for well above its considerable value, and she was wondering just how soon it could be replaced. Visions of an even more spectacular bauble floated before her like a juicy morsel in front of a hungry shark. Something with emeralds might be nice? Her dilemma also lay in judging the speed with which she could decently be seen to enjoy herself again after her display of sensibility. Ignoring the fact that her fellow guests were still under suspicion, she announced to Delia that she had decided not to spoil everyone's holiday, and would put the affair behind her.

Walking through the orchard to her favourite viewing point, before the sun set and darkness fell, Luciana caught a glimpse of Marnie dancing round the pile of stones again, while Kenneth squatted on his haunches, watching intently. The seed of a suspicion, not connected with her own problems, began to irritate Luciana's mind.

She went as usual to stand on the edge of the cliff and swayed a little as she stood there. The drop was very sheer, and the rocks below conveyed a dark invitation.

Returning to her room she was aware that she was being followed. She sat down at the dressing table to brush the long hair – Titian hair Carlos had called it – that had once been his pride and delight. She was so used to confronting a beautiful reflection in the mirror that she seldom noticed how that reflection had altered, but today she suddenly noticed another face beside her own, a small white face, not beautiful at all, staring back at her. It was the first time the child had actually entered her room.

'Can I stay while you get ready for dinner?' asked Marnie. 'Will you tell me some more stories? Tell me about your great big dog, and how your pony raced the wind and the house like a castle on the island. Tell about the round holes in the walls for the muskets to poke through and the openings for pouring boiling oil on the enemy. Tell about when you and your brother tipped your bathwater down the hole and your mom had people to dinner who got drenched in all their finery.'

Next evening, at the same time, the child appeared again, and Luciana was aware that she had been waiting for her arrival, and would have been disappointed had she not come. This evening visit became a ritual.

'What is that great black book?' asked Marnie. 'Has it got pictures?'

'No pictures, I'm afraid.'

'Is it only stories then?'

'Not stories no. It's entirely full of words.'

'What's the point of words if they're not made into stories?'

'Well, you can't have stories without words and this magic book tells you what every word in the language means. Can you read?' The child nodded. 'Look then, and I'll show you how to use it.'

They had taken it in turns to look up words for each other and guess their meaning. Marnie was entranced. When the light began to fade Luciana told her to take the book inside.

'Put it on the table by my bed and close it carefully, please. You should always treat books with respect because they'll be among the most important friends you have in life. I never like books being left open.'

'In case the words might get out?' asked the child, round-eyed.

'Certainly,' said Luciana, very much liking the idea. 'Imagine if you wanted to find the meaning of an important word, but when you came to look in the dictionary there were only blank pages inside because they'd escaped.'

They sat together on the veranda outside Luciana's

bungalow and watched the darkness enclose them, not creeping up as it did in England as though playing at grandmother's footsteps, but arriving with the suddenness of an unexpected visitor.

'Tell me about your house *again*,' said Marnie, moving her chair to be closer to Luciana. 'The house with the tall, tall tower like in the fairy tale and the tiny door on to the secret stone stairs where you hid from your nurse. Tell about sliding down the roof on to the battlements with your brother and how your mother fainted clean away when she saw you from down below. Tell about rowing the boat on the loch and catching the fish. Tell about the otter. I wish I could go there.'

'Perhaps one day you will.'

'Would you take me there?'

'Oh, I wish I could do that too,' said Luciana, absent-mindedly stroking the child's straight, mousy hair and tucking it back behind her ears. 'Oh, I wish I could . . . but listen now, because I'm going to tell you about the castle's secret room and how we used to try to find it by hanging handkerchiefs out of all the windows we knew about.'

One night Patsy did not attend dinner.

'The poor love, she's quite worn out with emotion.' Delia told anyone who enquired. 'She's staying in bed.' Reg wouldn't half have minded a glimpse of Patsy lying in bed. He wondered if she wore a nightdress.

Next day news spread fast that Patsy was ill, and Colin's strident tones could be heard demanding a doctor. 'A proper doctor, mind, not some local quack.' Stella's voice dripped solicitude. Inwardly she thought this was all they needed – some nasty virus running through the hotel. Colin made unpleasant suggestions about getting the kitchens inspected, but here Stella felt on safe ground. She had always been fanatical about hygiene, and in any case, it did not appear that Patsy's stomach was particularly affected. Pressed to describe his wife's symptoms, Colin could not come up with anything specific; Stella, going to visit the patient, did not expect to find much wrong, but what she did find filled her with foreboding. Patsy was clearly extremely unwell.

Stella telephoned the American doctor on the main island, not because she thought he was a better physician than young Dr Gladstone Henry, the highly qualified West Indian who had returned to give his native island the benefit of what he had learned in London, but because she guessed that the elderly Dr O'Connor would be more acceptable to Colin. She knew the doctor to be a drunken old soak, but he had an excellent bedside manner. Assured by Stella that fees were no problem, Dr O'Connor said he would get a pilot to fly him over later in the day.

When Marnie came to visit Luciana, she looked pinched, sallow and heavy-eyed. Luciana noticed that no one had made her change her clothes, which were creased and grubby. The skin round her mouth looked rough and sore.

'My mom is very sick,' said the child, twizzling a lock of her hair and then chewing it.

'Yes, I know. I'd heard.'

'The doctor is coming to see her.'

'I'd heard that too.'

'Do you think he will make her well again?'

'I should think that would depend on what's wrong with her, and whether he knows what that is.'

Luciana gave Marnie a penetrating look. The child did not meet her eye, but remained standing by the hammock grubbing a hole in the earth with the toe of her sandal. She shivered as if a cold wind was blowing round her, although it was stiflingly hot.

'Could I get in and lie beside you for a little bit?' she

whispered. Luciana eased over and Marnie manoeuvred herself in. Very soon she was asleep.

Lying with a slumbering child beside her was a novel experience for Luciana. She was surprised how heavy Marnie's head was, resting on her arm, but she did not move despite the discomfort.

The doctor arrived in the early evening. He sat with the patient for some time, and for even longer afterwards at the bar with Colin. He had not achieved a diagnosis, there seemed so little to go on, but he spoke reassuringly of the effects the climate could have on the very fair-skinned, of the patient's obvious sensitivity – and of delayed shock. Patsy must drink plenty of glucose and water but absolutely no alcohol, said Dr O'Connor, gracefully accepting a third daiquiri. He was sorry he would not be able to return the following day as he had to fly to the States for a conference, but he would leave a prescription and a note for the local fellow if they needed to call him in. If Colin liked to settle the bill now? suggested Dr O'Connor. Save everyone paperwork?

The doctor was baffled by Patsy's condition, but he knew a seriously ill patient when he saw one. He also knew how much more difficult it was to get an exorbitantly large bill paid, should the patient not recover. He thought it altogether more desirable to leave the case to Dr Gladstone Henry. He slapped Colin on the shoulder in a fatherly way and left.

The following day there was no sign of anyone else's succumbing to the mystery illness, but Patsy was worse. She seemed to be shrinking like an apple that has been stored too long; she did not speak, or recognise anyone. Stella telephoned Dr Henry, and all trace of honey had left her voice. Even Mike had sobered up.

When the doctor arrived, Luciana waylaid him in the car park. They talked for some time, until Stella rushed out to put a stop to the conversation. She thought it typical of Luciana's selfishness to try to sneak a free consultation without an appointment. Stella knew Luciana to be fabulously wealthy – and to all appearances in perfect health. She had not lived up to Stella's expectations as an asset to the hotel.

Like Dr O'Connor, the young black doctor immediately recognised the seriousness of Patsy's condition. Unlike the older man he had an idea of a possible cause for such a devastating and sudden collapse. It was not something he had learned in medical school in England.

He said he would keep Patsy under close observation. No, he didn't think she should be flown to hospital on the main island. On the contrary, she should on no account be moved. He asked Colin a lot of questions which seemed not only irrelevant, but also impertinent, though there was an authority about Dr Henry which Colin found compelling, if not reassuring. When he suddenly asked to see Marnie-Jane, Colin who had completely forgotten about his little stepdaughter, had to admit that he hadn't the faintest idea where she was.

'You don't think she'll get this bug too, do you?' he asked uneasily, wondering what his own chances of succumbing to it might be.

'I don't think she'll go down with the same complaint as your wife, no,' said Dr Henry. 'Nevertheless, I think you should be extremely careful of that little girl. She may be in some danger.'

He said he had another call to make in the hotel but would like to see Marnie as soon as possible. He emphasised that she needed to be found as a matter of urgency and he wished to be informed as soon as she had been located. Then he asked the way to the Contessa's bungalow.

But Marnie could not be found and no one could

remember when she had last been seen. The staff did not think she had come to breakfast. Stella walked round the grounds calling, 'Marnie? Marnie, dear, are you there?' on a note of rising hysteria. Dr Henry spent a long time with Luciana but had to leave without seeing the child, though he said he would be back later. It was hoped she would turn up when she was hungry – but Marnie, huddled under a bush, seeing and hearing everything, did not want food at all.

A rustle in the undergrowth and the feeling of being watched – that indefinable awareness of a presence – alerted Luciana, as she lay outside her room. When she sensed that the child was very close, she held out her hand and kept very still, as if in the presence of a timid animal. When she felt a small hand slip into hers, she closed her fingers very gently round it, and stroked it with her thumb. Then she reached out, put her arms round the child, and held her close. She could feel the thumping of a heart against her own and she thought it was a long time since she had been heart to heart with anyone.

'Marnie,' said Luciana, after a bit, 'do you really want your mother to die?'

Very slowly the child shook her head. 'I thought I did – but I don't any more. I'm . . . I'm scared.'

'Then,' said Luciana, 'I think it's time you showed me where her diamond pendant is. Shall we go for a walk together?'

'What will they do to me?' asked Marnie, twisting her hair into strands and pulling bits out. Luciana did not think she was referring to her parents or the hotel management.

'They won't do anything to you. For one thing they won't know, and for another, I shan't let them.'

'They . . . he . . . said you have to have something precious belonging to someone to give you the Power. But he . . .' She could not bring herself to say the name. 'What will he do to me?' she asked at last. 'Will he make the Jab Molassi come for me? He said if I ever told anyone . . .' She did not finish the sentence.

'But you have not told anyone,' said Luciana, 'and you don't need to anyway, because you see I know what's happened. Listen, Marnie, there's no spell that can't be broken if you know the way to do it. And I *do* know. I know a lot about magic – much more than Kenneth. Come, you will see . . . but you have to trust me. Can you do that?'

Slowly the child nodded.

Earlier that day Luciana had gone into the little town and withdrawn a large sum of money from the bank in cash. This she now collected from her room.

'I am going as usual to look at the sea,' she said. 'And then we might watch the pigs being fed together. Perhaps you would like to go your usual way and I will go mine, and no one will notice either of us.' They looked at each other in perfect understanding.

When it became known that Luciana had found the diamond heart somewhere in the garden, the general feeling of relief was enormous, though the lady-from-Purley thought the whole thing was extremely fishy. If people expected her to swallow a fairy tale like that, they had picked the wrong woman. She had always thought there was something sinister about Luciana. She had said so to Reg countless times.

Dr Henry found his patient improved in the evening, though apart from terrifying dreams she could not remember the last few days at all. The doctor said she could get up soon.

It was announced that Colin and Patsy had decided to cut their Caribbean holiday short after Luciana had had a long – and from his point of view very unpleasant – talk with Colin. As soon as Patsy was well enough, they intended to fly to the States, drop Marnie with her father, who had agreed to have her back, and then fly on to England.

Marnie paid a final visit to Luciana's bungalow.

'I'm going away,' she said, leaning against Luciana's chair. 'I'm going back to my dad.'

'I shall be going away shortly, too.'

'When will you be going and where will you go to?'

'I don't know exactly when, Marnie, but I think it will be soon, and it won't be anywhere I've ever been before.'

'How do you know that you'll like it, then?'

'I don't know,' said Luciana. 'That is a bit of a worry, but perhaps it will be a great adventure and I've always liked that; perhaps it will be the greatest adventure I've ever had.'

'When will I see you again?'

'I don't know that either,' Luciana stroked the child's face with her finger and pushed her fine, straight hair behind her ear, 'but I have something for you and it's the beginning of a treasure hunt. You could say it's the first clue.' She placed a small package in the child's hand.

'What's a clue?' asked Marnie.

'It's something that helps you to solve a mystery or to find something. A sort of helpful hint if you're on a quest.'

The child looked at the packet and then looked at Luciana. 'Can I open it now?'

'No, not yet. You can open it when you get home to your father. Keep it safe and think of me sometimes. Remember what we've shared together and remember that your visits made me happy when I didn't think I could ever be happy again. Will you do that?'

'I swear,' said Marnie solemnly. 'I will never forget you, not ever. Will you send me a letter? Nobody ever sends me letters.'

'Yes,' said Luciana. 'Yes, that I can promise you. I will write to you for as long as I can and each letter will be like another clue in a treasure hunt.'

When the sweet couple left, Luciana did not go to wave them goodbye as most of the other guests did. She had no taste for watching the departure of the child. She had not thought it possible that she could mind so much.

Dr Gladstone Henry had not only endorsed her opinion about Patsy's illness, he had confirmed some other suspicions that had nothing to do with Marnie or the diamond pendant. The grievance Luciana had been nursing so carefully and the lump which she had recently found in her body were one and the same: the cancer of the spirit had become a cancer of the flesh.

You sent me this, Luciana told Carlos, her husband. You caused it by dying first and leaving me alone. Soon I shall die too, so I will not need to fall over the cliff after all – but you had better be waiting for me when I come, wherever you are.

She looked at her reflection in the glass, and a stranger looked back at her – a stranger with white hair and a wrinkled skin, though inside she felt herself to be the same as she had always been.

Truly, Luciana thought, old age is a terrible disguise. We become unrecognisable even to ourselves.

Part Two

Glendrochatt

Chapter Three

There was always a sense of excitement before a new group arrived for one of the courses that were regularly run at Glendrochatt, the tall house on the hill, which looked out over rolling Scottish landscape to a stunning backdrop of mountains beyond. Surely the view in itself should be an inspiration to aspiring writers, thought Isobel Grant, who lived there and never got tired of marvelling at the beauty of her surroundings. A few years earlier, she and her husband Giles, spurred by financial necessity to do something – anything – to enable them to continue living in his old family home, had turned it into an arts centre and it was now a flourishing concern.

Isobel looked at the names of the expected participants on the list in her hand. Though the format for the courses had been tried, tested and honed over the last five years, it was the unknown factors that created the buzz of anticipation. You never knew what surprises were in store, what hidden talents might be discovered in seemingly unlikely people; what conflicts might arise from throwing a set of strangers – albeit ones with a common purpose – into close proximity in an isolated environment for several days; what unlikely friendships might be formed in a short space of time; what life-changing decisions could result from chance encounters and the opportunity to investigate secret aspirations in a supportive environment.

'What can you tell me about any of this lot?' asked Catherine Hickman, the respected poet and teacher of creative writing, who was to be the main tutor on this particular course.

'Not much really,' said Isobel. 'The usual mixed bunch, I suppose. There's the statutory retired schoolmistress who knows she's got a bestselling children's book in her but wants you to discover what it is – she has a breathless letter-writing style and is lavish with exclamation marks and little line-drawings of old-fashioned children bowling hoops; there's an ex-army officer who barked at me down the telephone and kept talking about "the admin"; there's a chap who says he admires your poetry, which is nice, but he didn't tell us anything about himself. He just scribbled N.A. across the voluntary questionnaire, which I thought was a bit arrogant. He could be a con man or a defrocked priest for all I know – perhaps he thinks he's the twenty-first century's answer to Gerard Manley Hopkins. There's a married couple from Yorkshire who want to share a room and a pair of friends from Cornwall who don't. There's really only one person I know anything about and that's Louisa Forrester who's a connection of mine – our mothers were cousins. We've known her and her family for ever and we used to see a lot of her when she was at university at St Andrew's and often came here for weekends. I haven't seen her for a bit, but she's lovely and I know you'll enjoy having her. Everyone always adores Louisa.'

'Hmm. I'll reserve my judgement, thank you,' said Catherine, laughing. 'I tend to be a bit allergic to people everyone else adores. Anyone else?'

Isobel ran her finger down the list of names. "Giles thinks he might have heard of the last female. I've no idea what age she is, though her voice sounded quite young when I spoke to her. She's called Marnie Donovan. She was a late booking but seemed particularly determined to come. We turned her down originally but offered her a place off the waiting list at the last minute after someone else dropped out – though I was half inclined not to, because when she first rang up to enquire about the course and I said we were full, she seemed to imagine that I ought to conjure up a place for her whether we had room or not. I thought then that she could be trouble. She gave an address in London but had an American accent. Giles has an idea that she's been in the news sometime – but can't remember why, so we don't know much about her either. Anyway, there'll be nine students in all. Sorry not to be more helpful.'

'Not to worry,' said Catherine cheerfully. 'It's probably better not to know too much before they come. We'll certainly have gathered a lot more about them by next weekend and nine's a nice number. Now just run through the timetable with me. What time are you expecting them to arrive?'

'Between five and seven. Some people are coming by car, but Giles is going to Perth to meet a train at six. I thought we could have supper prompt at half past seven and then Giles will introduce you to the group and hand over to you?'

'Fine,' said Catherine. 'We'll have an introductory get-together at about eight forty-five. I always think that first session is interesting but I've learned not to make up my mind about anyone too quickly. So often it's the little mousy person who looks boring who turns out to be a genius and the one who shoots their mouth off and says too much too soon who tends to have a crisis later. People ask me why I go on teaching when I could give it up to concentrate full time on my own writing, but when I tutor a course like this, I know it's the endless fascination of human beings that keeps me at it.'

'Oh, I do agree,' said Isobel. 'We always think the best fun is discussing everybody afterwards. Now I'll leave

you in peace to make your preparations and I'll head off
and check all the rooms are in order. Are you sure you've
got all you want?'

'Yes, indeed; everything's perfect, thank you. It's lovely
to be back. I always look forward to coming to
Glendrochatt. See you later then.'

'See you later,' repeated Isobel and the two women went
their separate ways.

Louisa Forrester felt a lifting of the heart as she turned off
the A1 at Scotch Corner and took the Bowes and Brough
road towards Penrith and thence up the M6 to Carlisle,
enjoying the shapes of the rounded hills above the road
and the green valley below, dotted with small white farms
which looked like toy houses from where she was driving.
Louisa felt full of optimism and initiative. Behind her she
had left the gritty ashes of a dead romance and the end of
an interesting job, both of which had lasted for several
years. It felt good to be heading north and she thought of
Tennyson's words, which her father used to quote to her
when she was a small girl:

> . . . bright and fierce and fickle is the South,
> And dark and true and tender is the North.

Ahead lay . . . who knew what? Certainly a change,
decided Louisa, and she put on a CD of Scottish songs to
endorse her mood and sang along with the music.

Her parents thought she was mad to have abandoned
both the man and the job – particularly the man. She could
understand their point of view and was truly sorry to put
them through such obvious anxiety – they had borne too
much of that in the past. They had been devoted to Adam
Winterton, who was kind and clever and dependable and
not without a sense of humour, a quality Louisa's father

said was vital for anyone who hoped to survive a relationship with his daughter. Adam had fitted into the Forrester family perfectly – too perfectly, thought Louisa. That was the trouble. There were no surprises about him and she had come to feel stifled by his predictability and increasingly irritated when everyone told her how right Adam was for her, how covetable all his excellent qualities were; what a wonderful *husband* he would make – how rash it was of her to make the break. And always she could hear the words 'and think how he stuck by you through everything . . .' even if they had not actually been uttered out loud.

The job had been covetable in many ways too. Her boss, an MP, had a northern constituency, which had enabled her to spend more weekends at home in Yorkshire than she might otherwise have done; it had taken her on trips abroad, and she had met people and done things that would not otherwise have come her way. But the world of party politics had never really enthralled her and recently she had found it increasingly difficult to identify with any particular party, something her employer had found amusing and challenging when she first came to work in his office as a junior secretary, but which, in his PA, he found less acceptable. His ego had inflated as fast as his career had flourished, and, thought Louisa ruefully, lately his sense of the ridiculous seemed to be deflating equally fast. They had parted amicably, not without some regrets, but on the whole with mutual relief. It had been a tidy ending.

The same could not be said of her parting with Adam, who had known her all her life and been deeply in love with her for most of it. He'd been devastated when she had first tried to break off their relationship and still obstinately refused to accept that it was over for good. 'I shall be waiting for you,' he said, and it infuriated her. It occurred to Louisa now that back in London, in the bright south, Adam was really the one who was *true and tender* while she, heading northwards in search of adventure, was *fierce and fickle,* but she thrust such negative thoughts aside. If she thought too much about Adam a lump came into her throat, because right as she felt their break-up to be she did still love him, even if not in what she described to herself as 'the right kind of way'.

'Oh, darling,' her mother had said, 'how can you do this to him? He's never looked at anyone else, not even at the worst times. Not even when . . .' Her voice had faltered and trailed away.

'I know,' Louisa answered. 'I know. But please don't say it, Mum. I can't help it. I need to be free . . . to take risks . . . to spread my wings. I'm restless. Perhaps I've got bored.'

'I should have thought there'd been enough uncertainty in your life already without going wilfully looking for it,' said her mother, quite sharply for her. 'There are worse things in life than being bored. You, of all people, should know that.'

'But it's *because* of that that I have to go and do something different – try out other life styles – experiment – because I couldn't do it at the age when all my friends were being irresponsible and light-hearted and making mistakes.' She had put her arm round her mother and hugged her. 'I'm truly sorry, Mum. I know you love Adam and a part of me does too and always will, but it's not enough. It doesn't satisfy me – and it shouldn't satisfy him. He deserves better and I hate the feeling that I'm short-changing him all the time but I just can't help it. If I don't manage to deal with this thing that still seems to colour my life and affects the way everybody treats me, I think I'll go mad. I have to go searching for something new. Perhaps find someone new too – someone who isn't affected by the past.' She had added passionately. 'Don't you *see* that?'

And her mother had looked at her and answered, 'Oh yes, darling, I see all right. I see only too well . . . and it scares the daylights out of me.'

Before she left home, Louisa had gone to say goodbye to Mr Brown.

Mr Brown had opened an eye at her for a brief moment but then gone back to sleep. 'You look after yourself,' she said. 'Don't you go and die or anything while I'm gone. I shall be back soon and I couldn't cope without you,' but Mr Brown spent much of his day snoozing and it was hard to tell how much he took in.

Louisa stopped for an early lunch at the first service station after she had turned onto the M6. She had been driving for two hours, which, for her, was usually the right time to have a break. Normally a conscientiously healthy eater, she eschewed the salad selection in favour of a plate of chips with bacon and eggs, and a leaden-textured chocolate muffin, and this cholesterol-rich meal added to her sense of freedom and escape. She carried her tray to a table by the window and thought about the week ahead.

She intended to try her hand at several creative possibilities before deciding what direction to follow in a new life and had been poring over brochures of various courses. The writing course had particularly appealed because she already knew Giles and Isobel Grant. The week sounded interesting; she thought it would probably serve as well as anything to set her on a new tack and she was much looking forward to going to Glendrochatt again. The last time she'd visited the Grants, they had just made the big decision to use their house as an arts centre and the whole place had been in chaos, crawling with builders, plumbers and electricians. Everyone had been buzzing with excitement, tossing out new ideas and arguing over plans. Now it was a running concern and she was looking forward to seeing what changes had been made. She had always liked the Grants and thought that if they'd managed to transfer to their business venture the relaxed, happy-go-lucky atmosphere that Isobel had created when the house was purely a family home, and then combined it with the exhilaration and enthusiasm generated by her more mercurial husband, it boded well for the week ahead.

She looked at her watch and reckoned that she had about another two and a half hours' more driving ahead. She hoped she might arrive before the other participants so that she could have a chance to see Isobel on her own first.

In fact she made such good time that she reached Glendrochatt soon after four, though as she sped along the A9 between Dunkeld and Pitlochry she was so deep in her own thoughts about the future that she nearly missed the turning to Blairalder, causing the car behind her to brake violently as she suddenly swerved off the dual carriage-way without any warning.

After a few miles she caught sight of Glendrochatt. She had forgotten what a landmark the old house was as it stood against the dark, wooded hills behind: a tall house, harled white, grey-slated and dominated by a central tower – a romantic house, almost a castle, really, thought Louisa. What a setting for creative writing! She wondered what her fellow students would be like, but if she felt a little doubtful about her writing capabilities in the week ahead it did not occur to her to be anxious about human relationships. Louisa, who had been loved and cherished all her life, had the happy gift of expecting to find friendship wherever she went and was seldom disappointed.

The wrought-iron gates were open and it was with a sense of adventure that she turned into the mile-long drive and rattled over the cattle grid. There were still a few primroses embedded in the moss on the shady side, but where the ground fell away on the sunny side, the sweep of daffodils which she remembered were always spectacular in April were now mostly over; the great beech trees had started to come into leaf and though it was too soon for the later azaleas and rhododendrons for which the grounds were famous to be at their very best, some early varieties made vivid splashes of apricot and yellow and pink. She wound down her window and breathed in their honeyed scent, together with great gulps of air that smelt of moss and peat and the coconutty smell of gorse. Halfway up the hill, where the drive divided, there were two notices. The one pointing right said TO GLENDROCHATT ARTS CENTRE, OLD STEADING THEATRE AND CAR PARK and the smaller one to the left simply said PRIVATE. After a moment's hesitation Louisa took the left hand fork and drove round to the front of the house. Stone steps arched up to the front door over what might once have been a moat but now held sunken flowerbeds that were filled with spring bulbs. Hyacinth and tulips were coming out and green *Alchemilla mollis* sprawled elegantly over the edge of the beds. Louisa happily tooted her horn, got out of the car and stretched.

'Louisa! Hi there!' Isobel Grant, a wooden garden trug filled with white 'pheasant eye' narcissi over one arm, was coming up through the rhododendron bushes below the house accompanied by two dogs. She was wearing ancient gumboots and a rather grubby fleece. Isobel might not be conventionally pretty but looking at her bright, amusing face Louisa was reminded again of how attractive she was.

'Oh, how lovely to see you,' said Isobel now, dropping the trug on the bottom step and giving Louisa a welcoming hug. 'I did so hope you'd manage to arrive before the others. It's far too long since we've seen you.

Giles and I were so pleased when you booked for this course. How are you?' She looked at the younger woman appraisingly. 'Goodness, you look well, Louisa – you look stunning!'

'I *am* well.'

'Of course you are . . . you always look wonderful but it hits me afresh each time I see you.'

Louisa stooped to fondle the ears of the little spaniel that was squirming at her feet, angling for attention. 'Hello, Flapper,' she said. 'I remember you, of course – but who's this other portly person? I don't think we've met before. Is she new?' and she indicated the extremely stout miniature wirehaired dachshund whose stomach almost touched the ground and whose rod of a tail was going like a metronome set for double tempo.

'Oh dear – that just shows what ages it is since you were last here,' said Isobel. 'This is fiendish but ingratiating Lozenge and she's four. Technically she belongs to Edward, but you know what it is with children's animals . . . I do all the caring and then when he comes home she switches allegiance to him in the most maddening way. I'm afraid she's addicted to eating baby rabbits, which is great for the garden but bad for Lozenge – and presumably not much cop for the baby bunnies either. This time of year she's at her most unattractive, poor darling, because she blows up like a balloon and gets these bald patches from excavating burrows.'

'I wondered if that hairless strip along her back was distinctive of a special breed,' said Louisa, laughing, 'a sort of short-legged opposite of a Rhodesian ridgeback – a Perthshire leatherback perhaps. Has she ever got stuck down a rabbit hole?'

'All too often – it's a constant hazard. We've several times had to dig for her and we all live in dread of her disappearing because Ed would be inconsolable if anything happened to her – actually we all would. You mightn't think so, but she's on a very strict diet at the moment!'

'Well, it can't be very successful,' said Louisa. 'I don't think Weight Watchers would approve. By the way, I hope it's all right that I've come round to the front?'

'Of course it is! You're *special* and I've given you a room in the main house with us so that you and I can have lovely gossips about everyone in between times – so we'd have to bring your things in this way anyway. Catherine Hickman's over here too, but the others will all be in the new accommodation we made out of the old steading. How about a mug of tea before we get inundated with everyone else arriving? I'm dying for one myself.'

'Tea would be ace.'

'Let's go and put the kettle on then and I can bung these flowers in water. It's such a shame you've just missed the daffs.'

Louisa followed Isobel up the steps to the front door, through the hall and into the big kitchen, once the billiard room in Giles's father's day, and now the hub of the house.

'Shall we take our tea outside?' suggested Isobel. 'I can't bear to waste a moment of this lovely day – you never know when you're going to get another one up here and you've been cooped up in the car all day too.'

They took a couple of cushions and sat together on the front steps, savouring the warmth of the spring sunshine and gossiping companionably while the obese Lozenge lay blissfully on a lower step having her bulging stomach massaged by Louisa's foot.

'How are the twins?' Louisa asked.

'Very well. Amy's about to do her AS exams. She's not sure yet whether to go straight to music college after A levels or read something else at university first and then go back to music later. Edward's still at his special-needs Camphill School, near Aberdeen. We've got difficult decisions about him ahead of us because he can't stay on in this particular school after he's eighteen. Technically he'll be an adult then but he's still a small boy trapped in a grown-up body.' Isobel sighed, then added hopefully, 'But we've got over a year before we need cope with that problem, so I'm sure something good will turn up.'

Like all their friends, Louisa knew that any fairy god-mothers who might have been present at the christening of the Grants' twin son and daughter had not divided life's gifts evenly between them. Bright, talented Amy was clearly fulfilling her early promise as an exceptional violinist, but Edward had always been different and fitted into no special category – he'd proved to be a child of heartbreak and triumph in fairly equal measure and Louisa could well understand that the difficulties, both for himself and for his parents, were unlikely to get any easier with approaching manhood.

'You've just missed them,' said Isobel. 'They're back at school now but you'll see both of them at the weekend. Amy will be playing in the concert Giles has organised for you all on Saturday night.' She hesitated for a moment and then added in a slightly constrained voice, 'But we're not without a child in the house at the moment, as you'll no doubt discover. We have my small nephew staying with us.'

'I didn't know you had a nephew.' Louisa was surprised.

'No? Well I have – my sister Lorna's little boy. Do you remember Lorna?'

'I certainly do. She's not the kind of person you forget! I knew her marriage had bust up but I didn't know she'd got any children. I thought Mum told me it was one of the reasons for the break-up – that Lorna was desperate for a baby. Last time I was here I think she'd just walked out on that marriage and was about to come back from South

Africa and descend on you here.' Louisa shot Isobel a sympathetic glance. Lorna, by far the more glamorous but much the less attractive of the two sisters, had always been a byword in the family as a troublemaker. 'You didn't seem to be looking forward to it much!'

Isobel gave her an unfathomable look. 'Yes, well, Lorna's apt to have that effect on me,' she said. 'Anyway she's married again now . . . she was always very good-looking, but in her forties she's turned into a serious beauty – with the help of a few tweaks here and there – and I can't describe how glamorous she is. She's become the trophy wife of an American senator, if you please – his third wife to be exact!' Isobel took a swig of tea. 'Anyway, the senator doesn't take kindly to stepchildren if they interfere with his plans. There was an SOS from Lorna and we were left literally holding the baby at very short notice, because they wanted to go travelling. There's no date set for his return to the States yet . . . not what we bargained for at the start of our busy season.'

'Goodness! How long has he been with you?'

'About a couple of months already . . .' Isobel hesitated. She said guardedly: 'It's a bit tricky all round at the moment, because Lorna seems to be incommunicado. Luckily I've managed to get a lovely girl from the village, who's on her gap year and eventually wants to be a teacher, to help me. She wants to earn money to go travelling and doesn't mind what she turns her hand to otherwise I don't know what I'd have done. She's been brilliant with him. Typical Lorna! *She's* busy so she dumps her child on *me* – a child I don't even know because Lorna went back to live in South Africa before he was born. It doesn't matter to her that we're busy too! Poor little scrap. It's not his fault and he really is a lovely child.' She added emphatically: 'He's a great addition to the household. We all dote on him.'

Louisa was just about to say 'Tell me more' when the dogs started to bark and went rushing down the steps as a small, fierce-looking young woman came stomping round the side of the house, carrying a large bag and looking like a thundercloud. She dropped the bag, and glowered up at them.

'Well, thank God I've found someone at last,' she exclaimed. 'Are you two on this course too, and if so how the hell did you manage to raise anyone in this godforsaken place? I was beginning to think I'd come on a complete wild goose chase. I've been ringing bells and opening doors and shouting myself hoarse for ages and there doesn't seem to be a sign of anyone about. What sort of a crap set-up is this?'

Isobel jumped to her feet and ran down the steps, beaming a welcome. 'Oh *poor* you, I'm *so* sorry. I'm Isobel Grant. Welcome to Glendrochatt.' She held out her hand, and asked: 'And which of our guests are you?' although she had a shrewd idea who it might be. The young woman ignored her hand.

'I'm Marnie Donovan. I've booked into a course here. Don't you have any staff around this place?'

'Indeed we do. I think you and I've spoken on the telephone and it's really good to see you, but you're a bit early so you've caught us on the hop. We weren't expecting anyone before five and it's only half past four now – but don't let that worry you in the least. It's great that you've managed to get here.'

Marnie Donovan looked slightly appeased. She nodded at Louisa. 'You on the staff here then?' she enquired.

'No,' said Louisa, indignant on Isobel's behalf at such unnecessary rudeness. 'I'm on the course too – so no doubt we'll be seeing a good deal more of each other during the next week.' She didn't sound as if she found this a pleasant prospect.

'How come if you're on the course and arrived even earlier than me that you managed to get some service?' demanded the young woman.

Louisa raised a disdainful eyebrow at her. 'Perhaps I don't demand such instant attention?' she said pointedly. 'This isn't a hotel.'

'Louisa's an old friend of ours,' interceded Isobel hastily. 'I'd asked her to come a bit ahead of everyone else so that we could get a chance to catch up on each other's lives and we were just having a gossip.' She hoped animosity was not going to spring up between Louisa and the new arrival, aware that, for all her charm of manner, one or two people found Louisa's ready social confidence and quick tongue daunting, and thought her arrogant.

'How lucky for you both,' said Marnie acidly. 'Sorry to interrupt your tête-à-tête and all that, but if it wouldn't be *too* much trouble I should like to be shown my room now please.'

'Of course.' Isobel willed herself to sound friendly. 'We'll go there straight away. Where have you left your car?'

'In what I assumed was the car park.'

'Fine. You're sleeping in one of the arts centre bedrooms so we'll go through the house and out the back way and that'll give you an idea of the layout. Let me help you with your bag – or you can leave it here and someone will come and pick it up shortly.' She looked at her watch and smiled at her unresponsive guest. 'It's nearly five so our helpers will be back on duty any minute.'

'I lugged it down here so I suppose I can lug it back,' said Marnie ungraciously, though she added a grudging, 'thanks all the same.'

'I'll come too,' Louisa said to Isobel. 'I can't wait to see all the alterations and what you've done to the actual theatre.'

'Good idea. I'm longing to show you everything.'

'Would you like me to take my car to the car park too, or is it all right to leave it here, Izzy?'

'Oh, leave it here – it'll be fine. Right, follow me then.'

Isobel led the way, back through the hall and down a passage to the covered way that led to the theatre and across a courtyard to the pretty old farm buildings that the Grants had converted into accommodation for the visiting artists, musicians or students who attended the various events that took place during the spring and summer. She chatted brightly away, explaining about the changes she and Giles had made and how they had based their idea for the centre on the original fortnight's summer music festival which Giles's parents had started years ago. Louisa, who knew the past history of Glendrochatt and was genuinely impressed at all the alterations, responded enthusiastically, but Marnie Donovan walked along in silence.

'Have you anything more you want from your car, Marnie, and if so would you like help to carry anything?' asked Isobel.

'I've got my laptop and a few bits and pieces – nothing I can't manage myself.'

'Let me take your bag for you then, and we'll wait while you collect whatever else you need.'

'Goodness,' said Louisa as they watched Marnie walk across the car park. 'What a charmer! Hope the rest of them aren't like her. I don't know how you managed to stay so friendly, Izzy, after she was so rude and disagreeable.'

Isobel laughed. 'Oh well, it's my job. We have to try to please the punters, you know! Wonder what's eating her though . . . she looks so unhappy. But she'll probably mellow – people usually do. She's not the first tricky customer we've had and I don't suppose she'll be the last. See if you can befriend her.'

'Hmm. I might.' Louisa looked noncommittal. 'I don't like grumpy people. I'll sit out here and wait while you take her in.'

After she had shown Marnie to her room, pointed out the bathroom and the facilities for making hot drinks, suggested that she might like to walk round the grounds – 'Please feel free to go anywhere' – and told her that she hoped she'd come over to the house for a pre-dinner drink at seven o'clock, Isobel collected Louisa and took her to look at the theatre.

Leaning on the windowsill of the charming little bedroom above, Marnie Donovan watched them go. They looked so relaxed and companionable, she thought, chatting and laughing together, with the dogs frolicking around them: the epitome of easy friendship. She could see two cars coming up the drive. Other participants, no doubt. More people to contend with . . . more people to offend . . . oh, God.

She turned back into the room, slumped on the bed and buried her face in her hands. 'Shit,' she said to herself, 'oh shit. Why, oh why have I done it again? Why do I always have to be like this, alienating people before I've even started to know them?' Isobel Grant had been conscientiously friendly, but there had been something about the way the tall fair young woman had looked at her that made her feel like a bit of flotsam washed up on a beach. Snooty cow, thought Marnie, who does she think she is with her wah-wah voice, her confidence and her airs and graces?

The temptation to leave was strong. But I will not be frightened away, Marnie told herself. This time I will not run away and I will do what I have set out to do. She thought of the person who had caused her to come to Scotland in the first place. You helped me once, more than you could ever know, whispered Marnie. Long ago, when we were both outcasts, and I have never forgotten it. Help me again now and I will not let you down. This place is just a stepping-stone. I will stay in Scotland until I have found what I am looking for.

Chapter Four

By seven o'clock all the would-be writers had arrived, been shown to their rooms and taken on a quick conducted tour of the premises; at eight thirty everybody was assembled in the smaller of the two conference rooms that opened off the enchanting little theatre for which Glendrochatt was justly famous. The theatre had originally been built so that Giles's actress mother could exercise her histrionic talents on the neighbourhood, but he and Isobel had resurrected and transformed it a few years ago, commissioning a delightful and witty backdrop for the stage from the designer and muralist Daniel Hoffman, and turning the farm buildings of the original old steading into smaller rooms for workshops and exhibitions, plus residential accommodation for participants in the various courses which took place from early May to the end of October. Giles, who had a flair for talent-spotting, was justifiably proud of having discovered Daniel Hoffman's work before he was well known and his prices had become correspondingly prohibitive. He liked to think the little theatre at Glendrochatt had been an important stepping-stone in Daniel's booming international career.

Catherine had opted to eat by herself for this first meal and not meet her prospective pupils till later, but supper for everyone else had taken place in the dining room of the main house.

Isobel, an excellent hostess, always tried to inject the

atmosphere of an informal house-party into any gathering to help break down barriers of reserve between the participants. She did not think the present group appeared to be a very homogeneous bunch so far, but as this was often how it seemed to start with she was not unduly worried about it. Giles, at the head of the table, appeared to be having a hard time between the retired teacher – a baby-faced blonde of uncertain age, dressed in a décolleté dress of mauve tweed worn with tangles of scarves and costume jewellery, from whose mouth a positive Niagara of words poured out – and Marnie Donovan, who responded to his efforts to draw her out as though she'd taken a Trappist's vow of silence. There was something about Marnie that made her instantly noticeable, though certainly not because she gave off encouraging signals for anyone to approach her. Marnie could be really attractive, Isobel decided, if only she would smile occasionally, but as it was she reminded her of an aggressive small dog – a terrier perhaps – who at the slightest hint of unfriendliness from a potential adversary would be ready to spring into action and go straight for the jugular. Unlike the garrulous ex-schoolmistress, she seemed impervious to her host's easy social charm, and Giles, she thought, looking at her husband with amusement, did not usually meet with such a lack of response from the female sex. She sent him a mocking look down the table and he laughed back at her, quick as always to pick up her unspoken message.

Isobel wondered what events in her life had caused Marnie Donovan to be so mistrustful of her fellow human beings. She made a marked contrast to Louisa who was sunnily chattering away to her neighbours, happily confident that they would all soon become the best of friends.

Isobel had seated herself between Colonel Smithson – the only man in the room wearing a tie – and a large lady from Cornwall called Morwenna Gilbert, around whom a gentle gloom seemed to hang like a permanently temperate climate; she started to spark a little once Isobel discovered her love of gardening and displayed an encyclopedic knowledge of plants, but whenever Isobel tried to show enthusiasm about any particular species she would shake her head apologetically and murmur: 'But I doubt if you could grow that here,' like the response to some mournful horticultural litany.

It had been a simple but delicious meal with a choice of delicately spiced Thai chicken with rice, or a vegetarian alternative, followed by Canterbury tart and home-made ice-cream. There was cheese for anyone who wanted it and what Giles called a good but uneventful Sauvignon Blanc to drink. Everyone always enjoyed the food at Glendrochatt, which the Grants took great trouble over and of which they were justifiably proud.

At exactly quarter past eight, Giles, who was good at keeping an unobtrusive eye on the clock, had caught Isobel's eye and brought the meal to a close by tapping on his glass. 'I expect you'd all like a chance to collect your notebooks and pencils,' he said, smiling at his motley assortment of guests, 'so let's meet in the conference room in quarter of an hour when it will give me great pleasure to introduce Catherine Hickman, our wonderful tutor for this week. Some of you may have heard Catherine read her poetry on the radio, or on that literary guessing game "Who Wrote That?", but I assure you that by Saturday morning she will also have discovered talents in all of you that you didn't know you possessed. Oh, by the way – I'm afraid this is a no-smoking house, but if any of you are longing for a cigarette you've just got time to go and have one in the garden – and for once you can do it in comfort because our unreliable Scottish weather is in a benevolent mood. See you all shortly.'

'Thank God for that,' muttered the tall man who walked with a noticeable limp and had been sitting on Marnie Donovan's other side. He'd made well-mannered efforts to engage her in conversation, but had received no more response than Giles had. 'Would you excuse me,' he asked her now, 'but I don't think I can hold out for much longer without having a smoke – pathetic, I know,' and he went off purposefully towards the front door where he stood on the steps gasping down restorative lungfuls of nicotine as though inhaling oxygen at a high altitude.

Earlier, when they had all gathered for a drink before dinner, Louisa, not one to suffer from social inhibitions, had made a beeline in his direction as soon as he had appeared, hoping to sit next to him at dinner. The moment she had seen him she had recognised him and remembered vividly the occasion when they had met before . . . what was his name? Christopher something? She had met him with Adam. Adam would know all about him – she must remember to ask him. At the thought of Adam she felt a pang of guilt because she recollected only too well that at their one meeting she had thought this man had all the glamour and edge – a faint but exciting whiff of danger – that Adam lacked. Perhaps the seed of her subsequent restlessness and disenchantment had even been sewn then? With his dark good looks and casual elegance, he stuck out in the present company like a particularly well-manicured thumb, but though he was of a type familiar to Louisa, it struck her that something about him had changed since their last meeting. She thought he now had a closed-in, almost wary, look that sat surprisingly with his otherwise sophisticated appearance.

'I'm Louisa Forrester,' she had said. 'I'm hopeless at remembering names but I think we've met before, haven't we?'

He had agreed immediately, though he looked taken aback at the sight of her.

'Yes indeed. Of course I remember you too. Did we meet at the opera or something like that? Anyway, what a surprise to see you again here,' and he smiled politely, though in reality Louisa thought that for a brief moment he had looked more alarmed than pleased and wondered why this should be so. Perhaps he was diffident about his writing ambitions and didn't want any mutual acquaintances they might share to find out about them – though she didn't really think he looked the type to lack self-confidence.

'We'll no doubt get plenty of chances to talk more later,' he had said smoothly and turned away from her to continue talking to the ponderous gardening lady to whom he'd been speaking before Louisa approached. Attractive men did not usually respond to Louisa in such an apparently lukewarm way and she was intrigued and challenged. Oh well, his loss, she thought wryly, amused at herself for feeling disappointed at his reaction – and he's right of course: there's lots of time to find out more about everyone. She decided that she must ask Giles and Isobel about him, but accepted it cheerfully enough when Isobel had not placed her next to him at dinner but had sat her instead between two women because, as so often happens on mixed courses, the women outnumbered the men.

At Catherine's request the chairs in the conference room had been set out in a circle. After eyeing each other uncertainly the group seated themselves, with much fiddling of pens, opening of notebooks, shuffling of feet and adjusting of the psychological space around them. Isobel, who usually attended the introductory session to make sure everything went smoothly, always found this a fascinating process and one that had little to do with either the distance between the chairs or the size of the individual. Marnie, for instance, physically the smallest person in the room, looked as though she had circled her chair with an invisible line, daring anyone to invade her boundaries, while the retired schoolmistress looked as though she had spent a lifetime popping in and out of other people's territory with entirely benevolent intentions but little sense of whether she would be welcome.

'Room for a little one next to you?' Isobel heard her asking the Colonel cosily, beads and bangles clanking as she billowed up to him.

'Ah, um . . . yes of course. Indeed. Delighted,' he replied, looking alarmed but stoical in the face of danger and leaping politely to his feet. He pulled out the chair she was about to sit on with a gallant flourish, nearly causing her to collapse on the floor.

When everyone was finally settled, Catherine came in with Giles and seated herself in the only vacant chair, smiling warmly at her assembled pupils who eyed her with varying degrees of hope or caution.

'Well, I'll leave you all to it,' said Giles after he had introduced Catherine. 'Please don't hesitate to let us know if there's anything you need. If you press the buzzer on the desk in the hall it will alert one of us that we're wanted and we'll come and find you. Breakfast will be from eight to eight forty-five in the dining room. You should each have a timetable in your room but there's one on the notice board as well. You'll find the usual assortment of drinks in the bar if you need fortifying after your session. Tea and coffee are always on the house – please help yourselves at any time – but there's a price list of other drinks on the counter so if you'd just jot down anything else you have in the little book that's provided, that would be helpful and you can pay at the end of your visit. Have fun and I'll see you all in the morning. Goodnight.'

'Now,' said Catherine, 'I think we should all introduce ourselves. We'll go round the circle and I'm going to ask each of you to tell us your name and where you come from and to say something – quite briefly, please – about what you hope to achieve during the next five days and what, if any, experience of writing you've had – whether you've had, or tried to have, anything published, for instance. It doesn't in the least matter if you've had no experience at all, it's just helpful for me to know.'

She looked round the room. 'So . . . as you know, I'm Catherine. I live in London. I used to teach English in a girls' school but now I'm a freelance journalist and critic, and I do some broadcasting as well. I've had six collections of poetry published and also edited a collection of excerpts from the diaries of explorers down the ages and I teach creative writing to mature students which I love doing. I'm constantly humbled and impressed by the talent of my pupils and I'm very pleased to be here with you all in this beautiful place. I hope we're going to have a really enjoyable and creative time together.' She looked at the person on her right, a smallish middle-aged man, swarthy of complexion, with hair parted so low on one side that the parting was level with his ear, from which point strands of his dark hair had been carefully plastered across the top of his head in a vain attempt to disguise incipient baldness.

Catherine gave him an encouraging nod. 'Now it's your turn,' she said. 'Will you carry on next please and tell us about yourself and why you've chosen to come on this course?'

'Well, I'm Stanley,' said her neighbour, 'Stanley Heslington, and this good lady on my other side is my wife Winifred, but just call her Win, because everybody always does and if she's not present we can say we're in a no-win situation.' He paused for the laughter which did not come, and then went on: 'We live near Keighley, in Yorkshire,

61

we're both retired, we've a grown son and daughter who've flown the nest, as they say, to follow their own bent, so I've got time for my little hobby, which is writing. I used to be in the textile trade but I've always had a fancy to write and I've had several pieces published in our parish magazine. I also pen a fair number of poems for local occasions – and I get many a good laugh when I recite them in the pub of a Friday night, I can tell you!' Several people shifted uneasily in their chairs, conscious that they had failed to respond to his first sally and wondering what might be expected from them next. 'I suppose I've always been gifted for words,' he went on modestly. 'I've written a great little book on local wildlife but I couldn't get any of the publishers to take it on. Mind you, as I said to Win, it's their loss, because if I say it myself it would have been of great interest to a lot of people and I think they made a big mistake. But one must move on and now I've got a fancy to try my hand at a *ro*mance. I reckon I could do just as well as some of these lady novelists that get printed nowadays. I've been a bit of a lad in my day – quite a Romeo, as you might say – and I could draw on my own experiences.' He gave a satisfied chuckle while everyone made unsuccessful efforts to visualise him in this unlikely role. Louisa who had caught Isobel's eye hastily looked away to stop herself laughing but Stanley Heslington sailed happily on. 'Then happenstance one day I saw an article on this place here, when I was waiting in the surgery to have my ears syringed out by the nurse – I make a lot of wax you see which is troublesome when I'm listening for birdsong – and when I got home I said to Win, "How about a trip to Bonnie Scotland? We'll have a go at this writing lark together, dear. Now Win may not be gifted for writing like I am, but I said to her don't you worry love because I'll be there to help you through and . . .'

Catherine laid a hand on his arm and gave him her

warmest smile. 'Thank you very much,' she said. 'That's most interesting, but I'm going to stop you there, Stanley, because though it's lovely that you've decided to come on this workshop week together, I do think it's important that you and your wife should each do your own thing and we'd really like to hear Win speak for herself. I'm going to suggest that you don't sit next to each other in future sessions and then you can both be free to listen to your own inner voice. Now, Win, your husband has given us an introduction but perhaps you'd like to add something to it?'

Win, a pleasant-looking, apple-faced woman shot Catherine a not unamused look.

'It's true I haven't any writing experience,' she said, 'but I've always loved reading and used to look forward to English lessons at school. I know it's a long time ago, but I got quite good marks for my essays then, so I shall enjoy having a go again – so long as I don't hold the rest of the class up, that is. Maybe like Mr Grant said at supper I'll surprise myself – and my husband – and turn out to have hidden talents,' and she beamed engagingly at them all, while her vociferous husband looked not a little put out at this sign of independence and, possibly, unexpected rivalry.

'Wonderful,' said Catherine. 'Thank you very much, Win. Next please?'

If Louisa expected to gather more information about her stylish-looking acquaintance with the limp, she was disappointed. There were no startling revelations from the man who'd been so desperate for a cigarette. He simply said he'd recently decided on a change of direction and thought he'd try his hand at writing. Everyone immediately wanted to know what he had done before but he gave them no clue. Perhaps he's been made redundant, thought Louisa. If so it didn't look as if lack of money was a problem – or not yet anyway – but it might account for his less than enthusiastic response at finding someone he knew on the course.

'I'm just here to learn as much as I can about writing,' he said, shortly.

'Could you tell us your name, and whether you've ever had anything published or done any writing at all?' asked Catherine, vaguely recalling that Isobel had mentioned that he hadn't filled in any of the questionnaire.

He hesitated for a moment and then said: 'I'm sorry – yes of course. My name's Christopher . . . Christopher Piper. I live in London. I've had the occasional poem published. Nothing much.'

'Fine,' said Catherine, easily, 'thank you too then, Christopher.'

Isobel wondered what significance, if any, there was in his reticence. She thought he looked interesting, possibly the most interesting person in the group, except perhaps the grouchy Marnie who was intriguing too.

The Colonel, who said his name was John, wanted to write a history of his regiment; the retired schoolmistress announced in a breathlessly girlish voice that her name was really Barbara but she did hope they would all call her Bunty because that's what her friends called her and she just knew they were all going to become the best of chums on this exciting venture. Her dearest ambition was to write stories for 'little ones' and she had brought several examples of her work, which she also illustrated, with her.

'Aren't we all really still children at heart?' she enquired hopefully, though looking round the guarded circle of faces about her, Isobel didn't feel Bunty was getting quite the response she was hoping for, any more than Stanley had.

Morwenna wrote a gardening column for a regional monthly magazine, which, she informed them gloomily, had a decreasing readership and was likely to go out of business soon, unless the newly appointed editor could dramatically increase the circulation; she needed to change her style of writing but hadn't the faintest idea how to go about it and didn't expect to be able to manage it anyhow. Her friend, Joyce, a toothy but well-groomed woman with smooth bleached hair and immaculate make-up, looked a much breezier character. She kept a gift shop, which, she said, left her plenty of time during the winter to take up some other occupation, though she had had to get a friend to stand in for her this week, the tourist season having already started. Morwenna had persuaded her to come along. 'I've no idea at all if I can write. I just thought the course sounded fun,' she said cheerfully.

'Excellent,' said Catherine. 'Fun is just what I hope it will be. A very good reason to try it.'

Isobel admired, as she often had before, the friendly way in which Catherine coped with her very varied students, dealing firmly with potential monopolisers like Stanley but quietly encouraging everyone, no matter who they were or what they were like. It was the third year that Catherine had come to Glendrochatt to run a writing course and places were always much in demand when she was the tutor. She had become a great favourite of the Grants who now regarded her as a personal friend and always looked forward to her visits.

It was Louisa's turn to introduce herself next. 'Like Stanley and Win, I come from Yorkshire,' she said, smiling towards the Heslingtons, 'though I live a bit further north than they do. I read English at St Andrews and always had vague dreams about writing a novel some day, but time has ticked by and so far I've never even started one. I've been a PA to a politician for five years but feel I need a complete change for various reasons. I'm at a bit of a crossroads in my life . . .' Her voice suddenly trailed away.

Unaccountably she felt a lump in her throat and tightness in her chest that made it difficult to speak.

'And the writing?' prompted Catherine gently. 'Have you done any at all since university? Might this be the right moment to have a go at the novel?'

Louisa gulped. 'I . . . I don't really know. I'm afraid I haven't got a plot or characters lined up or anything.'

'Everyone starts in different ways. Let's just see what happens over the next few days. Was it the idea of writing a novel that brought you here?'

Louisa struggled to speak while Catherine smiled encouragingly. What on earth is the matter with me, Louisa wondered, unused to being inarticulate.

'Yes, partly,' she said at last, and then went on in a rush, 'but it's also because I'm contemplating big changes in my life and I know I need to face some things that I usually try not to think about.' She paused again, feeling foolish, and then continued in a steadier voice: 'I'm on the Glendrochatt mailing list and have always wanted to come on one of their courses. I've never had the time before but when I looked at their latest programme and read about this week, I thought perhaps writing might help me to unblock something – but it sounds rather an odd reason.'

'Not odd at all,' said Catherine. 'It's an excellent reason. You'd be amazed if you knew all the varied reasons that make people sign up for a course like this. Writing can put us in touch with all sorts of parts of ourselves that we aren't aware of or have never really examined before and that can be a useful experience in itself – and who knows what may come of it? Look on it as an adventure.'

'Thank you,' said Louisa.

Catherine turned to Marnie Donovan. 'Now, lastly, what about you?'

Louisa glanced at her out of the corner of her eye,

wondering what she would learn about this unfriendly young woman to whom she had taken something of a dislike. Would she perhaps refuse to cooperate and tell them nothing? She was surprised to notice that the American girl, having screwed her handkerchief into a long twist, was now winding it round and round one of her fingers with great concentration.

'I'm Marnie,' she stated. 'I'm American by birth but when I was growing up I spent almost as much time in England as in the States.' She added with an ironic lift of an eyebrow: 'My mother made a hobby of marrying Englishmen.'

When she wasn't being aggressive she had an attractive, rather husky voice. She went on, 'I came up to Scotland for . . . for personal reasons. Then I saw this course advertised and decided to try it.' She paused for a moment and then shrugged. 'I hope it may help me find what I'm looking for . . . I guess you could say I'm on a bit of a treasure hunt.' she said.

'That sounds interesting,' said Catherine. 'Would you like to tell us more about it?'

'Not really . . . or not at the moment anyway. I'm a pretty useless sort of person and I've spent most of my time running away from people and situations. Perhaps I need to take a trip down memory lane as well and try to learn a few things from it. Perhaps writing will help me too.' She suddenly smiled at Catherine, and the smile transformed her face. 'I'll try to do as you suggested to Louisa and look on it as an adventure,' she said, and shot a cautious, questioning look in Louisa's direction.

'Fine,' said Catherine. 'That brings me neatly on to something important I want to say to you all. Writing is a very personal business and can indeed be like a journey into ourselves, but I'm hoping that most of you will be brave enough to share some of what you write with the rest of us and that usually takes courage. I'd like you all to agree that anything we hear in the next few days will be strictly between "these four walls" and ourselves. If we're dealing with personal feelings or getting glimpses of other people's lives, this has to be a safe environment. Do you all agree with that?'

There was a general murmur of assent. 'Good. I'll just outline what we're going to do in the next few days then. There'll usually be two workshops every morning and time for personal tutorials in the afternoons – I'll pin up a list of times on the notice board, and you can put your names down if you'd like to have one. Otherwise afternoons are free and we start work together again at five. We have a guest tutor coming to talk about the rival merits of rhyme and metre versus free verse – which will give you all a break from me – and the well-known author Jonathan Mercer, who lives in Edinburgh, is going to give a talk on crime writing one morning. Friday evening is performance night when you'll all have a chance to read to the group from your own work – if you want to, that is. It's entirely voluntary. Finally I know Giles and Isobel have laid on a delightful concert for you on Saturday – your last night. I know some of you have brought samples of your writing that you want to talk to me about. If you give them to me this evening I'll do my best to look at them before your individual tutorials – nothing too long though, please. Because you all have different needs and wishes I shall be suggesting certain exercises I think you'll all find useful and then we can have sessions reading out the results and discussing them. Let's meet in here after breakfast tomorrow morning at nine fifteen for our first session and please bring pens and paper with you. Any questions?'

Bunty put her hand up. 'But what about writing for *children*?' she asked plaintively. 'I don't want to do any other kind.'

'I hope all the exercises we do will help you with any kind of writing,' said Catherine, 'and you can use them afterwards in whatever way you like.' Bunty looked unconvinced, and stuck her bottom lip out like a child herself.

Catherine got up. 'Enough for tonight, I think. Some of you have had a long journey and may want early bed and some of you may like to follow Giles's invitation and go to the bar. I'll see you all in the morning.'

Most of the group followed Catherine's suggestion and drifted towards the bar. Christopher Piper walked over to where Louisa was standing. 'Can I buy you a drink?' he asked. 'I feel as if I need one myself and we could do a bit of catching up about our last meeting.'

Louisa was about to accept when Marnie, full of brave resolutions to be friendly, came up to join them both and Christopher offered her a drink too. He certainly has impeccable manners, thought Louisa approvingly, but though she would have liked to have a drink with him she still felt sufficiently antagonistic to Marnie not to relish her company as well, so she changed her mind.

'It's very kind of you, but I've had an awfully long drive today so I think I might have an early night,' she said. 'I'm staying in the main house with the Grants, who are cousins of mine, and though I've already had a lovely chat with Isobel, I haven't had a chance to talk to my host yet so I think perhaps I'd better go over with Isobel now and exchange family news with him before I go to bed. Lucky you,' she said, addressing Marnie, well aware how unresponsive she had been to Giles's social efforts at dinner. 'I noticed you sat next to Giles this evening – I hope you enjoyed talking to him as much as most people do. He's always fun to sit next to, so easy and amusing and such a marvellous host – so good about taking trouble with absolutely *anyone*,' and she looked pointedly at the other woman. 'I'll have the drink another time if I may?' she said to Christopher.

'Of course,' he said. 'See you tomorrow. Good night then.' If he was disappointed to have his offer accepted only by Marnie, who had been so uncommunicative at dinner, and not by the engaging Louisa, he was too polite to let it show, but Marnie, thinking he'd got landed with her by default, felt uncomfortable.

'Night then both of you – see you tomorrow,' said Louisa and went over to join Isobel, who had just said her goodnights and was about to take Catherine back with her to the house.

Marnie gave Louisa's disappearing back a distinctly unfriendly look and felt her resolutions to be sociable dissolving like morning mist when the wind gets up.

'Oh dear, I'm afraid I've just been rather horrid,' said Louisa, not sounding all that sorry, as she and Catherine and Isobel walked across the courtyard, 'but I hope I've evened things up a bit after that ill-mannered little cow was so rude to you when she arrived, Izzy.'

'Louisa, that's too bad of you,' said Isobel, half-amused but aware that despite her charm and usual friendliness Louisa could occasionally cause trouble if she took a dislike to anyone. 'Please don't start a feud. It's very kind of you to take up the cudgels on my behalf but I assure you I can fight my own battles and I'd much rather try to win Marnie over and get her to enjoy the week and shed her prickles.'

'I think she might prove interesting, that one,' said Catherine thoughtfully.

'Oh dear – well I'm sorry then,' said Louisa, pulling a face. 'I can see you neither of you approve, so I'll try to be nicer to her, but I don't promise anything if she goes on

70

being such a pain . . . and anyway I feel much better for having said what I did! I could see she knew exactly what I meant.'

'Yes,' said Isobel, laughing. 'Knowing you, I bet she did! You've never gone in for the Mona Lisa approach, have you? What did you both make of Christopher Piper? He's our mystery man – rather a dishy one though.'

Louisa grinned. 'Hmm – dark and smooth, like expensive chocolate!' she said. 'I bet he's got a little notice stamped on him somewhere saying *Guaranteed not less than 75% cocoa solids*. I've actually met him before but I was going to ask you to fill me in about him because I don't really know much about him – but you obviously know even less than I do.'

'But I think you fancy him rotten,' teased Isobel, who had noticed Louisa's manoeuvre before dinner.

Louisa laughed. 'He certainly seems very charming, but I'm generously giving Marnie a chance to get to know him first!' she said lightly.

Giles and the dogs were waiting for them in the kitchen, a tray with a decanter of whisky and glasses on the table and the kettle simmering away on the Aga for hot drinks.

'Now tell me how you got on and what everyone was like,' said Giles, ready to have a discussion about the evening. 'And guess what, darling.' He grinned at Isobel. 'You're going to be very pleased with me! I've remembered what it was that I read about the Donovan woman.'

'What?' they all asked.

'I think she recently inherited a lot of money,' said Giles. 'I knew her name rang a bell. At least we know we have one participant who can afford to pay her bill!'

And he looked at their surprised faces with satisfaction.

Chapter Five

The following morning by half past nine, the group had once more assembled in the conference room, this time seated round two oblong tables, which had been pushed together to form a square. Catherine was already seated when her class started to arrive.

There was already a much less constrained atmosphere than there had been the night before. Several people had chatted over drinks in the bar before going to bed, and they had all met again at breakfast. There was beginning to be a sense of camaraderie and a feeling that they were here with a common purpose, no matter how disparate their ages, backgrounds and talents might be. If there was not exactly a stampede to sit next to Stanley Heslington, this was something of which he was supremely unaware as he settled himself confidently next to Louisa.

'Aren't I the lucky one then?' he enquired, eyeing Louisa in a way that set her teeth on edge. 'I've stolen a march on the other chaps and landed myself next to the bonniest young lady in the room. Maybe I'll be able to give you a hint or two – seeing as I've had previous experience,' and he winked at her knowingly, though whether he was referring to his writing skills or his success as a self-styled Romeo, Louisa dreaded to think.

His wife went over to Marnie, who had sat herself down on the far side of the table with an empty chair on either side of her. 'Can I come and sit by you?' she enquired, unfazed by Marnie's unapproachable air.

'Catherine particularly told Stanley and me not to sit together.'

'Oh yes, please do. Of course you can.' Marnie treated Win to the smile that had so transformed her face when she had turned it on Catherine the previous night and she made room for Win to pull out the chair next to hers.

Across the table Christopher Piper noticed the smile and wondered what it required to receive one. He had certainly not been favoured with one the evening before, and although Marnie had been perfectly civil she had remained ill at ease and he had not managed to break through the barrier of her reserve. Since he was sometimes considered aloof himself he regarded her reticence with some sympathy but couldn't help thinking that the engaging Louisa would have been much more enjoyable company. He'd had his own reasons for not wishing to encounter any previous acquaintances at Glendrochatt and had been extremely surprised and far from pleased to bump into someone who knew him. However, now that it had happened and there was nothing he could do about it, he must make the best of it; he remembered how attractive he had thought Louisa when they'd met before. Marnie might prove to be interesting if you got to know her, he thought, but Louisa certainly looked as if she'd be a great deal more fun.

Louisa had also noticed Marnie's smile and been surprised. Though she had no particular desire to befriend the young American, she too was intrigued by her – and especially since Giles's revelations of the night before. Being one of those fortunate individuals who have never suffered agonies of shyness, Louisa didn't really understand the strange ways it can make sufferers behave, and she still felt a little piqued by what she considered Marnie's uncalled-for antagonism. She and Catherine and the Grants had enjoyed a happy time over mugs of tea in the kitchen, discussing all the course participants and especially Marnie, who didn't match their idea of a wealthy heiress. Giles had been unable to recall who it was that had left her the fortune or what the circumstances were, only that it had been unexpected. Louisa determined to discover more about her.

'Good morning everyone,' said Catherine when they were all settled. 'I thought we'd have a general talk about what we mean by creative writing and then I'm going to suggest that you all do an exercise which I think you'll find interesting – the first of several that we're going to try over the next few days.'

'But do we all have to do the same one?' enquired Bunty mistrustfully.

'Well, that's the idea. The point is that though you'll all start off with the same brief, I can guarantee that what you produce will be entirely different. That's the excitement of it and the challenge. I hope to encourage you to give yourselves permission to "go with the flow" – *your* flow, *your* thoughts, not anyone else's. I want you to cast aside preconceived ideas of what you ought to write, even what you *want* to write, and let whatever thoughts and memories come up take wing. I don't want you to say "I'm going to write a poem this morning" . . . or a children's story, or a piece of political reasoning. Later you may find you can use what you have written to become part of any of those things. To quote from a book on "freeing the writer within" by an American author called Natalie Goldberg, I want to get you to "write down the bones" of what you are and who you are and the interesting thing is that you will find it much easier to do if you don't have too much time to think about it.'

One or two people looked wary. The Colonel gazed down at his highly polished shoes and cleared his throat. 'I'm afraid I'm a feet-on-the-ground sort of chap,' he said gruffly. 'I don't think letting imagination take wing is quite my sort of thing.'

'Ever tried it?' asked Catherine.

'Er . . . no. No, I can't say I have.' He looked rather shocked at such a suggestion and Catherine thought she might as well have asked if he'd ever taken part in a sex orgy or snorted coke.

'Well, don't worry about it; it's not as dangerous as you think,' she said, giving him an amused and not unsympathetic smile. 'Try to reserve judgement until you've had a go. Look on it as a training exercise for your writing troops. A toning of unused muscles – a drill.'

Everyone laughed, including the Colonel.

'Hmm,' he said dubiously, 'I can see you're a very persuasive woman. Dangerous!' But he smiled back at her.

Bunty leaned earnestly towards him, displaying a good deal of crêpey cleavage in the process: 'I'm sure you must once have had lots of little imaginary friends to play with,' she said encouragingly.

The Colonel hastily averted his eyes from her bosom and returned to the safety of contemplating his shoes. Louisa had a vision of him in tweed jacket and tightly knotted tie, skipping round a fairy ring with a lot of pixies, and wished Isobel had been present to enjoy this exchange. Glancing up she was surprised to catch Marnie's eye and see a flicker of laughter there too. Perhaps a thaw was setting in?

'Do I take it then, Catherine, that you're of this modern school that doesn't hold with grammar, punctuation and rhyme and all the well-tried rules that my generation was raised on?' queried Stanley. 'Now when I was a lad at school . . .'

'Not at all,' said Catherine, interrupting hastily before Stanley could get up a full head of steam and start huffing on about every detail of his education. 'Of course all those things are very important too and we'll come to that in a later session, but this morning's exercise is not about rules. It's about finding a way to get past that inner censor that so often inhibits us from writing freely – or even writing at all.' Privately she thought that by the end of the week she might wish that Stanley's inner censor – if he had one – would shut him up completely. 'But before we actually start writing,' she went on, 'let's go round the table, name some of our favourite authors and think what it is that makes us enjoy them.'

Bunty said coyly that she still liked to read the Little Grey Rabbit books in bed and added roguishly that she'd always seen herself as Squirrel: 'I used to be a redhead too.' Colonel Smithson professed a preference for military history and Stanley said he wasn't much given to reading other people's writing, as he didn't want it influencing his individual style. 'No plagiarism for me,' he announced loftily. 'I don't hold with it.'

Jane Austen, Tolkien, Ernest Hemingway, Georgette Heyer, C. S. Lewis, Patrick Leigh Fermor and John Buchan all received mention, as did William Boyd, Anne Tyler, John Grisham, J. K. Rowling, both the Trollopes – Anthony and Joanna – and Dickens.

After some general discussion about books – a useful way of getting everyone to contribute, Catherine found – she asked them to get their pens and paper ready.

'Now,' she said, 'I call this exercise "I remember" and some of you may even like to start with those words, but the whole point is to go with what feels right to you. Again you may find it helpful to write in the present tense – some people don't like that, but it often has the effect of making your writing very immediate, very live. If you're not comfortable with it, then that's fine, don't use it, but it's a powerful tool. What I do want you all to do is to relive some defining moment in your lives – it could be a vivid early memory, nice or nasty; an encounter with a particular person; a moment of extreme happiness or fear; it could be something quite inconsequential. Use whatever springs immediately to mind no matter how surprising or even trivial. Don't stop to think, just dive in. I want you to keep your hand on the page and keep it moving. Don't stop to re-read what you've put or allow your inner editor to take over. Plenty of time for that later. You've got about twenty-five minutes, but forget about the clock because I will tell you when to stop, and when I do ask you to stop please put your pens down. Then I'll give you another few minutes just to finish a sentence but nothing more – we're not looking for polished work at the moment. If something scary or difficult or unexpected comes up – go with it. Right. Start now please.'

For the next twenty minutes the only sound in the room was the furious scratching of pens on paper, the ticking of the clock and occasionally some rather heavy breathing. When Catherine called 'Time!' none of them could believe that ten let alone twenty-five minutes had gone by and they protested that they had only just begun.

'Good,' said Catherine after giving them another five minutes to complete their sentences. 'You all looked as if you were getting something down on paper, which is wonderful. I think we'll take our break a bit early this morning so that we have time to share our writing before lunch. Let's meet back here in twenty minutes.'

After a break for coffee, the group reassembled and Louisa found herself walking back to the conference room with Christopher.

'We must find a time to catch up on each other's lives sometime,' she said. 'I have a feeling that you had some sort of disaster after we met? I seem to remember that Adam Winterton tried to get hold of you and your girlfriend to come to dinner with us, but you'd had an accident or something and couldn't come . . . and then I had to go abroad with my boss for a bit and we lost touch.' She looked at him questioningly. 'Am I right?'

Christopher didn't look very forthcoming. 'I was involved in a crash and it put me out of circulation for a bit,' he said. She thought he might say more, but he obviously wanted to change the subject. 'This next session should be interesting, don't you think?' he asked.

'Umm. But I'm not sure I'm looking forward to it if we have to read out what we've written,' said Louisa. 'I think I put down complete drivel.'

When they'd settled back in their places, Catherine smiled at them all. 'I hope some of you will have surprised yourselves,' she said. 'And I do hope most if not all of you will feel able to share what you've done with the rest of us. I repeat what I said last night: if anyone would be unhappy to do so, there will be no pressure – but if you will trust my experience, I think most of you will benefit if you can be brave enough. We need to test our writing against other people's opinions and if you're going to be successful writers you have to be prepared to expose your feelings. Also, as I said yesterday, this is a safe environment in which to try things out. Is there anyone who would definitely rather not read what they have put?'

There was an uneasy pause while most people looked furtively round the room to see what the general reaction was going to be, but no one put their hand up.

'Good,' said Catherine. 'Now, who will start?' Nobody volunteered. 'Right,' she said. 'No surprises there then – that's what usually happens. Marnie, would you be prepared to start, please?'

'Why me?' asked Marnie, looking at her least cooperative.

'Just because you happen to be sitting next to me and we

have to start somewhere, I'm afraid,' said Catherine mildly. 'So if you'll be the first, then we'll go round clockwise and it will be Win's turn next.'

Marnie hesitated for a long moment and Louisa wondered if she was going to share what she had written with the rest of the group or whether she would refuse point blank. Then, rather as though she had been wavering on the edge of a rock before plucking up courage to dive into deep waters, she started to read from the notebook in front of her:

'This might have been the story of a killing,' she began, *'and the fact that it's not is because a particular person, who's had a lasting influence on my life, intervened. I only met her for a few weeks, a long time ago, but I've never forgotten her. Now she's dead and I'd like to repay her for what she did for me, but I haven't decided how to do it.'*

She paused, looked up and glanced round the circle of listeners. 'But it's why I'm here,' she said gruffly, 'it's part of my quest.' Then, her voice gathering strength, she went back to the pages in front of her and continued: *'All through my childhood I loathed my mother. My feelings were a deadly combination of fear and boredom like watching a Hitchcock film and constantly waiting for something awful to happen. I've gotten over the fear of my mother now, though incidents from my childhood have left me with a legacy of other terrors that I still battle with. I still have issues with my mother but I don't spend much time with her. I even feel sorry for her at times — she's in the hands of the face fixers big time because she can't hack the fear of losing her youth and she's not a happy lady. I see her when I have to and we can be reasonably civil to each other for a short time — until she gets going on the dissatisfaction of having a daughter who is neither sociable nor pretty and who has always been a disappointment to her. I suppose she has a point. She was a stunner herself, and photographs tell me I was a hideous baby and a plain child. From the day of my birth I've* been the stone in her shoe. I thought my father was God when I was little, though I was scared of him too, in a different way. I love him very much now and in his way he loves all his children from his various marriages, but I've always felt a bit of an intrusion in his high-powered life – a bit of a cuckoo in the nest. He and my current stepmother have stayed together for nearly ten years, which is a record for him. Perhaps it's a sign he's getting old because he's certainly mellowed. He and my mother split up when I was three and then played pass-the-parcel with me for as long as I can remember.

'When I was seven I nearly caused my mother to die. I certainly intended to make her ill, if not actually to kill her, but we were both unexpectedly rescued and the fact that she survived is neither to my credit nor due to me. That incident has marked me because I've come to realise that life is a gift and no matter how difficult or unhappy it may be, we should not take liberties with it or wish it away either for ourselves or for anyone else.'

Louisa felt a sudden connection with the prickly young woman whom she had up to now regarded with suspicion. I must try to get to know her, she thought. I too have learned lessons about the value of life.

'When I think of that time in my childhood,' Marnie continued, 'I am back in the West Indies lying under a frangipani tree, almost drugged by its overpoweringly sweet scent; hearing the wind rustling the palms and the waves breaking on the reef far below so that it is hard to know which sound is which. From my secret hideout I watch a tiny iridescent humming-bird quivering in the air as it sucks nectar from the scarlet centre of a yellow hibiscus; black and yellow banana-quits flutter and jostle for crumbs round the bar and a magnificent frigate bird sails high overhead, soaring above the sea. I can tell it's the male bird because I can see the red blob on its throat. Kenneth has taught me that.'

As she switched abruptly to the present tense, it became clear to her audience that she was suddenly miles away from the highlands of Scotland or the other people in the room. She almost looked as if she was in a trance. *'There's a goat bleating in the distance,'* she said in a dreamy voice, *'and I can hear the persistent, repetitive cooing of a dove in the tree above me – but all the time I'm also listening to the laughter of grown-ups who are drinking planter's punches round the pool and do not know or care where I am. I don't care about them either. I like to be invisible. It feels safer. The old lady likes to be invisible too but I don't think it's because she's afraid. She hardly ever bothers to answer when anyone speaks to her – which they mostly don't – but I often watch her when she doesn't know I'm there. My mom says she's an Italian contessa and real wealthy and that she used to be a famous beauty – but I think she's gotten that bit wrong. I don't think the old lady is beautiful at all, though I like to look at her and I'd like to talk to her too. Her face is like a map.*

'Sometimes I help Kenneth feed the pigs; sometimes I sit on the baked earth as he leans on his rake in the hot, hot sun and tells me scary stories, which make me shivery in spite of the heat. The stories turn into terrors after I've gone to bed at night and the grown-ups have disappeared for dinner and often I scream and scream, but nobody comes. My mom locks me in when she and Colin go over to the main building for their dinner. I bang on the door but she takes no notice. How can I get away from the demon dancers if they come for me when I can't get out to run away? Once, when they came, they danced all round the bungalow and peered through the window and I thought I'd die. I can still see their painted faces and gleaming bodies in my dreams – and the masks and the feathers. Some of them wear leg shackles and shake their chains and I know they're coming when I hear the beating of the drums. If there's a moon, their shadows come first, flying over the grass like huge great bats, and I can't stop myself from yelling even though I'm feared the demons will hear me.' Marnie's voice had risen several tones so that she was speaking in a high childish voice quite unlike her usual

rather low register. She seemed short of breath and Louisa wondered if she was going to have a fit or an asthma attack. '*Perhaps it's a good thing nobody comes,*' Marnie went on, '*because Kenneth says I must never, ever tell his stories to anyone. He says if I tell, then Jab-Jab, the Jab Molassi, will get me. My mom says it's just a silly dream but I know it's real when the dancers come. I make myself as small as I can in bed and go to sleep with my fingers crossed to keep him away. Sometimes I wet my bed and my mom could kill me. Even though I've become brown in the last few weeks I'm still made to wear a sunhat all the time. Kenneth says God took the colour out of him when he was born as a punishment to his mother. A woman put a curse on Kenneth's mother for borrowing her man. It doesn't seem fair that Kenneth should be punished for what his mother did. My mom is always borrowing other people's husbands so maybe I'll get to be punished for that too. Maybe that's why the demons come. Maybe next time they come they'll take me away with them.*

'*Kenneth has crinkly white hair and funny red eyes and a face like ash but he is my particular friend and he likes me being with him. He knows everything about plants and birds and animals and he has a tame mongoose that can kill snakes, like Rikki-tikki-tavi in* The Jungle Book. *He looks after the fruit trees and the pigs and the goats and the chickens. He says I can watch him slit the throat of one of the goats one day but I don't want to. He says blood is very powerful and each day I'm feared it will be the day he'll want to show me the slaughtering of the goat. Sometimes he takes me to the little one-roomed, blue-painted house made of wood where he lives with his mother. The house is on legs like a table and Kenneth's mother's two black pigs live underneath it. She splits coconuts and gives me the milk to drink and she sings hymns to me. When she goes to church she wears a huge purple hat with a red feather. She says the Lord Jesus will always look after me but I don't believe her. I don't think he cares about me at all. He wasn't there when the demon dancers came because I prayed for him and he didn't help.*

'*Once I spent a whole afternoon in Kenneth's mother's house without my mom and stepfather noticing I'd gone. They'd be mad at me if they knew where I'd been, but I never tell them because I don't tell them anything. Sometimes people in the village come to visit Kenneth in his house and give him money to do things for them – but he hasn't got any friends apart from me. Kenneth says he and I can share secrets because we're both outcasts. I asked my mom what an outcast was and she said it's someone nobody wants, so I guess he's right. I don't think the old lady is an outcast though. I think it's her that doesn't want other people. I wish I were like that too. I wish I didn't care.*

'*Something interesting has happened. I have talked to the old lady. She doesn't like my mom either. We walked back from the piggeries together after she'd been for her usual visit to the cliff. She always stands very close to the edge and looks down. Each time I figure she's going to fall off but she never has. She doesn't know that I watch her. She talked to me as if I was a grown-up person and I didn't want to be invisible to her any more. I think I shall go visit her one day. I wonder if she's seen the dancers too? I wonder if she knows about Jab-Jab? Perhaps she is in danger too.*'

Marnie suddenly stopped reading. 'That's all I've done so far,' she said, not looking up. 'I ran out of time.'

There were murmurs of appreciation from the group, who had listened intently to her story.

"Thank you, Marnie," said Catherine, quietly. "That was fascinating. You had us all involved, and you've told us a great deal in a short time. You've really set our imaginations working and using the present tense certainly seemed to work for you. Were you surprised yourself at how the writing flowed once you got started?'

'Yes,' said Marnie. 'Yes, I was. It suddenly started pouring out and I could have gone on and on. I . . . I didn't expect it to happen like that and it wasn't what I'd intended to write about. I'd planned something different. It was weird. It was like I was a child again while I was writing.' She looked up then and saw that everyone was smiling at her. Cautiously, she smiled back. Then she muttered, 'Thanks for listening,' sat back in her chair and closed her eyes as if too much eye contact was more than she could manage.

Christopher Piper, who had been watching her face while she was reading, thought she looked completely drained.

'Now, Win?' prompted Catherine briskly. She knew from experience how easily emotions could get out of hand in the hothouse atmosphere of a writing class and felt it would be wise to take the spotlight off Marnie and leave her time to recover. 'Can we have yours next, please?'

'Well, it'll be very hard to follow Marnie,' said Win, 'but seeing as we're all in this together and she was so brave as to start us off, I'll have a go. I'm afraid I've not had an eventful life or done anything interesting, but when you suggested we might write about a particular person I immediately thought about going to tea with my grandma every Sunday when I was a little girl.'

'Excellent,' said Catherine. 'Please share her with us.' So Win read to them in her pleasant gentle voice, and conjured up a very different picture from the exotic setting of the West Indies. She transported her listeners to a smallholding in the Yorkshire Dales in the early nineteen fifties, presided over by an indomitable little woman, bent almost double like an old staple, who had a heart of gold, a will as enduring as the walls of millstone grit amongst which she lived and a wit like the crack of the Lone Ranger's whip.

When she had finished, there was a spontaneous little burst of applause – from everyone except her husband.

'That was *so* good too, Win,' said Catherine, noting Stanley's disgruntled expression and determined not to give him a chance to say anything belittling before she'd been able to give her own verdict. 'I couldn't have wished for two more splendid opening pieces or two more contrasting styles. This is just what I wanted to illustrate to you all – that you all have unique material available if you'll give it a chance to surface. Marnie intrigued and alarmed us – we felt her fear and loneliness and she took us to an exotic location. Win has shown us something equally vivid and completely different. We knew what those floury scones smelt like when they came out of the oven, we felt the chill of the icy outside privy in winter and the warmth of the old range inside the house – and we knew about the warmth of the welcome in that farm kitchen too. Thank you both . . . well done. Morwenna, could you read your piece now, please?'

As she listened to the various readers, Louisa became uneasily conscious not only of her own increasing anxiety about making public what she had written, but also of a feeling of shame that somehow she had not expected the general standard of writing to be so high – and what that told her about her own arrogant preconceptions made her blush.

Morwenna had written of the first small plot of garden she'd been allowed to call her own as a child; of how she had bought a packet of nasturtium seeds with her pocket money and of the lifelong love of growing things that it had engendered in her. Toothy Joyce made them all laugh with her hilarious accounts of the tourists who flooded her gift shop in the summer and the Colonel wrote about his pride in the men of his platoon, when he first saw action as a young subaltern, serving with the Northumberland Fusiliers in Aden during the early nineteen sixties. He wrote in short staccato sentences – not unlike gunfire, Louisa thought – which suited his subject well.

There would have been no prizes for guessing who had penned Bunty's offering, which turned out to be full of skipping elves, kindly gnomes and magic mushrooms – though not, her listeners presumed, ones with hallucinogenic qualities.

Christopher Piper, like Marnie, wrote in the present tense to describe the overwhelming impression that his first sight of the great stone figures on the northern porch of Chartres Cathedral had made on him when he'd first seen them as a schoolboy, giving him a sense of awe and an acute awareness of something 'other' which he'd never forgotten. 'But I'd also just read *The Hound of Heaven*, which I was studying in English for my GCSEs,' he said drily when he'd finished reading, 'so I was ripe for indulging in the fancy that I was being pursued by the divine. Not a feeling that's persisted.'

Louisa looked at him in surprise. It was not at all the sort of thing she had expected from him. She wondered if he really had once been a monk, as Isobel had suggested over tea last night.

'I think you have material for a poem in that bit of prose, Christopher,' Catherine told him seriously, 'but I suspect you already know that yourself.'

'Perhaps.' He looked pleased. 'I hope so . . . I shall work on it, anyway. It's interesting to write about a subject not of one's own choosing.' He grinned, suddenly. 'That hasn't happened to me for years – very salutary!'

Stanley Heslington was the only person not prepared to read out what he had written – possibly some people suspected because he hadn't actually written anything. Win looked agonised. 'I feel I've got a bit beyond all this elementary stuff,' Stanley said – an announcement that was greeted in stony silence by the rest of the group. He looked round defiantly, spoiling for an argument, clearly expecting pressure to be brought to make him change his mind, so that Catherine's cool: 'That's perfectly all right, Stanley. It's completely voluntary,' as she moved swiftly on to the next person, did not please him at all.

'Now, Louisa, it's your turn,' said Catherine, thinking that the bubbly young woman, whose confident vivacity seemed at odds with the fine-drawn fragility of her physique, looked surprisingly nervous. She had noted Louisa's sudden loss of equilibrium the previous evening, but that was nothing particularly unusual. During her years of tutoring, Catherine had got used to witnessing sudden emotional upheavals, even in the most unexpected people, when they started exploring a part of their past which they usually kept firmly submerged. 'Will you finish the session for us? It's always especially hard to go either first or last, but I hope you'll let us hear what you've managed to do.'

'Yes of course,' said Louisa, determined that if Marnie had been brave enough to go first, she was certainly not going to refuse to be last, and not wishing to put herself in the same uncooperative camp as Stanley Heslington either. She took a deep breath, looked at her notebook and began:

'*I shall never forget my seventeenth birthday because that was the day I first saw Mr Brown and it was Mr Brown who made me decide to go on living – to fight my illness and cooperate with the treatment I resented so much. When I first looked at his battered body in the cardboard box, he suddenly opened his huge dark eyes and I felt as if he was seeing into the depths of me. If a human had looked at me like that, at that particular time, I would have turned away because I was so fed up with being peered at and prodded and questioned and assessed, but this was different. More of an exchange between two scared creatures coping with unfamiliar circumstances and uncertain futures. Fanciful* perhaps, but that's how it seemed to me at the time. Anyway, we gazed at each other and I made a pact with him – sad, bedraggled pair that we were. If you will survive, I swore to him, then I will survive too. All or nothing. If you can pull through, then so can I, but if you die . . . oh! if you die, I vowed to him, then I will give up and die too and it will save everyone a lot of trouble. It was a terrifying oath to take but it was the beginning of my battle to live – and his. I had been warned that my hair would fall out, had been expecting it and absolutely dreading it – but I also hoped desperately that I might be the exception. You always think the lightning won't strike you and when I first started to find stray hairs on my pillow every morning and then great clumps of it, I gave way to self-pity. I wallowed in it. I felt like a moth-eaten relic and I didn't want to face my reflection, but at the same time I developed a morbid fascination for checking on my appearance in the mirror whenever I didn't think anyone else could see me. It was like an addiction. Of course it didn't help my state of mind that I felt so sick and awful as well, but there was more to it than that. I hadn't really felt ill before the cancer was diagnosed, just tired and listless, so the fact that it was the treatment rather than the illness that seemed to be doing these awful things to my body made me furiously angry. My poor parents had a terrible time with me. I don't know how they bore it. I wanted to give up the chemotherapy and was as uncooperative about everything as I could possibly be. I suppose the anger was at least a positive reaction, but when I started to lose my hair I turned my face to the wall. I know now that both my parents and the doctors were very bothered at my attitude. My mother has told me since how our GP, who had known me since I was little, kept telling her that she must somehow try to make me fight the disease myself – willingly cooperate in my treatment – but no one could get through to me at all.

'I'd always been the spoilt baby of the family, indulged and teased and protected by my older brothers, and adored and pampered by my parents. I had a blissful home in the country, with ponies and dogs and much love and laughter; I was popular at school and was used to being told I was pretty – goodness, I must have been insufferable! – but my world had always been a sunny place where there was someone ready to kiss me better if the smallest thing went wrong. I felt inviolable – and when I got sick I had no stratagems for coping with ordinary difficulties let alone real misfortune and I very nearly gave up on everything.

'Then on my seventeenth birthday a friend of one of my brothers, who was a bit older than me, found a fledgling tawny owl at the side of the road that had been hit by a car. He knew a lot about birds, especially raptors – he had a Harris hawk that he'd trained himself – so he realised that he shouldn't try to pick it up in his hands and that it could easily either die of shock or damage itself even more if it struggled, so he managed to gather it up, very carefully, in an old dog towel he'd got in the back of his car, and put it in a cardboard box and take it home. He'd always been brilliant at mending things and he managed to super-glue its obviously smashed beak together, but he didn't dare examine it more closely. He was on his way to the vet with it, when he suddenly thought it might interest me because, before I got ill, he sometimes used to take me out hawking with him. Anyway, he stopped at our house to show it to me. It was in an awful state, wet and filthy and injured and it only had half its feathers. I looked in that box and thought we were two of a kind because I only had half my feathers too. Adam – the friend – asked me if I'd like to go to the vet with him and I said I would, which was quite a decision for me because I hadn't come to terms with my mothy hair then and couldn't bear anyone to see me. Also I wasn't supposed to go anywhere where I might pick up an infection, but to my mother's great credit she encouraged me to go. I think she knew something important had happened. So I got in Adam's car with the box on my knee and we drove off to the vet.

'The owl had to have its leg set and one wing pinned, and though the vet thought Adam had done a spectacular job on the *smashed beak he didn't think it would pull through. Anyway, against all the odds Mr Brown, as we called him, survived – and so did I. I had no idea till then what tight regulations there are about keeping wild birds in captivity. We had to get a special certificate from the vet to show Defra, to say Mr Brown couldn't have survived if we'd let him loose. He still can't fly well enough to hunt properly though he can flutter up to a low branch. Adam gave him to me as a birthday present. Lots of people have wanted to buy him since, but luckily I'm restricted from selling him – not that I'd ever do that anyway because I'll never, ever part with him. The day after he came to us, I had my head shaved properly and when the treatment was finished my hair grew back in, just as I'd been promised it would. And Mr Brown's feathers grew in too. He's a very handsome person now. Sometimes I take him round with me – he loves the car – and sometimes he stays with Adam, but mostly he lives in his own aviary at my parents' house and he's extremely tame. He'll ride about on my shoulder when I'm at home provided I've got something padded on – owl claws are very sharp – and I can put my finger in his beak and he'll nuzzle it but never peck. I dread anything happening to him. He's still in very good shape but he's eleven now, which is quite old even for an owl in captivity – in the wild, seven would be a goodish age. He's my icon of recovery.'*

Louisa stopped reading and again there was silence in the room, but this time, unlike the response that Stanley had elicited, it was a friendly, encouraging silence.

'I'm afraid it's a bit disjointed,' she said apologetically, 'a bit of a jumble really.'

'I told you we weren't looking for polished work,' said Catherine. 'The point is that you had us on the edge of our seats, and I have a feeling it was important for you too.'

'Yes.' Louisa nodded. 'What Marnie wrote about life being a gift, something we should never take liberties with, that really rang a bell for me. I learned that lesson too, though in very different circumstances from hers.'

'Well, my goodness,' said Catherine, 'we have had some fascinating stories this morning! What a great start to our week. You've certainly all deserved your lunch and I should think you're very ready for a break after so much soul-baring. Thank you all for being wonderful students. Giles and Isobel have asked me to say that there will always be a buffet lunch in the main conference room, so please go and help yourselves. This afternoon is free. You may want to write or get inspiration from exploring the countryside. There are wonderful walks – up the hill behind the house, or round the lake. I'll see you all back here at five.'

There was a general move towards the main conference room and the promise of food. Louisa found herself standing next to Marnie as they queued for home-made soup and hot rolls. They looked at each other appraisingly, both aware that after the exposing and sharing of such intimate stories, the relationships of everyone in the room had inevitably changed. Surprisingly Marnie spoke first.

'We got off to a bad start, you and I,' she said gruffly, her longing for acceptance getting the better of her habitual defensiveness. 'I'm sorry if it was my fault.' She gave a little shrug. 'It usually is. I'm hopeless at first approaches. I can't seem to get the hang of them.'

'And I was an unfriendly cow,' said Louisa quickly. 'But I was fascinated by what you wrote. We've had completely opposite early experiences. I'd love to hear more. Shall we go for a walk together this afternoon? I need to blow some cobwebs away after all that introspection.'

She thought Marnie might refuse and was pleased when she nodded. 'Sure. I'd like that. I was quite unprepared for the fascination of all those personal revelations – makes you look at everyone in a completely new way and want to know more. You can tell me about your recovery icon – I've always loved owls.'

'And I want to know more about Kenneth and that old lady. I sensed she has become really important in your life. Am I right?'

'She's the most crucial part of my whole story – she's the reason I'm here.'

'Let's meet after lunch and I'll take you up the hill and we can sit by the burn and listen to curlews calling and put our worlds to rights.'

'Okay. I'll tell you about the old lady. It only takes one person to alter your whole way of looking at things and she did that for me.' She made a wry face. 'But old habits sure die hard – I'm still working on it after twenty years!'

They didn't attempt to sit next to each other at lunch, not wanting to start on their exchange of histories until they were alone, but as soon as the meal was over they headed up the hill behind the house.

Christopher Piper watched the two young women depart and set off in the opposite direction – something he seemed to be doing rather often lately, he thought. He too had been absorbed by the stories, looking at all his fellow students with new eyes and wanting to know more about them. In particular he would have liked to know more about the events in the West Indies – which must surely have been responsible for turning Marnie into such an awkward, distrustful character – and also about the unexpected shadows in Louisa's otherwise apparently sunlit life. Few people turn out to be quite what they seem on first meeting, and he thought wryly that this would certainly apply to him too. It had occurred to him before lunch that he would like to suggest to Louisa that they might go for a walk in the afternoon, but apparently

Marnie had got in first – and anyway he wasn't sure that he was prepared to get into a close conversation with Louisa Forrester, much as he felt drawn to her. It might prove awkward.

Chapter Six

As they walked up behind the house, through a small gate and out on to the open hillside, Louisa and Marnie chatted easily enough about the other participants on the course and the fascination of everyone's revealing pieces of writing. They agreed about the horrendousness of Stanley and the cleverness of Catherine in uncovering and encouraging the talents of Win. They agreed in liking the Colonel and Morwenna and Joyce.

'And Christopher Piper?' asked Louisa as they followed the burn uphill. 'What do you make of him? Bit of a dark horse? Answer to a maiden's prayer? Arrogant shit?'

'I don't really know what I think about him yet,' said Marnie cautiously, aware that she must sound stiff and dull to Louisa – and probably untruthful too, she thought ruefully.

'Didn't you enjoy having a drink with him?' asked Louisa.

Marnie shrugged, miserably conscious of how awkward and unforthcoming she had been with Christopher the evening before, when she had secretly longed to be as outgoing and amusing as Louisa seemed, quite effortlessly, to be with everyone.

'It was sort of okay,' she said. 'He was perfectly friendly but I didn't find him that easy. Probably my fault.'

'At least you have to admit he's attractive?'

'I suppose he's very good-looking – if you go for those sorts of looks,' Marnie said dismissively.

Louisa laughed. 'Oh, but I *do* go for them, don't you?' she said. 'Anyway, I certainly think he'll add to the fun of our week! I'm dying to know more about him because I think something must have happened to him since I met him a few years ago. I really, really like him.'

Marnie thought it extraordinary that Louisa was prepared to disclose her liking so openly on such short acquaintance. She could not in a million years envisage herself making such a statement about her hopes and desires to anyone. Louisa might or might not be a gambler, she thought – but she certainly wasn't a poker player.

They had reached a small stone bridge across the burn. 'If we go over to the other side,' said Louisa, 'we could sit against that rock – out of the wind but in the sun. You can see for miles up here, can't you? Keep your eyes open for an eagle.'

'Oh, I would so love to see one,' said Marnie. 'The old lady in the West Indies used to tell me about golden eagles – and otters and deer and seals – in her Scottish childhood. So . . . talking about birds, tell me more about your owl.'

'Okay. God, but I'm really hot after steaming up the hill like that! Must be out of training.' Louisa pulled her jersey off and they both flopped on to the mossy grass, which was surprisingly dry, and watched the clouds drifting across the brilliant blue sky. There was no sign of an eagle, but a buzzard wheeled and mewed overhead and curlews bubbled their spring calls like the noise of the peaty water purling over the rocks. Louisa told Marnie about her beloved owl, Mr Brown: how tame he was; what a character; how funny; how beautiful.

'When you see him from a distance you think he's just plain brown, rather a dull colour,' she said, 'but when you have him on your arm you marvel at the variety of shading in his tawny feathers; their delicacy; the way they overlap. People talk about "wise owls", but actually, I hate to tell you, they're among the least intelligent birds – real thickos. Sometimes Mr Brown forgets he's a bird and fancies he's a dog and tries to waddle after me with the rolling gate of a drunken sailor which is terribly endearing – providing he gets something tasty like a dead chick afterwards!'

'Does he love you too? Do you feel you have a two-way relationship?'

'Hard to tell. Perhaps he thinks I'm his mate – certainly a source of food. I don't love him for his brains, that's for sure, though he has a certain engaging guile connected with food, but I like to think we have an odd sort of rapport on another level. It may all be in my imagination.' She made a deprecating face. 'Don't laugh, but I tell him things . . . I ask for his help . . .' She shrugged. 'I know it sounds silly. I can't explain it.'

'Maybe he's the grown-up version of what teddy bears once did for us when we were kids – something that was vitally important as far as I was concerned. Perhaps he's your prayer wheel, your rosary . . . but also your touchstone to help you clarify your own thoughts. He's . . .' Marnie searched for the right word. 'He's your go-between; an intermediary between the everyday self and the spiritual bit that wants to communicate with the divine.'

Louisa looked at her with surprise. 'Yes,' she said. 'Thank you. That's it exactly. How did you know?'

But Marnie, having ventured with such unexpected empathy into Louisa's emotional world, seemed to withdraw again, shying away from the intimacy of the moment like a startled horse. Louisa half expected to see her gallop off across the hill.

'Tell about the hawking,' said Marnie. 'You mentioned that your friend, the one who rescued Mr Brown, was into falconry.'

'Umm . . . Adam. He's always been mad on it. He first got me hooked when I was about fourteen.' Louisa returned to more neutral ground and told Marnie about the thrill of flying hawks either to a lure or after live game. 'You feel you're not just spectating but have become part of the countryside, part of nature itself – exciting, sometimes brutal nature. You feel primitive – part of the wind and the moorland. Nothing to do with a sentimentalised version of wildlife. It's terrific. Adam first started with a kestrel and then got a Harris hawk, though he's flown black kites and eagle owls and various falcons too. He's brilliant at training them. I still love going out hawking with him but it doesn't happen very often now – only when we go home to our respective families in Yorkshire. We've been living and working in London for several years. Adam's a serious-minded lawyer but he becomes another person out on the hill.'

'And what's happened to him now?' asked Marnie. 'Not to Mr Brown, I mean, but Adam? Do you still have a relationship?'

'Did,' said Louisa, rather sadly. 'We did. But we've just split up – my doing. I'd still like to be friends but I need to move on. Unfortunately he didn't feel the same way and he was very upset. I feel terrible about him. He's been my rock for years – and now I've chucked him.'

'But you can't base a relationship solely on gratitude.' Marnie suddenly felt sorry for the glamorous Louisa. 'Do you still have to go for check-ups and things for your health – even after ten years?' she asked curiously, wondering what it must have been like to live under the threat of dying at such a young age; admiring Louisa's head-on attitude to life. 'Is that still a problem or are you completely in the clear now?'

But Louisa brushed this question aside. 'Who's ever completely in the clear about anything?' she said breezily.

'I'm fine and I've been very lucky. I do still have check-ups and it's a great relief whenever it's over for another year, but in between times I don't let myself think about it. Medical history's boring and I've had too much of it.'

From the expression on Louisa's face Marnie guessed that this was not as easy as she made it out to be, but since she was the last person to probe for more information than anyone wanted to give she did not press her about it.

'Let's not talk about me any more.' Louisa tossed a pebble into the pool below them and pulled her jersey on again although Marnie thought it was still pleasantly warm. 'It's your turn now. Tell me more about what happened in the West Indies. Something momentous obviously *did* happen.'

So Marnie told her about the strange events surrounding her mother's terrifying illness, of how the old lady had rescued her and how they had formed an unlikely bond that still represented the strongest attachment Marnie had ever sustained for anyone. 'Perhaps that's just because we were separated so soon,' she said bleakly. 'Perhaps it wouldn't have lasted if she'd known me better. I'm crap at keeping relationships going. I might have spoiled it.'

Just as she had when she read to the class, Marnie seemed to Louisa to enter an almost hypnotic state when she described the dark events that had taken place in her childhood. It was clearly a very vivid memory and they both became so completely absorbed in the telling of it that they lost all sense of time.

Earlier, when the sun had felt so hot, it had been easy for Louisa to be transported by Marnie's storytelling and imagine herself on a Caribbean island, but as the afternoon wore on there started to be a chill in the air. A sharp breeze sent the cloud-shadows racing across the hills, so that it looked as if the dark patches of the still winter-dead bracken were on the move, dragged across the surface of the land like an outworn carpet. Further away, a few of the high peaks were still capped with snow and little pockets of white clung in the hollows below rocky outcrops: a reminder that spring could still withdraw its favours, thought Louisa.

Marnie sat up, and hugged her knees. She felt as disorientated as if she had returned from a long journey, or woken after a particularly vivid dream and was still in the half-world between two realities. She gazed out over the unfamiliar Perthshire woods and fields. Windflowers, the tiny white wood anemones which still starred the grass in shady places, danced in the breeze and clumps of primroses nestled in the mossy bank above the rushing burn – but she half expected to see larger, more exotic flowers and hear the roar of the ocean and the clattering of the wind in the palm trees.

'So you never saw the old contessa again after you'd gone back to the States?' asked Louisa.

'Nope,' answered Marnie sadly. 'I never saw her again and it's a big regret – but she kept her promise. She did write to me. She went back to Italy after we left St Matt's. I had three letters from her after she got home. I've kept them all.'

She looked at Louisa, speculatively, as though assessing her trustworthiness as a future friend. 'She did more than write,' she went on. 'She left her diaries to me in her will. But they've only recently come into my possession so I'm still trying to piece her story together and learning things about her life. It's real difficult because she obviously wasn't a dedicated diarist and only wrote it spasmodically – and, as far as I can make out, quite randomly, for no obvious reason. She'll start on something interesting and then just stop. Her writing's also extremely hard to read, not to mention the fact that some of it's in Italian. There

99

appear to be huge gaps. It's tantalising but up to now I haven't wanted to let anyone else look at it. It may sound stupid but I've felt as if I'd be betraying a confidence, although I'm definitely going to need help. All the same, with what I have managed to make out, I get a feeling of what she must have been like. Headstrong, passionate – obviously capable of giving and inspiring great love. Courageous too – I think she had a tough time in the war. I guess she was pretty impossible to deal with if she didn't want to cooperate. Surprisingly funny – her comments about other people are sharp and hilarious. I'm totally fascinated by her.'

'When did she die?' asked Louisa. 'I imagined from what you said that she was quite old and ill when you met her.'

'She was. Well . . . she was certainly ill and of course I thought she was ancient, though I don't suppose she was more than seventy – old enough to a child, though. She died of cancer six months later. Apparently by then she knew she'd only gotten weeks left, but she went all the way out to the States to meet my father and talk to him about me, though I didn't know anything about it at the time. Sadly I'd just gone back to England. She'd expected to see me, but we just missed. I'd have been heartbroken if I'd known at the time. My father tells me now that she made a great impression on him – he was quite smitten with her and thought she had real style and dignity – very imperious, very *grande dame*. He's quite funny about her – my father's a powerful, scary man himself, the president of a huge international company, and people don't usually tear strips off him or cut him down below his considerable size. He says she left him in no doubt about what she thought of both him and my mother as parents. Imagine her doing that for a little girl she hardly knew – and a plain and rather disagreeable child at that!'

'She obviously didn't find you disagreeable,' said Louisa, surprised to find tears pricking her eyes, aching for the lonely little girl Marnie must have been. 'You clearly gave her something too – brought out some feeling of warmth at the end of her life that she thought she would never feel again. It can't only have been a one-way thing.'

'I hope not. What a comforting thing to say! Thank you for that.' Marnie gave Louisa one of her fleeting, under-used smiles. 'She told my father about the incident with Kenneth and her anxiety that dealing with such dark things might have been dangerous for me. I think she was probably right about that. I still get strange moments when I feel overwhelmed by something dark that I can't explain but which I know is linked to that time. She must have rattled my father because when my mother sent me back to him he insisted on keeping me for quite a long period. It was one of the more stable episodes in my childhood – until his then marriage broke up and it was all change stations for everyone again.'

'Does your mother know what you tried to do to her?' asked Louisa curiously.

'No. I asked my father about that. Apparently the Contessa made him promise not to tell my mom. She thought she'd be certain to use it against me if it suited her. Dad says the old lady had taken against my mother big time and was really scornful about her.'

'What else do you know about her story?'

'She wasn't Italian by birth. She was born and brought up in Scotland – in the house on the loch that she told me so much about as we lay in her hammock. I think she had an idyllic childhood, or so it sounded to me as a little girl. Lots of freedom; lots of animals; lots of laughter, lots of love – all the things I'd always longed for. She obviously adored her elder brother. Then, when she was eighteen, she was sent out to Italy to learn about art and culture, and also, so she told me, to learn how to behave like a polite young lady instead of the unruly wildcat her mother said she was turning into. Apparently it didn't work out as her family hoped. While she was there she met the love of her life, an Italian from an old aristocratic family, a landowner with estates in the south of Italy, whom she first of all ran away with – causing frightful scandal – and eventually married in the teeth of both families' disapproval.'

'Why did her family disapprove of the marriage so much? A landed count sounds rather a catch to me.'

'Because he was fifteen years older than her; because he was a Roman Catholic and her family were Protestants. Worst of all because he was married and he left his Italian wife for her – big disgrace as you can imagine with both families furious and unforgiving. Obviously not much Christian charity on either side.' Marnie paused.

'And?' prompted Louisa.

'And her diaries weren't all she left me,' said Marnie. 'It's unbelievable really but she left me . . . nearly everything. Everything that was hers to leave, that is. I believe there were estates in Calabria and an apartment in Rome and those had to go to a nephew of her husband's. You can't imagine the shock when my father told me all this only a few months ago. He broke it to me about her death at the time of course and was very sweet to me because I was extremely upset – but he never said a word then about inheriting money. I remember it vividly. I suppose everyone probably remembers the first time someone's death really touches them personally. The Contessa made him my trustee together with an Italian lawyer and swore him to secrecy. She left it up to him to decide exactly when I should be told but suggested it should be after my twenty-fifth birthday. She thought I ought to have more experience of life before I got control of what is a serious amount of money.'

Louisa gazed at her. So Giles had been right: Marnie had indeed inherited a fortune. 'What was in the parcel she gave you when she said goodbye to you? The first clue?'

'Two things. There was a little silver photograph frame with two faded black and white pictures in it: one is of a little girl of about six wearing a caped coat and leggings and standing with her arm round an enormous shaggy dog – a Scottish deer hound I should think, very Walter Scott, very Landseer – and on the back in faded ink is written *Lucy-Anne with Archer, 1920*. She's standing by a great door with some sort of crest or something carved in stone over the top. The second picture is of a house – a tower – on the edge of some water – a tower with an imposing arched doorway – the same door, I guess. It looks like a castle really. The other present was this – look.'

Marnie fished inside her jersey and pulled out a gold locket on a fine chain. It was engraved with the initials L.A.D.G. She pulled the chain over her head and opened the locket to reveal a miniature head-and-shoulders portrait of a little girl – obviously the same child as in the photograph – a little girl in a white lace dress; a beautiful child with brilliant blue eyes and long, red hair held back from her face by a bow tied on the top of her head. 'I always wear it,' Marnie said. 'It gives me a link with her because she showed it to me one time when I went to visit her in her room. You don't know how much I long to be able to thank her for what she's done for me . . . and I don't mean just the money. She had no reason to care for me, but for the first time in my life I felt someone liked me and valued me just for myself. I said this morning that it only takes one person to change your outlook. She changed mine.'

'You must have given her something special too,' insisted Louisa. 'She'd never have done all that if you hadn't made a huge impression on her. She must have loved you – and from what you say it doesn't sound as if she was used to loving children, only her Italian husband. Didn't they have any family of their own?'

'There was a little boy who died. I think he only lived for a few hours. Anyway, apparently she couldn't have any more. Her diaries of that period make heartbreaking reading. But there's no doubt her husband, Carlos, adored her and it was a great, great love for both of them that lasted all their lives. I can't imagine that sort of love. Apparently he died unexpectedly of a heart attack a few months before I met her and she couldn't cope with life without him at all.'

'Like Sir Henry Wotton's lines about the death of Lady Morton,' said Louisa. 'I remember crying over that when I was at school. I used to think it was the shortest and most romantic poem in the English language:

> 'He first deceased; she for a little tried
> To live without him: liked it not, and died.'

'Yes,' said Marnie. 'I've never heard that before, but just like that. That says it all.' She looked at her watch. 'Gee – look at the time! I've wittered on about myself most of the afternoon and it's half of four already! It's gotten a bit chilly. What an egomaniac you must think me . . . I do apologise. Thank you for listening to me but you should have stopped me.'

'No way!' said Louisa. 'I want to know more, but we'll have to dash now if we want to grab a cup of tea before we start the next session at five. You can't leave me in suspense for long, though. Will you promise to let me have the next exciting instalment soon?'

'Okay,' said Marnie, 'but only if you tell me more about your story too.'

'Hmm – perhaps,' said Louisa, after a moment's

hesitation. 'But mine's not nearly so interesting. Come on then. We'd better hurry.'

They hurtled down the twisty path by the burn, slithering and sliding on the loose stones at high risk of twisting ankles, but both finding it a release after the intensity of exploring the past.

They arrived back at the house laughing and breathless and Isobel, who was pouring out tea and dispensing home-made biscuits in the kitchen, thought she had never seen such a change in a short space of time as that which had occurred in Marnie. A testament to the curative powers of laughter and friendship, she thought, and sent a grateful, approving look in Louisa's direction. 'Well, you both look full of good Scottish fresh air,' she said, smiling a welcome to them. 'Come and stoke yourselves up before you start work again.'

All nine participants of the course had reassembled ready for the next session, and all except Stanley were looking forward to it. Win, like various other people, had put her name down for a tutorial with Catherine and had been allotted the first session at three o'clock that afternoon. In the teeth of her husband's discouragement she had taken several little pieces that she had secretly written over the years to show Catherine, and half an hour later had emerged in a glow of excitement at the encouragement she'd received. This she had unwisely shared with her husband and his ungenerous scorn and grumpiness had nearly taken her breath away, used as she was to disparage-ment from that quarter. But if Stanley expected his wife to give up the idea of writing and stick to warming slippers and making Victoria sponge cakes he had seriously under-rated her. She had quietly but firmly refused to be put off and had disappeared into the garden with pen and note-book to work on some of Catherine's suggestions, leaving her husband at a loose end with no one to bore or bully.

Morwenna and Joyce had taken Bunty with them and gone by car to explore the small town of Blairalder, where Bunty, succumbing to an acute attack of Highland fever with alarming results, had bought herself an outfit in gaudy Royal Stuart tartan, complete with matching tam-o'-shanter and, as Joyce had muttered to Morwenna, enough tins of Edinburgh rock to rot the teeth of all her relations for years to come.

Christopher had gone down to the loch in pursuit of solitude but found the Colonel had got there before him. Christopher thought that once he would have had no compunction in shaking him off, but the Colonel hailed the younger man with such genuine friendliness that he had neither the heart nor the bad manners to turn down the suggestion that they should go round the loch together. Before they were halfway round Christopher's leg started to play up, but he would have died rather than admit he would like to turn back. If, by the end of the afternoon, he felt he knew a great deal about the Colonel's regiment he was equally relieved not to be questioned about his own history.

They were all sitting in the kitchen, some at the big round table, some on the cosily squashy sofas and chairs at the far end of the room, fortifying themselves with mugs of tea and finding the brownies and shortbread that Morag, the Glendrochatt cook, had produced irresistible, when Giles came in holding the hand of a small boy.

'Hi, everyone,' said Giles. 'Look what we've got! How's that for a productive afternoon's work? Show them, Rory.'

The small boy rushed over to Isobel waving a minute brown trout, all of ten centimetres long, by the tail. 'I catched it all by myself,' he told her excitedly, and then added modestly: '. . . well almost.'

'How wonderful, darling!' Isobel sounded suitably impressed. 'Shall we ask Sheena to cook it for your tea?'

The small boy nodded enthusiastically, and then overcome to be the focus of so many people's attention, placed his catch carefully on the shortbread plate, climbed on to Isobel's knee and stuck his fishy thumb in his mouth.

Louisa thought he was the most sensationally good-looking little boy she had ever seen and was just about to say to Isobel 'So this is Lorna's son?' when she was struck by something which froze the words in her mouth and left her gaping like a fish herself. At this moment Bunty, lured by the presence of a child like a falcon to a day-old chick, swooped from the other side of the room and crouched by Isobel's chair, demanding to be told the full story of Rory's battle with Leviathan. It was easy to see why she had devoted her life to children because in no time at all she had him telling her the whole saga, from the delicious digging up of wriggly worms for bait to the dangling of the rod over the pool in the burn, the *ginormous* tug on the line, the crucial skill of the strike and finally the landing of the monster. Isobel couldn't help thinking that Bunty, dealing with an actual child, was much more attractive than Bunty trying to treat everyone she met as if they were one, and thought perhaps she should revise her opinion of her.

'Well you are a clever boy,' said Bunty admiringly, 'and I'm sure it won't be the only fish you and Daddy catch together either!' She beamed happily at the other spectators. 'Easy to see who's a real daddy's boy, isn't it?' she enquired, addressing the room at large, and then, turning to Isobel, she added, 'I don't think I've ever seen a father and son more alike in all my years of teaching – it's almost uncanny. You must be very proud of them both.'

Isobel froze. Across the room she and Giles held each other's gaze as though a magnet connected them and there was one of those silences, in reality mere seconds, that to a few people in the room seemed to go on and on, making a nonsense of the usual measure of time. Isobel had gone very white. 'Yes,' she said, her voice unnaturally bright and clear. 'I am very proud of them, but Rory isn't actually our son. He's my nephew.'

'Oh well.' Bunty was blissfully unaware that a chasm had just opened at her feet. 'That's even more remarkable then – but I suppose uncles and nephews can be just as alike as fathers and sons, can't they? After all, it's the same pool of genes, isn't it?'

'Rory is my sister's little boy.'

Isobel's words came out with a ringing clarity that might have won her a prize at a competition for elocution and even Bunty couldn't fail to notice the look on her face. Louisa felt her heart thudding in her chest, all sorts of uncomfortable scenarios suddenly opening up in her imagination and old gossip about Isobel's sister Lorna racing through her memory. She longed for the right words to switch the moment off, but it was Catherine who saved the day.

She banged loudly on her teacup with a spoon, though there was hardly a need to call for silence. 'I'm sorry to hurry you all,' she said briskly, 'but it's after five, and we have work to do. Could you all please make your way across to the conference room as quickly as you can? We need to get started.'

Then, feeling like a schoolmarm again, she shepherded her nine adult pupils out through the French window and across the courtyard to the conference room, leaving Isobel, Giles and Isobel's small nephew alone in the kitchen.

'Rory,' said Isobel, putting the little boy gently off her knee, 'why don't you run and find Sheena and ask her if you can have your bath now and then you can have your tea in the nursery and look at a video.'

She waited till the kitchen door closed and then turned on her husband. 'Oh, *Giles*,' she said. 'Oh, Giles, I can't stand this! What are we to do? This is the third time in a month it's happened. And you promised me – you've always sworn it wasn't so . . .'

'No,' said Giles, 'no, Izzy. I told you what Lorna told me when he was born.'

He came towards her and tried to take her in his arms but she shook him off and busied herself ostentatiously clearing the table, violently wiping the surface as if she was trying to scrub out Bunty's words.

'Look,' he said. 'We have to face the fact that we've both always known this was on the cards.' He added bitterly: 'It's obviously suited Lorna to play cat and mouse over it but it's suited us to accept her word, though with her record we should never have let ourselves be taken in.' He punched the palm of his left hand with his right fist. 'One single, stupid, much regretted night with your bloody sister and . . .'

'Well don't expect *me* to be sympathetic.' Isobel banged a cupboard door shut with such ferocity it was amazing all the china inside didn't shatter.

'Oh, Iz! Sympathy doesn't come into it. For God's sake don't let's allow ourselves to be thrown right back after all we went through five years ago and after the way we've struggled and succeeded in getting our life back together – then Lorna would really have won. She's deliberately lobbed a time bomb into our marriage, knowing it couldn't be long before it exploded. Now it has. What beats me is why the hell she's waited so long.'

'Isn't there some quote about revenge being a dish that's best served cold?'

'Ah,' said Giles, 'yes of course – that's it exactly. Come on, darling,' he went on urgently, 'we can't give Lorna the satisfaction of eating that dish. Somehow we'll get through this together.'

Isobel looked at him with great misery. 'Poor Rory,' she said. 'He's such a great little boy and none of this is his fault. But – oh, Giles, I hate myself for doing it, but every time I look at him I see you, and then . . .' She faltered and stopped, and at last came slowly over to her husband and stood looking up at him. 'And then,' she went on, almost in a whisper, 'then I see Ed. Darling, special, *different* Ed and the contrast with how he was at Rory's age hurts so much I don't know what to do with myself. All those might-have-beens come flooding back and overwhelm me.'

'I know,' said Giles. 'I know. Don't think I'm not dreadfully aware of it too.'

'But I don't need any DNA test to tell me the truth,' Isobel said fiercely. 'I look at the portrait on the landing by Carlos Sanchez of you at the same age. I look at the photograph on my dressing table of you in your kilt aged five that your father gave me. They're not just *like* Rory – they could *be* Rory. I can't stop looking at them. First at him, then at you, then at Ed – and I know that Lorna has finally got her revenge on me for marrying you. She's given you the perfect son we couldn't have together. And I can't bear it.'

This time when Giles put his arms round her she didn't pull away. He held her close, stroking her hair, feeling her shaking with emotion – miserably conscious of her distress; terrified that a chasm was about to open up between them; filled with foreboding about the future.

Chapter Seven

Christopher Piper lay on the bed in his room in the Old Steading, hands linked behind his head, and asked himself, not for the first time, what on earth he was doing in this place with these unknown people. What did he really hope to achieve? Was he adventurously moving forward to new and challenging possibilities, or was he, as his long-term girlfriend, Nicola, scornfully maintained, in cowardly flight from real life? His feet stuck out over the bottom of the mattress as they always did in any standard-sized bed, but he was used to that. At least this bed was a great deal more comfortable than other beds he'd been sleeping in recently and he thought wryly that his present companions, even though he might not have chosen any of them, were a good deal more congenial than the last group of people he'd been with.

After the evening session with Catherine, he'd received a text from Nicola, which read: *Have u come to yr senses yet?* He was outraged that she dared to consider she still had the right to ask such a question – what was it to her where his senses were, after she'd made it so abundantly plain that unless he were prepared to play the next stage of his life the way she wanted, she would have nothing more to do with him? The idea of Nicola's suddenly turning up unannounced and causing trouble – which would have been quite in character – filled him with disquiet. The thought of what her reaction to his fellow writers would be both filled him with amusement and brought him out in a cold sweat. Thank goodness she didn't know his address – at least he'd had enough sense not to tell her that. He viciously punched the one word *NO* into his mobile in reply, then thought better of it and erased it. It would be better to ignore her message altogether.

His leg was aching seriously now. He'd swallowed a couple of painkillers and got himself a whisky from the bar, which he'd brought upstairs so that he could think his own thoughts and escape for a bit from the increasing chumminess of the group. Too bad if they thought him unsociable, though he'd made a real effort to be friendly at supper and sat between bright, bird-like little Win, who was clearly developing unexpected talents, and jowly Morwenna, who wasn't. Nice women, both of them, and he'd been surprised to find how interesting they were to talk to, in their very different ways. Win had a beady eye for unexpected detail, a dry sense of humour and a shrewd way of summing people up which made her good company, though Christopher felt it might be as well to be a little guarded in her deceptively mild presence lest one should become fodder for a sharp little character sketch. She was the sort of woman in whom it would be easy to confide and give away more information than one intended. Despite the potentially undermining effect of the steady drip, drip, drip of her husband's barbed criticisms, he thought Win actually had far more self-assurance than Morwenna, who was clearly finding the demands of the course very taxing.

In the five o'clock session after tea, Catherine had presented them each with a postcard of Chagall's *I and the Village*, and suggested that they should write down their reactions to the painting. 'I want your *instant* reactions. Try to put down what really hits you, not what you feel you should notice or what you may already know about the picture,' she said. 'I don't want second-hand artistic criticism.'

'I can give you my instant reactions here and now,' Stanley had spluttered, rudely flipping his postcard back across the table to Catherine, 'but you won't like them. The artist's a lunatic and the picture's a bloody insult, that's what.'

'Well write that down then, Stanley. It doesn't matter whether I like it or not.' Catherine tried to keep an edge out of her voice; she was getting tired of Stanley's sniping. 'It's getting your imaginative response on paper that matters,' she said to the class as a whole, 'so that you can work it into something later – prose or poetry – if you want to.'

'Is it a fairy tale?' asked Bunty hopefully. 'I think it might be rather a scary one for children.'

'You tell us,' Catherine invited her.

Stanley had thrown his pen down and banged out of the room, fully expecting that there would be an instant move to persuade him to return, but no one followed him and his wife watched him go with a speculative look.

'What did you think about the Chagall exercise?' Christopher had asked Morwenna as an opening gambit at supper as she tucked into her piled plateful of poached sea-trout with watercress sauce and new potatoes. She let out a despairing moan.

'I had no idea what it meant at all and afterwards I was amazed at what other people found to say about it. I could only describe what I saw and I felt totally baffled by it – that huge, weird green face of someone wearing a hat and a crucifix and holding a little tree in his hand gazing, nose to nose, at a sheep which appeared to have someone milking a cow inside its head . . . incomprehensible! A nightmare.' Morwenna shook her head. 'I felt so envious because most of you seemed to be having such fun with your ideas, but I've never had any imagination myself.' She let out a sigh. 'When I was a child I was always the odd one out,' she told him. 'Other little girls seemed able to play any role at the blink of an eye, switching from wicked witch to beautiful princess as though they had an invisible script to read from, but I never had the slightest idea what I was meant to be doing let alone what I was expected to say, so I was always cast as a dumb animal or a servant, neither of which were required to speak and could be bossed around accordingly.' She shrugged her shoulders hopelessly.

'But I thought you already wrote a column for a newspaper? That's way ahead of what most of the rest of us here have achieved,' said Christopher, hoping to cheer her up.

'Oh, I can write about *facts*. I can tell you when to mulch your border, how to divide the rhizomes of your irises and what plants are least likely to die in your soil – but apparently that's not enough for our new editor. He talks about fresh approaches, firing the hearts of our readers with inspirational ideas and using more poetic imagery in our writing. Making the magazine *challenging*, he says. I don't really know what he means. I think it's quite challenging enough to get the planting times right and decide what shrubs will benefit from pruning without playing literary guessing games. It is a gardening magazine, after all.'

'Perhaps he'd like you to say your love is like a red, red rose, but you feel safer doing a Gertrude Stein and saying a rose is a rose is a rose?' suggested Christopher.

Morwenna, munching her salad as thoroughly as though she was shredding compost, chewed this idea over too. 'I suppose so,' she said gloomily, and added, 'but I've never been adaptable and I doubt if I can change now, so I also know I'm almost certainly going to lose my job even though I'm quite good at it. The readers want information . . . and I really do know about plants, so it seems a pity,' she said sadly.

'Why don't you run a question and answer column instead?' asked Christopher. 'Then the readers could send you their burning queries and you could give them the crisp, factual answers they need. You could get your friends to bombard the paper with interesting queries – or even send the questions in yourself to start with,' he suggested. 'It might become unmissable monthly reading: *Morwenna's Mailbag – Your Monkey Puzzles Solved.* You could sell the idea to your editor as a change of format for the magazine and then suggest he commissions non-horticultural writers, local celebrities perhaps, to describe their dream gardens. That would supply the purple prose he needs each month – and you could then write helpful comments on the practicalities of their schemes. How's that for a suggestion?'

Morwenna had looked at him out of her lugubrious brown eyes and said: 'That's not a bad idea. I might even give it a try,' which Christopher imagined, coming from her, was a positively lyrical response.

He'd been surprised at the varied approaches to the Chagall postcards, including his own. Marnie had written from the point of view of the young woman in the top right corner whose house has so disconcertingly turned upside down, leaving her head down, but mysteriously managing to defy gravity by remaining standing on the roof. She hoped it was a metaphor for coping with change and upheaval, for developing an ability to keep one's footing in unpropitious circumstances. Win had concentrated entirely on the huge face, which according to her had turned that curiously bright shade of green through an excess of jealousy. There were no prizes for guessing where that idea came from, though nobody liked to comment on it. Louisa had gone for an ecclesiastical view – the domed church, the rosary and crucifix round the green man's neck, the jewel colours and stained-glass window effect of the picture. Problems with the established church? Doubts about the trappings of religion? Corrupt cardinals? Papal fallibility? Louisa had let her imagination rip. The Colonel, trained not to give way to panic no matter how challenging the conditions, had attempted the exercise with grim determination but found it surprisingly enjoyable. He suggested that the painting might be symbolic of rural issues: the management of an outbreak of foot and mouth for instance, with the green man representing Defra. Warming to his theme he mentioned possible assistance by the military (though no one could see much evidence for this idea in the picture) and the colour coding of various restricted-access routes on agricultural land. He was rather pleased with this last notion. Joyce said the colours reminded her of eating fruit pastilles at the pantomime and that led her on to pantomime horses, and then to pantomime cows – something she knew about since she had once played the hind legs of one in a W.I. Christmas performance. Morwenna, despite her complaint to Christopher that she had no imagination, had come up with the suggestion that the tiny bejewelled tree in the green man's hand must have had its roots selectively pruned by a bonsai fanatic – a form of arboriculture she abhorred. Christopher himself had taken the view that the green man was psycho-analysing his prize-winning sheep in an attempt to cure it of its inconvenient conviction that it was really a cow. A question of identity crisis, he decided, indulging in a little self-mockery, caused by having your personal world turned upside down.

The session had ended in much hilarity. After only twenty-four hours together members of the group were beginning to feel they knew an extraordinary amount about each other. Bonds were beginning to be formed.

Though Christopher had initially been dismayed at the sight of Louisa Forrester, he found himself liking her more and more. Perhaps he should have realised that recognition was possible anywhere – given the publicity he'd received – but it had been disconcerting to bump into someone he'd met before in this unlikely setting. He had a vivid recollection of their meeting at Garsington: Louisa's wasn't the sort of face you forgot. He'd thought her charming then, and he found her just as delightful now. He could have kicked himself for not being more open with her on the first evening. He decided it would be best to confide in her as soon as possible and put an end to speculation. She was obviously curious, but what did it matter, after all? Sophisticated Louisa might epitomise the lifestyle he was trying to leave behind, but then she seemed to be seeking changes too. She gave the impression of being so carefree and light-hearted that it had been a surprise to learn what a struggle she'd had with illness. Her display of vulnerability had been unexpected too. The other young woman, Marnie, not so glamorous, but also possessed of that indefinable quality that makes someone's presence felt, intrigued him too. He had caught a glimpse of such unhappiness and uncertainty on her face the first evening that he had felt an urge to comfort her, but then felt he had come up against a brick wall. Huh! The new, caring Christopher, Nicola would have said mockingly – and it would not have been intended as a compliment.

Christopher had put his name down for a tutorial session with Catherine the following afternoon. He had taken her up on her offer to look at a piece of his work and realised that he was pinning a lot of hope on her reaction, though he doubted if she would have had time to do more than glance at what he'd brought with him. His future might depend on what she advised him to do. Christopher, who for years had relished taking decisions about important issues, who had prided himself on flourishing in the cut and thrust of a highly competitive business life, who had thrived in the buzz and excitement of the City, was uncertain what his next step should be. He only knew he had to change direction.

He looked at his watch. It was not quite eleven and though he felt exhausted and edgy as he so often did nowadays, he knew sleep was a long way off. He wondered if it would be one of those nights when he would relive past events; when he would fall briefly into a heavy slumber only to wake with a violent jolt a few moments later, hearing again the awful bang and feeling the sickening moment of impact – and then have to face what had happened all over again. Suddenly the dreaded and by now all too familiar physical sensations that had afflicted him since the car crash started to close round him, sucking him into a dark whirlpool. It was a horrible feeling, not initially violent, but rapidly accelerating into a nightmarish panic as he felt his heart start to pound, while a squeezing sensation in his chest made him convinced he would suffocate, the whole accompanied by a deadly nausea. Everything in the room seemed to be closing in on him yet he was incapable of fighting his way out as the walls appeared to tower over him. Breathe, said Christopher, doggedly forcing himself to remain calm, hanging on to this one word, this mantra, as if it were a rope flung to a drowning man. Breathe and count. Breathe in . . . hold . . . breathe out. Breathe in . . . hold . . . breathe out. Concentrate on breathing and you'll be all right. He lay there willing himself to focus on the slow in . . . out, in . . . out, and after a bit he realised that the black terror was indeed beginning to recede. His hands were less clammy and the walls of the room settling back to their comforting, ordinary safeness. The relief was enormous – but so too was the disappointment that after weeks without it, this physical horror had returned. Though it usually occurred last thing at night, when he was safely in bed, he had a horror that it might overtake him in public and the fear that others should witness his terror had been a constant nightmare in prison. His doctor was confident that the attacks would get better as the memory of the real trauma of being trapped in a crushed car gradually receded, but confessed that he didn't really know how long it might take.

When he was reasonably confident that equilibrium had returned, Christopher got cautiously to his feet and went over to the basin. He splashed his face in cold water and it steadied him. He flung open the window, which looked out at the back of the building over the park, and breathed in the peaty, spring-scented air. A nearly full moon was sailing in the sky, casting a criss-cross tangle of shadows from the branches of the great oak trees on to the grass below. A white rhododendron – he must ask Morwenna if she knew what variety it was – looked as if the silvery light was shining, not from the moon, but from its heavy flower-heads to illuminate everything round it. There was not a breath of wind, unusual for Scotland, thought Christopher, and it was so still he could hear the distant rumbling of the burn. Then he heard the sound of an engine and saw the lights of cars coming up the drive. He guessed it would be the rest of the group, back from the Drochatt Arms, and wondered how they had progressed in friendship – or possibly animosity. Soon car doors were being slammed, footsteps crunched on the gravel and there was the sound of a key being turned in the lock of the main door below; there was muffled laughter on the stairs. He thought with surprise that he was pleased to know they were all back.

Even more surprisingly, after he'd had a bath and gone to bed, he had the best night's sleep he'd had for a very long time

Chapter Eight

Isobel and Giles had not dined with their guests that night and Catherine made their apologies for them.

'I do hope it wasn't anything I said about the little boy?' Bunty had asked, eyes bulging with speculation, leaning eagerly towards Catherine – she had a habit of coming very close to whomever she was speaking to and was obviously longing to ferret about for more information. 'It may be that I'm over-sensitive – everybody always notices how sensitive I am – but I feel I might have been a weeny bit tactless?' Catherine had said firmly: 'No, of course it's nothing to do with that. The Grants always try to dine with their guests the first night, as they did yesterday, but they often have other commitments as I'm afraid they do tonight.' Bunty had looked unconvinced and would have liked to pursue the matter further, but pleasant though Catherine was there was something a little daunting about her that Bunty found disconcerting.

The evening session finished at half past nine. The Colonel, who'd arrived at Glendrochatt by car, had been studying the notice board on which various local attractions were advertised and now invited anyone who fancied an outing to come to Blairalder with him for a drink at the Rob Roy bar in the Drochatt Arms.

'We could all have a dram together,' he suggested, using what he felt was suitable jargon for the area, 'to let our hair down after school, as it were.' Louisa caught Marnie's eye and they exchanged an amused look: this could be difficult for the Colonel since the sparse fringe of grey surrounding his gleaming pate was cropped ultra close in the military fashion of his day. The Heslingtons were the first to accept the invitation, Stanley ungraciously saying that if he didn't get out from this bloody place for a bit he'd blow a gasket. He received a reproachful look from his wife, which he chose to ignore. Bunty, Joyce and Morwenna all said they'd like to go too if they could be given a lift and after a slight hesitation Marnie offered to take them in her car. She gave Louisa an enquiring look, hoping she would join them, but Louisa shook her head, mainly because she wanted to talk to Isobel but also partly because Christopher had declined the invitation and she thought it might be a chance to find out what had happened to him and get to know him better. It never occurred to her that Marnie might be hoping for support because she never found social situations at all threatening herself. Marnie was conscious of a twinge of disappointment after the unexpected closeness she and Louisa had achieved that afternoon, but she felt no particular surprise. Rejection, in however trivial a way, was part of her expectation of any attempts at friendship.

Catherine excused herself on the grounds that she had work to do. Just as Louisa was about to go in search of Christopher, she saw him escaping purposefully, whisky in hand, across the courtyard to his room, so she decided to look for Isobel first.

She found her in the old nursery. Giles had indeed had a genuine commitment, a practice session of the band which he both organised and regularly played in with various friends and his daughter Amy when she was at home. They were due to play at a big Highland ball in a few weeks' time and needed to run through their programme. Often they practised in the theatre at Glendrochatt with Isobel providing food and the whole rehearsal turning into a highly convivial evening, but because of the writing course they had arranged to meet in someone else's house tonight. Isobel had originally intended to dine with the group, but since the incident at teatime the idea of Bunty, oozing goodwill, but running on a burning scent of curiosity, had proved too much for her and she had taken her supper through to the nursery which had been Giles's refuge in his often lonely childhood, and which the Grants now used as their family retreat when the house was full of visiting strangers.

It was an infinitely comforting room, shabby by some standards, perhaps, with its faded chintz curtains and some threadbare patches on the carpet, which were mostly covered by sagging but comfortable armchairs: it was a room where small children could build dens under the tables and teenagers could sprawl on the floor; where dogs had their own beanbags but sometimes sneaked on to the sofa and piles of books balanced on windowsills – a room that had been lived in and loved by several generations.

A film was running on the television when Louisa poked her nose round the door, but Isobel wasn't looking at it. She was curled up in one of the big squashy arm-chairs with Flapper at her feet and Lozenge – indecorously showing a vast expanse of stomach – lying upside down beside her. Rory's toys were strewn all over the floor in a happy muddle, but tonight Isobel had neither inclination nor energy to tidy them up. She looked quite unlike her usual bright self, but at the sight of Louisa she got up at once, dislodging Lozenge with difficulty, and smiled a welcome.

'Louisa, how lovely! Come and tell me how you've got on and make me laugh. I need cheering up.' She turned the television off, threw a couple more logs on the fire that was still necessary most evenings, and then poked at them viciously, sending armies of sparks rampaging up the chimney.

'Oh, Iz! That bloody woman's really upset you, hasn't she?' Louisa perched on the club-fender in front of the fire. She didn't pretend not to guess what was wrong. 'Don't let anything she said get to you. She's not worth bothering about, nosy old cow.'

'It wasn't her fault.' Isobel ran her hands through her curly dark hair. She was one of those lucky women whose hair looked good no matter how rumpled or wind-blown it might become. She flopped back in her chair and said: 'I can't believe I was so *stupid* as to allow it to turn into an issue like that. If I hadn't gone and made such a thing about the relationship, nobody would have noticed anything . . . but Bunty Whatsit was so damn persistent I felt cornered. Oh, hell! What a mess. It's not the first time Rory's likeness to Giles has been remarked on and we can't go on ignoring it. I'm sure for anyone who's seen him it's *the* local topic for gossip. We have some dreadfully difficult decisions to take – not just for us but for the rest of the family – and for Rory himself.' She looked at Louisa through deeply troubled eyes. 'I suppose you realise that Rory really *is* Giles's son?' she asked.

'Well, it's impossible not to see the likeness,' admitted Louisa reluctantly. 'He is the absolute spit of Giles. How long have you known?'

'I suppose if I'm honest from the moment I clapped eyes on him at the airport,' said Isobel. 'But I've been trying to deny it to myself and to Giles and . . . and to anyone who could put two and two together and come up with a horribly accurate answer. The worst thing is that I'm pretty sure Amy cottoned on immediately. I think she's waiting for us to say something and now I suppose we'll have to.'

'And you didn't have any idea before?' Louisa was astonished.

There was a pause. 'Not . . . not for certain.'

'Wasn't he like Giles when he was a baby? How long was it since you'd last seen him?'

'Believe it or not I'd never seen him before. He was born in South Africa and though my mother used to go out there to help Lorna with him a lot, Lorna always had nannies as well so she wasn't dependent on Mum. We never went there because, after the awful trouble she caused us, we'd had a tremendous falling out with her and broken off all relationships with her. Later when my parents used to have Rory to stay for quite long periods in France without Lorna, they took great care that we never overlapped with him. I quite see why now! They must have known but it was never acknowledged. By the time my mother got ill and couldn't cope with him any more, Lorna had moved to the States and was becoming involved with her senator. The shock of meeting Rory at the airport was awful. I thought I might pass out or something, and then I had to witness the look on Giles's face when I got Rory back here. Nobody but my sister could have done anything like this,' Isobel said bitterly. 'Imagine putting your little boy – the child you were supposed to have longed for so desperately and then apparently couldn't cope with – on a transatlantic flight in the charge of a completely unknown nanny and shipping him out to relations he'd never seen in his life before and all because she didn't want to fall out with her new glitzy husband – who must be a real shit judging by his previous marital history. Their political life was very hectic at the time and Lorna thought Rory was better out of it. That's what she said anyway. Also she said she wanted to mend her fences with me – and I was mug enough to fall for it – or rather to feel it was wrong to keep a feud going indefinitely. In reality I'm now sure she's using the child as a weapon against me.'

Louisa was appalled. 'Do you want to tell me about it? Please don't feel you have to if you don't want to.'

'No, I think I might go mad or burst or something if I don't talk about it and I need an outside view. You're the perfect person, because you know about the characters in the drama without having actually been involved. Let's have a drink. What would you like? Wine or something stronger? I hardly ever drink spirits but I'm going to have whisky tonight.'

'Wine would be fine for me.' Louisa kicked off her shoes and curled up on the sofa and Isobel, once she had fetched their drinks, found herself going back to the time five years before when she and Giles had just finished converting Glendrochatt as an arts centre and were about to start their first season. Lorna, newly divorced from her South African husband, had arrived, uninvited, to spend the summer with them, announcing that she intended to help them get the new project off the ground.

'She said she had nowhere to go – not strictly true – and we'd just been let down by a newly appointed assistant administrator and were desperate for more help. Lorna's incredibly efficient but even so I was terribly against her staying,' said Isobel. 'I knew she'd cause trouble but it seemed too difficult to refuse under the circumstances. And my God! Did she excel herself! She's always had a genius for putting other people in the wrong and quite soon she'd practically taken over the place and set us all at odds with each other . . . not just Giles and me, but the wonderful staff we had working for us at the time – even the children. Well, especially the children really. Amy and Edward hated her from the word go. Amy because she tried to interfere over her music – playing her fiddle had always been Amy's special, happy bond with Giles – and

Edward because Lorna completely terrified him. I know Ed's not easy and I've learned to accept how difficult some people find it to know how to react to any kind of handicap, mental or physical – well, it *is* difficult. I've often found it hard myself, but since Ed was a tiny baby Lorna was never able to disguise her distaste for him whenever she saw him. Luckily that wasn't very often because she lived so far away but it always hurt.'

Isobel broke off and struggled to get her voice under control, and Louisa remembered how her mother had told her about Lorna's extreme, lifelong jealousy of her younger sister and her many small acts of unkindness. Despite her greater beauty and many talents, a few discerning people had felt sorry for Lorna when she was growing up, because everyone always liked Isobel so much better. Some of her parents' friends had tried to make allowances for her sharp tongue and manipulative ways, but Lorna hadn't wanted pity – she had only wanted to be loved, as Isobel was loved, happily and naturally and without effort. She had longed to laugh as easily and joyfully as Isobel seemed to do, but her own inability to find the quirks of life amusing made this a losing struggle.

'It might have been all right if only she'd just left Ed alone,' went on Isobel, 'but she wouldn't. It was a sort of bullying. She kept trying to set him tasks and make him do things which were quite beyond him, all in order to impress Giles, and we had one or two incidents when she nearly did him serious harm. Then she accused him of doing something he hadn't actually done. She shook him and screamed at him – Ed, who has always been so gentle and so nervous – and literally frightened him out of his wits. He ran away and went missing. It was a nightmare time.'

Isobel's grey-green eyes looked dark with misery. She

saw again the limp figure of Edward being carried into the house after he had eventually been found. She went on painfully: 'We'd had such struggles to get Edward, with his autism and his physical disabilities, to the point he'd reached, and then he turned right back in on himself and wouldn't speak for weeks – his fits started again and we came horrifyingly close to losing him. I felt it was entirely Lorna's fault and in the end we had to ask her to leave.' She looked at Louisa. 'I can't believe the family bush telegraph didn't drum some of this through to you. Did you know that Giles was Lorna's first boyfriend and that they went out together all the time they were at university? They were never actually engaged, though it turned out later that Lorna had always assumed that they'd eventually get married.'

Louisa nodded. 'I think Mum did tell me something about that,' she said cautiously, 'and I knew you'd had a bit of a hiccough a few years ago. Must have been terribly awkward for everyone.'

'It was ghastly. It seems extraordinary now, but I never met Giles while he and Lorna were going out. Of course I was away at school much of the time. I knew she had a man in her life, but Lorna was always terribly secretive and my mother used to complain that she never met any of her friends. Lorna often stayed here at Glendrochatt with Giles's scary old father, but she never invited Giles home to Edinburgh.'

If Louisa thought this might have been because Lorna was determined not to let any of her friends meet her bubbly younger sister, she didn't say so. 'So when did you first meet Giles, then?' she asked.

'Not till after they'd split up. It was Lorna who actually broke up the relationship, though I think that was a way of trying to bring Giles up to scratch. It was just before they both came down from Bristol. Giles thought it was all quite amicable and as far as he was concerned felt they'd outgrown each other. It never occurred to him that Lorna hadn't accepted the split as final. She went off travelling confident that when she returned she'd be able to get him back with a snap of her fingers. I didn't know all this at the time – though I certainly learned about it later. But in the meantime Giles and I had met each other . . . and that,' said Isobel, 'was dynamite.'

'I can't help envying you that, though I see you have an awful problem at the moment, Izzy,' said Louisa. 'I could do with a stick or two of dynamite myself right now. It's what I long for.'

'What about Adam? I've only met him once or twice and mostly at social occasions – weddings and things. He's always struck me as lovely.'

'That's the trouble. He *is* lovely . . . the nicest person I know, but not a whiff of dynamite. We've split now and it's been enormously painful because I don't think he's ever really looked at anyone else. He's stuck by me through everything – I might not have pulled through without him, and I'm terribly aware of it – but I've felt so stifled lately, and I've started to be beastly to him. You can't go on with a relationship that turns you into a horrible person – an ungrateful, sharp-tongued nag. He said he'd rather live with me even when I was horrible than not live with me at all – but the point is I can't live with myself under those circumstances and I resented him for making me so nasty. I know it's monstrously unfair but Adam has sort of become connected in my mind with my years of illness and I need a fresh start. He still says he loves me and always will, but I think he's beginning to accept it more now. Don't tell me I'm spoilt and selfish,' said Louisa sadly, 'because I know it.'

Isobel thought that it was Louisa's occasional ability to be ruthless – which sometimes made people think of her as spoilt – that had also given her the determination to fight – and survive – cancer. How complicated life was. She said seriously: 'Poor Adam . . . but isn't gratitude one of the hardest emotions to handle?'

'Umm – you're right. Funny you should say that, because Marnie said much the same thing to me this afternoon,' said Louisa. 'But go on about Lorna. I didn't mean to sidetrack you with my problems. What happened next?'

'Oh well, Lorna got home, full of expectations of marriage and children and life at Glendrochatt, only to be told by Giles that he was going to marry me – the much younger sister she'd always resented and bossed around. To make matters worse, she was not only still in love with Giles himself, but completely obsessed with this house and estate, and had set her heart on being mistress of Glendrochatt. Don't think I don't realise how dreadful it must have been for her, but when Lorna has a grudge, even a small one – and this one was mega – she's never been able to let it go and move on to other things. It grows into a complete obsession. Anyway, after our wedding she married a glamorous South African eye surgeon and we all hoped everything was all right. She had a luxurious lifestyle and masses of money but it didn't work out. He was unfaithful and the babies she said she longed for didn't happen. Because John had been married before and had children by his first marriage, and because Lorna had taken herself to endless doctors, we assumed she couldn't have any. Certainly that's what she told my mother. How wrong we were! Anyway, that summer after they split up, she came back from South Africa intent on paying off old scores with me and getting Giles back . . . and she very nearly did.'

Louisa could imagine Lorna's temptation. Giles was extremely attractive and though her own fondness for

Isobel would certainly have stopped her from flinging any lures over him herself, sisterly affection had obviously not been a sufficient deterrent to Lorna.

'Did you realise at the time that they were having an affair?' she asked.

'They only had one night together – and it was partly my fault.' Isobel sighed. 'I refused to go on a Suzuki music weekend with Giles and Amy – and Giles took Lorna in my place. But I couldn't throw stones because I was on the edge of an affair myself with Daniel Hoffman – the artist who painted the two backdrops for the theatre. He was spending the summer with us, mostly working in the theatre, but Giles also commissioned him to paint my portrait – very dangerous, that was. Exciting heart to hearts between the artist and the model during sittings.' Isobel pulled a mocking face and laughed, but Louisa could see the recollection was painful.

'Is the portrait good? Do you like it?'

'Everyone likes it, even me. It's wonderful – quite apart from me it's a sensational picture. It's hanging in the drawing room – do go and have a look sometime. Giles used to have ambivalent feelings about it because he says Daniel captured a look on my face that he thought was only ever directed at him. I wouldn't know about that – but I still feel very badly about Daniel because he fell for me in a big way and out of rage at what I could see was brewing between Giles and Lorna, I encouraged him. He got badly hurt. He was a fascinating character, great fun and quite unlike anyone I'd ever met before. The children adored him and he was specially brilliant with Ed – which of course particularly endeared him to me. He was several years younger than me so I suppose I was flattered to start with and it was just the morale boost I needed at a tricky time in my marriage. That's how it began anyway, but then I started to fall for him too and the whole thing nearly got out of hand. If it hadn't been for the drama with Ed I don't know how it might have ended. That brought Giles and me to our senses with a bang. So you see,' said Isobel with painful honesty, 'I'm not really in a position to take the moral high ground with Giles about his one-night stand with Lorna.'

'Perhaps not in theory . . . but that never seems to help much with how one feels,' said Louisa. 'I always thought you and Giles had such a cast-iron marriage.'

'I thought so too at one time, but now I don't think there is such a thing. Nothing in any relationship is ever quite what it appears to the outside world, is it? We've made a pretty good job of welding our marriage together again, and I'd thought it was stronger than ever till Rory was dropped into it. Now I'm so afraid, I feel as if an arctic wind was blowing round me.'

'Afraid of how Giles will react?'

'Afraid of what it'll do to us both . . . but mostly afraid of myself. Terrified of what may happen and whether I can cope. Look how I over-reacted to Bunty, and she's a total stranger and it doesn't really matter what she thinks.'

'How long is Rory here for? Won't it all blow over when he goes back to Lorna? Surely she can't expect him to stay with you indefinitely.'

Isobel groaned. 'I don't *know*. I don't know what she expects or even wants – but I'm not going to let the poor little boy be used as an emotional football and kicked to and fro across the Atlantic to score points for opposing sides. He's not just Lorna's responsibility now – he's Giles's too – a little cuckoo in our nest. And that,' said Isobel, 'makes it very complicated.'

At that moment they heard footsteps in the hall, the dogs rushed excitedly to the door of the nursery and Giles came in.

'Good heavens, what on earth are you two doing sitting

in the dark? You look like a pair of owls!' he said. Isobel and Louisa blinked in the unexpected glare as he switched on the lights. 'Hi there, Louisa. Hope you've had a productive day with the writing muse. Hello, my Iz. I'm afraid I'm a bit late, but we got carried away and started on something new. Still we had a wonderful practice.' As Giles bent to kiss his wife, Louisa watched him touch her cheek with his finger in a small gesture of private intimacy. He gave Isobel a questioning look.

'You look exhausted, darling . . . you all right?' he asked.

'Oh, wonderful, terrific,' Isobel's sarcasm was biting. She had been longing for Giles to come home, but at the sight of him the horrible, unwanted feelings of resentment seemed to rise in her gorge like bile. 'I've just been filling Louisa in about our little family dilemmas,' she said nastily.

'Oh well, tell the whole world, why don't you?' Giles was instantly furious. 'Louisa can alert our friends and relations to the latest Grant drama and you can announce it to the writing group tomorrow . . . since you made them so interested in the first place.'

Louisa sensed the tension between husband and wife simmering below the surface and felt caught in the cross-fire of matrimonial sniping that might easily ignite into a full-blown fusillade. Perhaps dynamite was not so enviable after all, she thought wryly. Aloud she said: 'Look, I think I'd better leave you to discuss this in private.'

'Oh, God! I'm sorry, Louisa.' Giles was instantly apologetic. 'That was unfair to you both. I was well out of order.'

Isobel gave herself a little shake as if to dislodge some foreign body. 'Me too. Sorry, sorry, sorry.'

'It's getting late. Bedtime for me anyway I think,' said Louisa lightly. She kissed her host and hostess a swift goodnight, for once thankful to escape their usually congenial company.

When she had gone, Isobel looked at Giles in horror.

'What is this doing to us? I didn't mean to react like that. I could kill Lorna. I feel as if she's infected me with a horrible virus and my immune system can't cope with it.'

'I know. But we will cope with it. We have to,' he said. 'Come to bed, darling. We have better ways of communicating than this.'

In the small hours of the morning Isobel woke with a terrific start to bloodcurdling yells. She and Giles had talked long into the night and then made love with a passion that would have been the envy of many long-married couples. She leaped out of bed and ran barefooted down the passage. The landing light was on and the door of the little room that had been Edward's before he was promoted to a larger one upstairs on the top floor was ajar, propped open by a book. Rory was sitting up in bed screaming hysterically. Isobel gathered him in her arms, murmuring all the old words of comfort that she had used to Amy and Edward when they were little. 'It's all right, darling. I'm here. It's only a dream. Wake up. I'm here.'

'The Hat! The Hat!' screamed Rory, incoherent with terror. 'Get him off! Take it away, take it away!'

'I will, darling. It's all gone now. No more Hat.' Isobel hadn't the faintest idea what, or who, the Hat was, but after years of practice, particularly with Amy, she knew about exorcising nightmares. Rory wound his arms so tightly round her neck she was nearly strangled, but his screams subsided to sobs, and the sobs gradually became intermittent, though with each one she could feel his bony little body shuddering. She rocked him and murmured to him until he was completely quiet and he leaned against her exhausted, thumb in mouth.

'There,' she said. 'That's a good boy. Would a drink of hot Ribena make you feel all better?'

He nodded, looking up at her through dark lashes from greeny-brown eyes that were so uncannily like Giles's – so unlike her sister Lorna's big blue ones. He took his thumb out of his mouth for a moment. 'Don't go,' he said, before jamming it back in again.

'I won't be a minute. I'll just go and boil the kettle and come right back and we'll have a hot drink together. I'll sit on your bed and talk and we'll have a picnic. Where's Rabbit?'

Rory burrowed down the bed and came up with the battered one-eared rabbit that was the most treasured possession he had brought with him from the States, though he'd come with a trousseau of immaculate new clothes to cater for every possible variation of weather or social occasion. 'I think you'll find he's got everything he could possibly need,' Lorna had said on the telephone, but Isobel thought he'd come without any of the things a child really needed – except perhaps Rabbit.

'You pop to the loo,' she said now, 'and by the time you've done that I'll be back.'

'You won't be long?'

'I won't be long.'

When she came back with two mugs, she sat on the edge of his bed and told him about the games Edward used to play; about the bag of plastic dinosaurs he had always insisted on taking with him wherever he went and how he and Amy had loved to play in the old wooden castle that had been made years before for Giles when he was a little boy too. When Rory had finished his drink she tucked him in tight and watched his eyelids beginning to droop as if they had become too heavy to hold open any longer. She went on talking softly until she judged he was really asleep before she got cautiously off the bed. She stood for a moment looking down at this small replica of her husband with his perfectly proportioned body, grace of movement and wonderful looks – so different from her own son. Two tears trickled slowly down her cheeks and her throat felt tight. He had called out for his grandmother in his sleep, but it occurred to her suddenly that not once, even at the height of his nightmare, had Rory called out for his mother.

She turned out the bedside light and slipped quietly out of the room.

Chapter Nine

The following morning, Christopher woke early and decided to go for a walk before breakfast.

No one else was about as he let himself out of the door into the courtyard. He thought how cleverly the old farm buildings had been converted by the Grants to provide the facilities for their flourishing arts centre – an example of good manners in architecture. He went round the side of the accommodation wing and came out at the edge of the park. The air was full of birdsong, and if, in the morning light, the rhododendron bush below his bedroom window had lost its magic, moonlit luminosity, it still looked beautiful: the heavy white flower clusters just touched inside with yellow as though some medieval monastic artist – a master of restraint – had dipped his finest brush in ochre paint and drawn barely perceptible lines down the centre of each petal. Across the valley below, transparent wisps of mist were draped along the river, giving the landscape the look of a Chinese picture painted on silk, with the tops of trees rising above the early haze and the far hills rolling into the distance. What a place to live, thought Christopher – lucky, lucky Grants.

He forked left up a mossy path into the wood above the drive. Some of the pointed buds on the branches of the ancient beeches were still only beginning to unfurl and show hints of the brilliant green to come, and those new leaves that were already fully out were crumpled and covered with fine silver down. The path soon petered out but after a steep scramble, which was testing for his leg, he reached a clearing and stopped to sit on the remains of a fallen tree trunk in the early sunshine. Below him, he could see the tip of the flagpole on the tower but the flag, with the Grant coat-of-arms on it, was hanging limp, with no breath of wind to lift it.

He thought what fun it must be to run a joint venture from home as Giles and Isobel did – how satisfying. No doubt there were tensions and difficulties for a married couple in working so closely together, but it seemed to him infinitely more desirable than the frenetic rush in which he and Nicola had led their lives and most of their friends still did. Many couples hardly seemed to have time to enjoy each other's company any more – even go on holiday together, if their careers clashed – but he didn't think the Grants' rural lifestyle was one that Nicola would appreciate. The buzz of the City, the pressure of cutthroat competition, was the breath of life to her and it wasn't only the resulting prosperity that acted on her like a powerful aphrodisiac – though money was very important – but everything it represented: not just purchasing power but influence; excitement; control; recognition. She had been fond of telling him that it was the thrill of the chase as much as the capture of the quarry that was significant to her in the pursuit of wealth, though Christopher suspected that she wasn't exactly lacking in blood lust either. And not so long ago, I was every bit as ambitious for the same things myself, he thought. It's not her fault that I've altered. I can't blame her because I've had a change of heart and mind and she hasn't – and some of the anger against her that had been festering inside him started to drain away.

It was his mother who had suggested he should come on this particular writing course. She had seen an article on 'Life Enhancing Vacations in Beautiful Places' in the glossy supplement of her Sunday paper and Glendrochatt had been one of the four venues suggested. There had been a walking week in Andalusia combined with bird watching; a painting holiday in Greece tutored by a well-known artist; a music and meditation course in Wales offering such enticements as spiritual detoxification and energy realignment . . . and the creative writing week in Scotland. 'Make use of your leisure to renew your creative vision,' the writer of the article had urged piously. 'Come home refreshed in body and spirit, with a new skill and a new perspective on life.'

'That's what you should do,' his mother had said with conviction. 'Go on a writing course. Remember all those essay prizes at school? Remember the excitement when you started to get a few poems accepted when you were up at Oxford? The writing bug has never really gone away, has it? We always thought you'd go into journalism before you got so smitten with the City. Now you've been given an opportunity to re-evaluate your whole existence and the time and chance to pursue a completely new direction.'

He'd raised an eyebrow at her. 'Oh, is that what this is all about? A great new chance for me?' he'd asked mockingly.

'Yes,' she'd answered. 'At least, that's exactly what it could be – if you choose to let it.'

'I see. Someone else's appalling bad luck turned into my good luck? Seems a bit unfair on them, to put it mildly.'

'Better than wasting a chance! Better than wallowing! You can't alter what's happened so you must make your own luck now,' she'd said fiercely. He could see she was on the edge of tears, and it was so unlike her to be critical – she who had been his staunch supporter through everything – that he'd felt ashamed. He thought with a pang that she'd got to look much older recently.

'I'm sorry.' He put his arm round her thin, stooped shoulders and gave her a hug. Then he said teasingly. 'Poor old Mum! Casting your pearls of advice before swine as always! But I expect you're right – you usually are. Give me the article then. I won't promise to go, but I'll promise to read it.'

She had handed him the paper. 'Go on a quest, darling,' she said. 'You may not find what you *expect* . . . but you never know what else you may discover.' She had added lightly, 'It might even prove to be a treasure hunt!' And she picked up the earthy wooden trug, which had somehow made its way into the drawing room – something that drove his meticulous father crazy – gathered up her ancient leather gloves and clippers, called up the dogs and headed off to her beloved garden before he could start raising objections to the idea. He had looked after her fondly and thought she bore a strong resemblance to a modern-day version of the White Queen in *Through the Looking-glass* – pearls, spectacles and dog-whistles tangled round her neck; hairpins cascading out of the knot of white hair, which was balanced as precariously on top of her head as a pile of ivory spillikins; the zip of her old skirt skewed round, off centre.

Where else had he heard that phrase recently, he wondered? Then he remembered. The first evening, Marnie Donovan had said she had come to Scotland on a treasure hunt. So that makes two of us, he thought, and he got up from the log, suddenly realising that he felt extremely hungry, and went down the hill to the house.

He had expected to be the first down to breakfast, but when he went into the dining room he found Marnie was there before him.

'Do you mind if I come and join you?' he asked, thinking she might have come early in order to avoid other people and might not welcome company. He wasn't particularly keen for her company himself, but thought it would have looked distinctly unfriendly to sit at a different table.

'No of course not,' she said politely, the glowering countenance of the first day gone, but not looking particularly welcoming either.

'So how was the Rob Roy bar?' he asked, sitting down beside her after he'd helped himself to porridge from the hot plate and noted the inviting-looking options of scrambled egg and bacon, mushrooms and fried bread that were also on offer. 'Did you have a scintillating evening with Stanley and Bunty and co.? What was the local night spot like?'

'Very much for the tourists – all clannish upholstery and rather mothy stags' heads.' Marnie giggled, suddenly, surprising him. He hadn't thought she had much sense of humour. 'Bunty was the only one of us suitably dressed for the evening – she looked like Rob Roy in drag. I think even the regulars were rather stunned by the sight of her in her new tartan outfit but oh brother! She certainly matched the decor! It was quite fun to start with – but I think there's trouble brewing in our little gang.'

Christopher thought that when she let her guard down, Marnie looked a different person. He guessed she must be in her mid or late twenties, but with her fine light-brown hair scraped back in a ponytail and her face devoid of make-up she could have passed for several years younger. He wondered if she had any Slav in her ancestry, something to do with high cheekbones and a wide but finely moulded mouth. Her straight dark eyebrows and thick, dark lashes made a surprising contrast to her very pale skin.

'What sort of trouble?' he asked.

Marnie piled butter and honey on to a croissant – obviously weight-watching was not one of her problems.

'Well,' she said, 'it was Stanley of course, so I guess you could say it was a trouble waiting to happen. He was okay to start with – boring, but okay. The Colonel insisted on standing us all drinks – and there were some pretty fearsome-sounding mixtures on offer, I can tell you! Mostly whisky-based concoctions laced with strange liqueurs and called names like *Monarch of the Glen* and *The Chieftain's Revenge*. Talk about breaking down barriers! Everyone got very garrulous. Even Morwenna became quite skittish, but Stanley soon became more and more belligerent. He was horrible to poor Win, mocking her writing efforts and accusing her of disloyalty to him. We all felt terribly embarrassed. The Colonel tried to intervene but made it worse by saying things like "Remember there are ladies present" and "We don't want any unpleasantness, do we?" ' Marnie had got the Colonel's staccato delivery off to a T. She grinned. 'You could see that Stanley was positively *ripe* for unpleasantness and the poor old Colonel's jolly decent old-school-tie-ishness was getting up his nose big time. It would have been funny if it hadn't been so awful. Stanley started shouting about what a rip-off this place was, how Catherine didn't know good writing when she saw it and the Grants were toffee-nosed parasites. Everyone else in the bar stared at us. Bunty started to sniffle, Morwenna looked as if she'd like to dig a hole and plant herself in it, but Joyce was brilliant – she started buttering Stanley up, massaging his ego and pretending to flirt with him, and managed to get him to quieten down a bit – and then luckily he passed clean out. But I fear there'll be repercussions today. Did we have problems getting him out to the car! First of all we couldn't budge him and then he started flailing about. I must say the Colonel was fantastic in the end but you should have come with us. We could have done with another man to help.'

'Well, what excitements I missed! I can see I'll have to give the Rob Roy bar a try some time,' he said, laughing at her, 'but I'm not going with the whole gang and certainly not with Stanley Heslington. I'll take you and Louisa out for a drink one evening if you'll come with me. How grim for poor Win, though I suppose she must be used to it by now.'

'No kidding. But I think he may have pushed her too far this time.'

Marnie's awkward constraint of the first day seemed to have vanished. She and Christopher had finished eating and were still chatting away over their coffee when the other members of the group arrived. Louisa came over to their table.

'Hi there,' she said, smiling at them both in her easy friendly way. 'You're a couple of early birds. Hope you've left some breakfast for the rest of us! I meant to be in such good time this morning too, but I overslept. This writing business must be more exhausting than I thought.'

'Can I get you something?' asked Christopher, getting to his feet. 'There's a marvellous selection to choose from.'

'Oh yes please, I'd love a cup of coffee. I can't face the day without my caffeine fix – but then I'll go and forage for myself.' Louisa sat down next to Marnie. 'I think you've stolen a march on me,' she said laughingly, nodding towards Christopher's back as he went over to the breakfast bar. 'You two looked as if you were getting on very well together.'

It wasn't said with any sort of barb, but, conscious that Louisa was attracted to Christopher and had met him before, Marnie immediately felt uncomfortable. She longed to say something light and airy – a soufflé of a joke – and tease Louisa in return. I'm no good at this sort of banter. I don't know the rules of the game, she reflected miserably, feeling her awkwardness creeping back. The thought of making a conversational threesome and either sitting gauchely silent while Louisa sparkled away to Christopher and discussed mutual friends, or finding herself saying something alienating or inappropriate as she sometimes did when ill at ease, filled her with dismay, though she despised herself for being feeble.

'I've finished my breakfast so I'll leave you to have yours in peace,' she said abruptly, liking Louisa, but feeling inadequate in her sunshiny presence. She got up and collected her used cup and plate to put on the trolley, as they'd all been asked to do, and walked out of the dining room with only a cursory greeting to the others and a nod of acknowledgement to Christopher as she passed him.

Louisa raised a quizzical eyebrow. 'Sociable type, Marnie,' she remarked as Christopher handed her a cup of coffee.

'I don't think she means to be rude but she certainly seems a bit offhand sometimes,' he agreed. 'Perhaps she's just chronically shy.'

'I can't make her out,' said Louisa. 'She can be really interesting to talk to – we had such a good walk together yesterday – and then she suddenly goes off the boil again and you're back to where you started with her.'

'Oh well, I expect we'll all get to know each other better as the week goes by,' said Christopher. 'By the way, I know exactly where it was that I met you. It *was* at the opera – at Garsington, at a performance of *La Cenerentola*. I was with Nicola Hornby and you were with Adam Winterton, whom I've met on business occasionally and always very much liked, though I don't know him well. We had seats next to yours and then found we'd all chosen the same spot in the garden for our picnics and we had a drink together.'

'Of course! When I saw the list of participants your

name didn't ring a bell, but the moment I saw you I knew we'd met somewhere before.'

Louisa's recollection of that evening was indelibly stamped on her mind. In fact it was all too vivid a memory, because from that one, fleeting encounter she could date the beginnings of her restlessness and dissatisfaction with Adam: with Adam as her lover and partner, and especially with the idea of him as the future husband he'd always hoped he would eventually become. She had noticed Christopher as they had made their way up to their seats in the covered stand, and then, finding herself sitting next to him throughout the performance, literally rubbing shoulders with him, had been acutely conscious of his physical presence.

'How is Adam?' asked Christopher now, wondering what Louisa might know about the events in his own life since then.

'He's fine. We're still good friends but we've split up now,' she said, wanting him to know this. 'Do you still see Nicola?' she asked.

'No,' said Christopher. 'We've split up too,' and they were both aware of a frisson of interest passing between them.

Nicola had not taken to Louisa at the time, he remembered, or vice-versa, he suspected.

'Huh! That leggy blonde didn't half fancy you,' Nicola had said afterwards when they were driving back to London. 'Bet you anything she and her worthy-looking escort get in touch and try to fix another meeting sometime – and it won't be at his suggestion. But don't you go along with it, because while she ate you up for dinner, I'd be stuck talking to him and he certainly doesn't look my type.' Nicola pulled a disparaging face. 'He's got N. *but D.* written all over him.'

Christopher had laughed. He could see that solid-looking, bespectacled Adam Winterton would not be Nicola's glass of champagne at all. 'Well he *is* nice, but I've never considered him in the least bit dull so you'd be wrong about the last bit. He's got a reputation for being extremely clever.'

'Oh, *clever*! What's that got to do with it?' said Nicola dismissively, though she was exceptionally bright herself.

He said teasingly: 'Perhaps we should take the initiative. I liked the "leggy blonde" myself – she's amusing. I might ring Adam and try to fix something for the four of us.'

But a week after that sunlit evening of music in the Oxfordshire countryside, with the heady scents of wisteria and mown grass mingling with whiffs of champagne and cigars, with swifts screaming across the garden and adding their own top notes to those of Rossini, life had completely changed for Christopher and Nicola.

Chapter Ten

By nine o'clock, eight people were seated with Catherine round the table in the small conference room with their pens and paper at the ready. Stanley Heslington was notable by his absence but Win was there. Catherine glanced at her watch, waited a moment and then sent her an enquiring look, but Win did not seem inclined to have her eye caught and appeared preoccupied with her notebook. Catherine decided it would be better to start without him. She was beginning to have her own ideas about who she thought might be going to benefit from the course, but Stanley was not one of them.

She suggested that over the next two days everyone should write a short piece about a journey. It could be a story or an article but it should be two thousand words long.

'What happens if we get so carried away that it's much, much longer?' asked Bunty, opening her rather protuberant blue eyes even wider than usual, a look she had worked on and perfected in her youth and still fancied gave her a kittenish charm. She was under the illusion that the Colonel might find this appealing.

'Then I'm afraid we mightn't have time to discuss it properly,' said Catherine, 'which would be a pity. Besides, if you want to write professionally it's a good idea to get a feel for the word count. So many magazines have to turn down good material because it's not the right length for their particular publication.'

'I think it ought to be the author's own instinct which decides the length,' objected Bunty, pouting like a thwarted child.

'Well, sometimes, yes – but if you were a dressmaker, you'd expect to make a garment the size and shape your client wanted,' suggested Catherine. 'We have to tailor our words in a similar fashion. If you find you've written too much, then cutting what you've done is always a useful exercise too. Most of our work is improved by cutting. You'd be amazed at how my poems always benefit from the knife – though I still find it very difficult. Have a go at two thousand words anyway.'

'Can it be a children's story?'

'Of course. I expect you'll all produce something completely different. So long as the subject and length are right it can be anything you like.'

Bunty perked up immediately.

'Bet they all travel by broomstick on that particular journey,' muttered Louisa to Morwenna who was sitting next to her.

'Hmm . . . or on a magic carpet,' agreed Morwenna, already planning how she could make her journey horticultural and finding to her own surprise that despite her usual lack of imagination she could clearly envisage a trip to Nepal with the Dendrologists Society, something she had always wanted to do.

'Just for fun, let's go round the table and each produce a word off the top of our heads which we'll all include in our story or article,' said Catherine. 'You start, Win.'

'Flapjacks,' said Win.

'Louisa? What's your word?'

'Owls,' said Louisa.

'Rhododendrons?' suggested Morwenna.

'Tanks,' said the Colonel.

'Fairies,' offered Bunty predictably. Joyce suggested

tourists, Marnie produced voodoo and Christopher said oysters.

'Fine,' said Catherine. 'Those are all nouns so I'll throw in an adjective. Let's go for spine-chilling.'

'Spine-chilling flapjacks! That should be a first,' said Christopher and everyone laughed. Catherine thought that her class were beginning to relax with each other and hoped it would give them the confidence to be adventurous in their writing.

At eleven o'clock they were just about to pause for a mid-morning break and troop off to the espresso coffee machine in the bar when Stanley burst through the door, followed at a slower pace by Giles. It was clear that Stanley was in a black rage. He scowled at everyone.

'Get your bag packed,' he said to Win. 'We're leaving. I want everyone to know that I reckon this place is a bloody con. You and me'll catch next train to York and I've told Giles Grant here that I'm demanding my deposit back in full and I won't be paying owt else neither.'

'I'm afraid we don't do refunds,' said Giles. 'If you have taken out the holiday insurance that was suggested on the booking form, then you will be able to take it up with the insurance company, though I'm afraid they're unlikely to pay except in cases of illness or emergency.' He added smoothly, 'But we'll be delighted to arrange a taxi to take you to the station if that's what you want.'

'You won't get a penny out of me,' shouted Stanley. He glared furiously at Catherine. 'Call yourself a teacher,' he said rudely. 'You don't know good writing when you see it. Come along Win. We'll not waste more time.'

There was an embarrassed silence. Everyone's eyes turned to Win. She sat down again in her chair and looked straight at her husband. 'You go, Stanley,' she said quietly. 'You go on home if that's what you want, but I'm learning more from Catherine than I've learned from anyone in years and I shall stay and finish the course.'

Catherine, touched by Win's bravery, but not wanting to be the cause of a domestic break-up, said, 'I'm sorry you feel like that, Stanley. Why don't you both discuss this in private? We were just about to break for coffee now anyway. We'll leave you to talk it over together.'

'Nowt to discuss.' Stanley looked like a stocky black bull, such a bad-tempered gleam in his bloodshot eyes that Christopher quite expected to see him start pawing the ground prior to a charge. 'You heard me, Win.' He stood in the doorway, blocking everyone else's line of retreat. But his wife stayed where she was.

'No, Stanley. I agree there's nothing to discuss. You go home, but I won't be coming back with you. Not this time.'

He looked at her for a moment in disbelief, then turned and blundered out of the room without another word.

'Oh, well done, Win!' There was universal approval.

'You'll have to excuse Stanley,' she said, suddenly looking very distressed. 'It's just that he's finding his retirement ever so difficult. We . . . we both are. He's not been used to having time on his hands and his writing's always been his pet little hobby, his special pride, so it's hard . . . especially as I've taken to it so well. He wasn't expecting that. Bit of a break from each other may be a good thing.' Though her words to her husband had sounded so calm, now that he'd gone Win's voice shook. She gave Giles an uncertain smile. 'I'm ever so sorry he was so rude to you. If there's a problem about the money I can pay my own fee.'

'Don't you worry about that,' said Giles quickly. 'We'll sort something out. I'm delighted you're going to stay on with us, and I know Catherine will be pleased too. She's been singing your praises as one of her star pupils.' Catherine nodded assent. Giles went on: 'I'm sorry

Glendrochatt hasn't been a success for your husband, but these courses aren't for everybody. You stay and get on with your writing and we'll take care of you. I'll go and see that Stanley gets taken to whatever train he wants to catch. Don't worry. I won't fall out with him.' He gave Win a reassuring smile and went off to see that Isobel wasn't suffering an earful of Stanley's abuse and make sure that he was helped on his journey away from Glendrochatt as swiftly as possible.

Christopher went over to Marnie, who was standing on her own, looking uncertain. 'Shall we collect some coffee and take it outside?' he suggested. 'It's too nice a day not to make the most of it while we can. I don't think we can help much here.'

Marnie nodded, pleased and surprised that he should seek her out. The other women had immediately clustered round Win in a supportive group like a swarm of bees around a queen, but she – as usual, she thought despairingly – while longing to make the right sympathetic gesture had hung back just too long and now felt she would be intruding if she muscled in on the rest of them. Louisa, she noticed, had immediately gone over to Win and given her a spontaneous hug – and doubtless she would now be saying exactly the right thing, thought Marnie enviously. She followed Christopher through the swing doors into the bigger room next door with a sense of relief.

'Where shall we go?' she asked when they'd collected their coffee.

'Let's go and find somewhere to sit that overlooks the loch.'

They went across the courtyard to the front of the house and found an old white seat, the paint flaking somewhat, under one of the huge beech trees. They sat in silence for a few moments, drinking in the view, inhaling the honeyed scent of azaleas and enjoying the peace.

'My mother tells me that the feel of the sun on one's back is one of the physical pleasures that remains undiminished with old age,' said Christopher.

'How old is she?'

'Nearly eighty – though I find it hard to believe. She seems to have remained exactly the same for such a long time that I've always taken it for granted. You don't often notice changes in the people you love if you see them all the time, but I suddenly looked at her the other day and realised how much she'd aged lately. It gave me a hell of a jolt. Ageing isn't like going down a gradual slope, it's more like a staircase, don't you think? People stay on the same step for a long time and then suddenly they seem to go down several treads.'

'I'd never really thought of it before. Perhaps I've never been close enough to anyone to feel like that. Do you love your mother very much, then?'

'Oh, my mother's special. She's amusing and wise and kind – and completely scatty. She drives my high-powered, pernickety father mad, but he adores her. We all do. You'd like her.' Christopher laughed at Marnie's expression. 'You would, I promise you. She'd make you laugh. What's more, I think she'd like you.'

Marnie was conscious of feeling quite absurdly pleased that he considered that someone he clearly both deeply loved and had respect for too might like her. She was also intrigued: the concept of anyone driving their husband mad and still being adored was a novel one to her. In Marnie's experience, once the glitter of a marriage started to wear thin, the spouses invariably split up.

'People often *don't* like me,' she said seriously. 'I'm so hopeless with most people – I can't seem to say the right things. I'm often so sharp; so unfriendly. I would have liked to go over to give Win a hug just now like Louisa did, but I had no idea what to say about Stanley and I was afraid of getting it wrong and making her even more upset – so I chickened out and said nothing.'

'It's not true that you can't say the right thing,' said Christopher. 'I've been envying things you said the first day we met.'

She looked at him in astonishment. 'What do you mean?'

'You were so open in what you said and wrote about yourself. You and Louisa were both so honest – everybody else was too, except for me, but you two seemed especially so.'

'Weren't you honest then? I know you didn't tell us much about yourself, but after all, why should you? Did you make it up about being moved by Chartres Cathedral?'

'No, of course not. That was perfectly true as far as it went – but I missed a perfect chance to admit to something about my life that it would have been better to acknowledge straight away – and now the obvious moment has gone and I wish I'd had more guts. When Win showed such courage this morning, I despised myself.'

'Would you like to tell me more now?' she asked, wanting to try to help him because he looked so troubled; very surprised to think he might need help in any way at all. There was a silence. He appeared to be considering the possibility. 'There's no need to tell anyone about your personal life if you don't want to,' she went on, although she was dying of curiosity. 'Why do you feel you have to say anything at all?'

Christopher lit a cigarette and inhaled deeply. 'Partly because I think it's going to come out anyway – which is a very poor reason, I know. You see, I've been the object of quite a lot of publicity off and on, but I thought that here I would be completely anonymous. Then I found that Louisa and I had met before and we both remember where. I can see she's curious about me and she could easily find out what there is to know if she wants to.'

'And you want to be able to get in first?'

'Yes. I suppose I do.'

'So? Go on then.'

'So,' said Christopher, 'I'm having a session with Catherine this afternoon – she's kindly been looking at some writing I brought with me and I shall tell her the reason why I've come to Glendrochatt . . . but perhaps I could tell you first?' He gave her a quizzical look and she wondered what was coming. 'I do want a new career. I do want to try to write – and I do urgently need to change my lifestyle.' He took a deep breath. 'But . . . I've only recently come out of prison,' he said, gazing across the loch to the far hills. 'I've served half my sentence. I'm still on probation.'

'What did you do?'

'I killed someone.'

'Did you mean to?' she asked, showing interest but no surprise, as if it were quite an everyday occurrence.

'God no! No, it wasn't *murder*. It was "death by dangerous driving" – which, if you're convicted, carries a mandatory three-year sentence."

'If my mother had died all those years ago, I would have committed murder,' said Marnie.

'Nonsense! Of course that wouldn't have been murder,' he said firmly. 'An unhappy little girl of seven who was manipulated by a strange and very sinister grown-up to take part in some dodgy ritual! No way! Put that right out of your head – but thank you for trying to identify with me all the same. You see you *do* say the right things.' He smiled at her then, though she thought the expression in his eyes was bleak.

'Did you feel a sense of injustice for being sent to gaol for what must have been an accident?' she asked curiously. 'I think I might have done.'

'No,' he answered. 'No – quite the contrary. In a weird way it was a kind of relief. Nobody in their senses *wants* to go to prison, of course they don't. It's not an experience I'd recommend to anyone – it's a complete nightmare – I didn't mean *that*, but I did desperately need to pay a price. In some ways the sentence didn't seem enough. It's a terrible, terrible thing to take a human life. Nothing could bring back the guy I'd killed, but I suppose the awfulness of prison has helped me, just a little, to live with the guilt.'

'Were you drunk?' she asked.

'Not on alcohol – though I easily might have been – but I was blind drunk with rage, which was quite as bad – no . . . it was worse: it was unforgivable. I'd just had a furious row with my girlfriend, and I stormed out of the house in a towering passion, roared off in my very powerful car, cornered far too fast on a twisty country road and met an oncoming car head on. The other driver was killed instantly. He hadn't got a hope.'

'And you?'

'Oh, I cracked a few ribs and a few other bits and pieces of minor damage – but I smashed up my right leg good and proper. They thought they were going to have to amputate, and I had to have another big operation quite recently, immediately after I came out of prison, and was in plaster and on crutches again for several months. I was fortunate that the medicos managed to save my leg and I was incredibly lucky to escape with my own life. Not much justice in that for the other man.'

'I'd noticed that you limp. Do you still get a lot of pain?'

He made a grimace and shrugged. 'It's a salutary reminder of priorities. My right leg is held together by metal but it's far better than anyone expected it would be, and after the last operation it's still improving. I might not make a very good stab at climbing Everest and I wouldn't choose to jump off a wall, but there's not much in the way of ordinary mobility that I can't manage now, even if I'm not as nimble as I once was. I try not to limp because it can become a habit, but if I'm tired or have walked too far, I know I still do it.'

'Do you know anything about the other driver?'

'I didn't know him personally, thank God. He was an elderly man – a widower, I believe, but in perfectly good health. Someone's father and grandfather; lots of people's friend – many people attended the trial. The press had a field day: *Wealthy Playboy Businessman Kills Much Loved Local Senior Citizen* . . . that sort of thing, though I've never actually been a playboy. I suppose it would have been even worse if it had been someone young, or the parent of small children – but you can't start weighing people's lives in a balance of dispensability. He didn't deserve to die, his relations didn't deserve to be bereaved and I didn't deserve to live.'

'But you *are* alive,' she said, quite fiercely. 'So you'd better make use of the rest of your life. Wasting it won't bring him back.'

'Yes,' he said, looking at her with respect. 'That's exactly what my old mum says too. That's why I'm here.'

'I guess we're both on a quest,' she said. 'Looking for new lives; banishing shadows. What a challenge! I haven't killed anyone but I've messed up big time . . . my own life and other people's.' She gave a sad little shrug. 'I'm a litter lout – when things get difficult I usually run away and leave a mess behind. Perhaps I'll tell you sometime.'

'I hope you will. I'd be honoured.' Christopher looked at his watch. 'Meanwhile, I've burdened you quite long enough. We're going to have to hurry or we'll be late. Thank you for listening, Marnie. I feel much better for telling you.' He touched her arm lightly and let his hand rest on her arm for a moment.

'Thank you,' he said again. 'Thank you more than I can say.'

As they walked quickly back together towards the Old Steading, Marnie wished she'd asked him what had happened to the girlfriend with whom he'd had the blazing row.

Chapter Eleven

Isobel and Giles had provided a room in the main house to be available for tutorials. It was known as the tower room and was reached by a stone staircase in the oldest part of the house.

In the days of Giles's grandparents it had been the butler's bedroom – a butler who was said to be so good at his job that he was kept on despite bouts of extreme drunkenness when he terrorised the entire household. So great was his competence – when not in thrall to the whisky bottle – at running the house, cleaning the silver, looking after the considerable cellar and generally organising the lives of his employers that after Giles's grandfather died his grandmother had preferred to keep a lead-weighted cosh hanging by her bed in case she ever had to deal with her butler on an off-day, rather than give him the sack and lose his services. She had not apparently had to resort to wielding this fearsome weapon but one winter night, after a drunken orgy, he had descended the stairs head first and fallen to his death. Ever since, his ghost had been said to haunt the tower room, several people over the years claiming to have heard sounds of uneven footsteps and stentorian breathing when there was no one to be seen. No servant had been prepared to sleep there since, which was hardly a problem nowadays, Giles said, because there were seldom any living-in staff at Glendrochatt, most of the Grants' helpers occupying cottages on the estate. It seemed an ideal room for occasional use by visiting instructors – during daylight hours. So far neither Catherine nor any of the other tutors had complained of an unwanted presence during their tutorial sessions, though no one was very keen to go up the stairs alone at night.

At two o'clock, unconcerned about drunken butlers, live or dead, but very anxious to hear Catherine's professional opinion of his writing, Christopher climbed the steep steps and found her waiting for him with the door ajar. The room had been pleasantly furnished with an oak refectory table in the window on which Catherine could lay out any papers she was working on, and there were several comfortable chairs. Ancient tartan curtains hung at the long, narrow windows and some dark oil paintings in heavy gilt frames embellished the walls, though it would have been difficult to hazard more than a guess as to their subject matter. Giles had long indulged a fantasy that if he ever felt rich enough to have them cleaned one of them might turn out to be a Rembrandt, though no art connoisseur had so far given him any grounds for hope.

Christopher could see immediately that the manuscript he had left with Catherine the first evening was on the table. The years seemed to roll back and he felt as if he were waiting outside his housemaster's study at school.

'Christopher – do come in. Nice to see you.' Catherine always looked forward with interest to the one-to-one sessions with her varied mature students; they gave her an interesting insight into the personality behind the writing, and occasionally a chance to view their written words in a more illuminating light. Christopher intrigued her. Urbane was the adjective that sprang to mind on first meeting, and yet he seemed full of contradictions. She and Giles and Isobel, discussing the intake, had agreed that he was the dark horse of this particular group. Behind the outward social aplomb, there was a guarded quality about him.

'I hope you've recovered from Stanley's onslaught?' he asked politely. 'It was too bad that he was so rude to you. Quite unwarranted.'

'I was a bit shaken,' she admitted, 'but at the same time I couldn't help feeling rather sorry for him, poor little man. It can be a dangerous disappointment to mix wishful thinking with cold reality.'

'Yes, indeed.' Christopher wondered if she thought he was in danger of this himself.

'Not, however, in your case,' said Catherine, reading his thoughts and coming to the point at once. 'I told you the other day – you can write. I think you know it yourself anyway.'

'I imagine that's what Stanley thinks too,' said Christopher drily. He nodded towards the stack of typed A4 sheets of paper. 'I suppose I do think – or hope – that I have a feeling for words, but whether I can ever turn it into something that might be publishable in a commercial market is quite another matter. I feel guilty to have presented you with such a large chunk of writing. I'm sure you won't have had time to do more than glance at it. It would be quite unrealistic to think you could read everybody's magnum opus in a couple of nights.'

'Well yes – although I do read extremely fast. I have to in my profession. Normally I would have read some sample bits and done a bit of skimming to form a general impression and we'd take it from there. However,' Catherine paused and looked at Christopher's face, which gave nothing away. 'I have to tell you that in this case I have not only read your book – all of it – but I couldn't put it down.' She added: 'And that's most unusual, I assure you.'

'But that's amazing! Wonderful!' Christopher walked over to the window, hands in pockets, and gazed out for a moment. He was astonished to discover how shaky he felt, a measure of how much her verdict meant to him. 'I can't tell you how pleased I am,' he said. 'Thank you. That's made my day.'

'It's exciting for me too. We often see some surprisingly good work on these courses, but it's unusual to find something that you immediately know could find a market. Your novel has got a few things wrong with it, of course, but nothing a good editor couldn't point out to you. Nothing you couldn't easily improve. It's a thrilling – not to say alarming – read. You had me jumping at every little creak on the stairs or bang of a door. I was glad I wasn't alone in this rather spooky old house when I read it! You have a good sense of pace and dramatic tension and the characterisation is excellent. I particularly liked the character of Ted. Also . . .' Catherine paused as if searching for the right words, 'the setting seems entirely convincing and *Inside Knowledge* is a good title for a thriller set in a prison.'

Christopher shot her an amused look. 'How satisfying to have chilled your spine,' he said, 'but the setting should be convincing. You probably guessed. I do have inside knowledge. I wrote it in prison.'

'I did wonder,' said Catherine, smiling at him. 'The small details are so credible and it's written with such authority that you know the writer must either be familiar with the ambience or have done very thorough research. How satisfactory to have made such splendid use of what must have been a very traumatic time.'

'I've just been telling Marnie how much I regret that I wasn't open about it on the first night when it would have been so easy, but now that I'm out, I've discovered that it's quite difficult to know how to play it. Some people find it acutely embarrassing and don't know how to react to one at all.' He grinned. 'Marnie was brilliant. She just looked interested and asked me what I'd done.'

'And what had you done – if that's a permissible question to ask?'

'I drove my Aston Martin at an unforgivable speed, in a foul temper, misjudged a bend and the bloke in the car coming the other way hadn't a hope. I don't remember much about the actual accident – but the horror of the fraction of a second before the impact, when I knew the car was out of control, will always be with me.'

'What do you do for a living?' asked Catherine. 'Is that going to change now? Did you lose your job through all this drama?'

'I worked in the City. I had my own company with a partner and we specialised in buying ailing businesses, turning them round to become highly profitable outfits and then selling them again. We worked very hard but we made an indecent amount of money – by some people's standards. But the accident has only served to endorse a decision I was already contemplating – to sell the company. We'd received a very good offer for it and I wanted to give up the rat race of London, move to the country, raise a family – and try my hand at writing. My girlfriend saw things differently. We had a terrible row and we said some unforgivable things to each other, but what happened after that was in no way her fault. I should never have driven in the state I was in.'

'Does she feel terribly guilty about it now?' asked Catherine. 'Not about the actual accident, I mean, but for her part in the row. It takes two to have a major quarrel.'

Christopher shook his head emphatically. 'I don't think she feels guilty at all. I think she was always very clear that I was entirely to blame . . . and she's absolutely right.'

'Are you still together?' Catherine had been conscious of the undercurrent of attraction between Louisa and Christopher and also, she thought, though this was much less easy to pick up, of Marnie's less obvious responsiveness to Christopher. She thought she might be the only person to have noticed this, and couldn't help wondering if it spelt further rejection in Marnie's life. If I were twenty years younger, thought Catherine, I would be responding to Christopher too.

'No, we're not together any more,' said Christopher. 'She broke it off.' After a moment he added with a not very convincing attempt at lightness: 'She's probably well shot of me. It turns out that we don't want the same things out of life. I think that's been a shock to us both.'

'Did she come and visit you in prison?' Catherine asked curiously.

'No – no, she didn't do that. Can't say I blame her,' said Christopher but Catherine could tell she had touched on a nerve. 'Look – about this book . . .' he said rather awkwardly after an uncomfortable little silence. 'I'm so cheered by your encouragement, but what do you think I should do next?'

'I'm sorry. I shouldn't have asked you such a personal question,' said Catherine. 'That was very unprofessional of me. Yes, let's get back to the book. I have a suggestion to make. You may remember me telling you all on the first evening that Jonathan Mercer is coming to give a talk on crime writing. I don't know if you've ever read any of his books but he's been extremely successful. I spoke to him last night and he's coming over on Thursday morning. He'll give his talk at eleven instead of our usual second morning session. I think Giles and Isobel said there are some locals coming in to hear him too which will be nice and make the talk more stimulating, so I gather it will take place in the theatre, and then when they've all gone he's going to stay and have lunch with our group so there'll be a chance for anyone who wants to talk to him to ask him questions then. He's a good friend and colleague of mine and he owes me a professional favour or two anyway. I'd

163

like your permission to show *Inside Knowledge* to him and ask his opinion. I'm fairly confident he'll like it and I think he might be very helpful to you. Would that be all right?'

'It'd be more than all right! I'm a tremendous fan of his. I've read all his books.'

'Good,' said Catherine. 'I'll organise that. I think your book will specially intrigue him because he was Writer in Residence at a Scottish prison for a year. Can you spare this copy of the manuscript? I hope you've got another one?'

'I have . . . and I most certainly can!'

Catherine looked at her watch. 'We've got a few minutes left before my next appointment with Bunty, so let's talk about another aspect of your writing. I think I suggested that you might bring me a short poem. Have you brought anything?'

He handed her a sheet of A4 paper. 'I've brought an embryonic one and I'd love your opinion on it before I take it further.'

They sat at the table while Catherine read it. 'Hmm. Too much unnecessary detail,' she said firmly, 'and I don't think we need that last line at all – much more telling without it. Credit your reader with more perception and don't explain too much. It's certainly got the makings of a poem – possibly two different poems. I think you need to cut it fairly drastically and reorganise some of the lines. The secret of a good poem is often in what you plant in the reader's mind, but don't actually *say*. The trick is to get them reading between the lines.'

Christopher grinned at her. 'Yes, ma'am,' he said, thinking that after her unexpected but extremely welcome enthusiasm for his book he was probably due for a little deflation. He got up. 'Life is looking up for me again,' he said. 'I mustn't let it get away from me. Thank you more than I can say. I don't intend to make an embarrassing point of banging on about my prison sentence in the future, but neither do I want it to be any sort of mystery . . . so if by any chance anyone is speculating, it's quite all right by me to be open about it. I'll probably mention it to the Grants. Just thought I'd like you to know that.'

'Thank you. That sounds a good decision. We'll keep our fingers crossed that Jonathan agrees with me about the book.'

At that moment there was a series of frisky little taps on the door and Bunty poked her head round it without waiting for a response to her knocks. 'Only me,' she said cosily, pattering in on the little feet that looked far too small to support her weight. She was so heavily endowed in front that Christopher thought it was amazing she didn't overbalance and fall on her face every time she got up. Perhaps she was specially weighted internally like those toys that babies can't push over.

'Oh, *hello*, Christopher.' Bunty, who had just overheard a most interesting bit of gossip, gave him an unmistakably beady look of unveiled curiosity. Before finding her way up to the tower, she had popped into the kitchen, the hub of the Glendrochatt household, where there was usually something interesting going on, primarily to check if Rory might be around, but ostensibly to search for her reading glasses, and found Isobel, who was making shopping lists, being regaled with a riveting piece of information. Bunty had hardly been able to believe her ears and – naturally not wishing to intrude – had managed to stand in the doorway for several minutes before she was noticed.

She favoured Christopher with her warmest smile – and Bunty's smiles could be very warm indeed – in which compassionate understanding and burning interest were about evenly balanced.

'And how *are* you, dear, after all your ordeals?' she asked solicitously.

'Very well, thank you,' said Christopher, a gleam of

amusement in his eye. Bunty looked so pregnant with speculation that he knew immediately that he must have been the subject of a very recent conversation. He felt a twinge of disappointment – it obviously hadn't taken Marnie much time to spread his story, and though he had not told her in confidence – rather the reverse, he realised ruefully – he was, all the same, surprised. While it was clearly as natural for Bunty to gather and spread rumours as a bee collecting pollen, somehow he had not expected it of Marnie.

'I didn't know you were going to have the appointment before me, but it's so nice to see you,' Bunty improvised, trying to play for time in order to delay him. 'Have you had a lovely session with Catherine?'

She eyed Christopher hopefully, willing him to disclose more about himself. Bunty might be irritatingly nosy, he thought, but there was something innocent about her that made it hard to be actually offended. She reminded him of a greedy little dog, begging for titbits.

'Lovely,' he echoed, smiling at her but not throwing her any juicy morsels all the same. He was relieved to see that Catherine had deftly turned the manuscript of *Inside Knowledge* over so that neither the title nor his name could be read by Bunty's gimlet eyes.

'You must be enjoying being here so much. It's all so interesting and stimulating, such lovely people, especially after . . . um . . .' Bunty beamed encouragingly.

'Oh, I am,' said Christopher. 'Especially, of course, the food.'

'The food?'

'After the diet of bread and water,' said Christopher gravely, raising an eyebrow at her. 'It's such a welcome change.'

Catherine tried not to laugh and Bunty had the grace to look a little disconcerted.

'I mustn't encroach on your tutorial time,' said Christopher. 'Thanks so much again, Catherine. See you both later,' and he went down the steep stairs, conscious of having enjoyed himself greatly.

He went out of the front door and stood for a moment on the arched steps over the moated flowerbeds. He could see Marnie still sitting under the big tree on the white bench where they had talked earlier. She had a notebook on her knee but she wasn't writing in it, just gazing dreamily at the view. She looked lost in thought. He walked over to join her.

'Hello there,' he said, coming up behind her. She gave a little start and turned round.

'Oh gee, you made me jump! I was miles away. So how was the tutorial? I hoped you'd come out this way – I've been wanting to hear how you got on.'

'Better than I dared hope,' he told her, sitting down beside her, surprised and pleased that she should be there, waiting for him. 'I can't believe it. Catherine has actually read all of my book – and she likes it! She was really very enthusiastic – I'm on a high.'

'You didn't say you'd written a whole *book*. That's awesome! Tell me about it. What kind of a book? Are we talking academic research, a slim vol of high-minded Miltonian sonnets or a bodice-ripping blockbuster?'

He laughed. 'It's just a thriller. I've always been a fan of whodunits.'

'Me too. Did you write it all when you were in prison?'

'Yes. It was my salvation. Probably saved my sanity.'

'Did you scribble away in longhand or did you have access to computers?'

'Oh, all in longhand. You don't exactly get to have your own personal laptop in jug, you know! There were computers in the education block, but not for use in free time. You can usually get hold of adequate writing

167

materials though there are a few restrictions – no spiral backed notebooks, and no staples, for instance, in case you might be tempted to use them for some sinister purpose, and you can't have pens brought in to you from outside in case they're used for smuggling something. You can get felt-tip pens and pencils and paper in the shop, but paper can disappear at an alarming rate. Popular for lighting spliffs and fags – and there's the sabotage factor, of course.'

'Sabotage?'

'Oh, just petty spite, but a bit frustrating until I learned to play the system. I lost the first few chapters several times.' He shrugged. 'Nicked or just vandalised; sometimes it disappeared completely, sometimes it got torn up – or what I'd written was made unreadable by having some pretty colourful additions scrawled all over it. Once I got wise to the hazards, I used to give it to the chaplain for safekeeping, a chapter at a time. He was very helpful.'

'How awful.' She looked at him with respect, thinking how un-self-pitying he was. 'Your background must have been against you,' she suggested. 'Were you picked on because of it?'

'You can be picked on for absolutely anything – but contrary to what you might think I was much better equipped to cope than some.' He laughed and said lightly, 'The English private boarding school system is quite good training for prison, you know. If you've been away to prep school aged eight and then on to a public school – not to mention a short-service commission in the army when I came down from university – you learn how to look after yourself. How to keep your head down at certain times and especially not to rise if you're baited – how to laugh it off or give as good as you get without provoking. Of course I was called Mr La-di-da from the first moment I opened my mouth, but in the end it became a not unfriendly nickname.' He grinned at her. 'Being over six foot certainly helped a bit too,' he said.

'Were you ever really scared?' she asked.

'Of course,' he said soberly. 'There's a good deal to be scared about – and not always from the people you'd necessarily suspect. Very unpleasant things can happen. I was lucky. Anyone who's been to prison and says they were never scared is almost certainly lying.'

She wanted to ask more, but something in his expression made her feel it would be better to change the subject. 'What are you going to do about your book now?' she asked. She hoped he might offer to let her read it, but didn't like to suggest it.

'Ah,' he said. 'That's the exciting bit for me. Catherine is going to show it to this crime novelist who's coming to talk to us. But that's enough about my affairs. What have you been up to? Have you had a go at this piece about a journey we're all supposed to do?'

Marnie pulled a face. 'I can't seem to hack it. I've come to the conclusion that writing isn't really my thing.'

'Oh, come on! We all enjoyed hearing about the West Indies – the voodoo, the old lady. I have to know more. It was riveting stuff.'

'Perhaps . . .' She shook her head doubtfully. 'But that was because of what happened to me – the issues I still have – not because I have a vivid imagination or a compulsion to write. It was all *there*. I didn't have to conjure anything out of thin air.'

'Well, you had us all very involved. You've obviously led a fascinating life so far. You've travelled, so write about a real journey you've had. Why don't you put your name down for a session with Catherine and talk it over with her? She's very helpful. Bunty's with her now – no doubt giving her a tremendous bashing about children's literature.' He laughed. 'By the way . . . you didn't waste much time spreading the buzz, did you? Bunty was agog – running on a burning scent, positively drooling at the mouth!'

'What do you mean? What about?'

'About my past. Don't think I mind,' he added hastily, seeing the expression on Marnie's face. 'I told you I wanted to have it out in the open. Who did you tell?'

'Did she say I told her about you?'

'Lord no. It was quite funny, though, because the minute she saw me she was popping with curiosity. I just assumed you must have said something because I didn't think anyone else knew – but don't look like that,' he said quickly. 'I really don't mind. In fact I'm quite grateful.'

She leaped to her feet, eyes blazing, and all the angry defensiveness back.

'I don't care whether you're grateful or not,' she flashed. 'How could you "just assume" I passed on what you told me!' She snatched up the jersey she'd hung over the back of the seat and gathered up her writing things.

'Hang on, Marnie – please don't go. I'm really sorry if I've upset you. I certainly didn't mean to . . .'

'Well you've sure succeeded. I don't go spreading gossip about people.' She put her chin in the air. 'I'm not *that* interested in your past anyway – don't kid yourself,' she said cuttingly, and without looking at him again she headed rapidly back towards the house, shoulders hunched, her very walk expressing indignation.

Christopher watched her go and cursed himself for a clumsy fool.

Chapter Twelve

Adam Winterton missed Louisa intolerably. During the years they'd lived together he'd often wondered how he would cope if the moment came when she fell for someone else – something which he'd secretly regarded as inevitable. Now he didn't know whether it was worse or better that it hadn't been – as far as he knew – for another man that she had left him.

In one way, he told himself, it was a comfort that she hadn't succumbed to a grand passion against which he would have felt helpless, but on the other hand the fact that she'd decided to end their relationship because the love he gave her clearly wasn't enough for her (or rather, as she put it, because it was becoming too much) could hardly be regarded as reassuring. He had known for a long time that she was restless and unsatisfied and would have given anything to make her happy but had no idea how to change himself sufficiently to do it. His dogged-ness, his reliability, his kindness, all good qualities in themselves, added up to a sum total that read 'boring' when Louisa was doing the arithmetic. What he had to offer was simply not stimulating enough. There were plenty of other women who had made it plain that they would calculate the sum differently, but it wasn't other women that Adam wanted. He was also aware that having loved and supported her all through her illness, he had become associated in her mind with the part of her life she most wished to forget.

Like Elizabeth Barrett Browning, he could count the many different ways he loved her and knew that for him one of them would always be 'to the level of every day's most quiet need'. But he knew also that his ways of loving did not measure up to the thrills and passion she longed for. She had once told him, in a temper, that he must have been born middle-aged and though she had apologised later, and said she hadn't meant it, Adam knew that however sorry she was to have *said* it – and it was part of Louisa's charm that she was always genuinely sorry for her sharp tongue – she certainly *had* meant it at the time. Her words had stuck in his memory like flies to a scroll of sticky paper. 'And before you were born, I bet you just sat there in the womb like a lump of lard, longing to have a good old wriggle but too bloody considerate to give your mother a kick,' she had said, goading him, irked by his gentle forbearance.

As to why he loved her, thought Adam, who can ever answer that question completely? He knew he loved her for her courage and her honesty; her enthusiasm and sense of joy; the bursts of generosity that were uneasily twinned with selfishness and the laughter that was never far away; for her ability– so lacking in himself, he thought – to create excitement, and of course for her beauty; but above all he just loved her for being Louisa. Always had. Always would.

He tried not to ring her too often though she usually sounded pleased to hear him. If she rang him – which she did surprisingly often for someone who had said she wanted a complete break – and left a message on his answerphone, he would play the message, however mundane, again and again just to hear her voice, that light, amused voice he loved so much. If I had more guile – or sense – thought Adam, I wouldn't ring her so often, I'd keep her guessing. But the theory was so much easier than the practice, and though he despised himself for giving in to temptation he knew he would be dialling her mobile in his lunch hour to find out how the course at Glendrochatt was going.

Louisa was sitting in the kitchen chatting to Isobel when Adam rang. She fished in the pocket of her jeans for her mobile, stretched her enviably long legs out on the big squashy sofa at the end of the room and prepared for a pleasurable exchange of news. Despite her craving for excitement and for new experiences and also, she hoped, for a new relationship, it was unthinkable that she should not know what was going on in Adam's life. She enquired about his work and about various mutual friends. They asked after each other's families; they talked about Mr Brown, whom Adam promised to visit when he went to Yorkshire the following weekend. If Louisa's parents should happen to be away when she was away too, he'd agreed to have Mr Brown in London, as he and Louisa had often done in the past.

'Oh, Adam, talking of Mr Brown,' she said, 'we all had to write about a really important person or event in our lives as our first exercise. I wrote about you giving me Mr Brown and how that not only changed my life but literally saved it.' Adam felt his throat constrict, more moved than he cared to let on. Could he have judged things wrongly? Could this be a tentative overture from Louisa signalling the possibility that she might be having a change of heart? He schooled himself not to reveal the small spark of hope her words kindled.

'How's the writing going?' he asked.

She laughed. 'Oh dear! I think my search for a creative outlet is proving a bit like Tigger's breakfast,' she said. 'Sadly I don't think my future lies in being the new Jane Austen, so it will have to be something else. But this is a heavenly place. I'm having a fascinating time, being fed like a prize pig, and so enjoying seeing Giles and Isobel again. Some of the people on the course are hilarious.' Her character sketches, which amused Adam very much, would not have flattered some of her co-writers. 'Oh, and by the way,' she said after she had regaled him with the saga of Stanley's thwarted genius and Morwenna's gentle gloom, and made him laugh about Bunty's girlish skittishness, 'do you remember that couple we once picnicked with at Garsington a few years back – I think she was a stockbroker or something – and you told me afterwards that he'd made a fortune buying and selling some upmarket mail-order food company? We tried to fix a date to meet again but nothing came of it and we lost touch.'

'I remember.'

'Well, you'll never guess,' she said with exaggerated casualness, 'but that chap, Christopher Piper, is here on the course too.'

Alarm bells rang in Adam's head. He remembered all too well Louisa's obvious, instant attraction to Christopher and how she had pressured him afterwards to invite him and Nicola to dinner. He recollected also his shameful feeling of relief at hearing from Christopher's secretary that Christopher – whom he'd always liked – was in hospital following a serious car accident and would be out of circulation for some time. His heart sank now, but he said, easily enough. 'Yes of course I remember – and then he had a car crash and they couldn't make it. And then there was all that publicity because the poor guy killed someone in the accident, and got a prison sentence for it. The City was buzzing with gossip at the time but you may not remember it because you were working in Brussels when it hit the press.'

'You never told me that!' Louisa sounded accusing.

'Didn't I? Well, you could easily have read about it for

yourself in the papers,' he said mildly. 'How is he now? Is he okay?'

'Well, he seems okay apart from a slightly gammy leg – and he's as charming as ever.'

'Oh well, give him my regards, then,' said Adam. 'I must go now. I've got a client coming to see me at two. ''Bye then, Louisa . . . glad you're having such a lovely time,' and Adam put the telephone down rather quickly.

'That was Adam,' Louisa explained unnecessarily to Isobel, 'and guess what? He was telling me about Christopher. Did you and Giles realise the poor guy has been in prison? He killed someone in a car crash and got sent down.'

'Oh my God,' said Isobel, appalled. 'How ghastly. That explains a lot. I certainly hadn't put two and two together, but now you mention it I think I do remember reading something in the *Daily Mail*.'

They were both unaware that Bunty had been standing in the doorway for some time, until she ostentatiously cleared her throat and came tripping in. 'I hope I'm not interrupting anything private,' she said, though obviously only too pleased to have done so, 'but I'm just looking for my specs. I'm always losing them – it must be a sign of old age!' She clearly didn't believe this for a moment herself and waited for the contradictions that did not come. She made a token effort to search round the kitchen hoping Isobel and Louisa would go on talking, but when they didn't she was driven to saying: 'Oh, Louisa, dear, I couldn't help overhearing what you were saying to Isobel about Christopher as I came in. Isn't that tragic? A man like him to have been to prison!' Her eyes misted over with pity. 'How brave of him to come here. How he must have suffered. We must all make extra efforts to cosy him along and help him feel at home, don't you agree?'

'I hope I try to make everyone feel at home – whether

175

they've been to prison or not,' said Isobel tartly. It was unlike her to be acerbic, but the distress Bunty's nosiness had caused her over Rory was still fresh in her mind. 'By the way,' she added, 'I suppose those glasses hanging round your neck aren't the ones you've lost, are they, Bunty?'

Bunty clapped a hand to her bosom and gave a little yelp of surprise as it encountered her glitter-framed reading glasses tangled in the many loops of a shell necklace which cascaded down the tightly fitting front of her sparkly, lurex jumper. 'Silly me! To think they were on me all the time! How clever of you to spot them! Thank you so much, dear.'

'It's a pleasure,' said Isobel truthfully and Louisa gave a muffled snort.

'I must be on my way,' said Bunty. 'I'm going to have a session with Catherine at half past two, and,' she lowered her voice thrillingly, 'who knows what I may discover about my future in the next half hour?' She sounded as if she was on her way to a séance with Madame Za-Za at the local fair rather than a tutorial on creative writing. She lingered for a moment longer, hoping to glean more information, but as none seemed to be forthcoming she eventually pattered off on the dangerously slender kitten heels that looked unequal to the burden they supported. They could hear her steps tap-tapping down the stone-flagged passage.

'Off to become J. K. Rowling the second, one presumes,' said Louisa. 'Poor Catherine. I don't envy her.'

'And poor Christopher too!' said Isobel. 'He's obviously going to be in for the third degree from Bunty when she next sees him. Bet she tries to sit next to him at dinner this evening. I must try to forestall her.' She looked at Louisa. 'Are you going to tell Christopher that you know about his past?' she asked.

Louisa wrinkled her brow. 'I think I ought to tell him, don't you?' she asked, looking bothered. 'It might be a bit unfair otherwise and I really like Christopher. I thought he was amazing the very first time I met him.'

'Oh, Louisa – don't go and cause trouble, will you?' said Isobel impulsively.

Louisa looked indignant. 'In what way?'

'Well, I'm sure you wouldn't *intend* to,' conceded Isobel, 'and it wouldn't be about the prison episode if you did, of course – and yes I agree, you'll have to tell him – but I think you could stir up a hornets' nest in other ways without meaning to. You're such a flirt and you're so attractive but you don't always realise the strength of your own effect on people.'

Like Catherine, Isobel had picked up on Marnie's reaction to Christopher, and though she had no doubt that Marnie, in certain situations, could fight her own corner fiercely and effectively if she had to, she couldn't help feeling the dice would be heavily loaded against her if Louisa decided to make a play for Christopher's attention and pit her own sophisticated confidence against the lack of self esteem that led Marnie to be so chippy and ungracious. Also, now that she knew what Christopher had been through so recently, she thought he might easily fall seriously for Louisa and get hurt himself if she was only looking for a light holiday flirtation.

'Of course I won't cause trouble,' said Louisa, rather upset that Isobel should think she might do so.

'Just so long as no one gets hurt – yourself included.' Isobel glanced at the clock. 'I must be off. I have to pick up a ham from the butcher in Blairalder and then I've got to collect Rory on the way home. It's Sheena's day off and he's been to play with our farm manager's little grandson. It's so good for him to have a friend to play with. He's so unnaturally well behaved compared to most other children that it's great to see him whooping and screaming and running a bit wild.'

'Well, I think you're amazing, Izzy. I really don't know how you cope with the drama about Rory as well as everything going on here.' Louisa got up. 'Back to school now. I'd better do my homework. We're all supposed to write a piece about a journey. 'Bye for now, then . . . I'll keep you informed about all your interesting guests. Regard me as your personal undercover agent!'

'Undercover, my foot!' said Isobel. 'You'd never be any good at undercover anything. You'd always get noticed. Just heed my words of wisdom and don't go stirring any pots.'

'I'll do my best!' Louisa stuffed her writing paraphernalia into her capacious, soft leather bag – battered but expensive looking – swung it nonchalantly over her shoulder, blew Isobel a kiss and sauntered off across the courtyard, humming 'I Know Where I'm Going'.

Isobel felt deeply sorry for Adam Winterton. Though she could see he didn't ignite Louisa's smouldering passions or fulfil her yearning for steamy romance, she thought it was unfair to call him dull. Whenever Isobel had met him – admittedly only a few times – she had found him an interesting and amusing conversationalist with a dry sense of humour, and liked him enormously.

Since the night following Bunty's uncomfortable probing about Rory, Isobel had tried to put that situation on hold till the end of the week, but the question about the little boy's future, and her own and Giles's responses to it, nagged at her like a sore tooth. She had to keep testing it out, deliberately biting on the tooth to gauge the pain factor. She wondered if Giles was doing the same, though they hadn't spoken of it again. She knew he had a better ability to play at ostriches than she had, but both Amy and Edward would be coming home shortly, and she and Giles needed to have prepared some sort of joint statement before perspicacious Amy got in first and quizzed them on the subject. Edward was different. Though he could still look alarmed at the very mention of his Aunt Lorna, complications about the biological facts of Rory's parentage would mean nothing to him. Indeed she thought he would be thrilled to be told he had a little brother. Despite his sixteen years, he was still at his happiest playing the imaginary games more suited to an average six-year-old, and from the start of Rory's visit had adored having him to play with and boss around. Isobel and Giles had watched with helpless anguish over the years as all his childhood contemporaries – the children of their friends – had one by one outgrown Edward as a playmate, and though many of them were still touchingly fond of him, and often extremely good with him, they had long since ceased to be on equal terms. It had given Isobel a dreadful pang to watch Edward and Rory playing together and know that in terms of ability, the twelve years that separated them were non-existent. Strangers meeting Edward for the first time saw a cumbersome adolescent who needed to shave (though he could not yet manage to do this for himself) but Isobel saw the vulnerable small boy she knew him still to be inside.

She had no idea where Lorna was at the moment. There had only been two picture postcards addressed to Rory by way of communication from her in over a month. Both had just had *Love from Mummy* scribbled on them, with no other information whatsoever. Isobel had sent a brief progress report every week and had rung the Washington number several times but so far had only managed to speak to Lorna's 'personal assistant'. Senator and Mrs Congleton were away travelling, she said evasively. No, she was sorry she couldn't give out their telephone number or their addresses.

'But I'm her *sister*,' objected Isobel. 'I'm looking after her child.'

'I assure you that any message will be passed on,' said the voice, 'and I'm sure Mrs Congleton will be pleased to hear that Rory is well. I believe she has your number.'

'Of course she has. Please ask my sister to ring me as soon as possible,' she said coldly. 'I really need to speak to her about arrangements for Rory.'

She resisted the temptation to invent some spurious drama about the child that might kick-start his mother's maternal instincts into action – if she had maternal instincts. So far there had been no response to her call. What was Lorna playing at? What sinister motive was behind her behaviour? One thing was certain: no actions of Lorna's were ever uncalculated.

Isobel whistled for the dogs, and went round the back, where her ancient Volvo estate car was parked. 'Come on, Flapper. Bad luck, Lozzie, I'm afraid it's slimming time. You can get in at the bottom,' and she set off down the drive whistling for the dogs to follow. It was a wonderful way of exercising them when she was busy and Flapper, despite her advancing years, still loved tearing after the car with her ears streaming in the wind. Poor Lozenge, who adored riding in the car and hated to be left behind, was less enchanted with the idea, but trundled gallantly along behind, her short legs going like a clockwork toy, the gap between her and the car getting ever wider. At the end of the drive Isabel stopped and got out to open the back for Flapper, who leaped straight in, while Lozenge was still a grey speck in the distance. Eventually she appeared, panting but triumphant.

'If you didn't eat so much you wouldn't need to do that, you old greedy guts,' said Isobel severely as she lifted her in. Lozenge gave her a reproachful look and started noisily slurping from the water bowl in the back of the car, making a great deal of mess. Isobel's car was usually a tip – the worst mess was confined behind the dog-guard, but old shopping lists and sweet papers tended to litter the floor, not to mention a miscellaneous collection of boots and waterproof jackets belonging to various members of the family, which seemed to breed on the rear seat. Now there was also Rory's car seat, and some of his books and toys had lately been added to the general clutter. Rory . . . I'll get this week over and then, Isobel vowed to herself, then Giles and I will have to sort the situation out and come to some decisions.

She wondered how Christopher Piper would react to the fact that Louisa had been checking up on him and was certainly going to let him know. At least nobody could call my life dull, she thought wryly, and as always she sent up a prayer of thanks for the home and family she loved so much. It had been threatened with possible break-up once before. She had no intention of letting it happen again.

Later in the afternoon, Christopher was still sitting on the seat under the big beech tree when Louisa came out of the house looking for him. He was busily scribbling in a notebook, but she decided it would be a perfect moment to have a talk with him while he was alone, and possibly tell him what she'd heard from Adam.

'Just the person I wanted to see,' she said coming up behind him.

'Oh, hello Louisa,' he said, obviously pleased to see her. 'How are you doing – do you want to sit down?'

'Umm. Why not? It's so lovely out here. You look mighty industrious – I hope I'm not interrupting.'

He screwed the top on his pen, put it in his pocket and closed the notebook. Louisa would have loved to see what he'd written.

'If you are, then I'm delighted to be interrupted! I had a

poem torn over by Catherine earlier this afternoon and now I can't stop tinkering with it and think I'm making it even worse.'

He wondered what scent Louisa used – something fresh and delightful, so that her fragrance always lingered faintly after she had been in a room.

'You're taking the writing really seriously, aren't you?' she asked, sitting down beside him. 'Now that odious old Stanley has buggered off, I get the feeling that you and Win are the only two of us who really mean to continue with it after this week is over. It's fun; it's interesting; we're all learning unexpected things about ourselves, but none of the rest of us is really good enough to take it any further.'

'I don't think it's a question of anyone being better than anyone else. I think it's more about whether any of us really want to try to get published and make a career out of it.'

'And you do?'

'Yes,' he said emphatically, wondering if he would have had the courage to admit this without Catherine's earlier encouragement. 'Yes, I really do. I was a bit dubious about coming here, but I'm so glad I did. I think Catherine's an outstanding teacher and it's a marvellous place.'

She hesitated a moment and then said: 'I've just been talking to Adam. He sent his regards to you.'

'Then do give him mine when you next speak to him,' he said, guessing what this must be leading up to and on the whole feeling relieved. He gave her a not unamused look. 'And what did Adam tell you about me?' he asked.

'He was telling me about your recent troubles. I am so sorry.'

'Ah,' he said lightly, raising an eyebrow at her. 'I thought someone had been spreading the glad tidings about me, but I didn't know it was you. I thought it was Marnie.'

'I'm really sorry if you didn't want anyone to know. I've only told Isobel because she was there when Adam rang and heard bits of our conversation anyway.'

'Oh, don't be sorry. It's no secret – how could it be? These things are public knowledge. My fault for not wanting to talk about it earlier. I should have said something to you on the first day.'

'Why did you think it was Marnie?' she asked.

'Because she was the only person I've told about it, and I thought she must have said something to Bunty . . . because Bunty obviously knows too.'

She said: 'I'm afraid that was my fault – I certainly didn't intend to tell her, but unbeknownst to me she was standing in the doorway, ears flapping, and overheard what I was saying to Isobel.'

'I'm sure she must have lapped it up. Oh well, you've saved me a lot of trouble and now I shan't need to tell anyone myself,' he said. 'What a relief! Please don't worry.'

'It's very nice of you to take it like that,' she said. 'I'd have hated to make things difficult for you. I'm glad you're not angry with me.'

'Of course I'm not angry with you. Only cross with myself for being so stupid in trying to keep it dark in the first place, and even crosser with myself for wrongly blaming Marnie. She was very hurt with me for presuming she'd betrayed what she obviously regarded as a confidence. That I do mind.'

'Well at least I can put that right for you,' said Louisa. 'I'll go and tell her it was my fault.'

'No thank you, Louisa,' he said firmly. 'It's very kind of you but I'd rather do it myself. I owe her an apology.'

She felt a small, unworthy pang of jealousy. Why had he chosen to confide in Marnie? What had gauche Marnie got that she hadn't?

'What will you do when the course is over?' he asked.

'I haven't decided yet. Even though I doubt if I'll continue with the writing, I'm enjoying the course so much I might well do something else. It's opened up a lot of new ideas. It's good for one to do something completely different.'

They were both relieved that there was no awkwardness between them after Adam's revelation. After a bit, Christopher looked at his watch. 'It's suddenly getting a bit parky out here, don't you think? The sun's been so hot one forgets it's only May and this is the north of Scotland. Shall we go and grab a cup of tea before the five o'clock session begins?'

'Good idea. Wonder what Catherine's got in store for us next? I'm not so keen on reading out my own efforts but I do love listening to what other people have written – you get such surprises.'

They got up and walked together back round the side of the house towards the Old Steading, chatting easily about their fellow participants and their possible future plans. Christopher told Louisa about Catherine's favourable reaction to his book, and she told him how much she wanted to travel and see more of the world. Neither of them noticed Marnie standing at the bottom of the front steps, watching them.

Chapter Thirteen

After collecting the marmalade-glazed whole ham on the bone, which was one of the specialities of the excellent butcher in Blairalder, Isobel drove into the yard at the back of Mains-of-Drochatt, Giles's farm manager's house, to collect Rory. She knocked on the half-open back door and called out: 'Anyone there?'

'Hello there, Isobel. Come along through.' Mrs MacDonald, a stocky, fresh-faced woman with short grey hair which still showed traces of its original auburn, was in the kitchen sitting at the old-fashioned scrubbed table in the middle of the room, which was piled, not with the plates of home baking that might have been on display a generation ago in the days of her mother-in-law, but with papers. Janet MacDonald was a well-respected judge and breeder of working Border collies.

'You look busy as usual,' said Isobel. 'It's so kind of you to have had Rory when you have so much to do yourself.'

'It suited me just fine,' said Janet. 'It's kept Robbie happy all morning too – and out from under my feet! They've been playing with Jessie's latest litter of puppies and Alick took them off up the field in the trailer which was obviously a thrill for Rory – so apart from giving him a bite of lunch, which I had to do for everyone else anyway, it's left me free to start to tackle some of this paperwork. We've got a trial coming up in May for novice handlers and dogs. Giles has agreed that we can have it in the park as usual, which will be great. Rory's a grand wee lad, Isobel. He's been no trouble at all.'

'How much longer have you got Robbie with you?'

'For another week I think – but he comes over for the day often enough anyway. They only live the other side of Pitlochry but you'll have heard that he's got a new baby sister, so it helps a bit if I have him to stay occasionally. What with the twins as well, our Jeanie's got her work cut out with four children under six.'

'My goodness yes,' said Isobel. 'That's a real handful. All the same, I envy her having you to call on. We're a bit short of grannies in our family. I wouldn't be looking after Rory now if we still had a granny. He spent a lot of his early life with my parents when my sister was abroad.'

Janet MacDonald gave Isobel a shrewd look. She thought the younger woman was looking tired and strained – not her usual bubbling self at all. 'I was sorry to hear about your father's death after Christmas,' she said. 'It must have hit you very hard coming less than a year after you lost your mother.'

'Thank you – I must say I do miss them both dreadfully. It seemed bad enough when they first moved to France after my father retired and gave up the house in Edinburgh where I was born. I hated that, but at least they were always popping over to see us, and we used to go there too. Amy and Edward adored our visits to them. It was a real shock when my father collapsed and died so suddenly. We'd always thought he was indestructible and there'd never been any mention of heart trouble before as far as we knew. He did find it very hard to cope without Mum. They'd always been so close, and it always seemed as though she relied on him completely, so it was a surprise to find he was quite so lost without her. He'd been so strong and wonderful all through her illness – and so decisive about everything all his life. It just shows you can never really know the inside of any marriage except your own. Everyone keeps telling me it's a blessing he's gone too, but it's hard to see it like that sometimes.'

'Other folks are wonderfully good at telling you how you should feel, but only you can really know,' agreed Janet comfortingly. 'He was a fine man, your dad. There's many round here have reason to be grateful to him. No one's troubles were too small or insignificant for him to take on. My family thought of him as something of a hero.' Isobel and Lorna's father had been a much loved and respected family solicitor with something of a Robin Hood attitude to his wealthy and less wealthy clients.

'When we were children my father was a hero to us too,' said Isobel, smiling at Janet. 'My sister and I used to vie with each other for his approval. His word was law in our childhood – which seems rather appropriate! It was for their sake rather than my sister's that I agreed to have Rory to stay at such a busy time for us. My mother adored him and always seemed to be having him to help Lorna out when he was a baby. I must be getting back – leave you to your paperwork and get on with my own. We've got one of our courses going on this week – the first of the season, which always makes life hectic until we get back into the swing of it again. One or two people are staying on for a second week, but it'll be much less busy next week. Perhaps Robbie'd like to come over to us for a day then, if he's still with you?'

'I'm sure he'd love it. They've got on so well.'

Isobel got out her diary and they fixed a date. She wondered what the older woman, who had known Giles all his life, thought about Rory's striking likeness to his uncle-by-marriage. Janet MacDonald was not one to spread local gossip, though Isobel was well aware that there were plenty of other people who were. She had no doubt at all that Rory's paternity must be the talk of the village.

'Ach well, just be thinking of all your good memories of your father then, Isobel. I'll go and give the boys a shout.' Janet went out into the yard and Isobel could hear her calling: 'Robbie! Rory! Come along in now, boys. Rory's auntie's here.'

Isobel was suddenly struck by an idea – a possible explanation for something that had been puzzling her. Of course, she thought. Why didn't I think of that before?

When the two little boys came running in, Rory flung himself on Isobel, his face glowing. He looked dishevelled, grubby and happy, the knees of his jeans muddy, and the laces of his trainers undone – just how a little boy ought to look, thought Isobel, complicated mixed feelings almost choking her.

'I don't need to ask if you've had a lovely time!' she said, touched by his welcome. Rory looked at her with shining eyes. 'You'll never, ever guess what's happened, Aunt Izzy.'

'Something pretty exciting by the look on your face!'

'Well . . .' Rory took a deep breath, the news almost too momentous to be given words. 'Well . . . guess what's happened to Robbie's guinea pig!'

'You picked it up by its tail and its eyes dropped out?'

'Course not!' Rory gave her a horrified look, obviously not familiar with the old nursery joke.

'Tell me then.'

'It's going to have *babies*. And that's not all,' said Rory impressively. He paused dramatically to let the full impact of his announcement sink in, and then said: 'Robbie says when they're borned I can have one for my very own. I've never, ever had an animal of my own.'

'Oh, Rory.' Isobel hated having to be a wet blanket. 'It's a lovely idea and perhaps we can come and see them, but I really don't think you'll be able to take a guinea pig back to Washington with you.'

'But I don't live in Washington any more,' said Rory. 'I live here now. I live with *you*. Please say I can have one, Aunt Izzy. *Please.*'

Isobel realised that it was the first time Rory had voluntarily made mention of where he lived. He seemed to have blanked his previous existence from his mind. Initially she had presumed this was because homesickness might be too painful to bear, but now she had got to know him, she thought otherwise, and her heart sank.

'I'll be very good if you let me have one,' said Rory earnestly, gazing up at her with Giles's dark eyes. 'I'll look after it all by myself. I promise I will. I've never had a pet of my own.'

Janet MacDonald came to the rescue. 'I'm afraid we'll have to wait to see how many babies Snuffle has first, Rory,' she said firmly. 'She may only have one baby and if so, Robbie's little sister's been promised that. Unless she has several babies there might not be one to spare. But we'll certainly let you know when they arrive and you can come and look at them and then we'll have to see.' And with that Rory had to be content. He didn't think Mrs MacDonald was the sort of lady you argued with. He said polite goodbyes and climbed into the car, and Isobel strapped him in.

Janet MacDonald watched them go. Five years ago when Lorna Cartwright, as she had then been, had spent the summer at Glendrochatt there had been plenty of rumours flying round regarding her possible relationship with her brother-in-law. Lorna had been heartily disliked locally not only for her high-handed and abrasive approach to everyone – only thinly masked by a surface sweetness that hadn't deceived many people – but for her blatant attempts to steal her sister's husband. Giles was a popular landlord and Isobel was much loved locally. Not much doubt, by the look of things, that those rumours had been true, thought Janet now. Surely Isobel herself must be aware of the child's uncanny resemblance to her husband? A difficult situation, she thought – but thank goodness it was none of her business, and she returned to the more pressing task of selecting a suitable dog to sire her young Border collie bitch's first litter of puppies – the controlled line-breeding of dogs, in Janet's opinion, being a much more rewarding preoccupation than the uncontrolled breeding habits of certain humans.

On the drive back to Glendrochatt House, Rory, clearly having had a blissful day, prattled on happily about puppies and tractors, but kept returning optimistically to the subject of guinea pigs.

'What would be a good name for a baby guinea, Aunt Iz?' he asked.

'If the mummy's called Snuffle how about Hawk?' suggested Isobel, but such a catarrhal connection was lost on Rory.

'What about Daffodil?'

'Umm. Nice,' she conceded, her mind half-occupied with questions of catering, but slipping easily back into the old ability to carry on one conversation with a child while thinking of something completely different. 'But it doesn't seem very guinea-piggish somehow.' Against her better judgement she allowed herself to be beguiled into a discussion of suitable names for Snuffle's expected progeny which lasted them all the way back to Glendrochatt.

'Run along in to Sheena now, darling,' she said when they had driven up to the back door, 'and she'll give you your tea because I've got a lot of boring grown-up things I have to do.'

'I shall tell Sheena I'm going to have my very own baby guinea pig, and she'll be very excited,' said Rory, looking up at his aunt under the unfairly long lashes that any girl would have died for, the beguiling dimple, which was so like Edward's, quivering in his cheek.

'You tell her what you like, you bad boy,' said Isobel, laughing at him. 'I'm afraid it won't make any difference.'

'Will you come up and say goodnight when I've had my bath?'

'I will.'

'Promise?' he asked anxiously.

'I promise . . . now *scoot*.'

What am I getting into, she asked herself as she lugged the ham into the kitchen, followed by the dogs. Lozenge, who had been driven nearly crazy with desire by the tantalising whiffs of ham in the car, gave her a reproachful look as she plonked it safely down on the kitchen table, well out of reach of small, portly dachshunds with insatiable appetites but disappointingly short legs, and went to check on arrangements for this evening's dinner.

She felt as if a self-protective coating of enamel round her heart was being slowly and inexorably chipped away.

Chapter Fourteen

Isobel was luxuriating in a hot bath when Giles came up to change for dinner. She had just poured in some more of her favourite Jo Malone lime, basil and mandarin bath essence and was lying back in the water, reviewing her day and pondering on the idea that had struck her earlier, when he came in.

'Hello, my Iz. So how's my love then?' he asked, as he invariably did after only the shortest separation.

'Thinking,' said Isobel.

'Novel experience?' Giles grinned at her and perched on the edge of the bath. 'About anything in particular, may one ask?'

She hesitated. 'About Rory,' she said at last. 'About the past . . . and the future.'

'Ah.' Giles got up and went to look out of the window, hands in pockets, jingling coins.

She watched him, not sure whether this was the right moment to attempt a discussion that might have unforeseen consequences, like walking down a track where suspected landmines might lie in wait.

'Must get that grass cut. It's already far too long,' said Giles, taking out the little leather-bound notepad he always kept in his pocket and scribbling a reminder to himself, but Isobel didn't think his mind was really on the mowing.

'I've had an idea that might explain a few things that have been niggling at me,' she said, 'but I don't know how to check it out and I'm not even sure whether or not to test the theory on you.'

He turned round to face her. 'Well, before you decide,' he said, 'I have something to report to you – and for once I'm not sure how you're going to react. There's been a development.'

'What sort of development? Chuck me the towel, will you?' Isobel did not want to be wet and naked if there were going to be disclosures about Rory. Giles passed her the towel and watched her as she stepped out of the bath, this woman he loved so much but had once nearly lost through his own folly and vanity.

'There's been a message from Lorna. Sheila took a call from the States while I was at the trustees' meeting in Perth. She looked for you, but you'd just gone to fetch Rory and she had to go home before you got back.' Sheila Shepherd was Giles's long-standing secretary, much loved by all the family. She had loathed Lorna when they had briefly had to work together during the turbulent summer when Lorna had tried to reclaim Giles from her sister and install herself as mistress of Glendrochatt.

'I bet it wasn't Lorna herself who rang.'

'No, it was her PA, but she condescended to give Sheila a list of times and numbers when we might catch Lorna. Bloody cheek! Apparently Lorna and her creepy old senator are coming over to London soon and it "might be convenient" for them to take Rory home with them. Decent of them to let us know,' said Giles with heavy irony. 'It's lucky I wasn't there. I might have blown my top.'

Husband and wife looked at each other, both aware that complicated, unresolved issues were bound to come up; both unsure of what they really felt about the child; both afraid of saying something that could never be unsaid and might inflict lasting damage on their relationship.

Isobel spoke first. 'Poor Rory,' she said, 'poor little boy! Shoved from pillar to post – a pawn in a spiteful grown-up game.'

'You've been so good with him . . . so fair; so loving. You're very generous, Izzy, don't think I'm not deeply aware of it, but it does make for difficulties. You must be itching for him to go.'

Isobel took her dressing gown down from the hook behind the door, wrapped it round herself and tied the sash tightly round her waist with a look of great concentration, as though she feared she might be scrutinised by hostile, prying eyes.

'I thought I was,' she said. 'It will certainly make life a whole lot easier to be without him . . . and oh, Giles, I shan't have to fight myself over this awful jealousy thing the whole time – about you and Lorna, about you and Rory, about Rory and Ed. You can't imagine how I dislike myself sometimes at the moment. It's a nightmare.' She paused, and looked at him. 'But do you know,' she continued, on a note of surprise, 'all I feel right now is dread at the thought of telling him he's going back. I only agreed to have him because I knew Mum and Dad would have wanted me to . . . and now there are no grandparents to come to his rescue any more and I hate to think what sort of life he'll have with Lorna.'

'You don't think perhaps he'll be anxious to see his mum again?' Giles suggested cautiously, much moved by her words.

'I don't know – he may be. But I think he'll be awfully bothered too. I think he feels . . . *safe* with us. Something he said this afternoon made me very uneasy.' She told Giles about the guinea pig episode.

'Oh, Lord,' said Giles. 'I suppose one of us had better actually speak to Lorna before we tell him anything. It would be too awful if he got all thrilled and excited and then she let him down. That seems highly likely to me. I think one of the suggested times to catch her is about nine o'clock tonight, our time. Will you try her – or do you want me to do it?'

She laughed suddenly and went and put her arms round his neck. 'No, I most definitely don't want you to do it, Giles Grant! She'd be thrilled. Anything rather than that! I'll try her after dinner and leave a sizzling message if I don't get her. We'll think together how to approach Rory after that. We need to sleep on it.'

'We most certainly do,' said Giles, laughing back at her, loving as always her lightning change of mood. 'I just wish we didn't have to do other things first!'

'You know that's not what I meant! You're incorrigible,' she said severely, but she returned his kiss. Giles held her close and laid his cheek against the top of her head. 'I love you so much, Iz,' he whispered. 'I couldn't exist without you. You do know that, don't you?'

'Hmm,' she said. 'I'll have that in writing. Oh, God! We're going to be late for dinner if we don't hurry. I wish we hadn't got to chat up all these people, though I have to admit to being quite intrigued by this lot. I have a feeling there are deep emotional issues being worked out among our band of writers. At least it takes my mind off our own troubles.'

It didn't take unusual powers of perception to pick up that something was amiss with Marnie. Isobel thought she resembled a volcano – heavy clouds hanging around and the possibility of an explosion an alarming threat. Her chippy unfriendliness seemed to be back in place and Isobel marvelled that anyone's looks could be so altered by their frame of mind. Marnie reminded her of one of those visual tests made up of little dots: look at her one way and you saw an attractive young woman – pretty would be the wrong word – with good bone structure, a beautiful skin and, when she let her guard down, something both touching and beguiling about her; look at her in another way and she appeared as plain as the proverbial pikestaff and rather disagreeable. Isobel noticed how she turned away from Christopher when he came into the room and ostentatiously went to talk to the Colonel. She did not of course know about the misunderstanding between them, or that before dinner Christopher had gone in search of Marnie to make an apology for his assumption, but she had not been in her room and he had failed to locate her. Isobel didn't imagine the atmosphere in the writing class could have been enhanced by Marnie's surly negativity, but thought that Catherine, who had taught in some tough places over the years and had a useful capacity for detachment, would have been well up to handling it; it just seemed a pity that, after the welcome departure of Stanley, other frictions had cropped up. She threw a questioning look at Louisa, wondering if there had been some trouble she didn't know about.

Dinner was to be in the dining room tonight, and as Isobel shepherded everyone in, she managed to say to Marnie: 'Do come and sit next to me tonight. I've been so hectic, and Catherine's kept you all so busy, that I don't seem to have had much chance to get to know everyone properly. I know you're staying on for our "Enjoy Scotland" week so I'd welcome the chance to tell you what the options are and find out what you'd particularly like to do. I love trying to tailor it as far as possible to individual requirements.' Her easy friendliness was difficult to resist and Marnie responded in spite of herself, as most people usually did to Isobel. She had that rare gift of bringing out the best in the people she was with and quite soon had the younger woman laughing at accounts of some of the dramas that had occurred since they had decided to put

Giles's ancestral home to commercial use: of invasions by bats which had eventually been discovered to be nesting in the drawing-room chimney and had mysteriously appeared from nowhere, night after night, to swirl round the heads of disconcerted guests at dinner; of the hysterical horror of a well-known concert pianist who was giving a week of master classes in the newly refurbished theatre and had insisted on dining in a hat for the rest of the week; of the fraught occasion when Glendrochatt's antiquated water system, fed by its own reservoir up in the woods, had failed when the house was stretched to capacity with a group of journalists on whom the Grants particularly wished to make a favourable impression; of the time when the stout leader of an ensemble from Hungary had gone exploring on the roof – Giles having rashly told him about the sensational panorama to be seen from the battlements – and had failed to secure the heavy lead-covered trapdoor after he'd squeezed through it and had been trapped on the roof for several hours before he was located.

'When we eventually tracked him down we thought we were never going to be able to get him back into the house again.' Isobel laughed at the memory. 'He got stuck in the opening like Mr Jackson in *The Tale of Mrs Tittlemouse* and we had to do a lot of undignified pushing and pulling to get him back through it. Now we take care to shove crumpled newspapers up the drawing-room fireplace in July and August to stop any bats attending late-summer soirées – but that's yet another hazard because we nearly set the room ablaze once when we forgot to pull the paper out when we suddenly wanted a fire in the evening – as one's apt to do in Scotland at any time of year. We also keep a huge water container permanently filled and have lots of buckets handy to fill up loos et cetera in case we have another major water crisis and there's a large No

Entry sign at the bottom of the stairs that lead to the roof to deter exploring musicians – but we still never know what dramas are going to hit us next. The penalties and pleasures of living in an ancient house, I suppose!'

'Well nothing's gone wrong with this week yet anyway,' said Marnie, laughing. 'In fact I'd say everything is going just fine.' She added gruffly: 'I don't think I've ever been made to feel so welcome anywhere.'

'Oh Marnie – *thank you*. I'm so glad.' Isobel guessed that this sort of tribute didn't come easily to her prickly guest and it made it all the nicer. 'But we haven't got through the weekend yet, when the twins will be at home. Amy's taking part in the Saturday concert and can get very histrionic when she's performing and Edward . . . well, with Edward at home anything can happen, especially when we're busy and have a house full!'

'Tell me about them. I gather from Catherine that your daughter's a talented violinist. Does your son play an instrument too?'

Isobel found herself telling Marnie something about Edward's difficulties and was surprised to find what a good listener she was.

'But goodness me . . . this is not what I meant to talk to you about at all,' she said apologetically, stopping suddenly, mid-sentence. 'I didn't mean to burden you with family problems.'

'It isn't a burden,' protested Marnie, touched that Isobel should have confided in her. She would have liked to ask more about Edward, but was afraid of appearing nosy and intrusive like Bunty. 'I think your son sounds a fascinating character,' she said, 'and I shall look forward to meeting both the twins.'

'Well you'll certainly do that . . . but let's get back to thinking about next week. Tell me if there's anything special you'd like to do – any particular interest you may have?'

'Well, there *is* something.' Marnie hesitated, then: 'If you wanted to track down a particular old house – possibly a castle – in this part of Scotland, but you didn't know who it belonged to, what it was called or even exactly where it was, how would you set about finding it?' she asked.

Isobel considered. 'That sounds a bit of a tall order. Literally tall if it's a castle, I suppose, but they're almost two a penny in some parts of Scotland. Anything with a bit of turret stuck on somewhere can get glorified with the title of castle; some are called towers and some, of course, like this one, are just called house. What have you got to go on?'

'A couple of old black and white photographs – rather faded and crumpled – and some verbal descriptions from when I was a little girl.'

'Well, I've never tried to do anything like that, but I suppose I'd probably go to one of the big estate agents like Strutt & Parker or Finlayson Hughes in Perth who specialise in selling or letting those sorts of properties. I'd certainly make enquiries with Historic Scotland – the government organisation that deals with old buildings and heritage matters. It'd be a bit of a long shot, but it might be worth looking in back numbers of magazines like *Country Life*, or *The Field*. I'd ask around friends in case anyone came up with an idea. Why? Are you researching something?'

'Well, I'm hoping to, in a way – but I don't quite know how to go about it.'

'Giles is always full of unexpected bits of local knowledge and has lived here all his life. It sounds right up his street. I'm sure he'd love to help.' Isobel thought for a moment. 'I know who else would be a brilliant person to ask,' she said, 'and that's my sister's old godmother, Evelyn Fergusson, who lives near here and is an absolute mine of information about Scotland's old houses and families. One of the things I was going to suggest that you and the others might like to do next week is to have a privately conducted tour of her fabulous garden and arboretum. It's a bit early to be at its best – June would be better – but there'll be some rhododendrons and azaleas out and the bluebells will be fantastic. It's a heavenly place anyway. It's open to visitors at weekends but we often take people there on one of the days when it's closed to the general public. Evelyn mightn't manage to take us round the grounds herself this year because she's pretty arthritic now, but her head gardener is hugely knowledgeable and a great raconteur. She enjoys meeting any guests we bring over and lays on marvellous home-made Scottish teas and a tour of the house as well. The house isn't normally open – just occasionally for charity – so it's a fun thing to be able to offer our guests here. We could pick her brains about your lost castle. Do you think you might like to do that?'

'I'd love to. That sounds wonderful. You are kind, Isobel.'

The wary, sullen look had vanished as though it had never existed, and Isobel wondered if it could ever be banished for good. From her vantage point at the end of the table she could see Louisa sparkling away to Christopher and wondered if she had yet told him of her discoveries about his life. It certainly didn't seem to have caused a rift between them if she had. Marnie would have her work cut out if she wanted to compete with Louisa for Christopher's attention, Isobel thought, but if she achieved it, it might be life-transforming. Aloud, she said: 'Good. I'll talk to Giles and we'll get that organised. I know Morwenna would love to see the garden. Is it a family connection you're trying to research?'

'Not exactly. Did Catherine tell you about the West

Indian episode in my childhood that I wrote about the first day?'

'No,' said Isobel. 'Catherine's always very particular that whatever anyone writes is confidential. Tell me more.' So Marnie, in her turn, found herself telling Isobel about her encounter with the old lady who had become such an unexpected benefactress. 'I want to find the Contessa's childhood home. I have a fantasy that I might buy it with the money she left me and do something worthwhile with it – and that would be my thank you to her memory,' she explained. 'Of course it may not even exist any more. It could have been pulled down or anything. It may be lived in but not for sale, so this might all be a complete wild goose chase. I wouldn't want to become a nuisance to you both,' she added diffidently, 'but it would be fantastic if you could help me.'

'Of course you wouldn't be a nuisance. I think it's a wonderfully romantic idea and I love chasing wild geese. Can I tell Giles about it?'

'Sure – that would be great.' In view of Isobel's enthusiasm and interest Marnie felt ashamed of her previous ill humour. How lovely it must be to be possessed of Isobel's easy friendliness – or Louisa's come to that, she thought with a pang. She had been on her way to make amends to Christopher for her unwarranted touchiness – and apologies did not come easily to Marnie – when she had seen him laughing and talking with Louisa on the white seat under the tree where she had left him, and all her old insecurities had kicked in. She was conscious that further down the table Christopher was seated next to Louisa now, but because they were on the same side as her she couldn't actually see how they were getting on together – but she could hear their laughter.

'Who else is staying for the second week?' she asked,

hoping that if Christopher was one of them, she might have a second chance to put things right.

'Only you and Louisa, the Colonel and Morwenna,' said Isobel. 'The Heslingtons were originally booked to stay on, but Win feels she's got to get back to Stanley now – rather her than me – and Joyce has to return to her gift shop. We usually have a waiting list of locals who would like to join in the events we've planned, but the residents have first say in choosing which options we go for. I'm glad you're staying, Marnie. I think you'll enjoy it.'

Isobel, a practised hostess, then turned to the Colonel on her other side, which left Marnie to talk to Joyce. It was impossible not to get on with Joyce. Despite her rather brassy appearance, everyone liked her and she was soon chatting away with Marnie as if they'd known each other for years. Isobel glanced at Giles at the other end of the big mahogany dining table, which had been in this room for over two hundred years. At the window end, where the sun caught it, the wood had faded to a mellow, almost golden colour but Giles liked this reminder of its presence in the same spot for so long, and resisted suggestions to have the table resurfaced. Fully extended, it seated twenty-four people in comfort, and the spare leaves which could be inserted to bring it to its maximum length, were of a much darker colour altogether. Isobel always longed to have a time camera that could record scenes from the past – show a film of other people's conversations and laughter, their political arguments and enjoyment of good food round the big table over the years.

She caught Giles's eye. He was listening with apparent attention to Bunty, though Isobel was very sure his mind was more likely to be running on grouse prospects or the availability of some new singer he had heard on one of his talent-spotting expeditions. She hoped Bunty was steering clear of the intriguing subjects of either Rory or

Christopher Piper, but had no doubt that her husband would be capable of steering her off dangerous topics if necessary.

As soon as dinner was over, Catherine herded her class off for the day's last session and Isobel braced herself to make a transatlantic call. This time, she was put through to Lorna almost immediately.

'Iz! We've managed to get each other at last,' said Lorna, who'd made no efforts whatsoever to speak to her sister so far. She sounded all sweetness and concern, but Isobel, who was inured to her sister's devious ways, was not deceived.

'So how's my little man then?' asked Lorna, honey dripping from her tongue.

'He seems fine,' said Isobel. 'He doesn't appear to have been homesick at all.'

'Oh well, he's a much travelled child,' said Lorna. 'He takes life as it comes.'

'Just as well – under the circumstances,' said Isobel tartly, and then thought, I must not be goaded into playing verbal games. Lorna's always been able to wind me up.

'Yes . . . I'm very lucky he's got such an easy temperament. Otherwise,' continued Lorna blandly, 'I wouldn't have felt able to ask you to come to my rescue when Brooke and I had so many important commitments.' Like hell you wouldn't, thought Isobel. 'And what does Giles think of Rory?' went on Lorna. 'Have they got on well together?'

Don't rise, don't rise, Isobel told herself. 'Fine,' she said coolly. 'Giles has always been a pied piper to children.'

'And who do you think Rory's like?'

In ordinary circumstances it would have been the most natural of questions from one sister to another, but it made Isobel see red.

'Actually I think he's rather like Ed,' she said. She heard

with satisfaction Lorna's little intake of breath at her answer. Bull's-eye, she thought. 'Now tell me your plans for getting Rory home,' she said after a highly charged pause.

'Well, we're hoping to be in London for a visit soon so I thought you could put him on a flight from Edinburgh to Heathrow. I might be able to meet him there myself unless Brooke needs me that day, but the temporary nanny I've booked to fly back to the States with us could meet him if I can't.'

Isobel felt outraged, but managed to refrain from saying that the person who needed Lorna after six weeks' absence was her little boy. Instead she said: 'And who is coming to pick him up at Edinburgh airport?'

'Surely he can travel as an unaccompanied minor? It's only a forty-minute flight.'

'No,' said Isobel. 'No, Lorna, that's too much to ask of him. He's only five. I wouldn't be prepared to do that.'

Lorna sighed audibly. 'I'd forgotten how terribly fussy and over-protective you always are with children – still, I'm not complaining. I'm sure you've taken good care of Rory.'

As Lorna had always liked to keep up the fiction of scatty, disorganised little Iz, the perpetually inefficient younger sister, this was a complete volte-face.

Isobel said coldly: 'I'll ask Sheena Graham if she'll go with him. She might even welcome a trip to London, but you'd have to pay her expenses.'

'Of course. Whatever. Naturally I'll see she's not out of pocket.' Lorna sounded bored, as though such mundane considerations were beneath her. 'I'll get my secretary to go ahead and book the flight and she'll ring you with a firm date. It'll be in the next ten days. Thank you so much for having him,' she added graciously.

'You didn't give me much choice,' said Isobel. 'Talk about do first and ask second . . . putting him on a flight like that and then telling us he was on his way. You knew I'd never leave a child stranded, but we might have been away or anything.'

'And I'm very grateful.' Lorna had got herself in hand again and, as so often in their past, gave the impression of speaking patiently to a difficult child. 'But after all that's what families are for, isn't it?'

What else do you think families are for, Isobel longed to ask . . . for sharing husbands? Instead she said, 'Do you want to speak to Rory tomorrow and tell him yourself that he's coming home?'

'Oh, I don't think so. The telephone's such a bad instrument for communicating with children.'

'Well you obviously think so anyway,' Isobel was goaded into retorting. 'I'll tell him, then.'

'Yes, do. 'Bye then, Izzy. We'll speak again soon,' and Lorna Congleton, millionaire senator's wife, Washington society's latest beauty – and long-time jealous, manipulative sister – rang off.

Isobel found Giles in the drawing room, listening to a new recording of a youth orchestra playing Prokofiev. He turned the sound down and got up as soon as she came in. He thought she looked exhausted.

'So you spoke to Lorna,' he said. 'I can tell because you've still got steam coming out of your ears. How did it go?'

She came and stood in front of him. 'My jaw hurts,' she said, leaning her forehead against his chest and closing her eyes.

'Your jaw?'

'Yes. I've just spent ten minute talking through gritted teeth, and you've no idea how painful it was.'

He put his arms round her and rocked her gently. 'Tell me about it.'

'I've done something I'm so ashamed of that I despise myself.'

'He stroked her hair. 'In what way?'

'Lorna asked who I thought Rory was like – who in the family he most reminded me of. I felt as though I was a fish she'd hooked,' said Isobel in a strangled voice, 'as if she was slowly, slowly reeling me in.' She looked up at him with brimming eyes and blurted out: 'I said I thought he was very like Edward.'

'Well that's true in a way,' Giles comforted her, aching for his wife, but filled with misery himself. 'He *is* like what Ed would be – ought to be – if . . . if things had gone otherwise when he was born. You've told me that several times. That's not such a terrible thing to have said.'

'Not to *us* it wouldn't be – not to you and me or Amy or any of the many people who love Ed, and see all the lovely things about him that are there despite his problems,' she said passionately, 'but you know how badly Lorna's always reacted to him – how physically repulsed she's always been by him since he was a tiny baby. I wasn't going to admit what she wanted to hear me say – that Rory's the living spit of you – and I knew it was the worst thing I could possibly tell her. I don't mind about Lorna – she asks for it – but oh, Giles, I feel she's made me stoop so low. I feel . . . polluted. I've deliberately used Edward as a *weapon* and that's what I mind. I've let him down.'

At that moment there was a knock on the door. They looked at each other in dismay and stepped apart.

'Come in,' said Giles.

Christopher Piper put his head round the door. 'Is this a bad moment?' he asked, sensing something in the atmosphere that made him feel he might be interrupting. 'You said if I looked in after the evening session . . . ?'

'Of course! I was hoping you'd drop in,' said Giles untruthfully but with a commendably welcoming smile.

He'd completely forgotten that after dinner Christopher had asked if he could have a word with him sometime, and Giles had suggested he should come and have a nightcap after the last session. 'What will you have to drink? I'm just about to have a glass of whisky – or would you prefer brandy?'

'Whisky would be great – with water please.'

'What about you, darling?' Giles gave Isobel, who was busily putting an unnecessary log on the fire, a questioning look – as much to check that she'd managed to get herself in hand again as to offer her a drink.

'No thanks, I'm fine,' she said, answering both queries. She realised that she hadn't had time to tell Giles about Louisa's disclosure and guessed that was what Christopher might have come to talk about. She hoped he wasn't going to drop out of the rest of the week.

Christopher looked round the room, a charming, peaceful place with a timeless air of faded elegance. He guessed that most of the things in it had probably remained more or less unchanged for generations – except for the picture over the fireplace.

'What a stunning portrait!' he exclaimed. 'Who painted it?'

'I'm so glad you like it.' Giles handed him his drink. 'It's by Daniel Hoffman. He did it five years ago when he came to paint the backcloth we'd commissioned for the theatre. You can see that tomorrow when Jonathan Mercer gives his lecture in the theatre. We were lucky to get him so early in his career. He was already making a name for himself in theatrical design, but portrait painting was a new venture. He's become very sought after now. Lots of people up here wanted him to work for them after he'd done Izzy. He's done a fantastic portrait of a rather oddball neighbour of ours called Lord Dunbarnock, who's our most important patron. He presented the theatre with a second backcloth and Daniel Hoffman had already caricatured him, along with various other people including ourselves, on the first, but the serious portrait is brilliant because it acknowledges all Neil Dunbarnock's undoubted eccentricities but manages to convey the deeply kind and cultivated person he is too. Apart from the fact that he's got Isobel to the life, it's a delightful picture, isn't it?'

'It certainly is. I've admired Hoffman's witty stage designs for Glyndebourne, but I went to an exhibition of his about three years ago in London and discovered what a notable portrait painter he is too.' Christopher studied the big oval portrait with appreciation. It showed Isobel in informal pose sitting on the front steps of Glendrochatt. Flapper was curled up at her feet, an open book and a cup of coffee were on the step beside her and she wore the alert, amused expression, head slightly on one side, which was so typical of her when she was listening to anyone. Five small roundels spaced round the edge showed her in other poses including one in full evening dress with a tartan sash knotted on one shoulder. 'Has he painted anyone else in your family?' Christopher asked.

'He painted Isobel's sister Lorna for the exhibition you went to,' said Giles. 'It was called *Woman in Black*. It's very striking – you may remember it.'

'I remember it very well – it was quite remarkable. It dominated the whole room. Do you own that too?'

'No,' said Giles. 'No I don't. I asked him to paint Izzy – but Lorna's picture was nothing to do with me.' Something about the way he spoke made Christopher think there must be a story attached to the painting.

'My sister's picture wasn't a commission,' explained Isobel. 'She's the beauty of the family and was staying with us when Daniel was painting me and he asked her if she'd sit for him so that he could exhibit it. He didn't want to sell it originally, but in the end he let her buy it on condition that he could still have it to exhibit. It was a sensation the first time it was shown – and made his name as a portrait painter. Lorna lives in the States, so I imagine it's hanging in her new husband's house in Washington now – which should do wonders for Daniel's career. Lorna is Rory's mother,' she added.

'Well, lucky Rory,' said Christopher. 'He'll no doubt inherit an heirloom one day – but I think your own portrait is even more delightful.' Privately he thought this was because Isobel was so enchanting herself and the artist had managed to capture her warmth and humour so well that anyone seeing the portrait couldn't fail to be beguiled by the personality of the sitter. He clearly remembered thinking that, striking though the picture in the exhibition had been, he would not at all like to meet the woman depicted in it, however beautiful she might be. There had been a sense of menace – malice almost – that was disturbing. Christopher, who had been a witness to the little drama in the kitchen triggered by tactless Bunty, decided that there must be complicated relationships and unresolved problems in the Grant family. How deceptive appearances can be, he thought – we are none of us quite what we seem. It gave him courage to make his own admission to the host and hostess whom at first meeting he had envied as a gilded couple with a charmed lifestyle.

'There's something you should both know,' he said. 'I should have told you at the start of the week – it was very remiss of me. I've recently come out of prison, but I'm still on parole. I cleared my trip here with my probation officer before coming – but I should have told you. I'm sorry.' He added, 'I don't think you need worry that I'm any sort of risk to your other guests. I killed someone in a car crash and got the statutory sentence.'

Giles said quickly: 'Well, thank you for telling us now.

You didn't have to do that – your private life is none of our business.'

Christopher pulled a self-deprecating face. 'I'm afraid I might not actually have told you,' he admitted, 'if Louisa hadn't recognised me, but we'd met before.' He looked at Isobel. 'I believe she's told you about it?'

'Yes,' she said, liking his honesty. 'She did, but I agree with Giles. It's none of our business, unless you want to talk about it.' She added quickly, 'Louisa won't have meant to make trouble, you know – she was just curious.'

'Like Bunty?' he suggested drily.

Isobel giggled. 'I don't think she'd thank you for that, but yes, I suppose so. If I'm truthful I have to say I'm intrigued too. You don't immediately conjure up one's image of an old lag.'

'Well thank God for that! I have to say this week is proving the best therapy I could have. I couldn't be more grateful to you both.' He told them about the thriller he had written in prison and his delight at Catherine's reaction to it.

'She won't have been flattering you,' said Giles. 'I can promise you that. Catherine's always very kind but she never raises false hopes. How exciting that she's going to give it to Jonathan Mercer. You'll like him. He's great fun.'

They talked easily of writing and prison and the turning of Glendrochatt from a beloved but dilapidated white elephant of a home into a flourishing business concern. They discovered several mutual interests and quite a few mutual friends. When the grandfather clock in the hall started to chime eleven o'clock Christopher got up hastily.

'I must go,' he said apologetically. 'I didn't intend to stay like this but it's been so good talking to you both. I've been a bit starved for conversation where I've been! Thank you so much for the drink – and the company. Glendrochatt is helping me to feel human again.'

'That's a lovely thing to say. Do you really have to go at the end of the week?' asked Isobel. 'Why don't you stay on for the second rather different and less structured week? Several of the others are staying. I think you'd enjoy it. We'd love to have you, wouldn't we, Giles?'

'We certainly would. Is that difficult – do you have to get permission for that sort of thing?'

'Well, I'd have to ask my probation officer. He has to know where I am and approve of what I'm doing. I certainly don't want to break any regulation and find myself back inside. I don't think I'd cope with that very easily, but he's a decent bloke and I'm not considered at risk of re-offending. I don't think there'd be a problem in staying here so long as I ask him. That's very kind of you. Can I think about it?'

'Of course you can. But I hope you decide to stay. You can help us in the search for Marnie's vanished castle,' said Isobel. 'That's going to be quite a challenge. Has she mentioned it to you?'

'No,' said Christopher. 'But it sounds intriguing.'

'You should ask her about it. And Louisa is going to stay too.'

When Christopher had gone, Giles grinned at his wife. 'Matchmaking?' he asked.

'Umm,' she said thoughtfully. 'Perhaps. He's such a charming man – I really like him – and after what he's been through I think he might need a helping hand. Besides, it will take my mind off our own troubles.'

'And which one do you think would be best for him, O scheming one?' asked Giles. 'Marnie or Louisa? I think you favour Marnie, but I'd back Louisa to get her own way if she wants something badly enough. And from the signals I've been picking up I'd say she was more than a little interested in Christopher.'

They turned off the lights in the drawing room, let the

dogs out and stood on the steps looking out over the misty moonlit garden.

'We're very lucky, aren't we, Giles?' she whispered. 'To live here in this beautiful place and have each other and our children.'

'Yes,' he echoed. 'We're very lucky. And we'll hang on to it. We won't let Lorna or anyone else spoil our happiness, or make us forget it.'

Chapter Fifteen

Christopher walked slowly back to the Old Steading feeling more at peace than he had for a long time; hoping that he might be able to put the awful time behind him and look to the future – a future which, he was becoming increasingly convinced, was unlikely to include Nicola. For the first time he confronted the idea that even if she were prepared to try to get together again, he might be the one who felt unable to go back to their old relationship.

After he had been released she had announced that she wanted to see him for the first time since the end of the trial. She had not been pleased to learn that the meeting would have to take place at his parents' house in the country, which he had chosen to give as his place of residence rather than his London flat. He had explained that the terms of his release, as a model d-category prisoner who had served half of his statutory three-year sentence, clearly stated that he must live at a fixed address and would have to ask permission to leave it.

'Why can't you come up to London for the night? Surely they'd let you do that. You're hardly likely to abscond – and anyway I don't see why anyone need know,' Nicola had said. Christopher could see that now that he was safely out of prison and she couldn't be called on to face meeting in such distasteful surroundings, Nicola might have enjoyed the thrill of an illicit rendezvous. It would, for her, have added zest to a moribund relationship. 'It's not as if you're tagged or anything,' she went on impatiently. 'I really do want to see you – of course I do – and there are lots of things we need to talk about, but I don't see why I should have to come down to Nether Pacey to do it. You've no idea how frosty your mother was with me for not coming to visit you in the nick. I thought she might be pleased to be shot of me but she kept offering to drive me there and come with me "if it would make it easier" as if I wasn't perfectly capable of getting there by myself if I'd wanted to! I tried to explain that I just can't *do* that sort of thing – prisons, hospitals, visiting the sick – anything like that makes me feel ill – but she doesn't get it at all. It's okay for someone like her who actually enjoys *ministering* to people . . .' She made it sound like a dirty word.

Christopher had not realised that his mother, who'd always had her reservations about Nicola, had tried so hard to get her to visit him, but thought it was typical of his parent that she had not attempted to make capital out of Nicola's desertion of her son. He could have told her that trying to change Nicola's mind on this score would be a lost cause, but it hadn't stopped him feeling bitterly hurt himself. Over the eighteen months of his incarceration they had spoken occasionally on the telephone – painfully stilted, unsatisfactory calls, always at his instigation and always under threat of his precious prison phone card running out in the middle of the conversation, since incoming calls to prisoners were not permitted. He thought, ruefully, that it would have been better for everyone if he'd accepted that their relationship was over before his conviction, but during the first traumatic months of his sentence he had hung on to the possibility of keeping it on hold, albeit in deep freeze, until he could deal with the situation in person. That Nicola might have been faithful to him during his absence seemed highly improbable and it was therefore no surprise when they eventually met to hear that she had been having an affair, about which she made no secret, honesty being one of Nicola's best qualities, though not one she ever felt the need to economise over. What had surprised him was that she seemed to think that they could just pick up again where they had left off – or rather where they had been before his own disastrous loss of temper which had led to the accident, and which he now so bitterly regretted.

'We can have a bit of fun together again – which I'm sure you need – and see how things work out,' said Nicola breezily, brushing aside her affair as an irrelevance, easily disposed of. The fact that none of the issues between them which had caused the row before the crash had been resolved didn't seem to bother her in the least.

'You can't seriously think we can take up as if nothing has happened?' he asked in astonishment. 'We couldn't agree on anything about the future *before*. We're two years older now, and I for one have undergone a huge change.'

'Exactly!' she had said. 'You're bound to have changed. All that unrealistic rubbish about marriage and children and giving up our London life! I was never going to be that sort of person and I never pretended otherwise – but you wouldn't have it. You had to nurture an unrealistic hope that I might suddenly turn into a cradle-rocking little Miss Muffet character. Surely now you've had all this time to brood about what a fun thing we had going between us, you must realise how crazy it would be to chuck it away for guaranteed boredom. Why do you always have to make such a big deal out of everything? Provided you don't still hanker to settle down by an Aga to breed children and write books I'm prepared to give things another go. I can't guarantee that it'll last any more than you can, but before you started getting broody and idealistic we used to have a great time – and that's good enough for me.'

She had been amazed when he said that it was no longer enough for him, and when he told her about the book he had written in prison she had looked at him in horror.

'You'd have thought the last two years would have brought you to your senses,' she said. 'You're such an impossible romantic. All right, maybe you might be able to get your thriller published – I can see that your prison sentence could make great publicity' – Christopher winced – 'but as for *poetry*,' scoffed Nicola, 'forget it! Where did that ever get anyone? Why can't you stick to what you're good at and let me do the same?'

'How do you know I wouldn't be a successful writer?' he demanded, unnerved to feel his temper beginning to rise again. Nicola had shrugged.

'I don't *know*, but I can only say that if you choose to chuck away your flair for economics and throw up a highly profitable and exciting career – which you could easily get back – to satisfy a schoolboy daydream, then don't expect me to hang about for you.'

'Expecting you to hang about is the last thing I'm likely to do,' he had said furiously. 'Experience has shown me that the minute things go wrong for me, you're off like a rocket with another man.'

'And you're becoming a pompous prig,' she flashed. She'd gone on to tell him that he always wanted everything his own way and took himself far too seriously.

Thinking of this exchange now, Christopher was inclined to think she had been right on the last score, anyway. He also thought, uncomfortably, that after accusing Nicola of falling into the arms of the first man who came her way when he was behind bars, he had been far from averse to the company of both Marnie and Louisa, the first two women – other than prison officers – who had come his way for a long time. Despite these disturbing reflections, his mood of optimism persisted and he decided that if there were no objections from his probation officer, he would stay on at Glendrochatt for the second week.

As he walked across the garden to the Old Steading, he could see a light still on in one of the upper windows – Marnie's. He wondered how she would react if he tapped at her door, offered an apology and asked if she felt like taking a moonlight walk round the garden. He could ask her about the vanished castle that Isobel said she was looking for, which sounded intriguing, but even as it occurred to him, the light went out and he thrust the thought aside. It was a stupid idea anyway. It was far too late and she'd probably think he had lecherous intentions. As she clearly took offence extremely easily he didn't want to get off on the wrong foot a second time.

He didn't know that when she'd turned her light out, Marnie had looked out of her window and seen him walking across the courtyard, illuminated by the security lights. She thought of calling out to him but was afraid he might misinterpret it as an invitation to something more, so she stayed silent while foolishly hoping he might look up and see her. She watched as he let himself in at the door.

And he did indeed look up, but an old habit for concealment made her step back so he didn't see her. She heard him come quietly up the stairs and then go on down the passage. There was the sound of a key turning in a lock and a door opening and closing and then silence. Stupid of her to think he might want to see her. She would have loved to talk to him about her proposed search for Luciana's childhood home – the house that had so lit up the imagination of a lonely little girl in the West Indies all those years ago. She felt instinctively that Christopher would understand and appreciate her romantic folly in looking for this castle-in-the-air and, as so often in the past, she cursed the inbuilt lack of self-confidence that prevented her from making approaches to other people. She would have liked to wish him luck for the following day when the manuscript of his book, which was clearly so important to him, was to be handed to Jonathan Mercer. It's such a little thing to wish someone luck, thought Marnie. So natural; so easy. Why can't I do it? Louisa, she felt sure, would have had no such inhibition.

Isobel rang Evelyn Fergusson the following morning. The old lady sounded pleased to hear her, and was enthusiastic about the idea of a small group coming over to see the house and garden the following week, especially when she heard that one of them was a gardening correspondent. They fixed a day and discussed the timing.

'Oh, and there's another thing I want to consult you about, Evie,' said Isobel. 'I'd like to enlist your help for a young American woman in the group whom you'll meet. She's trying to look up old roots and wants to locate a particular house in these parts. I'm not quite sure whether it's a fortified house or a proper castle – or even if it still exists – but you've got such a vast knowledge of historic buildings and such an encyclopedic memory for all the ins and outs of old Scottish families that I thought you'd be just the person for her to talk to. She's rather unusual, a bit of a one-off. She's quite reserved until you get to know her, but I think you'll like her. We do.'

'Then I'm sure I shall like her too and I'll certainly do my best to help – but that isn't what I thought you were going to say. I thought you were going to ask me about something quite different.'

'Like what?'

'There's something I need to discuss with you and Giles that I don't want to mention on the telephone. I've been thinking about it for quite a bit and I'd had it in mind that it might be a good moment when you brought your next Glendrochatt group over. You and I can have a blether over a cup of coffee while Hamish takes your visitors round the garden.'

'I'm not sure that Giles was planning to come,' said Isobel. 'Do you need him too?'

There was a pause, while Evelyn considered for a moment. Then she said: 'Perhaps not. In fact it might be better if it was just you and me.'

'That sounds mysterious. Ought I to know what it's about?'

Isobel paused encouragingly, hoping the old lady might elucidate a little, but Evelyn Fergusson was not to be drawn and just said: 'Perhaps you know, perhaps you don't. I'll look forward to seeing you next week then, Izzy. Do make sure all your group have sensible footgear this time. There are quite a few boggy places even after this dry spell and if we get any rain before they come the dell could become a quagmire. We don't want any more disasters like the time you brought that silly woman who came in stiletto heels and sprained her ankle.'

'I'll try to see they're all properly kitted out,' promised Isobel meekly, thinking that Morwenna, at least, would be suitably shod. She resisted the temptation to question her robust old relative any further because she knew it would not be the slightest use trying to pump Evelyn Fergusson for information once she had made up her mind to say nothing more.

Evelyn, who was her father's first cousin, had been an important part of Isobel's life for as long as Isobel could remember. Since she had no children of her own, Evelyn had regarded her favourite cousin's daughters with special affection, and though she had actually been Lorna's godmother, not Isobel's, she had always treated the two girls with the same interested generosity. As they grew up, however, it had been Isobel to whom she had become closest and over the years a special bond had formed between them – something that was yet another bone of contention for Lorna to add to the great pile that she was constantly collecting. Lorna was not one to be bothered by elderly relatives – unless there was something in it for her – but she greatly resented her younger sister's easy intimacy with her godmother.

Isobel was too busy for the rest of the morning to give any further thought to Evelyn's words. There was the lecture by Jonathan Mercer to prepare for, and last-minute arrangements for the concert on Saturday evening to organise. Amy, who was to be the chief performer, was coming up from school the following day so that she would be able to rehearse, and Edward was coming home for the weekend too.

It was another gloriously sunny morning. After her tutorial with Catherine the day before, Bunty, newly fired by the idea that self publication might be the best route for her to follow and full of unfounded optimism about her future career as the Beatrix Potter of the twenty-first century, had popped into Blairalder for a little shopping spree. She rather hankered for a genuine St Columba's teardrop brooch (as wept, a label assured her, by the saint) to put in her new tartan tam-o'-shanter. She had also found, in the chemist, some high factor sun-cream advertised as specially designed for children – safe but fun – and therefore, to Bunty, an irresistible purchase. She had been much taken by the prettily decorated, easily applied little push-up sticks and bought several of them; after breakfast she had anointed herself liberally with this protective potion before sitting on one of the stone seats, eyes closed, confidently soaking up the ultra-violet rays outside the conference room, preparing to 'tan without tears' before the first session.

Christopher and Marnie, who had avoided each other at breakfast, came across the courtyard at the same moment and gazed at her in astonishment. Then they looked at each other and constraint between them was instantly banished as they both doubled up with laughter. Bunty presented a very strange sight. Not only was she wearing a skimpy little sundress quite unsuited to either her age or the uncertainties of the Scottish climate, but all areas of flesh – of which there was much on display – appeared to have been decorated with brightly coloured green and blue squiggles like a cross between urban graffiti and Red Indian war paint. Bunty's face was especially arresting.

'Do you think she *knows*?' whispered Marnie, awe-struck.

'I wouldn't put anything past her,' said Christopher, 'but it can hardly be an accident. Let's find out.'

As they approached, Bunty opened her eyes and beamed at them, favouring Christopher with a specially cosy smile to reassure him that he would not find her censorious about what she privately thought of as his *sad past*. All her years in teaching had made her aware of the importance of encouragement rather than censure and she felt a great urge to give Christopher the full benefit of her support no matter what he might have done.

'Good morning, Bunty,' said Christopher, feeling he was about to get his own back for her nosiness. 'I do admire the rococo decoration. Does it have special significance? Runic writing perhaps? Messages for the fairies?'

Marnie gave a muffled snort but Bunty looked nonplussed – until she caught sight of her arms. 'Well, silly me!' she said brightly, 'It must be the Fun-in-the-Sun-for-Kids cream I bought yesterday – I had no idea. Perhaps I'd better go and wash my hands before our class. I wouldn't want anyone to think I was eccentric.'

'Then I think you might need to take a look at your face too,' suggested Marnie trying unsuccessfully to keep her own face straight.

Bunty opened her bag and peered at her reflection in her make-up compact. 'What a lovely idea for children!' she said delightedly. 'Whoever thought of that must really know what they enjoy. How clever! It restores my faith in the pharmaceutical companies. I've always feel they've got a bit too big for their boots. I shall give it to Isobel for little Rory,' and Bunty, not at all put out, heaved herself to her inadequate feet and pattered happily off to remove her war paint.

'I bet she'd still have bought it even if she'd realised what it did. You can't help admiring her,' said Marnie when she and Christopher had finished laughing as they watched her go tap-tapping blithely over the cobbles in her kitten heels. 'She's so completely herself.'

'Unique, I should think,' grinned Christopher. The clock over the theatre struck the half hour, but neither of them felt ready to go inside yet.

'Marnie . . .' he began, but she interrupted him.

'I know you must be mad at me, but don't say anything,' she said. 'Not until I've apologised for being so dumb yesterday . . . and not until I've wished you luck for this morning about your book. I really hope this thriller writer likes it.'

'Thank you,' he said, guessing the effort this speech was for her. 'But there's nothing to forgive. It was entirely my fault and I was the spiky one. And you helped me so much just by listening to me. You've no idea.' He looked down at her. 'Friends?' he asked, suspecting friendship was something she had always felt short of; something, he thought, that he had taken for granted for most of his life but had recently come to realise was the most important possession one could have.

'Yeah,' she said, 'friends,' and this time she gave him the brilliant smile that so transformed her whole face and which, on the first day, he had wondered how to earn.

Then, hesitantly, she held out both her hands to him and he took them in his.

They were standing gazing at each other when Louisa came through the archway.

Chapter Sixteen

The first impression of Jonathan Mercer, whose best-selling crime novels were occasionally erotic, usually dark and often violent – though never without a certain black humour – was not what most of the students at Glendrochatt expected. Joyce and Marnie were the only two who had never read any of his books. Christopher, Win and the Colonel pronounced themselves ardent fans, while Bunty said disapprovingly they weren't at all her sort of thing and she couldn't see why they were so popular but she had just dipped into the odd one occasionally to keep herself informed of the current literary scene.

'Just reading all the juicy bits more likely – the old hypocrite,' muttered Louisa to Isobel.

Morwenna admitted that she could easily become addicted to them, but found them so scary that she could only allow herself to read them when staying in other people's houses and had to forgo them when alone in her isolated Cornish cottage.

'He's the sort of writer who makes you jump at the sound of a falling leaf, and hesitate to pass your own totally unalarming broom cupboard under the stairs,' she said. Morwenna might look stolid and unimaginative but her new acquaintances were discovering that her facade of stodgy practicality in no way corresponded to the gentle and vulnerable character who lurked inside. They were all becoming very fond of the gardening correspondent –

especially the Colonel. Beady-eyed Win had noticed that he usually managed to seat himself next to Morwenna, though Bunty always rushed for the chair on his other side, making the seating of the class resemble a competitive game of musical chairs.

Tickets for Jonathan Mercer's talk had sold out weeks before and the little theatre was full. Daniel Hoffman's delightful backdrop, which depicted not only the romantic setting of Glendrochatt and the immediate Grant family members, but one or two of the arts centre's chief patrons as well – wittily representing their various quirks and enthusiasms – had been let down at the back of the stage. Isobel had done two spectacular arrangements of young beech leaves, 'pheasant eye' narcissi and the yellow mollis azaleas that grew, semi-wild, all over the garden. She had put the two big urns she kept for these occasions on pedestals at either side of the stage and the whole theatre smelt delicious. The buzz of conversation stopped as Giles and Isobel came into the theatre accompanied by a small, round teddy bear of a man, with thick pebble glasses and an ill-fitting jacket of a peculiarly unbecoming shade of ochre. He shambled on to the stage with the absent-minded look of one who has mislaid his car keys, is finally driven to searching for them in rather an unlikely place, and then can't remember how he came to be there.

After an affectionate introduction from Giles, who clearly knew him well, he proceeded to hold his varied audience of hundred and fifty spellbound for an hour, without any assistance from notes, slides or other visual aids. Fascinated silence was interspersed with gales of laughter and when he finished speaking the applause was extremely enthusiastic. In answer to a question as to why he had given up his career in forensic medicine he had scratched his bald head and said he supposed he'd got a bit tired of dead bodies, which made everyone laugh. 'And of course by then, I'd started to make money from my novels,' he admitted. 'That helped the decision along no end, but it wasn't till after my third book that I dared to rely on my pen as a source of income. My wife and I have five children. She's a doctor too but I don't think she'd have been very keen on me giving up my medical career unless I could help her put some bread on our table.'

'What qualities do you think you need to be a successful writer of fiction?' someone asked.

'Luck, timing, perseverance and a sense of enjoyment,' he said promptly. 'Don't go into it to make money – go into it because you can't help it. You *may* make money. I've been very lucky, but it took a little time. Perhaps, above all, you need to be a bit backward.' He smiled benignly at his audience. 'Most of us who write fiction haven't outgrown the childish ability to live in an imaginary world and have constant companions unseen by anyone else.'

The questions came thick and fast and eventually Giles, who had successfully managed to ignore Bunty's wildly waving hand, decided to call a halt and carry his popular speaker off for drinks and lunch in the main house. But Bunty, seated in the front row, was having no such brush-off. She got to her feet with surprising agility and called out, 'I have one more question for Mr Mercer, Giles dear. I don't think you've noticed my signals.'

'One more question then,' said Giles resignedly, 'but I'm afraid it will have to be brief.'

'I just wanted to know,' said Bunty 'why it is that Mr Mercer who seems such a *nice* man should write such *horrid* books?'

'What an excellent question,' said Jonathan Mercer, beaming kindly at Bunty. 'I've always wanted to know the answer to that myself. If I ever find out, I'll let the lady know!' and he followed Giles off the stage to more applause.

'Game, set and match to Mr Mercer,' said Christopher to Marnie and Morwenna who were sitting either side of him.

'We've still got lunch to get through,' Marnie reminded them. 'I'm not sure who I'd back for the last word, but Bunty sure has staying power!' She giggled. 'Perhaps she should have kept the blue war paint on – that would have been a good puzzle for a mystery writer to solve.' They told Morwenna about Bunty's decorative efforts at deflecting ultra-violet rays.

'I wouldn't have thought the sun would have caused her a problem anyway,' said Morwenna with uncharacteristic tartness as they made their way over to the house to meet Jonathan Mercer over lunch. 'Bunty strikes me as amazingly thick-skinned. Everyone's always snubbing her or laughing at her but whenever I start to feel agonised on her behalf I realise that she hasn't even noticed. She goes crashing on completely unaware of the effect she has on everyone.'

'Lucky her! I'll bet she manages to sit next to Mr Mercer at lunch,' said Marnie. 'Just look.' They looked and watched with amusement as Bunty tunnelled her way through the throng of the departing audience with a dedication that would have done credit to a mole bent on wrecking a grass tennis court. But if buttonholing the guest speaker was her intention, she was to be thwarted, because Isobel, a practised hostess, had done a careful *placement* for the dining room and put little name cards by each setting.

Christopher found himself next to the guest of honour and sent Isobel an appreciative smile. He also raised an eyebrow at Catherine who was sitting on the other side of the table, and she nodded at him encouragingly. She had obviously primed Jonathan beforehand, because immediately they were all seated he said: 'Ah – my rival crime writer I believe? I hear I've got a treat in store and possibly some serious competition in the future. I'm usually very cautious about accepting requests to read the manuscripts of first novels, because it can be so awful dashing people's hopes and yet it's unforgivable to give false expectations. It's a tough, over-subscribed and highly commercial market. However, Catherine is an old friend and colleague. We've taken creative writing courses together and know how each other's minds work. I have a huge respect for her opinion.' He shot Christopher a shrewd look through his thick spectacles. 'In fact it's rare for her to ask favours – so you must be exceptional. I'll do what I can to help. If your book is as gripping as she says, I think my agent might be interested. I gather you've recently had some useful background experiences too,' he added with a twinkle.

Christopher laughed, very much liking his neighbour. 'You could say that. Not voluntary ones, as Catherine will have told you – a question of trying to put a bad time to some sort of use!'

Jonathan nodded. 'Which politician was it who used to say that fulfilment in life came from practising "the art of the possible"? Anyway, I'll read your book within the next few weeks and we'll take it from there.' They discussed other topics after that, discovering shared enthusiasms for fly-fishing and music until it was time for Jonathan to turn to his other side and talk to his hostess.

Apart from the members of the course and Jonathan Mercer, Giles and Isobel had invited Lord Dunbarnock, an old family friend, the chairman of the trustees and certainly Glendrochatt's chief benefactor. His caricature was painted on the backdrop, but in real life he seemed even stranger than his depiction. His passion for vintage cars, of which he had a famous collection, sat uneasily alongside a lifelong phobia about germs – the legacy of an over-zealous nanny in his childhood – so that he spent his life getting his hands covered in engine grease and general grime while he tuned throttles and tinkered with carburettors, and then obsessively scouring them for fear lurking bacteria might smite him with some dread disease. It was rumoured that he kept antiseptic wipes in his sporran and his hands always had a raw, chapped look even in summer. Today, despite the balmy weather he was dressed in his habitual garb of kilt, tweed jacket, hairy shooting stockings and vast brogues. He presented a tall and cadaverously thin figure, but it was his long grizzled hair worn in a pigtail down his back that was the real surprise about his appearance. In his youth he had taken a bet that he wouldn't go a year without shaving or having his hair cut. He had won the bet, but the hirsute habit had remained: his one gesture of defiance to his terrifying old gorgon of a mother. Recently he had stunned the locality by having his beard shaved off for the first time in over forty years. Giles, who was extremely fond of him and took liberties that no one else dared to do, had suggested that the Scottish Tourist Board had listed a sighting of an unshaven Dunbarnock chin as one of the great moments of Scottish wildlife watching – almost on a par with a glimpse of the Loch Ness Monster – and that kind-hearted Neil Dunbarnock had only shaved to give the summer holidaymakers a better chance of observing this mythical attraction. It would have been easy to write him off as an oddball aristocrat, not to be taken seriously, but he had a close circle of devoted admirers who knew the extent of his erudition, the kindness of his heart and the generosity of his pocket. The fact that they loved him, however, did not stop his friends from laughing about him and regaling each other with tales of his latest eccentricities. As Giles and Isobel often said to each other, life would be much, much duller without him.

The uninitiated, however, could find him conversationally taxing. There were plenty of subjects about which he knew a great deal – sometimes unexpected ones – and on which, once launched, he could be extremely interesting, but he was painfully shy and it wasn't easy to get him going. Giles maintained that he was like one of his own cars – you had first to know how to swing the sometimes unyielding starting handle, and then how to adjust the choke to feed in the right conversational mixture.

Isobel, who had placed Lord Dunbarnock on her left, had taken a deliberate gamble in putting Marnie on his other side. Giles thought she should have put Louisa, who had met him several times before, next to him. Louisa's social skills were well up to the challenge of flirting decorously with Lord Dunbarnock – enough to flatter, but not enough to alarm him – but Isobel wanted to see how Marnie would cope with the challenge. She had a hunch these two awkward but curiously endearing characters might take to each other. She was not disappointed. It was not the elderly or the peculiar that Marnie found threatening, but the glamorous and socially confident. From the moment when Isobel switched her attention from Neil Dunbarnock to Jonathan Mercer, he and Marnie got on famously. By the end of lunch Neil Dunbarnock, enchanted to discover a fellow blues and jazz enthusiast who could match him fact for fact on such details as the Mississippi river boats on which "old Satchel-mouth" Louis Armstrong had first played and sung, had suggested that she come over to Dunbarnock to inspect his collection of jazz recordings, which included such legendary New Orleans' blues greats as Bessie Anderson and Billie Holiday – a rare invitation for a new acquaintance – and Marnie had confided in him about her search for a particular and possibly non-existent ancient house.

'I hope you find it,' he said. 'I will give it some thought. How much longer are you staying here?'

'Another week. We've been too busy writing to do any exploring yet, but Giles and Isobel are going to show us something of the neighbourhood next week.'

'Then I'll talk to Isobel and see if they could bring you all over for a drink. You might enjoy seeing my house. It's what is sometimes called a "fortalice" – a fairly typical fortified house with a tower and a good hotchpotch of styles. Most of my ancestors have meddled with it in some way over many generations. You have to realise that there are many so-called castles in this part of the world. Anything with pretensions to a tower and sprouting a few bunion-like turrets here and there gets called a castle – as mine is. Some of them are the genuine article and some of course are purely Victorian.'

'What bits of yours have you meddled with?'

'Not a great deal structurally.' He smiled at her. 'Being a confirmed old bachelor I'm pretty resistant to change and the inside of the house is much as it was in my parents' day.' He added drily: 'And equally cold and inconvenient, so I'm told, but I don't really notice those things. Not being a hunting man – unlike most of my forebears – my contribution has been to convert the old stables into garages for my collection of cars. I prefer engines to equestrianism.'

'Oh me, too!' Marnie decided that she liked her eccentric neighbour very much. 'Could I see your cars if I came over, as well as the records?'

'You *could*, I suppose,' he said rather doubtfully, 'but in my experience, most women seem to find them rather boring.'

'I wouldn't,' said Marnie decisively. 'I've been driving since I was a kid of eleven – not on the highway, of course – but my father's a real car freak. He's got his own racetrack back home in Virginia. He had me and my half-brothers practising on skidpads as soon as we could steer an old banger round the track. My father's got a 1933 Packard V12 which comes out on state occasions. It's known in the family as "Dad's mistress" – though goodness knows he's had plenty of the real variety too. And he adores roaring round in his old Ford Mustang. I enjoy driving that too. But then I love driving . . . almost anything.'

'What is it you specially like about it?' Neil Dunbarnock looked at her with interest.

Marnie considered. 'Perhaps it's because it frees me up. I feel in control behind the wheel,' she said at last. 'When I was little, speed terrified me and I hated going out with my father – he used to scare the daylights out of me – till he had the bright idea of teaching me to drive myself. It was a revelation! I don't know who was more surprised or pleased, him or me, and it's been a great bond between us. Now it's one of the few things I do that I'm really confident about. I've always been afraid of things happening that I couldn't handle. In the English bit of my childhood we had ponies. My mother has always ridden and one of my stepfathers was an MFH, but I was terrified. My pony bolted with me once when I was about ten, and oh boy, was I shit-scared then! I lost my nerve so completely that I even faced up to my mother and said I wouldn't ride again – and that took some courage, I can tell you. But when I'm behind the wheel I feel . . .' She paused. 'I suppose I feel I'm in charge,' she said. 'I even enjoy going fast – so long as it's me doing the driving. It's what other people may do that always panics me.' She laughed and pulled a mocking face, but her companion, who was far more observant than most of his acquaintances gave him credit for, thought she looked sad. 'I guess that goes for other things as well as driving,' she said. 'People just tend to frighten me . . . full stop!'

'People frighten me too,' said Lord Dunbarnock, smiling at her very kindly. 'I'm much better with engines. I know what I'm doing with those. And, yes, I'd be pleased to show you my cars as well as the records if Giles and Isobel bring you over.' He looked at her thoughtfully. 'I might even let you drive one.'

Marnie guessed this would be a very unusual honour and was touched. It gave her a warm little glow inside to think that this eccentric and allegedly antisocial elderly bachelor should have found her company so pleasant – and an even warmer glow to know, instinctively, that across the table, Christopher was aware of this too.

Christopher, having finished talking to Jonathan Mercer, had turned to Louisa, but both were unobtrusively watching Marnie while simultaneously conducting an enjoyable and light-hearted conversation with each other.

The moment she had seen Christopher and Marnie standing under the archway holding hands, Louisa had sensed immediately that something must have shifted in their reactions to each other, but was not sure how significant it might be.

It had seemed too good to be true to find Christopher Piper at Glendrochatt just when she so badly wanted a new relationship, and she couldn't help feeling that it must be fate that had brought this particular man back into her life at this particular moment. She was amazed at how quickly the whole writing group were getting to know each other despite such a short acquaintance. It reminded Louisa of her father's propagating frame in his greenhouse at home – Glendrochatt was proving a sort of forcing house for relationships, she thought. The group discussions during each session, the shared emotions triggered by individual pieces of writing – these produced an intimacy that would have taken far longer to achieve through ordinary social intercourse. Since their conversation by the burn, she had found herself becoming increasingly intrigued by the American girl and liking her more and more – but she also liked Christopher more and more and was conscious of a little stab of dismay at the idea that Marnie and Christopher might be attracted to each other. It caused Louisa, who was normally blessed with the happy gift of self-confidence, an unusual moment of self-doubt. She saw that the socially diffident Marnie was clearly making a hit with batty old Lord Dunbarnock and, what is more, looking as if she was enjoying his company, which was even more surprising. Louisa recalled an expression from her native Yorkshire – "Nowt so queer as folk" – and there were certainly some rum folk in this place, she thought, looking across the table at the eccentric peer.

'Marnie seems to be having a good time,' she said jokingly to Christopher. 'Americans are suckers for the aristocracy. Perhaps she's on the lookout for a tame laird?'

'Perhaps she is,' said Christopher, amused but not reacting to the tease. 'Good luck to her. But it certainly looks as if the aristocracy are equally beguiled by the Americans today.'

He was pleased to see Marnie chatting with such animation to the unusual-looking chairman of the Glendrochatt Arts Trust. What an interesting face Marnie had, he thought, looking at her with much closer attention than he had when they first met: a face that you would not get tired of looking at. Goodness, thought Christopher uneasily, what is happening? I hardly know her. How unexpected to find two such attractive young women on the course. He certainly had not come looking for romance. He had been conscious of the appeal of Louisa from the start, but was surprised to find himself increasingly drawn to Marnie. Is it just a reaction to the last two awful years? Am I going wild, like a horse let out to grass after being stabled all winter, he wondered – but he didn't think so.

He remembered a conversation in the early days of his infatuation with Nicola. He had been perversely trying to goad his mother into criticising her – something she had steadfastly refused to do – so that he could have the satisfaction of arguing with her. His mother had been infuriatingly resistant to his provocative needling, but had eventually silenced him with a question of her own.

'If you look at Nicola's face, are you moved?' she had asked suddenly.

'Moved? Moved by desire, do you mean?' he'd hedged, deliberately misinterpreting her.

'Of course I'm not talking about *desire*. Don't be stupid, Christopher. I'm talking about emotion. Does she move you?'

'Oh, *Ma*!' he'd said irritably. 'You do talk in riddles sometimes. I really don't know what you're talking about.'

But of course he had known very well. Now, he thought, if she asked me the same question about Marnie, my response might be different. Marnie does move me. But I mustn't get carried away, he thought. He couldn't fail to be aware that Louisa was interested in him and he certainly didn't want to hurt her, though he didn't for a moment think it represented anything more serious than an invitation to enjoy a flirtation, possibly leading to a light-hearted affair. He had no doubt that an affair with Louisa would be enormous fun – that word that Nicola set such store by – but it wasn't what he wanted any more. Perhaps they could all three just become good friends.

'Why don't I take you and Marnie out one evening next week?' he said to Louisa. 'I can't offer to drive, but I'd love to treat you both to a really good dinner somewhere. I gather you're staying on and Isobel's persuaded me to stay too. I'm looking forward to it – I don't feel ready to say goodbye to everyone here so soon after meeting them.' Louisa wondered if this was to be taken at face value, or was it a veiled hint that he was really referring to Marnie – or did he mean herself?

'We might get Morwenna and the Colonel to come with us too,' he went on. 'Nudge their budding romance on a bit.'

'Are they having a romance?' Louisa looked surprised.

'Not yet, perhaps – but I think they might . . . given some encouragement.'

'Well lucky them,' said Louisa, laughing. 'I have to say I hadn't cast you in the role of Cupid, Christopher, but who knows what romantic situations might develop in another week? Anyway, it's a lovely idea,' she went on. 'How good that you've decided to stay for the extra week too. That will be fun. Let's suggest the plan to the others then.' But at that moment Isobel got up and brought the lunch party to a close, so the conversation ended there.

Before he departed Jonathan Mercer came to find Christopher. He tapped the large package he had tucked under his arm. 'All safe and sound,' he said. 'How can I get hold of you? I've just realised that I haven't got your address. How much longer are you here for?'

'Only another week. I'm sure you won't have time to wade through it by then.' Christopher fished in his pocket for a card, crossed out the details of his London flat and scribbled down his parents' address on the back. 'I've put my mobile number as well, but that's where I'm based at the moment and where I can always be contacted.' He grinned ruefully. 'My movements are still a bit restricted.'

'Of course – due to the "useful background experiences", no doubt. Don't worry. I'll track you down, but don't expect anything too soon. By the way, if I think it might be helpful, would you mind if I showed it to someone else?'

'*Mind*? I'd be only too delighted. You don't know how grateful I am . . .'

But Jonathan Mercer waved his thanks away and the two men shook hands before Jonathan went in search of Catherine and the Grants to make his farewells. Christopher watched him walk away with a heart full of hope.

Chapter Seventeen

On Friday Isobel had arranged that Amy, who usually flew to Edinburgh from school, should come on the London to Inverness train that stopped at Perth, so as to coincide with Edward's bus from Aberdeen. It was a new venture for Edward to undertake even such a comparatively short journey on his own and it still made Isobel anxious, but both Giles and his school felt he was ready for this experiment in independence; provided someone actually put him on the coach and there was someone waiting to receive him at the bus station the other end, it had so far been a success. Isobel still worried that he might panic if there was any sort of hitch on the journey, but knew she had to help him towards as much self-sufficiency as was possible and this represented a huge step forward – something that even a year ago would have seemed out of the question.

Giles was going to meet them both in Perth.

'You will be there on time, won't you, darling?' Isobel asked. 'Promise me you won't get distracted by anything and run it all too fine?' Though Giles frequently had the devil's own luck over timing, he was not one to allow for emergencies and hated having to wait about for anything or anyone.

'Panic not, O ye of little faith,' said Giles, grinning at her. 'I shall check on my watch every two minutes.'

'You'll have to meet Ed first. Have you got Amy's mobile number in case his bus is late?'

'I have – and a parachute, a compass, a water bottle and my bag of pemmican.'

'I'm sorry, darling,' she said. 'It's just that it's so important he shouldn't lose confidence. You know what he's like if he gets a fright. When he's done it a few more times I'll get more relaxed about it. I don't mean to fuss.'

'I know.' He kissed the top of her head, noticing for the first time, with a wrench of the heart, a few silver strands in her curly dark hair – his laughing, once-so-carefree Iz who had whistled her way through life with bright confidence until Edward was born.

'Would . . . would you like me to take Rory with me for the ride?' he asked cautiously, not wanting to activate the lurking jealousy Isobel had confessed that she battled with over the beguiling little boy – his son, but oh, not hers. He felt he walked a tightrope between his own growing pride in, and love for, the little boy and his fervent wish not to cause his wife any extra hurt. 'I could take him off your hands for a bit?'

'Oh, do. He'd love to go with you and Ed will be thrilled to see him again. That's one of the good things about this whole difficult situation. It's Amy's reaction I'm much more worried about. I think we need to talk to her about it this weekend – explain a few things before she hears hints from anyone else.'

'Let's wait till Sunday then,' Giles temporised, dreading the thought of the explanations he would have to give to his daughter, remembering how passionately she had resented her aunt during that ill-fated summer, five years ago, when Lorna had succeeded in coming not only between husband and wife, but between father and daughter too; jeopardising the special bond they'd always had over Amy's music. He remembered ruefully how furious his fiery little daughter had been with him for falling prey to Lorna's manipulative wiles; how perceptively she had picked up on private temptations and hidden agendas without fully understanding what was going on.

'I think we should get the concert on Saturday night over first,' he said. 'I wouldn't want Amy to be upset before her performance. A lot of people are coming to hear her and it would be a shame if she didn't give of her best.'

'Just so long as we don't put it off till she's gone away again,' said Isobel drily.

She watched him go off, with Rory skipping along beside him, overjoyed at the idea of seeing the two big 'cousins' he had only met so recently – especially Edward. It was a revelation to those who had only come up against Edward's occasionally tongue-tied and frequently mysterious conversational approach to hear him playing with a much younger companion. For adults, talking to Edward could be like trying to solve clues in a crossword puzzle because he often chose to speak in a kind of code of his own making – fun if you knew the form and enjoyed playing word-games, but completely baffling if you didn't. However, this never seemed to be a barrier with younger children with whom he could employ a fluency of speech and a fertility of imagination that sometimes astonished even those who knew him well. From their very first meeting he and Rory had established a bond, and Isobel had found it both touching and tormenting to hear the two of them – twelve years apart in age – playing together on such equal terms, each appearing word perfect in the unwritten script necessitated by their imaginary games.

Isobel wondered, as she did whenever Edward was about to encounter anything or anyone new to him, what he would make of their visitors – and they of him. Bunty, she thought gloomily, might be brilliant with him, as she was with Rory, who irritatingly gravitated to her side whenever he saw her. Years of dealing with small children had immunised Bunty against the boredom of the repetitive questions that were still such a part of Edward's conversation too – but what of the other members of the writing group? How would they react to his archaic choice of language and amazing vocabulary; to his professorial style inquisitions or the occasional unsuitability of his chosen topics for discussion? What would they make of his obsessional behaviour and, as his twin so bluntly put it, 'Ed's general weirdness'? Edward could also take inexplicable likes or dislikes to people and usually made his feelings extremely plain, which, either way, could prove embarrassing.

With Edward you could never tell how things were going to work out: surprise was of his essence.

At eleven o'clock on Saturday morning, Marnie and Louisa came into the kitchen in search of coffee, the bar being temporarily out of bounds while preparations were made for the buffet supper which was to follow the evening concert. Catherine had arranged for the second morning session to be taken by the editor of a well-respected poetry magazine who had agreed to talk about his own view of the rival merits of strict rhyme and metre versus free verse, air his own editorial prejudices and then preside over a discussion. As neither Marnie nor Louisa felt that writing poetry was quite her thing and there was to be a small local attendance too, they had decided to give this talk a miss, and each secretly welcomed the chance to get together and possibly recover something of the friendship they had been on the brink of discovering on their walk up the burn on the first full day at Glendrochatt – which seemed an age ago now. They were both conscious of the fact that during the next, less structured week, with a smaller group, they would be thrown together even more and there was an issue between them which might make this extremely uncomfortable if not resolved – or at any rate faced. Though Christopher was the only one of the group to have serious poetic ambitions, the others had all expressed themselves keen to attend the session, possibly more because they wanted to hang on to the comradeship engendered by the classes than from any real interest in the particular subject. No one was looking forward to saying goodbye the following day.

Edward was sitting on a beanbag, watching an old video without the sound on. Everyone in the family hated watching television with Edward who had the curious knack of being able to read books or look at films out of sequence and still follow a story line; he was always pressing replay or fast forward in a random way that drove everyone else mad.

'Morning, Ed,' said Louisa cheerfully. 'Nice to see you again. Is it lovely to be home from school?'

Edward looked up at the two young women.

'So,' he said, ignoring this question and fixing both Louisa and Marnie with a challenging gaze. 'So . . . what was the great event that happened in Thcotland last Thunday then?'

Louisa noticed that though he still had a trace of the speech impediment that had made him so difficult to understand as a small boy, he no longer spoke as if his mouth were impossibly filled with soapsuds and the remaining slight lisp was now rather endearing. Speech therapy and enormous family input had worked a miracle.

'I've no idea,' she said. 'Something to do with football? Or was it that a band of literary geniuses arrived to stay at Glendrochatt?'

Edward gave her a quelling look and shook his head.

'No. So . . . what was the weather like on Thunday?' he

242

asked in the patient tone of one trying to simplify things for the intellectually challenged.

Louisa and Marnie looked questioningly at each other.

'Spring-like?' suggested Marnie. 'It was certainly a lovely day – it was real hot when we arrived.'

Edward nodded encouragingly. 'So . . . what elthe then?'

'Windy?' asked Louisa. 'It so often is windy up here, but I really can't remember. Was it a specially windy day, Ed?'

Edward shrugged, frowned impatiently and cocked his head at Marnie. He reminded her of an inquisitive sparrow hoping for crumbs. 'Don't know. So . . . what elthe then?'

Marnie, intrigued, remembered that Isobel had told her how difficult Edward sometimes found direct contact, though it didn't seem to be bothering him at the moment. She was aware that she and Louisa were being challenged in some indefinable way and suddenly very much wanted to pass the test – whatever it was.

'If it was hot then it must have been sunny,' she said, not looking at him, half-turning to gaze out of the window, but clearly considering the question very carefully.

'*Yeth*.' Edward looked pleased. 'So what elthe?'

'Something to do with the sun, perhaps?'

'Umm.' Enthusiastic nods.

'Sunny . . . hot, certainly. Oh, okay, okay . . . that's obviously not right.' Edward was shaking his head reprovingly. 'We-ell . . . let's think then. Bright, perhaps? Shiny?'

More nods. Edward was now looking at Marnie with keen expectation.

'Orange? Yellow?' she tried, feeling she was on the verge of a breakthrough. 'Golden?'

Edward beamed at her and started to jig up and down on the beanbag. 'So go on.'

'Umm. Well . . . *gold* then?'

'Yeth, yeth, yeth. So what else is gold?'

'Jewels . . . a crown . . . a . . . let me think now . . . some sort of a medal?'

'*Yeth!*' Edward punched the air.

Amy, who had come in during this inquisition, looked at Marnie with respect. 'Brilliant of you,' she said approvingly. 'Ed won a gold medal at his weekly school swimming session in the Aberdeen baths last week, didn't you, Ed?'

'I did. I was the most glorious thwimmer of the day,' said Edward modestly. 'I out-thwam everybody else.'

'Gee! Well, that must have been awesome,' said Marnie. 'I hope I'll get to see that medal someday.'

'I will show it to you mythelf,' said Edward, his whole face lighting up. 'And I will also show you my jam jar collection and my postcards and my football strips and my dead bugs and . . .' but Marnie didn't discover what other treats might be in store for her, because Edward, who had spied Rory in the hall, lost interest in the conversation as abruptly as though a light switch had been snapped off and disappeared out of the kitchen without a backward glance.

'You two haven't really met each other yet, have you?' said Louisa. 'Amy, this is Marnie Donovan. Marnie, this is Giles and Isobel's daughter Amy.'

'Hi there, Marnie.' Amy gave Marnie a friendly grin and perched on the edge of the big kitchen table, swinging long legs in extremely tight jeans. A lot of bare midriff was exposed between skinny T-shirt and the top of the jeans and a small diamond stud glinted from her navel. 'Oh good . . . yummy,' she said helping herself to a couple of the chocolate cookies that had been put out for the writing group. 'We never get these in the morning unless there's a course in residence! You mustn't mind that Ed went off the boil and walked out like that,' she went on, through a mouthful of crumbs. 'Mum would go spare if she knew he'd done that to you because she tries so hard with his manners – and he really tries too – but if he gets distracted he forgets what he's doing and then does something else. He'll probably remember just as suddenly another time that he wants to show you his treasures and then there'll be no stopping him until he's dragged you off to inspect them – whether you want to or not!' She looked anxiously at Marnie. 'In fact you're amazingly honoured. He's obviously taken one of his shines to you and he won't have *meant* to be rude. Etiquette is like a foreign language for Ed – he's just no good at making the right social noises at people.'

'I'd be the last person to criticise anyone for that – I'm not too brilliant at it myself,' said Marnie, liking Amy for this defence of her twin. She thought it would be difficult to guess the relationship between them if you didn't know what it was. Frail, shortsighted Edward, with his powerful pebble glasses, lopsided body and awkward ways seemed as unlike his sophisticated sister as it was possible to be. Amy had inherited the best of both her parents' looks, Marnie decided. She had Isobel's enviable hair and amused, expressive grey eyes, but she was a good deal taller than her mother, with something of her father's unsettling aura of glamour. As Marnie had watched Edward scuttling, crab-like, out of the kitchen and across the hall to join his little cousin, she had been conscious of a lump in her throat and thought that Amy's easy grace underlined a heart-rending contrast with her brother's jerky movements. Marnie's admiration for the Grants went up even further. How do they do it? she thought. How do they appear so cheerful and amusing – so *interested* in everyone else, when they must so often be full of private anguish? She resolved to get to know Edward better and try to enter into his different but intriguing world on his own terms.

'I'll look forward to seeing his treasures another time then,' she said, smiling at Amy. 'Sounds a real varied collection and – truly – I *am* honoured. Thanks, Amy. I hear you're going to play for us this evening?'

Amy grinned. 'Dad likes to make me sing for my supper when I'm home,' she said.

'What are you going to play?' asked Louisa.

'Well, I thought I'd start with the FAE sonata for violin and piano by Brahms and Schumann. It's the one they collaborated on as a birthday present for their friend Joseph Joachim who was the great violinist of the day and the notes FAE are a sort of code for Joachim's motto – *Frei aber Einsam* – Free but Lonely. Don't you think that's a tragic motto for anyone to have?'

'Sounds just like me!' said Marnie, laughing. 'What made you choose that piece?'

'Oh, it's huge fun to play, lots of whirling off-beat syncopations – nice and showy-offy! Then I'm going to play an arrangement of Lalo's *Symphonie Espagnole* and after the interval a Mozart concerto for violin and piano. Dad's made me write the programme notes so I hope I haven't made any bloomers.'

'Sounds great,' said Louisa. 'Who's accompanying you?'

Amy rolled her eyes. 'That's the really scary bit. Did you ever meet Valerie Benson – my old violin teacher? She's going to be very critical and think I haven't practised enough. She should be arriving any minute to rehearse and I know she'll put me though a tremendous inquisition about what my plans are for the future.'

'I think I remember her,' said Louisa. 'A forthright lady with hair screwed up in a knot? The iron hand in a see-through lace mitten? I seem to remember she had your father taped.'

'That's her!' Amy laughed. 'She even got the better of

Aunt Lorna a few years ago when she tried to interfere with my music and generally muck things up for everybody in the family. I owe Valerie so much and she's asked a whole lot of high-powered music friends to come tonight so I badly want to do well for her.' She darted a look at Louisa. 'Do you know Aunt Lorna, Louisa?' she asked.

'Not like I know your mum.' Louisa was not deceived by Amy's nonchalant tone and was relieved to be able to answer truthfully. 'I've met her at some family dos but I haven't seen her for years.'

'Well you haven't missed much,' said Amy. 'She's a real pain – as unlike Mum as anyone could be.' She peered out of the kitchen window. 'Oh, cool – that's Valerie's car now,' she said. 'I must go and greet her and take her over to the theatre. Nice to have met you, Marnie. See you both at lunch,' and she whisked off.

'Let's make ourselves a drink. I could murder some coffee.' Louisa put the kettle on. 'Well . . . so now you've met all the Grant family.' She looked speculatively at Marnie as though she were trying to assess her in a new way. 'You were amazing with Edward,' she said. 'How on earth did you know what he was trying to tell us? I had no idea what he was on about. I always find him rather difficult, though I'd hate Izzy to know.'

'Isobel told me about the way he likes to talk in riddles – but me guessing what he meant was just luck.' She gave a little shrug. 'Could be because I'm so bad with people myself that I identify with anyone who finds it hard to communicate.'

'Oh, come on . . . you're not really bad with people,' said Louisa, handing Marnie a mug of instant coffee. 'You've got into a habit of thinking no one will like you and it's rubbish. You should trust yourself more.'

'Safer not to. Free but lonely, like Amy's violinist, and

I've gotten pretty used to it by now,' said Marnie, following Louisa over to the big sofa and sitting down beside her. 'You're so darn friendly to everyone – seems to come so easy to you. You *expect* to get along with people – and you do. I've noticed how everybody looks pleased when you sit next to them. You make them laugh – you make them feel special.'

'Oh well, thank you – but everyone likes you too and one person seems to like you very much,' said Louisa. Marnie flushed painfully, stirring her coffee with great concentration and not looking at Louisa.

'It won't last,' she muttered. 'Nothing ever does with me. I'm a disaster area – sooner or later I do something stupid and bang goes another relationship.'

'Oh, for heaven's sake!' Louisa almost wanted to shake Marnie. 'I think Christopher likes you very much indeed. Wherever you are in the room he's aware of you.' She laughed at Marnie's frozen expression. 'Come on, Marnie, be honest . . . I think you like him too.'

Marnie started to twiddle a strand of her hair and then went on hesitantly, as if even putting such thoughts into words might be tempting fate, 'I . . . yeah, well, I suppose I do like him, but whatever you say, I don't dare count on it – and Christopher's been through such an awful experience he was probably going to start falling for the first woman he met anyway.'

'He met us both at the same time and I don't think he's fallen for *me*,' Louisa pointed out rather sadly.' She gave a rueful little laugh. 'Unlike you, I've been giving him signals that I'm interested in him and it's not often I get a negative response. Okay . . . I *do* expect people to like me. Why shouldn't they? I was born optimistic and until I got cancer when I was nearly grown up – which seemed to go on for ages and take a great chunk out of my life – I never doubted that things would turn out the way I wanted. I don't take that so much for granted now, but I still *believe* it's possible, and that bad experience has left me with a determination to make my own luck and a sort of urgency about going all out for what I want. I still have faith in myself – but,' she said, shaking her head in mock puzzlement, 'I think I've come up against a *force majeure* as far as Christopher's concerned – and it's you.'

Marnie looked at her curiously. 'Forgive me if I'm nosy,' she said, 'but I get the feeling your cancer still weighs heavy on your mind – even after all these years. Is the fear of a return something you don't dare lighten up about?'

Louisa was silent for a long moment and Marnie was afraid she might have offended her. She thought how elegant she was, how effortlessly she drew attention wherever she was – like an outstanding portrait in a gallery which always seems to dominate a room.

'Most of the time I don't think about it now, but you're right. I suppose I don't dare completely forget about it either. It's like touching wood.' Louisa was moved by the concern on Marnie's face. 'It's a case of keep swimming or go under – and I don't intend to go under. I got myself back together ages ago but it gave me a terrible shock at the time and the anxiety never completely goes away. It's why I feel the need to break away from my old life and do something different which has no connections with an old illness.'

Despite the brave words, Marnie thought of all the fear and private anguish they must conceal. She said awkwardly: 'Must be kinda weird. Wish I could help.' She longed to show her concern in a positive way – to make some meaningful gesture of support. 'What about Mr Brown?' she asked. 'Your icon of recovery?'

'Mr Brown's fine. I take comfort from that. I have to tell myself that one day he'll die of old age and I'll have to come to terms with that as best I can, but if anything should happen to him in any other way, if he were to have an accident or something . . .' Louisa let the words hang in the air. 'Anyway,' she finished fiercely, 'I mean to go on living for a long time yet . . . and exploring and laughing and loving.'

'But not loving Adam?' Marnie couldn't help feeling sorry for the unknown Adam.

'I'll always love him – but not in the way he wants. He's been terrific and I feel miserably guilty about him but I have to have my freedom.'

'And do you have feelings for Christopher?' asked Marnie, afraid to ask but needing to know. They looked at each other, liking each other despite their rival interest in the same man. Marnie felt as if her future depended on Louisa's answer.

'Well I'm certainly not *in love*,' said Louisa honestly. 'But I do find him wildly attractive and I could easily fall for him. I'd *like* to fall for him – and I'd certainly like him to fall for me! What about you?'

'I really like him too,' said Marnie, astonished to be making such an admission to anyone, even to herself – let alone to Louisa. 'I guess I'm not too qualified to talk about love.' And they looked at each other with understanding and some apprehension.

The concert in the evening was a great success. Amy played like a dream, and Isobel, a lump in her throat, thought she was being shown a glimpse of the future as she watched her gifted daughter gracefully acknowledging the applause, with just the right combination of youthful modesty and professional confidence. Even critical Valerie Benson was delighted with her former pupil's performance. After a delicious buffet supper most of the audience departed but the Grants had invited a few special friends to stay on. The chairs were cleared from the theatre and the students of the creative writing week found themselves herded on to the floor to dance reels.

'We can't let our special guests leave Glendrochatt without taking part in our tribal dancing,' announced Giles from the stage. 'We must end on a carnival note. Amy will now transform herself from a mere violinist into a proper Scottish fiddler and Valerie and I will join her. For those of you who've never done it before, we'll walk through each reel first and there are plenty of old hands to guide you through it.'

'Old tribal custom or not, I can't possibly dance reels,' protested Morwenna. 'I'm like an elephant! But I'd love to watch.'

'I'll watch too,' said Marnie quickly. Her palms suddenly felt clammy, her heart had started to thump and the old familiar screw of fear was twisting in her stomach, the reference to tribal customs setting sinister shadow figures of other carnival dancers leaping through her brain and the fearsome masked face of the Jab Molassi peering into her soul.

'No chance,' said Giles firmly, completely unaware of the demons he was releasing. 'Everybody takes to the floor and you'll both be fine. We'll start with something really easy and then once you've got the hang of that, we'll have a go at an eightsome. Apart from Louisa – who's been doing it since she first learned to crawl – have any of you danced a Dashing White Sergeant before?'

The Colonel and Christopher both said they knew how to do it.

'Wonderful,' said Giles. 'That's a great help.'

Marnie, checking how near she was to an exit, started backing to the edge of the room, the ringing in her ears so loud she thought everyone must hear it too – hear the beating of drums and the wild shrieks – but most people's attention was fixed on Giles as he showed the visitors how to do a basic pas-de-bas step and then gave a demonstration with Isobel of how to set to a partner.

Keep breathing. Unclench your hands. Concentrate on something else . . . the voices of various therapists also rang in Marnie's ears. Don't let anyone notice me, she prayed, unaware that Christopher had unobtrusively followed her to the door.

'Now please form threesomes,' Giles was saying. 'It doesn't matter if it's a man with a girl each side or the other way round – and stand facing another three. I'll call out what to do while you pace it through once and then we'll have a go to the music.'

Christopher quietly reached for Marnie's hand and hung on to it. 'Dance with me?' he asked, smiling at her in a way that in other circumstances would have made her heart turn over, rightly guessing that she was about to bolt from the scene – recognising the signs of a condition that, since his car crash, he knew all about too. 'Please dance with me,' he said. 'I promise I won't let you go wrong. Don't look so panic-stricken. *It'll be all right.*' He drew her back into the room where Louisa was standing talking to a friend of the Grants. 'Come on, Louisa,' he said. 'Will you do this with us?'

'Of course,' she said, privately thinking it extraordinary that a light-hearted social activity could cause anyone to look as scared as Marnie did – like a rabbit caught in the headlights of an oncoming car, she thought: Marnie at her plainest and least attractive. Louisa took Christopher's other hand.

'We'll make a threesome then,' she said. 'Let's go and dance with Izzy.'

Marnie felt as though she were a zombie, unable to protest or resist as they went over to join Isobel, who had scooped up the Colonel and Morwenna. After the walk-through, Giles, in his element issuing instructions, joined Amy and Valerie on the stage. After some tuning up, there was a rousing chord from the fiddlers, Christopher gave Marnie's hand a reassuring squeeze, then the music started and they were off.

It was immediately obvious that Christopher was a sensational dancer. As everyone started to move to the irresistible rhythm Marnie felt as if a spell had been cast on her by both the man and the music – not the terrifying spell of Kenneth the pig-man and the carnival dancers of her childhood, which had so darkly affected her, haunting her dreams and paralysing her confidence, but a spell that released inhibitions and set her feet flying and her spirits free. When the dance finished Christopher was stunned by the transformation in her face. She looked a different person.

'Thank you,' she murmured wonderingly. 'Oh, thank you so much. You don't know what you've just done for me. I wouldn't have missed that for the world and if you hadn't stopped me I'd have run away – but I adored it. It's the best fun I've had for ages.'

Louisa, looking from one to the other, guessed, with a pang that was infinitely more painful than she expected, that she was witnessing a defining moment between Marnie and Christopher. She turned back to Marnie and said brightly: 'There, you see – that was terrific. You picked it up brilliantly. As for you, Christopher – you really are full of surprises! To dance reels like that you must have been brought up to it!'

'I was indeed,' he said, 'and it comes back like riding a bicycle. My mother's Scottish and years of staying with my grandparents on Mull saw to it that we all learned as children – and later on when we were growing up we went to endless reel parties and Highland Balls.' He grinned at her. 'And you're not so bad yourself, Louisa!' Then he turned to Marnie. 'As for you,' he said, 'you're just a natural – do you know that? You dance beautifully.' She blushed with pleasure.

'I'm so glad we were both persuaded to do that. I'd never have believed I could enjoy it so much,' said Morwenna to Marnie, 'but then we were lucky in our partners, weren't we?' Like many people of statuesque proportions Morwenna had proved surprisingly light on her feet, and the Colonel, if not achieving Christopher's distinction, had been a dignified and reliable partner. Bunty on the other hand, gathering momentum like a runaway truck, her bosom bouncing unnervingly with each over-sprightly step, had thrown herself into the dance with such fervour that it seemed as if she might easily run over little Mr McMichael, the stout but diminutive partner Giles had paired her with, who was a valuable member of the Friends of Glendrochatt. He was seen scuttling off towards the bar after the Dashing White Sergeant, the whites of his eyes gleaming with alarm, not to reappear till the reels were over.

There was no time for further conversation before Giles started organising everyone to do an eightsome, which was such a success with the novice reelers that by popular demand they danced it again and then went on to end the evening with a hectic Duke of Perth. As Christopher whirled Marnie down the set, her feet hardly touching the ground, she thought she had never felt so happy in her life.

The evening was brought to an end by the singing of 'Auld Lang Syne' in honour of Bunty, Win and Joyce, who would be leaving Glendrochatt in the morning. Bunty brimmed with emotion, the week blending in her mind into a delightful collage of Highland cattle, leaping salmon, rutting stags and soaring eagles – none of which she'd actually seen.

As Louisa watched Christopher and Marnie walking back to the Old Steading together, she saw him put his arm round her shoulder and couldn't help wondering if the second week, to which she had been much looking forward, would now prove to be as enjoyable, as far as she was concerned, as she had hoped.

'Would you believe it,' she complained as she stood at the foot of the stairs after kissing Isobel goodnight: 'Sod's Law! It's the most annoying thing, but I'm getting to like Marnie. And that . . .' she said over her shoulder as she turned to go up to bed, 'makes things rather difficult.'

Later, when Giles and Isobel lay in bed enjoying a post mortem on the week, Isobel said: 'I think you're going to lose your bet on Louisa to win the Christopher Stakes, darling. It looks as if the outsider is galloping up on the rails at the last lap.'

'Oh, I don't know,' said Giles. 'There's still another week to go. Anything could happen.'

'Well I hope it doesn't,' said Isobel, 'because as far as Louisa's concerned I'm sure it's just wanting pastures new and the grass being greener and all that stuff . . . but with Marnie it's serious. I have a feeling that she's had so many rejections in her life that if this went wrong she'd be completely devastated.' She added: 'So you're not to do any stirring, you old control freak.'

'We've got enough problems in our own lives without my wanting to get involved in theirs,' said Giles. 'There was a telephone message from your dear sister while we were reeling. She's going to ring tomorrow. Apparently she and lover-boy have arrived in London – and that's far too close for comfort, so our guests will have to manage their own romances without my help or hindrance. Goodnight, my darling. I think that was a highly successful week, and didn't our little daughter do us proud at the concert?'

He kissed her goodnight, turned over and was asleep almost immediately, but Isobel lay awake for a long time, her mind a turmoil of conflicting thoughts.

Chapter Eighteen

Isobel had informed the writing group that a help-yourself breakfast would be laid out in the bar area between eight o'clock and ten thirty on Sunday morning for anyone who wanted it and that the Glendrochatt minibus would be ready at nine to take the three departing guests to Perth station. Those staying on for the second week were very welcome, she assured them, to remain at Glendrochatt during the day and make themselves at home in the house, or the garden; tea and coffee-making facilities would be available as usual but she would be grateful if they would make their own arrangements for lunch. She and Giles hoped to see them all again for dinner in the main house at eight o'clock.

Louisa, Christopher and Marnie, welcoming the thought of a lie-in on Sunday morning, made their farewells to their fellow writers on Saturday night after the dancing had finished, with promises to keep in touch, but Morwenna and the Colonel both appeared for breakfast at eight fifteen. In the Colonel's case this was because a lie-in was not something that had ever been in his vocabulary of luxuries and in Morwenna's because she felt she should be there to wave Joyce off on the long journey back to Cornwall.

Originally she had been disappointed that Joyce could not stay on with her at Glendrochatt, but she was now conscious of a secret relief that she would no longer feel compelled to try to include Joyce in her unexpected new friendship with the Colonel. In fact, breezy Joyce never had the slightest difficulty making friends of either sex and led a very sociable life, but with Morwenna it was far otherwise. Never having received the slightest encouragement from her family to have much opinion of her own charms, Morwenna had been enchanted in her late twenties to find love. A supremely happy marriage had followed – that happiness only to be snatched away when her charming, gentle clergyman husband had been found lying face down among the old grey gravestones in the churchyard of his country parish, dead of a heart attack aged forty.

Though they had still not given up praying for a baby at the time of his death, they had failed to achieve this longed-for blessing, so the desolate trudge through widowhood was especially bleak. Without the incentive to keep going for the sake of the children or the opportunities for making friends that a young family can provide, it was hard to make the efforts required to get going again alone, but Morwenna had got on with her life with a stolid lack of fuss or self-pity that people often mistook for self-sufficiency. Her green fingers had come to her rescue and she had turned for support to the one thing at which she thought she was any good. Urgently needing to earn some money, she had become a jobbing gardener working for more affluent neighbours, a business that had flourished way beyond her expectations, so that her advice started to be sought by local garden enthusiasts and her various employers turned into clients. From this small beginning had also sprung the gardening column that was responsible for her current attempt to improve her writing skills.

Given that there was an enduring hollow left at the core of her being by the departure of her beloved Dennis, she nevertheless considered herself reasonably contented, responding to the rhythms of the changing seasons with pleasure and finding genuine joy in growing things . . . but attempting, less successfully, to find comfort for an inner loneliness by eating too much. Morwenna, a large middle-aged lady, not ill-favoured but with no pretensions to glamour, had now been alone for nearly twenty years and had long ago given up hope that she might find another man to love and be loved by in the second half of her life. She had certainly not come on the writing course in search of romance so it had come as a surprise to find her company consistently being sought out by the Colonel. Louisa might consider the Colonel rather a dull old stick, but he possessed great kindness and a dry sense of humour. Morwenna knew she made him laugh – without always being quite sure why – and as she had never thought of herself as at all amusing this was a novel and delightful experience. What is more, with his old-fashioned, courtly manners, he made her feel feminine, something that hadn't happened in a very long time. The results were amazing – Morwenna began to bloom like a parched plant that has started being given regular doses of water to which nourishing pinches of Phostrogen have been added.

Two invitations had been issued the night before. The Colonel, who had privately consulted the Grants about what sort of outing they thought Morwenna might enjoy, had suggested that he should take her out to lunch at a restaurant recommended by Giles and then go to the rhododendron and azalea nurseries at Glendoich – which Morwenna had told Isobel she wanted to visit since she had so often ordered plants from them but never been there – and Christopher had asked Marnie to spend the day with him. Both these invitations had been accepted, so after they had said goodbye to Joyce, Win and Bunty and watched the minibus go off down the drive, Giles and

Isobel left the Old Steading to its own devices and walked slowly back into the house.

Giles took Edward and Rory out on the loch in the boat after breakfast to troll for trout; Amy, after the excitement and tension of her performance the night before, was still just a hump under her duvet, surrounded by a wild assortment of clothes strewn all over the floor of her bedroom; Catherine, who was leaving after lunch to spend a few nights in Edinburgh with the Mercers, was packing. Isobel, counting her as family, had invited Louisa to spend the day with her and the two of them were enjoying a leisurely gossip together in the kitchen, discussing every detail of the course and its participants, when the telephone rang. Isobel picked up the receiver.

'Lorna? Where are you are you ringing from?' Louisa heard her ask in an uncharacteristically sharp voice. Then: '*Tomorrow*? You must be joking! That's ridiculously short notice. Well, yes . . . of course we could have him ready, but that's not the point. It just doesn't give him time to adjust to the idea of another sudden change and I have to say that next week would be very much easier for us this end . . . we've still got a group here.' It was clear that a heated argument was ensuing. Isobel started to pace about the kitchen. 'That's totally untrue! I never said I'd be glad to see the back of him!' she exploded, running her free hand through her hair so that it looked at as if she were facing a force nine gale. Louisa got up and made for the door, feeling uncomfortably like an eavesdropper, but Isobel waved her back and mouthed 'Don't go' at her.

'Oh, all right, *all right*,' she said eventually. 'No I most certainly don't want you to come here. If you've booked their flights, so be it, we'll take him to Edinburgh and Sheena will come with him to Heathrow – but you'd better be there yourself to meet them and don't blame me if you have a very bothered son on your hands.' She slammed the telephone down, slumped in a chair and looked at Louisa with despair.

'I don't know anyone, *anyone* who can get me worked up the way Lorna can!' she said. 'They're staying at the Ritz all this week before flying back to the States – and what it'll be like for Rory cooped up in a grand hotel I can't think. Other people would think of lovely things to do with their child but I'll bet Lorna and her husband will be too busy networking in high circles to have any time for him. What's so awful is that I don't think for one moment that she really wants him there. I think she just wants to wind me up – or else she has a hidden agenda that I haven't cottoned on to yet. She says if we don't put him on the flight tomorrow she'll hire a car and come and fetch him herself, which is blackmail because she knows I'd do anything to stop her setting foot in this house again. Oh, shit, shit – where's that box of tissues gone?'

'In spite of everything, you really love him, don't you, Iz?' Louisa looked at her curiously as Isobel seized a handful of tissues from the box she held out. 'You couldn't be this upset if you didn't.'

Isobel nodded. 'He's twined himself round my heartstrings,' she said sadly, mopping at her eyes. 'And I dread telling him he's going back home because he was such a nervy little scrap when he arrived here and he's settled so happily with us. Despite all my grumping and grumbling and jealousy I can't help loving him, but oh! you don't know how much I wish that he were my son too . . . as well as Giles's.'

'I suppose,' suggested Louisa tentatively, longing to comfort her but very much afraid of saying the wrong thing, 'that he must have almost identical genes to your own children even if he isn't actually yours. Aunts and uncles can be very much resembled, and he's got every bit as much of your lovely parents in him as Edward and Amy have. Does that make it better or worse?'

'I'm not sure . . .' Isobel blew her nose violently. 'I hadn't thought of it that way. I'm probably being thoroughly unreasonable about the whole thing. It's what Lorna does to me. She brings out my worst self – the bits I don't like to admit are there.'

'Well, I think you're a bloody marvel, and who wants to be reasonable?' asked Louisa bracingly. 'Being reasonable's a dead bore.'

At this moment a yawning Amy appeared through the door wearing a pair of boxer shorts and an old T-shirt. She twined herself round her mother in a bear hug, all the sophistication of last night's concert performer vanished. Louisa thought she looked about twelve. She felt a sudden pang of envy for Isobel – so loved and so loving; so needed. A round peg who'd discovered and settled into her round hole at an early age and, despite the inevitable storms and demands of family life, still fitted her chosen space to perfection. Surely I can't be getting broody, wondered Louisa with surprise.

'Hi, Louisa,' said Amy. 'What's for breakfast, Mum?'

'Breakfast! You're hopeful.' Isobel laughed. 'It's nearly lunchtime!'

'No lovely weekend bacon?' wheedled Amy. 'I'm *starving*.'

'You're always starving. There might be some bacon left in the Aga if Dad and the boys left any – finish it up if there is. We're only having larder scrapings for lunch because I thought we could all forage for what we feel like and use up all the bits before we start again on proper meals this evening.'

'Great,' said Amy, taking a dish out of the oven and demolishing crispy slices of pancetta in her fingers. 'You

OK, Mum?' she asked, looking suspiciously at her mother. 'You look a bit weird.'

'I'm fine. The pollen count must be high or something.'

At that moment Giles and the boys came up to the outside door and Giles tapped on the glass and indicated two wet figures, both Edward and Rory having succeeded in stepping into the loch while getting out of the boat. They were full of happy giggles as Giles attempted to pull off their sodden wellington boots. It was such a happy, casual, outdoor scene, such a normal sort of Glendrochatt occurrence, that as Isobel went out to help remove wet garments – Edward's lack of coordination still making occasional assistance necessary with tricky clothing – she dreaded the thought of what she had to say to Rory. Her heart lurched further when she wondered how Edward, whose stability was always a precarious balancing act, would take the news that this newly acquired boon companion was about to be taken from him.

The boys padded into the kitchen in bare feet, making satisfying wet footprints on the floor.

'No fish?' asked Amy.

'Edward had a pull,' said Giles, 'but the trout had other ideas and they were giving Rory the cold shoulder today. We'll have better luck next time.'

'Can we go again tomorrow?' asked Rory.

'Yes, can we, Dad?' echoed Edward. 'Tomorrow I will give those fish the shock of their lives. Tomorrow I will catch Leviathan. Tomorrow I will be Angler of the Year. I shouldn't be surprised if I get another medal!'

'Well, not tomorrow, darling, because you'll be going back to school, and,' said Isobel, plunging in, 'because something rather special is happening for Rory tomorrow.' Across the kitchen Giles's eyes met hers. 'I've just had Mummy on the telephone,' she continued bravely, 'and can you guess what she had to say?'

'No.' Rory froze.

'Well, Mummy's arrived in England and she wants you to fly down to London to join her there. Isn't that exciting?'

'When will I be coming back?'

'We'll have to plan another visit for you very soon.' Isobel's voice was bright as polished glass. 'But first you'll have a fun time in London with Mummy . . . and then go home to Washington with her. Won't that be lovely?'

'No! This is my home. I live with *you* now.'

'Oh, darling, this can always be your *second* home. I hope you'll come and stay often – but your real home is with Mummy and Brooke. They want you back with them.' Isobel tried to take the little boy in her arms, but he fought her off, flailing at her with desperate small fists.

'NO! NO! NO!'

Edward's face had started to twitch. 'Is his mummy the spider lady?' he asked, this being the unfortunate name he had given his aunt the ill-fated summer, five years earlier, when he had become so afraid of her.

'Yes,' said Amy.

Without another word, Edward started pulling saucepans out on the floor and then got down on hands and knees and stuck his head in the cupboard – an ostrich ritual he hadn't displayed for a long time.

'Come on out, Ed. There's no need for that,' said Giles firmly, pulling him out and then holding him, while Amy, her face expressionless, put the saucepans carefully back and shut the cupboard door. Rory burst into hysterical sobs and clutched Isobel round the knees.

'I won't go-o-o,' he wailed. 'I want to stay here with you. You promised I could have a guinea-pig! I won't go!'

Sheena, arriving at this moment, made a welcome interruption in the hullabaloo and eventually she and Isobel managed to get both Rory and Edward out of the kitchen and up the stairs to change out of their wet clothes, though Rory's pathetic wails could still be heard in the kitchen from the top of the house.

When Isobel eventually returned to start getting lunch, Amy and Louisa were laying the table and Giles was carving ham. Louisa thought Isobel looked terrible. Giles put his arm round her and she leaned against him for a moment.

'Oh, Giles!' she said, giving herself a little shake and pulling away from him. 'That was even worse than I thought. Rory's in a frightful state – it's heart-rending. I've left Sheena reading him a story till lunchtime but he can't stop crying. I don't think I can bear it.'

'And you can't *do* it, either, Mum,' said Amy fiercely. 'You can't possibly send him back to Aunt Lorna. He's terrified of her. I know he is. Think of the effect she had on Ed.'

'I have to send him, darling,'

'You *can't*. How can you be so cruel? She'll wreck his life. Have you forgotten how she practically killed Ed? How she literally frightened him into fits and he nearly died?'

Isobel knew she could never forget the havoc her sister had once caused. She thought of Edward's limp, unresponding little body after he'd run away from his aunt and been lost; of how the police had been talking of dragging the loch before he'd been discovered in the woods; of his subsequent regression back to the baby habits they'd worked so hard to overcome and of his terrifying two months of total silence before speech returned – these images could still cause her heart to pound and her mouth to go dry. 'Of course I haven't forgotten!' she said sharply. 'Don't be silly, Amy.'

'Then ring Aunt Lorna up and tell her you're keeping him – or better still just don't put him on the flight! Serve her right if she had to worry about him for a change!' Amy glared at her mother.

'Oh, Amy, darling, we have to let him go!' said Isobel wearily. 'This is different. She's his *mother* for heaven's sake. She has something called parental rights.'

Across the room, Amy, white-faced, stared directly at Giles.

'And what about his father?' she asked, her voice very quiet but piercingly clear. 'What about *him*? Doesn't he have rights too – and responsibilities?'

There was a deadly silence. Then Amy rushed out of the kitchen and slammed the door so hard that everything on the newly laid table rattled as though the house had suddenly been hit by a hurricane.

Chapter Nineteen

Isobel sat down at the table and buried her head in her hands. Giles had looked stunned at Amy's utterance. Then with an obvious effort he got himself in hand.

He turned apologetically to Louisa, mortified that she should have had to witness such a private family scene. 'I'm desperately sorry about all that – thank goodness you're family and there's no one else here.' Trying for a lighter note, he said: 'Imagine what Bunty would have made of it! Look after my wife for me for a bit, Louisa – I need to go and find my daughter.' He touched Isobel lightly on the cheek. 'Don't wait lunch for us, Izzy,' he said, 'we'll come and help ourselves later. And don't look so agonised, my love. You told me I needed to clear a few things up with Amy. Looks like I've got my chance. We'll sort things out. Will you be all right?'

'I suppose so.' Isobel gave a watery smile. 'Not much choice – but oh, Giles, poor little Rory.'

'I know,' said her husband. 'I know . . . we have to do some serious thinking about the future.'

He found Amy where he thought she might have gone – down below the south terrace, through a small gate and into the wild garden that had always been the children's special play area.

Here was the wooden castle designed by Giles's father as a sixth birthday present for his small son. In it, Giles, a solitary but imaginative only child, had commanded armies and slain dragons; in it, some thirty years later, Edward, with his passion for history and store of unexpected information, had also become a crusader, or a Roman centurion; St George, Prince Caspian, Harry Potter or an alien. It was one of the surprises about Edward that though he could barely do more than write his name, he'd read fluently from quite an early age. During the last April holidays it had been a joy to Isobel to see the teenage Edward, so uneven in his development, so out of step with his contemporaries, blissfully re-entering his childhood world again, with Rory, a very willing participant, brilliantly playing minor parts to Edward's starring roles – though frequently without the foggiest idea about the characters he was supposed to be portraying. Here, in a circle of grass, was the seesaw on which talented Amy, as a small girl, had balanced precariously to practise her fiddle, music pouring forth with all the unselfconscious abandon of a bird singing in a tree. Here also was the old wooden swing, slung from a branch of the immense cedar tree that provided either shade or shelter.

Amy was sitting on the swing now, kicking at the bare earth with the toe of her trainer, her shoulders hunched, her heart deeply troubled. She eyed her father stonily as he approached.

'Hi, darling,' said Giles.

'Hi,' said Amy, unsmiling, not giving an inch.

'We need to talk,' said Giles, straddling the seesaw and perching in the middle of it, his heart sinking even further at the sight of his daughter's face. 'Or rather I need to talk to you. I need to talk about something that I now think I should have discussed with you weeks ago – about possibilities of which you are clearly already aware. Perhaps I should have guessed that too – but anyway I didn't. I need to ask your opinion. Maybe I need to ask for your forgiveness.' He paused. Amy said nothing. Giles watched her face, understanding the dichotomy between opposing loyalties, between love and furious resentment; aching for her distress. 'Are you prepared to listen?' he asked quietly.

Amy shrugged. 'I suppose so,' she said grudgingly, longing to make peace but not knowing how to do so without loss of dignity; wishing she could recapture the untroubled relationship of her childhood when her father had been her unquestioned hero, her musical mentor, her adored companion . . . until her Aunt Lorna had arrived at Glendrochatt, set the whole family at odds with each other and, in Amy's view, tarnished something special, which had never quite recovered its shine.

'You obviously realise Rory might be my son?' he asked.

'Only might be?' Amy's voice was cutting.

Giles winced. 'No – you're right. There *is* a doubt – but it seems more like a certainty. When did it first occur to you?'

'From the moment I first saw him, of course. I'm not stupid. It's just so obvious. Dad . . . did you . . . were you . . . you *must* have known about it before he came?'

'I'd . . . wondered.' Giles paused miserably, not sure how much to tell Amy. Then he said: 'I was afraid it was a possibility. By the time we discovered your aunt was pregnant she'd left her flat In Edinburgh and decided to go back to South Africa – that was a surprise in itself – but I desperately needed to know. I flew down to London to see her just before she left and confronted her. She denied, point blank, that I was the father.'

'Did Mum know that?'

'Not before I went. I told her when I came back.'

'And you believed Aunt Lorna?'

Giles hesitated. Then he said: 'I very much wanted to believe her – not least for your mother's sake – but Lorna has always bent the truth so I admit I wasn't entirely convinced – but I wouldn't have been convinced if she'd said the baby was mine either. Then when we heard from your grandparents that the baby had been born it was easy to accept – because either the baby was premature or the dates didn't quite fit.'

Amy twisted the ropes of the swing, and slowly spun round as she let them unwind. Then she said: 'It was that awful Suzuki weekend that went so wrong for me, wasn't it? When Mum didn't come with us and you took Aunt Lorna in her place?'

'Yes,' said Giles. 'It was then. I made a huge mistake.'

'*Mistake*?' Amy snorted scornfully.

Giles knew he must keep a hold on his temper and not be goaded into attempting justifications or discussing Lorna's devious tactics. Above all he must resist the temptation to mention Isobel and Daniel Hoffman. He said, 'All right, Amy – you have every reason to be angry. I behaved very badly. I'm not excusing myself but I'd like you to know that it only occurred once and I immediately made it plain to Lorna it must never happen again. And it never did – though not for want of her trying.'

'I hate her,' said Amy. 'I really hate her. How could she do that to Mum?'

'Jealousy's a terrible thing,' said Giles. 'It can be responsible for some awful actions. Lorna's always been insanely jealous of Mum. All through their childhood Mum was the better loved – by everyone. It must have been hard. Then Lorna not only wanted to marry me but – and this I only discovered afterwards – had set her heart on Glendrochatt too – had a completely false picture of herself as its chatelaine. And Mum got both. Then we had you and Edward, and Lorna, who'd always said she longed for children, was desperately envious of that too.'

'She certainly wasn't envious of Edward,' said Amy resentfully. 'She was always dreadful about Ed. Horrible.'

'No, not about Ed,' he admitted. 'Which makes it all the more difficult to understand why, when she'd always professed herself desperate for children, she could turn out to be such a rotten mother when she got a beautiful baby of her own like Rory. In South Africa there were always nannies and staff to look after him but Granny and Grandpa looked after him more than she ever did to begin with. They went out there and he spent long periods with them in France – but never when we were there.'

'So how come you and Mum can send him back to her now?' asked Amy accusingly.

Giles sighed. 'It's very hard for your mum. How do you think she feels to see the evidence of my unfaithfulness under her nose all the time? How do you think I feel when I respond to him as my son, and see the pain in your mother's face?'

'But she loves him,' said Amy doubtfully, looking very troubled.

'Yes . . . because she's an exceptionally generous person and because he's a very endearing child. But how generous are you, Amy?'

'What do you mean?'

'You weren't exactly thrilled when he arrived – and I didn't blame you. You probably feel very resentful of him now.'

Amy swallowed. 'But Ed will be devastated if he goes now. He adored playing with Rory . . . and Rory hero-worships him.'

'Yes, that's all true . . . for now. But Rory will outgrow Edward as all his playmates do,' said Giles inexorably. 'How will it be for Ed then?'

'I don't know. I don't know.' Amy was on the verge of tears. 'I only know I hate the thought of him going back to Aunt Lorna . . . but you make it all so sound so complicated,' she muttered.

'Because it *is* complicated. Because the cruellest thing of all would be to try to keep Rory for a bit longer now . . . and then abandon him. Even if we managed to get Aunt Lorna to agree to give him up – which would be very out of character – it still wouldn't be easy. We'd all have to make a huge commitment to him and that would mean you too, Amy.'

'So what are you going to do?' she asked.

'I don't know,' said Giles. 'I really do not know. But whatever happens you will be consulted – that's a promise – and you'll need to think carefully about your own answers.' He stood up and held out his hand. 'And I'm very sorry, Amy darling – more sorry than I can say – that actions of mine should have put us all in such an impossible position . . . but as Mum keeps telling me, it's not Rory's fault. Don't say anything more now, but please think about what I've said.'

Amy got off the swing and came and stood beside him. 'Thanks, Dad.' She slipped her hand in his and gave it a quick little squeeze before pulling away again. 'I will brood about it . . . but I wish it didn't all have to be so difficult.'

'Yes,' he said feelingly. 'So do I.'

She said: 'It was good fun playing together last night, wasn't it?'

'Terrific. Like old times. We always made a great team, didn't we?'

Suddenly she grinned at him. 'Guess what?' she asked. 'I'm absolutely starving!'

'Then let's go and see if they've left us any ham,' said Giles.

And they walked back up the hill together.

Chapter Twenty

Marnie woke early on Sunday morning to a feeling of contentment, after the best night's sleep she'd had for ages.

She lay in bed, drowsily savouring this sensation of well-being, conscious of being exactly the right temperature, of the softness of the pillows and the warmth and lightness of the duvet; watching pale sunlight slant across the wall and the curtains sway gently at the open window. A positive orchestra of birds was serenading outside. She could hear a wood pigeon's soothing, monotonous coo from somewhere near, while a pair of oyster-catchers, screeching urgently in the distance, sounded like paramedics speeding along with alarm bells ringing. She could identify the outpourings of blackbird and thrush and a particularly vociferous wren – that smallest of musicians which has the decibels of an amplified timpanist at its disposal; she could hear a willow warbler fluting diminuendos in the garden and picked out the demanding *teacher-teacher* call of a great tit. From the other side of the courtyard, Don Quixote, Edward's bombastic cockerel, was noisily greeting the new day. Not all visitors to Glendrochatt appreciated the Don's dawn reveille and there had been curmudgeonly complaints from Stanley at breakfast on the first day, but on this particular Sunday morning it sounded delightful to Marnie.

The crowing cock triggered old memories and in her drowsy state she wondered what other sounds were missing. Surely there ought to be the bleating of goats and the braying of a donkey in the background – and instead of the great tit and the wren there should have been a pearly-eyed thrasher singing *chocky, chocky, chocky* from a frangipani tree.

She waited for the disturbing combination of longing and fear which accompanied recollections of the West Indies to overwhelm her as usual – the nostalgia for an enchanted childhood place mixed with the terror of a malign but hidden menace . . . but it did not come. Then she remembered the evening before and how the threat of taking part in Scottish reels, which had sent her into such a spin of panic, had been transformed when she and Christopher danced together, and how a very different kind of magic from anything she had experienced before had cast a new spell over her – and exorcised an old one. She remembered his suggestion that they should go off together somewhere for the day. She stretched luxuriously and sat up, pushing her hair back from her face, and reached for her watch. After nine o'clock already! She flung the duvet back and got out of bed. She had just finished dressing when there was a tap at her door.

'Marnie?'

'Yes?'

'It's Christopher.'

'Oh hi – come in,' she said.

He peered round the door and smiled at her and she smiled brilliantly back. 'Hi there,' she said, conscious of a quickening of her pulse at the sight of him. 'I'm just about to go down to breakfast.'

'It looks like being a glorious day so I thought I'd check if you were awake.' He stood in the doorway. 'I reckon Bunty et al will have gone off by now and I wondered when you'd like to plan our day together – unless you've had second thoughts about it, that is?'

'Of course I haven't.'

'Great.' He hesitated for a moment and she wondered what was coming. He said abruptly: 'Look, Marnie, I feel badly that if we go off somewhere, the driving will all have to be on you. It's not only that I haven't got my car here, but I wasn't sure if you realised that I haven't got my licence back yet? It goes against the grain to invite you out for the day and then not be able to transport you wherever we decide to go, or at least offer to share the driving.'

'Is that all?' She laughed. 'I thought you were going to cry off. Not being able to drive may be lousy for you, but it certainly won't worry me,' she assured him. 'I love driving.' Then, thinking that the after-effect of the crash might have left Christopher with serious backseat-driving problems, she added: 'I'm a very good driver – even my father tolerates being chauffeured by me, and that's some recommendation, I can tell you. It'll be great to have someone to map-read for me and tell me where to go. I'm hopeless at carrying a route in my head. It'll be a nice change from being on my own.'

'Thanks – that's a relief then,' said Christopher, touched by the tact and sensitivity that lay behind the defensive thorn hedge she had planted round herself. He wondered what sort of adult relationships she'd had since her traumatic childhood and what had gone wrong with them – clearly something must have done, to turn such a potentially attractive young woman into someone who seemed to be so alone. 'I'll see you downstairs then,' he said. 'I just want to find Catherine before she disappears to thank her for all she's done for me, but otherwise the day is ours, so don't rush.'

But though the day might be theirs, they were both acutely aware of how little they really knew about each other. Each wondered if their relationship was about to take a huge leap forward; whether, without the rest of the

274

group to act as an echo sounder, the attraction that existed between them would flourish into something much stronger, or whether, with the opportunity to be alone together, it would wither away. Both were looking for a fresh start in their lives, both wanted something more than a light-hearted holiday romance, but there were issues to be sorted out and wounds that needed to be healed. There were hopes and possibilities but no certainties. Christopher felt very aware that he was dealing with someone who'd had her trust in human beings eroded at an early age and decided he must be careful not to make any wrong moves.

Marnie had wondered if Christopher would attempt to sleep with her when they reached the Old Steading the night before. There had been a moment as they had stood on the stairs on their way to their rooms when anything might have happened, but they had both held back; too many unresolved issues hanging between them; each afraid of inflicting or receiving more hurt.

'Goodnight, beautiful dancer,' he had said, softly. 'Thank you for helping me to come back to life again. Sleep very well. See you in the morning.' Christopher had been amazed at how the evening had gone. Earlier in the week it had been Louisa who had set his pulses racing, but the sudden magnetic attraction he now felt for Marnie was something much deeper altogether.

'Goodnight,' she whispered. 'Thank you too.'

After she had closed her bedroom door, she had leaned against it almost afraid to take another breath because she did not want to lose the moment. She had read somewhere that people who are drowning can have a whole life's review in a few seconds. She almost felt as if she were drowning now and thought with surprise that it was an entirely pleasurable sensation. She had intended to go over every detail of the evening in her head, analysing each word spoken, each glance exchanged – and each, surprising step danced – but when she got into bed she had fallen asleep almost immediately.

Christopher was talking to Morwenna and the Colonel when Marnie joined him. A supply of rolls and croissants, together with an assortment of home-made jams, marmalade and local honey had been left on the counter in the bar; there was a choice of yogurts and cereals, a big bowl of fresh fruit and a jug of freshly squeezed orange juice; tea and coffee were on the hot plate.

Morwenna and the Colonel, who'd breakfasted earlier with the departing members of the group, were finishing second cups of coffee and regaling Christopher with an account of Bunty's parting stroke of literary genius. Inspired by the reels at the party the previous evening, she announced that she'd been smitten by an idea for the plot of a gripping new Highland saga for children's television, a stirring drama about the adventures of the Dashing White Sergeant as a little boy. According to Morwenna she'd been bubbling so enthusiastically with this brilliant notion that it had been difficult for Isobel to steer her towards the waiting minibus, and Giles, despite frantic faces from his wife, who feared Bunty might make the others miss the train at Perth, had been unable to resist informing her that the origins of that particular reel were not Scottish at all – that the tune had been written by Sir Henry Rowley Bishop, English composer of 'Home Sweet Home', and the steps were actually based on a circle dance of Swedish origin.

'I bet that didn't stop her,' said Christopher, much amused.

'It didn't even stem the flood,' said the Colonel, 'but she's worryingly torn between the rival merits of *The Magic Kilt* and *A Sprig of White Heather* as a title for the series.'

'Oh, it'll have to be *The Magic Kilt*,' giggled Marnie. 'Think of the possibilities.'

Morwenna added that Catherine's face of polite resignation had been a study as Bunty, brushing these pedantic considerations aside, had breathlessly promised to let Catherine be the first to see the script as soon as she'd got more of it down on paper. 'Lucky for Catherine that at least she had you and Win on the course as well as the rest of us,' she said to Christopher. 'Not bad, I suppose – two genuine undiscovered talents out of eight – if you don't count the dreaded Stanley. I know Catherine has promised to help Win find some outlets for her snappy, evocative little sketches, if she manages to survive reunion with her horrible husband. Are you going to keep in touch with Catherine too, Christopher?'

He nodded. 'I certainly hope so. She's suggested I should come to some of her poetry workshops in London, which I fully intend to do, and of course I want to tell her about Jonathan Mercer's verdict – though I dare say she'll know about that before me. But don't underestimate your own writing, Morwenna. After all, you were the only one of us to have been published before – and you know how encouraging Catherine was to you in our final session.'

'Yes – she was very kind. But I owe a lot to your ideas and encouragement too,' she said gratefully. 'You've all given me the boost I need to try to keep going with my horticultural writing as well as with the actual practical gardening – at which I know I'm good. I'm definitely a hands-on gardener first and a journalist second.'

'What about you, John?' Christopher looked at the Colonel. 'Do you reckon you've got anything out of the week?'

'I certainly have – I shall peg on with my regimental history and Catherine's given me some helpful suggestions about how to make it a bit more accessible – and a little less boring, which,' he admitted with a twinkle in his eye, 'I gather was a very real danger.' He went on gruffly, 'But I think I've gained a great deal from the whole week in other ways – not just from the writing,' and he glanced towards Morwenna, who suddenly seemed preoccupied with gathering up her bag, her raincoat, and the gardening notebooks that she took with her everywhere. 'Shall we go then, Morwenna?' he asked, clearing his throat and straightening his perfectly straight and tightly knotted tie. 'If you're ready, let's take ourselves off and go and see what we can find at this famous nursery garden and you can give me a crash course in dendrology.'

'At least I don't think we'll find any garden gnomes there,' said Morwenna. 'But I'm sure Bunty's garden, if she's got one, must be seething with toadstools and little red men with fishing rods. 'Bye then, you two. Have a lovely day. We'll compare notes this evening.'

'There goes a pair of very nice people,' said Marnie as they watched the two solid, sensibly clad figures walk towards the car park. 'I thought they both looked dread-fully dull that first day – and I was wrong. I've got very fond of them both.'

'And he's right, you know,' said Christopher. 'It's not just the writing – encouraging though that's been for me – that's made this week so special. If I hadn't come, I wouldn't have met you . . . and that,' said Christopher, looking at Marnie across the table, 'seems unthinkable.'

They decided to head up the A9 to Blair Atholl and go round Blair Castle.

'If you want to start hunting for a missing castle,' said Christopher, 'I think you'd better see an example of the real thing and get your eye in. I believe Giles and Isobel have arranged for us to go to Glamis later this week and you couldn't have two more romantic Highland castles than those two. Then after we've culture-vultured all morning and read up on massacres and private armies and gazed at great halls decorated with fearsome arrays of weapons, how about some upmarket retail therapy by way of a contrast? I thought we could have lunch at the House of Bruar, a couple of miles further on, which has very good self-service food, wonderful country clothes and a marvellous gift department. It's an irresistible lure to my sisters whenever they're anywhere near here, much to the gloom of my brothers-in-law. How does that sound as a programme?'

Marnie said it sounded perfect.

'I have an ulterior motive for going to the House of Bruar,' said Christopher as they walked to Marnie's car. 'I hope you might advise me about a thank-you present for Catherine. It seems the ideal place to buy her something as a token of my gratitude but I don't know what to get. Will you help me choose?'

'I'd love to. That's a great idea.'

'And I also want to get a present for my old mum. She's been a rock through all my troubles. I can't ever begin to thank her – not that she'd want me to – but I'd like to take something home for her too.'

Marnie privately thought she would be much less qualified to choose presents for a mother – the rock-like variety being quite outside her experience. Memories of her own mother's bored and off-hand acceptance of lovingly made childhood offerings still made her wince.

They set off in Marnie's nippy little Audi 3. Christopher adjusted the passenger seat to accommodate his long legs and prepared to enjoy the trip because it was immediately obvious that Marnie drove with all the sureness that was so lacking in her social skills.

'Just be warned about speed cameras,' he said as they turned on to the A9 and headed north towards Pitlochry.

'No reflection on your driving, but this stretch of road is notorious for catching one out – as I've learned to my cost in the past. I'd hate you to get points on your licence on my account.' He hoped he wouldn't have offended her, but this was obviously not the sort of thing that made her touchy.

'Okay. Thanks,' she said, and then, 'Wow! What stunning country! What's the river down there?'

'Well, it's been the Tay and it's just about to become the Tummel. I knew you'd like it,' said Christopher, pleased with her reaction.

She was equally impressed by Blair – from the first glimpse of its white walls and turrets standing above and to the right of the road.

'Now that really *is* a castle – no kidding!' she said. 'All my childhood stories rolled into one. Who lives there, for the Lord's sake – Snow White, Mary Queen of Scots, Rapunzel, King Arthur?'

'It belonged to the Dukes of Atholl – no actual duke there now, but it's still owned by the last duke's family.'

'I hope the Contessa's ancestral home, if I ever find it, won't be quite that vast!' she with mock horror.

'Oh, castles in Scotland come in all shapes and sizes,' said Christopher cheerfully. 'Some of them are little more than fortified farmhouses.'

He thought her a beguilingly enthusiastic companion as they toured the interior, admiring its fine plasterwork and fascinating, varied contents. And all the time their enjoyment of everything was heightened by their acute awareness of each other, so that anything that amused them seemed funnier, every colour appeared brighter and anything beautiful became more breathtaking, just because they were together. The electricity between them was so strong that Marnie almost expected to see sparks flying and wondered if they might accidentally set off all the burglar alarms every time they brushed against each other.

Christopher found himself comparing Marnie to Nicola, for whom neither history, literature, romance or the natural world rated as interesting topics – though he knew she would have enjoyed their next port of call. He tried to think back to the days when he and Nicola had first got together and wondered rather guiltily what had made their relationship last as long as it had. There was sex, of course – that had always been good – but Nicola was also sassy, intelligent and witty and he'd found her drive and ambition an exciting challenge; they'd shared a fascination for the world of finance and big business and they'd had a lot of fun together, but cracks had started to form in the relationship well before the disastrous car crash which had brought it to such an acrimonious end. Quarrels had started to become more frequent, and instead of being stimulating as they had once been, increasingly he found them tedious. He and Nicola did not want the same things out of life and their views on how their future together should progress no longer tallied. We should have split up much sooner, he thought, and it was my fault that we didn't.

Marnie could hardly bear to leave romantic Blair Atholl, but in fact the House of Bruar, which advertised itself as Scotland's most prestigious country store, was an equal success with her. Even though it was so early in the season, it was already hotching with people, and they had to park in the overflow car park.

They decided to shop first and then have a leisurely lunch.

'What a dangerous place! This is every serious American shopper's dream,' said Marnie, surveying the beautifully laid out expanse of luxury goods. 'All this classy tweed and cashmere and leather – all that lovely kitchen stuff! It's the epitome of what we think of as ever-so-British classic good taste. My mother, who's a complete shopaholic, would go bananas here!'

'Oh, Lord – does that put you off?' Christopher teased.

Marnie made a rueful face. 'I guess I must have more of her in me than I bargained for,' she said, laughing. 'What was it Oscar Wilde had to say about mothers?'

'All women become like their mothers. That's their tragedy. No man does. That's his,' quoted Christopher. 'Sounds relevant to us both!'

'That's the one. Let's hope my likeness to her stops with the addiction to cashmere, then!'

She bought a cashmere scarf for her father, socks for her half-brothers and a pair of gloves for her stepmother – nothing, Christopher noticed, for her mother – and they each bought themselves a jersey. Marnie was torn between a bright blue polo neck and a pale pink one.

'Which do you like best?' she asked, holding them up against herself.

'Get the blue,' advised Christopher. 'It will match your eyes' – so of course she did. He chose a dark red sleeveless pullover, but she picked out one in a soft raspberry colour. 'This one's cool. Go on – live dangerously! Break out of the conventional mould,' she mocked. 'And how about revving up your sock situation while you're about it?'

'What's wrong with my socks?'

'Incredibly sober. Brighten up your life by bursting into stripes or spots!'

'You're as bad as my sisters,' he complained, but he bought the pink pullover and two pairs of colourful spotted socks and they laughed at each other, well pleased with their purchases. She vetoed his suggestion of buying Catherine a cardigan.

'It'd be a great present and I'm sure she'd love it, but she is one very big lady,' she objected. 'I could probably make a fair guess at the right size but it seems a bit personal if you don't know someone that well. Do you really want to give a present which says *Extra Large* on the label?'

'Oh, Lord, perhaps not! What do you suggest then?'

'Why not get her a throw instead? It'd be just as luxurious to wear but there wouldn't be issues about size. I could see her striding off to classes with it tossed round her shoulders. There's something a bit swashbuckling about her, don't you think? If she'd been born in an earlier age I see her dashingly riding astride while everyone else rode side-saddle, or galloping across the desert on a camel with a turban on her head.'

'Surely not in a cashmere throw?'

'Oh, I don't know – nothing but the best.'

So they bought a wonderfully soft serape for Catherine in a rich dark green and Christopher went on to buy his mother a very expensive pair of secateurs from the Country Living department, which he thought would be perfect for pruning and easy for her increasingly arthritic hands to manage. After paying for the secateurs, Christopher said he wanted to look at some gardening books so Marnie took herself off to the shoe department and bought a pair of tasselled loafers in red and navy-blue calf, with which she was extremely pleased.

'Lunch now,' he said, when they met again in the food hall. 'I hope you're hungry?'

'Starving. What an awesome spending spree! There's something about shopping that always makes me ravenous.'

'I'll remember from now on and avoid the combination,' he grinned, and Marnie felt a swift glow of pleasure to hear him talk about the future.

The restaurant was a cafeteria, but a far cry from the motorway variety. Christopher couldn't resist the joint of roast beef, just the right shade of pink, carved at the counter and served with all the trimmings – the sort of food, he told her, he'd dreamed about in prison – and Marnie chose the creamy-looking macaroni cheese with a choice of crisp and colourful help-yourself salads. 'My favourite thing,' she said. 'The ultimate comfort food.'

'Do you need comforting?' he asked.

'Not at the moment – far from it. I'm having a wonderful time.'

'Me too,' he said. 'Me too.'

They carried their lunch out to a table on the terrace at the back, where they could hear the river Garry's babbling even above the babble of the other lunchers. The food was delicious and they sat over coffee and made each other laugh inordinately about nothing in particular.

'What would you like to do this afternoon?' he asked. 'How energetic are you feeling?'

'I'm feeling terr-rific,' she said, twisting her fine straight hair back into a knot. 'What are you suggesting?'

'I thought we might follow the track by the river and walk up the Falls of Bruar. It's quite a climb in places but there are some spectacular rock pools and cascades. Would you like that?'

'Sounds great. I love walking, but will it be okay for your leg?' She had noticed him surreptitiously taking a couple of painkillers with his lunch.

'It'll be fine. It'll be good for it. Come on, then.'

After leaving their shopping in the car, they set off – hand in hand for the first time – up the steep path, which was rutted by tree roots, studded with buried rocks and covered by a slippery brown carpet of old pine needles. It was full of surprises, with sheer drops round corners where the ground suddenly fell sharply away, and unexpected stiles and bridges. Christopher had to duck his head to get through a tunnel where the track went

284

underneath the Perth to Inverness railway line. They paused to lean over the first narrow bridge and watch the water hurtling down over the dark rocks below them.

'It's like something out of *Lord of the Rings*,' said Marnie. 'With all this weird grey beard stuff hanging off the trees you expect to see a hobbit pop down a hole. And have you ever seen such clear water – perhaps it's really whisky? You can see every rock and pebble even though it's such a long way down. You don't know what magic you might see reflected in those pools.'

'The future perhaps?' he suggested, looking at her.

'Let's go on,' she said, very conscious of his gaze.

'I'm glad I haven't got either of my unruly small nephews with me,' said Christopher as they passed yet another yellow hazard notice warning of the dangers of walking too close to the edge. 'Right or left?' he asked, when the path suddenly divided.

'Right,' answered Marnie, instantly. 'Always turn right, my father says.'

So they crossed over another stone bridge and continued up the other bank where the river grew narrower and fiercer until they came to a natural viewpoint and gazed up at a series of fantastic waterfalls, deep in the gorge above them.

'Let's stop here for a bit,' she said, thinking of his leg. 'It's so beautiful and I could do with catching my breath.'

They flopped down on the rough grass among the wild blaeberries and bracken, with the sky an alpine blue above the pines, and the spray of the tumbling water silver against the black boulders.

Christopher lit a cigarette. 'Tell me more about this place you're looking for – I've only gathered bits of the story so far,' he said. So she filled him in about her terror of the faces peering through her windows at night in the West Indies, the sinister voodoo episode and the intervention of the Contessa, and then, years later, the unlikely legacy that had come as such a shock.

'You're going to be horribly disappointed if you can't find it, aren't you, Marnie?'

'I suppose so,' she said. 'You'll think I'm absurdly superstitious, but I feel I'm at a turning point in my life and I have this conviction that if I can find her childhood home things may take a turn for the better.'

'Perhaps it's the search itself that's important. Perhaps the fact that you've set out on your quest matters more than what you find at the end of it. Travelling hopefully and all that?'

'Maybe.' She shot him an anxious look, wondering whether he thought her cranky and obsessed. 'But twice in my life she's rescued me at a very critical time. I need to make repayment – not directly to her, of course, but in her memory – in her honour.'

'Yes,' he said. 'I completely understand that. I know about wanting to make reparation. But you didn't tell me there was a second time when she rescued you.'

She hesitated. His good opinion was important, but honesty seemed more so. 'I've made a mess of my life so far,' she said. 'I've done stupid things – things I'm not proud of.'

'Haven't we all? Want to share them with me? I shared my big mistake with you.'

'Yes,' she said, 'you did, didn't you – and I was honoured.'

'So?'

'So I was the worst kind of rebellious teenager. I gave my parents one hell of a time – even my mother got worried about me!' She rolled her eyes, emphasising the abnormality of this, and went on: 'Drinking too much, eating disorders, experimenting with drugs and relation-ships – longing for love and doing everything in my power to drive it away. In and out of jobs, in and out of therapy – you get the picture. After that I guess I started to grow up a bit and settled down some, but I was still pretty wild. Then when I was twenty-three I met and fell in love with a much older man – a fellow American. Glamorous, charming, sophisticated, wealthy. I'd been working in London for one of my father's companies and we met at some big charity function and he asked me out to dinner. We started a relationship. I was wild about him. To please him I'd have done anything. He came over to London often, but was away on business a whole lot too. He'd disappear, sometimes for months at a time. He'd phone me up from all over the world and that would keep me going – but I lived for his returns. He hinted vaguely at some tragedy in the past and said he'd never remarried – it was too painful to discuss. I hoped that if he ever did plan to marry again, it would be to me. He talked of a time in the future when he'd be able to ease up a bit on the business front and could be more settled, but he said he didn't want to tie me down too young. I was touched by that. I thought he was holding back because he was thinking of my happiness, but I assured him I was ready whenever he was. I started to get broody. I wanted a baby. Then one day when I'd had to go back to the States for a family occasion, I met a young woman of my own age at a friend's house for a book club lunch and we got talking about authors we liked. We clicked immediately.'

Marnie sat clutching her knees with both hands and gazed at the view with great concentration. Christopher could see that her knuckles were white.

'When she told me her name,' she said in a flat, unemotional voice, 'I suddenly knew what was coming. So, with hindsight, I guess you could say there must have been warning signals but I was so dumb I didn't pick them up. She was his daughter. The reason he'd never "remarried" was because he already *was* married – with five children. And as far as his daughter was concerned, very happily married too. "You'd just love my parents," she said. "My dad often goes over to London on business. I must have him call you up." I don't know what excuse I made to get away before lunch was over but I never told her I was her father's mistress . . . I went home and took an overdose instead.'

'Thank God someone must have found you in time! Did you really mean to kill yourself?'

'Oh yes,' she said. 'I meant to do it all right.'

'So what happened?'

'I was staying in my father's New York apartment and he'd gone down to Long Island where we have a house. I knew my stepmother had a stash of sleeping tablets in the bathroom closet so I took the lot . . . but she had a dental appointment or something and unexpectedly came back and found me, only just in time. What followed was a nightmare. Stomach pumps. Doctors. Hospitalisation – and questions, questions, questions. I felt as if I was being turned inside out. I had a complete breakdown and a spell in a clinic.'

'Oh, Marnie, I'm so very sorry.' Christopher leaned forward, put his arms round her and pulled her back against him. She felt like a coiled spring. He held her close, occasionally rocking her slightly as one might comfort a frightened child, longing to hold her even closer but not wanting to break the flow of her reminiscences.

'I know now,' she whispered at last, 'that what I did was cowardly and wrong and gave a lot of people a load of anguish and trouble. I'm probably not the person you thought I was at all.'

'Oh, but I think you are,' he said. 'I think you're brave and kind and funny – and beautiful, and very, very special. We all have secrets and put on disguises to hide from the outside world. It's a question of finding the person on the inside.'

'Odd you should say that, because in her diary the Contessa wrote that old age was like a disguise. She felt she'd become invisible – no one saw who she was any more.'

'Like wearing a mask?' he suggested. 'Like your carnival dancers. Was it the thought of them that panicked you so much about dancing the reels? I knew it was something more than fear of making a fool of yourself by not knowing the steps.'

'Yes,' she said. 'My old enemy. My demons. The spectre of the Jab Molassi. I thought I was going to freak out when Giles started using all my trigger words . . . carnival and tribal dancing. And then you transformed it for me. I shall never forget that, ever. How did you know how near I was to bolting?'

'Perhaps it takes a panicker to know one. Since the crash I get them too – different causes from yours, different triggers, but deeply disconcerting and unpleasant. Once I'd have laughed anyone to scorn if they told me I'd ever get panic attacks . . . what *me*?! . . . but now I know they're quite common and the most unlikely people are secretly afflicted by them. I suppose it was the crash that started it but being locked up in prison made it infinitely worse. It's getting better and I can usually stop it happening now. I've learned a lot in the last few years, but it's been a long journey.'

He felt her start to relax. He said: 'Tell me about the second time the old lady rescued you. I thought you never saw her again. When was that – and what did she save you from the next time?'

'Oh,' she answered, 'It wasn't when she was alive – and I suppose you could say she saved me from myself. After my twenty-fifth birthday, when my father was free to inform me about the legacy, he rightly guessed that knowing someone had cared for me enough to do something so unexpected might be just what I needed to help me get myself back on track – and it was. I'll show you the letter she left me sometime. I determined that I'd make something of my life and do something worthwhile with her money. I still don't quite know what or how yet, but yes you're right. I'll be gutted if I can't even locate that house. It's become symbolic. My whole trip to Scotland is a sort of pilgrimage in her honour. Of course we all *know* what pilgrimage means, but I love words and I'm a sucker for exact definitions so I looked it up in the dictionary. The first meaning was the one about a journey to a shrine or sacred place, but the second example said: "a journey or long search made for exalted or sentimental reasons". That's exactly what I feel about looking for my Contessa's childhood home.'

'I'm glad you love words,' he said, inordinately pleased at this evidence of further shared ground. 'I'm a word junkie too.'

'Shall I tell you about another superstition of mine?'

'Go on then.'

'You'll think I'm a nutcase!'

'Try me.'

'Well,' she said, 'the old lady was always doing crosswords and one day she had this dictionary on the table beside her and showed me how to use it. She played a game with me of finding words, inventing meanings and making each other guess – a "true or false?" sort of game. It was great. Then she'd make me put the book away and told me that if I left it open the words might fly off!' Marnie laughed. 'I guess it was pretty clever of her because it made me very careful with books and the habit's stayed with me. If I pick up a book that's been left lying open I still half expect the pages to be blank! How's that for a neurosis?'

'D'you know,' said Christopher, 'you've reminded me of something. When we used to stay with my Scottish grandparents on Mull, there was a 1909 edition of Grimms' Fairy Tales illustrated by Arthur Rackham in the old night nursery. I can still see its red and gold cover, and smell the musty scent of its pages . . . it gives me a shiver of terror even now. Some of the pictures were beautiful but some were incredibly scary. It was fine by day, but as soon as the light was put out I used to imagine that the giants and witches and goblins might escape. I used to keep a torch under my pillow and creep across to the bookcase to check that the book's covers were safely shut and it was tight in the bookcase. I haven't thought about it for years, but . . .' he laughed down at her, 'I can see all the pictures clearly in my mind's eye and do you know, one of the illustrations reminds me of you.'

'Well thanks! Some gnarled old witch, I suppose.'

'Not at all – you're Rackham's goose girl! If you come and stay at my old home I'll have to get hold of it and show you. My mother took the book after my grand-mother died.'

She leaned back against him. 'Better be careful,' she teased, secretly very flattered. 'Release the goose girl and you might let out more than you bargained for.'

'What a pair of shipwrecked mariners we are,' he said, after a bit. 'I'm trying to come to terms with the fact that I took a human life. You're facing the fact that you tried to take your own. Do you think it's just chance that we've washed up on the same shore?'

'I don't know.' Marnie's heart began to thump discon-certingly. 'I suppose it depends if you believe in destiny. What do you think?'

'I don't *know* either. It seems to me that knowledge is a luxury we often have to do without. But I do believe in instinct – my mother's forever telling me I should trust it more – and . . .' He looked down at her, hoping he was right to trust it now.

'And what?'

'And I have this feeling that you and I are meant for each other,' he said, quietly.

They sat in silence. Marnie, afraid that she might spoil the moment by saying the wrong thing, said nothing for so long that Christopher began to fear he'd been too precipitate and frightened her off.

'Have I upset you?' he asked at last. 'I know we've only known each other for a week and that you've been very badly hurt, but I just want you to know how I feel. Perhaps that's selfish, but I promise I'm not going to pressure you, or ask you to make any quick response – let alone a commitment at this stage. Tell me you're not angry with me.'

'*Angry*? How could I be? I think you know I feel the same. But I am very scared by it,' she admitted. 'Scared of being hurt again – scared of hurting you. My record's pretty awful. I find it hard to have faith in anyone and most of all myself. Hard even to trust the idea of happiness. I'm not a good bet for a relationship . . . and I haven't had one since my last disaster.' She turned round in his arms to look up at him. 'This girlfriend with whom you had the blazing row before the crash . . . what's happened to her?'

'She gave me the push when I was sent to prison.'

'And now?'

'Oh well, now that I'm no longer in trouble,' he said, 'she wonders if we should try to get back together again for a bit . . . "just for fun" as she puts it. I've told her there's no way I'd be prepared to do that. I was thinking this morning when we were going round the castle how little she and I have in common now – and how differently I feel about you.'

'And Louisa?' she asked, looking down again, and

pulling herself gently away from him. 'Louisa who's so pretty and amusing and attractive – so socially accomplished – what do you feel about her?'

'Nothing,' he said promptly, and then amended it. 'No, that's not true or fair. I like her very much. I can see she's very attractive and she's all the things you say – but she isn't *you.*'

'She fancies you, though.'

'Perhaps she thinks she does, because, like the rest of us in our different ways, she's come to Scotland searching for something or someone, and I happened to be there, like the classic reason for climbing a mountain. I don't flatter myself that it has much to do with me as a person.' He cocked an eyebrow at her. 'If Stanley or the Colonel had been more her type it might just as well have been either of them.'

She stood up and he was relieved to see the tormented look had gone. 'And you don't think Stanley might have tempted me if only he'd stayed on a bit longer?' she asked, laughing and holding out a hand to pull him up.

'God help you if he had! Now that would be something to be scared about!' He took her in his arms. 'We'll take things as they come – no demands or promises,' he said, 'and meanwhile we've got all of this lovely week ahead of us. Let's enjoy it together. Let's go searching for your house. Let's be light-hearted.'

'Yes,' she said. 'Like you said – we'll travel hopefully.' She gave him one of her sudden, transforming smiles. 'That'll be a new departure for me!'

He took her in his arms and they exchanged a long and highly satisfactory kiss before setting out down the steep and slippery path back to the car park – with wings on their feet.

And despite his words of caution, they both felt that a commitment to the future had been touched on.

Chapter Twenty-one

Drinks were served in the drawing room before dinner on Sunday evening and Giles opened a couple of bottles of champagne to celebrate the start of the visitors' second week at Glendrochatt. On the surface all was convivial but the atmosphere was charged with some very varied emotions.

The Colonel and Morwenna radiated a quiet contentment that spoke of a happy day and a gently ripening relationship, though there was nothing about either of them that demanded particular attention. It was as though a pair of functioning but slightly rusty hinges had been given a lubricating spray with WD40 and were beginning to loosen up.

This was in contrast to Christopher and Marnie. It would have been impossible to miss the current that was flowing between them, to ignore the private looks they exchanged or the way they stood so close to each other, and though Louisa was ashamed to find herself minding so much, she suddenly found it hard to bear. It wasn't that either of them ignored her – far from it. They had both made a point of seeking her out as soon as they returned from Bruar and appeared particularly pleased to see her, but for Louisa, used to being the centre of attention and – in the most charming way – the instigator, rather than the receiver, of acts of social kindness, this only emphasised the situation. It wounded her pride, on top of what she felt to be the rebuff she'd already had from Christopher, and in consequence she seemed distinctly unenthusiastic in response to Marnie's effort to be friendly.

Marnie, eager to share her new-found happiness, and having thought that she and Louisa were on the verge of genuine closeness, longed to tell her all about her day and show her the beautiful book on fortified Scottish houses and their gardens which Christopher had secretly bought for her in the Bruar garden shop while she was buying shoes. She could see that Louisa was on edge and, guessing the reason, was afraid such a gesture on her part would be insensitive, and might even be misinterpreted as deliberate gloating. As a result she automatically withdrew into her old shell, and became spiky as a sea urchin herself. I never know where I am with Louisa, she thought, or is it just me, reading the signals wrong as usual? It's like playing Snakes and Ladders – I land on a square that takes me up a little ladder, then I throw the dice again and – whoosh! – I'm on a great open-mouthed snake and back where I started.

Christopher, seeing Marnie's troubled expression, had directed a coolly critical look in Louisa's direction, which had hurt.

For her part, Louisa felt achingly envious of his obvious solicitude for Marnie, which she knew was unreasonable, since not long ago it had been Adam's protective attitude that she'd found so stifling. She was miserably aware that she was behaving unfairly and ungraciously, but that knowledge didn't help her to snap out of her mood or make her feel any happier. The fact that Isobel had invited Neil Dunbarnock – not Louisa's favourite man – to dinner, in order to make the numbers even, did nothing to soothe her spirits, especially when she found herself seated between him and the Colonel. She felt very much the odd one out – a state that might be familiar to Marnie, but was not one to which Louisa was accustomed. She wondered ruefully if she looked as ruffled as Mr Brown when he was in a huff. If she'd had feathers instead of hair, no doubt they would be standing on end for all to see. She had a choky feeling that she might be going to cry, and for the first time for ages longed for Adam to be with her. Perhaps I'll ring him later, she thought, just for a talk; just to let him know how much I still value him and need to keep in touch even though I don't want to get back together. Then she thought, but I can't ring him just because I want solace and reassurance about another man's lack of interest in me, especially when I'm not prepared to give anything in return.

I'm behaving like a spoilt child, she thought wretchedly. How can I rush to Adam for comfort only to abandon him if the going grows smooth again? She decided to make a real effort with Lord Dunbarnock, for Isobel's sake. She knew Isobel had endured a terrible day and had no wish to add to her difficulties by being a disruptive influence at her dinner party.

After Rory's disastrous reaction to the news of his impending return to his mother, Louisa had decided that the Grant family could do with time to themselves and despite Isobel's insistence that she was more than welcome to stay around had firmly taken herself off for the afternoon. She would have liked to go to the House of Bruar for a spending spree herself, but had no taste for playing gooseberry and the likelihood of running into Christopher and Marnie was too strong. She was normally perfectly happy to go sightseeing or exploring on her own, and had often found it positively enjoyable to get away by herself when she'd been juggling the conflicting priorities of a high-powered job, a demanding boss, a hectic social life and a committed relationship. But it's one thing to choose solitude for temporary escape, quite another to be alone because you feel yourself unwanted. Happy, resilient Louisa, who prided herself on her powers of recuperation and believed passionately in the near-magical benefits to health and well-being of positive thinking, had set off up the hill where she and Marnie had walked on their first day at Glendrochatt, sat on the same rock by the burn, taken the lid off her cauldron of secret fears and longings – and peered inside.

I've got everything going for me, she thought . . . why have I hit such an unexpected down *now*? I set off with such optimism. Where has it disappeared to? I'm free to travel, which I've always wanted to do. I could belatedly explore all those gap-year places I longed to visit but couldn't manage when I was the right age. She reviewed other exciting possibilities: a new job, not perhaps as well paid as her last one, but reflecting her personal interests more – in publishing, say, or the art world? She might do a course on fine art at the V&A and become a lecturer on the Nadfas circuit, something she had considered and been drawn to before. She didn't think an attempt at a novel was a serious option at the moment, though it might remain on the back burner. She had always shied away from thoughts of having babies; for a long time the uncertainty of her future health – now she hoped a thing of the past – had made her afraid to contemplate maternity in case it would eventually be denied her and she'd turned down the chance of marriage and children with Adam, telling herself – and him – that it would be too restricting, too demanding. Yet underneath these ideas for her future was a continuous, steady ticking which she did not want to hear, as the pendulum on her biological clock swung to and fro . . . to and fro . . . with maddening persistence.

Though Isobel and Giles were too conscientious a host and hostess to allow private tensions to make them anything other than attentive to their guests, they were both as taut as fiddle strings themselves. Isobel looked exhausted. Rory had followed her miserably round all afternoon, clutching his beloved rabbit and sucking its one remaining ear till it finally came off in his mouth and Isobel had to administer instant surgery and sew the sad and soggy appendage back on to Rabbit's threadbare pate. She and Giles had both read him a bedtime story, but whereas he usually fell asleep within minutes of his head touching the pillow, this evening she'd finally had to give him a dose of Calpol and then sit with him while he whimpered himself to sleep. To make matters worse she'd been driven to shouting at Edward, who had asked her with the regularity of a clock chiming the quarters why Rory had to go away.

'I'm not going to tell you *again*, Ed,' she'd snapped, more sharply than she intended, anguished for Edward's own puzzled misery at Rory's impending departure. She knew it was from his own rather than Rory's point of view that he was so upset, because Edward had problems identifying with other people's emotions. He found all changes very hard to cope with, and because he also found his anxieties impossible to articulate, he usually drove everyone demented when he was upset. 'I've explained to you a hundred times already. We none of us want him to go, but he has to go back to his mum and that's that – now SHUT UP!' Edward, who had never outgrown the need to suck something himself in times of stress, had stuck his curiously long, misshapen thumb into his mouth and withdrawn into his own world. He sat in front of the television fast-forwarding and replaying a video of *Buffy the Vampire Slayer* without really looking at it, as distant and uncommunicative as if no one else existed.

Amy had come to the rescue. She put her arm round Isobel's shoulders and gave her a hug. She couldn't bear to see her bubbly, laughing mother in such a state of distress.

'Poor old Mum, don't let it get you down. The Fortescues have asked me to supper this evening because Emily's home this weekend and one of the boys is going to collect me. Why don't I suggest they come early and we all go to a film and take Ed too? It'd take his mind off Rory and get him out of your hair for a bit. You know how he loves going to them.' Emily's family were particular friends of all the Grants' and lived a few miles away, the other side of Blairalder.

'Oh, darling, that would be wonderful,' said Isobel gratefully. 'You're a star. What a horrid end to your weekend this is proving to be. I'm so sorry. There has to be some solution and I don't intend to let Aunt Lorna get away with all the misery and havoc she's causing – but if we put ourselves legally in the wrong by not returning Rory now, it could make things much more difficult in the future. I expect that powerful senator husband of hers, who's a lawyer anyway, would chew us up for breakfast and then spit us out again.'

After dinner, Giles outlined arrangements for the week. The following day, he would escort them all to Edinburgh himself, where he had laid on specially conducted tours of the National Gallery and Holyrood Palace, lunch at Duck's at Le Marché Noir followed by a visit to the castle and a tour of some of Giles's own favourite small galleries and little streets. On Tuesday Isobel would take them for the planned private visit to Evelyn Fergusson's house and garden, which Giles thought would be of special interest to both Morwenna and Marnie. 'I have hopes that we may find some clues for Marnie in her search for her missing castle and I know Morwenna's going to be fascinated by the garden, but I think John and Christopher and Louisa will all find something to enjoy too.'

Other events he'd planned were an expedition to Glamis including a tour round the castle and lunch afterwards in the castle restaurant; there could be a trip round a whisky distillery or a visit to a sporran-maker; one day, weather permitting, they might go for an expedition up Glen Tilt and picnic by the river. The programme could be flexible, he said, and there would be opportunities to cater for individual requests if they arose. Might anyone like a day's fishing? The Colonel was not a fisherman, but Christopher said he'd jump at the chance if it were on offer. 'Only I'd have to borrow the kit from someone because I never thought of bringing my rod or anything with me.' Giles said that would be no problem and he'd see what he could do. 'You can borrow my rod and waders. You may be an inch or so taller, but we must be much the same size.'

The wonderful weather which had helped to make the first week at Glendrochatt so delightful deserted them and Monday dawned dull and chilly, with outbursts of drizzle – not a good day for scenic routes, said Giles cheerfully as he organised everyone on to the minibus, so isn't it lucky we've chosen to go to Edinburgh today? What could be more enjoyable, he asked, than a visit to an art gallery on such a grey day, to see the Reverend Robert Walker, as depicted by Sir Henry Raeburn, elegantly skating on the loch – an isolated figure in his clerical black and neat little bladed shoes, but with something saucy about the angle of his hat that made you wonder what unacknowledged passions might lurk beneath his trim exterior; what better chance to study Titian's *Diana and Actaeon* or walk round Canova's *Three Graces* as they indulged in a schoolgirly group hug?

While he discoursed so enthusiastically on the delights of Edinburgh, Giles's mind was also running on schemes about Rory. The more he saw of his newly discovered son, the more he loved him, and the more he loved him the more he wanted to keep him and bring him up in his own old childhood home. What he most emphatically did not want was to have direct dealings with his predatory sister-in-law. He was enormously touched by his wife's generosity towards the child. How could he convince her that she had no need to feel jealous of her sister? He knew he would never be personally tempted by Lorna again, but he also knew how scheming, ruthless and devious she could be. If she were to agree to let them see more of Rory, would that open the way for her to cause more trouble in their lives? He didn't know, but it brought him out in a cold sweat to think of it.

Though Giles gave no outward indication of the inner turmoil he felt about Rory's departure or his anxiety over Isobel's unhappiness, Louisa, who knew how bothered he was, admired the way he managed to give the impression that a trip with his guests to 'the Windy City' on a wet day was what he wanted to do above anything else. Perhaps she should make an effort to mend her fences with Marnie, whose offhand 'Good morning' nod and folded-in expression spoke of wounded feelings? Hmm, thought Louisa to herself, her dark mood persisting like fog. I'll see.

Six local members of the Friends of Glendrochatt were joining them for the day, lured by the excellent guides Giles always managed to lay on to lecture at each of the venues, since one of the perks of membership of the Friends was the opportunity to partake in events organised by the arts centre. Amy had decided to come along too, go round the National Gallery with them, and then peel off at lunchtime to meet a friend, before catching her train back to London. Isobel was going to put Edward on his bus in Perth before taking Rory and Sheena to the airport. She was dreading her day.

It was after six o'clock when the minibus got back to Glendrochatt after a highly successful day. Fired by Giles's knowledge and enthusiasm, Marnie, the Colonel and Morwenna professed themselves in love with Edinburgh and both Christopher and Louisa said they had learned more about the city in one day with Giles than on various longer visits over the years.

The only trouble in an otherwise smooth-running day had been the slight but perceptible undercurrent of tension between Louisa and Marnie. As Giles put it, after he and Isobel had escaped to the privacy of the old nursery and he'd brought her a glass of wine and given himself a glass of whisky, Louisa had been 'as nice as nuts' all day to Christopher, the Colonel and Morwenna, but distant and frosty with Marnie, who in turn had looked first agonised and then huffy.

'They nearly succeeded in spoiling the atmosphere. I wanted to shake them both,' he complained, 'but thank God they thawed a bit as the day went on.'

'Oh dear, I wish Louisa wasn't making it so plain that she minds that Christopher and Marnie are so obviously falling for each other.' Isobel looked distressed. 'It isn't as if Marnie had pinched him from her. I don't quite know what to do. I don't think Louisa's at all happy at the moment. The trouble is that I don't think she knows what she wants herself. I've never seen her like this. Under all the froth I feel she's at a crisis point.'

Giles shook his head at her. 'You can't always sort everybody's lives out for them, darling,' he said. 'Much more important, tell me how it all went for you. Did Ed go off on the bus without a drama, and how was the parting with Rory? You look whacked.'

'Well,' said Isobel, curling up on the sofa. 'Ed was fine. Full of endless questions about Rory and when he'll be coming back – but no problems about the bus. I rang Agnes and Karl at Ed's house to warn them that he might be a bit unsettled and asked them to keep an extra eye on him, but oh, Giles – Rory was *pathetic* . . . so white and silent and clingy. Just before the flight was called he said he felt sick. Thank goodness Sheena is with him. But . . .' said Isobel, 'I spoke to Lorna from the airport. I rang the Ritz to leave a message to say he was actually on the flight and I was put straight through to her.'

'That was a turn up for the books.'

'Wasn't it just!'

'And?'

'And I expected she'd be either provocative or aggressive – but she sounded sort of guarded.'

'What about?'

'I don't quite know . . . she was *almost* conciliatory. Said how grateful she and Brooke were to us, and how wonderful we'd been to see them out of a difficulty. A really sisterly thing to have done – blah, blah, blah. Sisterly, for God's sake! Very unlike Lorna. I have a hunch that Brooke was in the room with her and the performance was all for his benefit. I nearly asked her some very direct questions, but the airport didn't seem the best place for a confrontation. I do wonder what Brooke thinks about Rory? Anyway, I made her promise she'd ring tonight to let us know he's all right.' She looked at Giles. 'She must want something,' she said. 'There's always a hidden agenda with Lorna.'

They looked at each other with foreboding.

Chapter Twenty-two

'Don't forget to bring your photographs and any other clues about the Contessa's family,' Isobel reminded Marnie before they all piled into the Land Rover the next morning. 'I do trust you're not in for a disappointment, but I'm very much hoping that my cousin Evie may have some ideas for you to follow up.'

Giles had meetings all day in Perth, so it had been decided that Isobel should drive the five visitors over to Evelyn Fergusson's house and garden, taking the slower but more scenic route to Tillydrum, stopping on the way to visit Auchterlonie & Sons, the still family owned sporran-makers at Craigdennie. Giles wanted Isobel to pick up a sporran which he was having made for a godson's eighteenth birthday present, and the workshop, now run by Miss Auchterlonie, great-granddaughter of the founder of the firm, was an unusual and interesting place to take visitors. They could then have an early pub lunch at the excellent little Craigdennie Hotel before arriving at Evelyn's in the afternoon, where they would certainly be regaled with a spectacular tea.

Isobel had had two telephone calls from London the night before. The first was from Lorna's secretary to say that Mrs Congleton had asked her to inform Mrs Grant that Rory had arrived safely, was naturally a little 'overdone' by all the excitement of returning home but was perfectly all right; she would be in touch again before the family flew back to the States in a fortnight's time, and

Mrs Congleton particularly wished to renew the senator's and her thanks to her sister for having Rory to stay. Though Isobel's heart always sank at the sound of Lorna's voice, she couldn't help feeling outraged that her sister had once again managed to avoid speaking to her personally.

The second call was from a very indignant Sheena, ringing from her aunt's house in Twickenham. There had been a chauffeur-driven car to meet them at the airport, Sheena said, but no sign of Lorna herself until they arrived at the Ritz. The reunion between mother, son and stepfather had taken place in the Congletons' private suite. Lorna had opened her arms dramatically but Rory had failed to fly into them. Lorna had clearly been very put out and Sheena got the feeling that she had wanted to impress her husband with a touching tableau of a maternal reunion with a beloved child but that the scene had not gone according to plan. A huge pile of presents on the sofa had eventually got Rory thoroughly over-excited and silly, reported Sheena disapprovingly, but not *happy*, and when, shortly after their arrival, the smartly uniformed temporary nanny turned up Sheena thought she looked more like a gleaming bathroom tile than a warm human being with a love of children. 'No lap,' she told Isobel. 'Poor wee mite – he might as well cuddle up to an ironing board.' Sheena herself had an ample lap – indeed she was ample all over, spilling over like a cornucopia. Isobel couldn't help wondering what sort of sartorial impression her extremely tight jeans, snug-fitting lime-green stretch T-shirt, silver nose stud and magenta-streaked hair would have created on the senator. Warm hearts were possibly not high on his list of priorities. When Sheena had discovered that Lorna and her husband were going out to dinner that night and that Rory would be left alone with a strange nanny in a grand hotel, she had offered to ditch her own plans for the evening, help put Rory to bed and stay till he was asleep – an offer which was firmly turned down. 'I felt like a traitor when I left him,' she told Isobel. 'He was like so reproachful and I don't think he'll ever trust me again. He goes "Don't go, don't go" and your sister looks furious and that senator or whatever he calls himself made me feel like he'd got something nasty on his shoe.'

'What was he like?' asked Isobel curiously.

'Who was that bloke with a flowery name we learned about in Primary – one who kept looking at himself in a pond?'

'Narcissus?'

'That's him. Well the senator kept peering at himself in this great gold mirror on the wall and smoothing down his silver hair on either side of his head as though he liked the feel of it. I'll bet he's never gone tatty-picking or wrung a chicken's neck.' Sheena sounded scornful. 'You can tell he fancies himself rotten but he'd never get me to vote for him. My dad would say he was a real nancy boy. Rory'd be better off with a jelly piece for a stepfather!'

'Well, I can't thank you enough for taking Rory down.' Isobel couldn't help laughing but her heart sank for the small boy who had twined himself round her heartstrings. 'How Rory must have hated seeing you leave! I hope he doesn't have one of his nightmares tonight.'

Altogether Isobel had a lot on her mind as she drove down the drive at Glendrochatt, but she determined to put her worries on hold and give her visitors as entertaining a day as possible.

The sporran-maker, Judith Auchterlonie, was an unlikely-looking proprietor for a long-established family firm in the Highlands. Marnie had imagined a little, stooped, white-haired man with a leather apron and gold-rimmed spectacles, like an illustration of a cobbler in an old children's book, but the figure who greeted them was a sensational blonde with a figure like Marilyn Monroe's, immaculate make-up and an extremely short skirt. When they arrived she was at the front of her house taking delivery of a dead badger that had been run over on the road, but she looked as if she would have been equally at home taming tigers, taking to the high wire in a circus or receiving an Oscar in a Versace dress.

She greeted Isobel affectionately. 'I have the sporran all ready for you. I think Giles will be pleased with it,' she said. 'Please take your friends on through to the workshop and I'll be with you in a moment.'

The walls of the lean-to shed behind her house were lined with signed photographs of kilted male members of the royal family, bagpipe-playing sergeants of Scottish regiments in full ceremonial dress and various celebrity film stars of Scottish descent; there were pinned up newspaper cuttings of teams of dancers competing at Highland Games and a picture of Miss Auchterlonie herself, wearing an eye-catching hat, shaking hands with the Queen at a Holyrood garden party.

'You've obviously danced reels before, Christopher. Do you have all this regalia?' asked Morwenna.

'I have indeed – though I haven't worn my kilt for a few years now. Not much opportunity recently and it was a bit strained round the middle last time I wore it – too many City lunches,' confessed Christopher and added with a grin: 'I could probably get into it again now – eighteen months in prison is a great slimming aid, though not one I'd recommend. My sporran is an otter's head – a bit old and moth-eaten, but then it did belong to my great-grandfather. Otters weren't an endangered species in his day.'

'I'm rather relieved we haven't still got Bunty with us,' said Isobel, laughing. 'Despite her idealised view of all things Scottish I'm not sure she'd cope with snarling fox and badger masks. I bet she clings to an anthropomorphic view of otters in velvet coats with lace collars as in *Little Grey Rabbit* or Mr Badger in carpet slippers handing out wise advice in *The Wind in the Willows*.'

Miss Auchterlonie proved to be an entertaining guide to her esoteric trade as she showed them examples of the range of hand-made sporrans she and her two sons could produce – from glamorous tasselled regimental ones for the Black Watch to synthetic creations in psychedelic colours to appeal to a less traditionally minded younger generation. Christopher told her he thought his great-grandfather would spin in his grave at the idea of a fluorescent pink sporran.

'Och well – we have to move with the times,' she said tolerantly. There were drawers full of samples of the different types of leather, horsehair and fur that could be used.

'Bring me your granny's old mink tippet and I'll make you a sporran out of it,' she joked, and then explained about cantles – the metal D shape at the top of the purse which could be either something really simple or highly ornate engraved silver: a Celtic rune, a family crest, a Masonic symbol. Auchterlonies, she told them proudly, could produce sporrans for anyone and any occasion and a lot of their orders, she said smiling at Marnie, came from Americans.

The sporran they had made for Giles's godson was a very elegant affair – silver-mounted white horsehair with black tassels which was much admired by everyone.

'That's brilliant,' said Isobel. 'Giles will be delighted with it. Now we mustn't take up any more of your time. Thank you so much for letting us come.'

Tillydrum, where Evelyn Fergusson lived, was a large,

stone Victorian house, impressive rather than beautiful, at the top of a long wooded drive carpeted with bluebells. Isobel turned the dogs out of the back of the Land Rover after they'd crossed the cattle grid at the bottom and let them run after it, Flapper tearing along with lolloping ease and portly Lozenge puffing gallantly along behind.

A stocky figure in corduroys and a green sweatshirt with *Tillydrum Gardens* printed on it was standing on the steps as they drove up to the front door.

'Hi, Hamish. Lovely to see you again,' said Isobel, climbing out of the car. 'I know you're going to give my visitors a wonderful tour. This time I've brought a real expert to appreciate your garden. Meet Mrs Gilbert who writes a gardening column and lives in Cornwall – and this is Colonel Smithson, and my cousin Louisa Forrester, and Christopher Piper who tells me his mother is a great gardener too, and finally Marnie Donovan who's come from the States. How's Miss Fergusson?'

'Not too brilliant.' Hamish shook his head sadly after shaking hands with everyone with bone-crunching enthusiasm. 'She can't get about as she'd like and that's verra, verra frustrating for her. She's got this electric buggy which helps, but . . .' he gave a chuckle, 'I reckon it's really intended for pavements and such, and it gets some rough treatment here, I can tell you. She got it bogged down in the dell the other week and it was pure luck I found her when I did, because of course she didn't have her call-aid on her, did she?' Hamish sounded like a doting parent talking about a talented but wayward child. 'She asked if you'd go straight on in to her, Isobel – she'll be in the library – and we'll set off from here and join you later.'

Isobel waved her visitors off, put the dogs back in the car and went into the house.

Strong men had been known to go to bed in their

shooting stockings when staying at Tillydrum in the winter and even in May, after an unusually hot spell of weather, the stone-flagged hall with its mock-Jacobean panelling and balding tiger-skin rugs struck chill. Though Evelyn Fergusson's father – known locally as Sweetie Fergusson because his family fortune had been founded on the confectionary industry – had been a generous benefactor to many good causes, he was notorious for his parsimonious ways on the home front. Isobel's own father had been full of stories of breaking ice on the drinking water in freezing bedrooms in his boyhood, when staying with his wealthy but penny-pinching uncle. Evelyn, who had lived in the house all her life and was inured to its rigours, could well have been described as a hardy perennial – her short, springy hair resembled a snow-covered tussock of couch grass and the network of fine broken veins on her pleasantly weather-beaten face looked like the root system of a small but vigorous plant. Old family photographs showed her to have been extremely pretty in her youth and some hint of former beauty remained like a distant echo, though arthritis had taken its toll and steroids had given her face a telltale hamsterish look.

Isobel found her in the comfortable, cluttered library, a room with few concessions to conventional ideas of interior decoration, but a fine example of what the French like to refer to as *le désordre Britannique*. Piles of books and magazines, leaning drunkenly like the Tower of Pisa at gravity-defying angles, were an obstacle course that needed to be carefully navigated. Evelyn was sitting in an electronically operated chair upholstered in a hideous dung-coloured stretch material, surrounded by gardening catalogues, her ancient West Highland terrier, Jock, stretched out on the rug beside her. Isobel gave him a wide berth as she went to greet her elderly cousin – Jock's temper was untrustworthy at the best of times and particularly uncertain if he was suddenly roused from sleep. His wiry, theoretically white coat had acquired a yellowish tinge with age as though he'd long been addicted to nicotine and he wheezed as he slept like a pair of leaky bellows. An old Meissen chamber pot containing a bottle of Dettox spray was kept permanently on a window seat to cope with his unfortunate tendency to be sick on the carpet without warning. Jock was an inescapable hazard of visits to Evelyn.

'Izzy! How lovely! Forgive me if I don't get up. This marvellous new contraption ejects me like a cartridge if I push the right button but I'm still a little wary of pressing it too hard. I'll save it up for later when Hamish brings your group back, then he can field me if I get catapulted across the room.'

Isobel stooped to kiss the mottled cheek. 'It's so good of you to let them come, Evie. I know Hamish will give them a marvellous afternoon but oh, how I wish you could go out with them too! Tell me how you really are? How's the pain?'

'Oh, not too bad – it varies a bit. Luckily I'm almost entirely synthetic anyway. Not much of the original frame left now, but thank God for all these wonderful spare parts. I'm hoping they're going to redo my right knee again soon. Put another log on the fire, darling, and then make yourself comfortable.'

Isobel perched on the wide club-fender. 'If I was dropped into this room blindfold, I'd always know exactly where I was,' she said, closing her eyes and sniffing. 'Azaleas and daffodils and wood-smoke; leather and old books and your special potpourri. It brings my childhood straight back – me lying under the piano sucking your treacle toffee and reading *Lorna Doone* and *Jock of the Bushveldt* and half listening to you and Pa arguing about everything under the sun after Sunday lunch.'

'When you get old, people suddenly start agreeing with you – to your face anyway. It's very dull. I do miss your father,' said Evelyn, 'and not just for the arguments.'

'Oh, so do I! Whenever something funny happens I still want to ring him up and tell him. I miss Mum too, of course, but Pa was my guiding star . . . my yardstick.' She looked at the old lady. 'I badly want his advice right now,' she said, 'and for the first time in my life he isn't there when I need him.'

'Ah.' Evelyn Fergusson shot her a piercing look. 'It's partly about your father that I want to talk to you.'

'What's the other part?'

'The other part is about Lorna.'

'I rather thought it might be.' Isobel picked up the heavy brass poker and jammed its point into one of the big logs in the grate, sending an army of sparks marching up the chimney. 'Did you know that Giles and I've had Lorna's son, Rory, staying with us?' she asked.

'Yes.' Evelyn gave a snort of laughter. 'Hamish's wife had it from their daughter-in-law, who had it from Janet MacDonald's daughter whom they'd met at the tup sales – I think the little boys played together when Janet had her grandson staying. So the bush telegraph is in good working order, you see.'

'And? I think you know something about Rory, Evie.'

'How much do you know yourself?' countered Evelyn.

'I know he's Giles's son and that's enough of a problem to be going on with.' Isobel looked at the old lady to see if this came as a shock to her, but she remained inscrutable.

'Did Lorna tell you that herself?' she asked.

'Not in so many words. She very definitely hinted at it but I think she's enjoying a game of cat and mouse with me. But I *know*.' Isobel stabbed the fire again. 'He's the living spit of Giles, for one thing,' she said. 'But I still had to be sure.' She looked up rather defiantly, Evelyn thought, as though expecting disapproval. 'I've had a DNA test done,' she said. 'Two, actually, to be on the safe side. It's very easy at the moment, but I discovered that the law's going to change soon, and it'll require the mother's consent in the future, so I thought I'd get in quick while it's still possible.' She shrugged her shoulders. 'The results have just come through. Of course they matched. I knew they would.'

'And have you told Lorna that you've done this? Have you actually told Giles?'

'I haven't told Lorna. I've told Giles the result, though I know I should have asked him first before getting it done. He had every right to be cross with me for not telling him sooner,' she admitted. 'But actually I think it was a relief to him because he was as certain about it as I was from the moment we clapped eyes on Rory. We both needed confirmation – it could be important. When we first heard Lorna was pregnant, Giles went to see her to tackle her about it, because . . .' Isobel paused and said painfully, 'because we knew from the dates that it had to be a possibility that the baby might be his. I can't tell you how difficult I found that. I was convinced that Lorna would make all the capital she could out of the situation just when we'd got our marriage back on track, but then, astonishingly, she denied to Giles that the baby was his. And then, to our huge relief, she went back to South Africa. I don't think we were either of us really convinced by what she said,' she added honestly, 'but it suited us to go along with it. When we heard from my parents that the baby had arrived, very early for the dates, we let ourselves accept the story Lorna put out, and hoped that he could – just conceivably – be the child of her first husband before she'd come back to Scotland. It's amazing,' she added ironically, 'what you can make yourself swallow if you want to believe something badly enough.'

'And now?'

'Now Lorna's sent for Rory to go back to her. And instead of feeling relieved, I'm miserable. It was awful. He's clearly terrified of her and he begged to stay with us. Shocking really, and you won't believe this, Evie – I can hardly believe it myself – but after being so upset to think he was Giles's son and not mine, when it came to it I could hardly bear to let him go. What a mess! Five years ago Lorna nearly succeeds in wrecking our marriage. Then against all the odds she takes herself off the scene. Now it seems she's back in trouble-making mode again, though I don't know what she's after this time, but it suddenly occurred to me the other day that this had all started up again since Pa's death and there had to be a connection. You and Pa were always very close and Lorna is your goddaughter . . . am I right in thinking he told you something?'

'Yes,' said Evelyn. 'Your father was always afraid that if anything happened to him Lorna would get up to her old tricks again and try to make life difficult for you and he wanted someone else to know what he'd agreed with her. It's very sad, because Lorna has got so much, if only she'd let herself enjoy it: talent and looks and now a child and a rich second husband. But nothing is ever enough for her. She was always a deeply jealous little girl – her own worst enemy – and she's grown up into a jealous woman who's capable of being extremely vindictive. Over the years I think your father's managed to act as a brake on some of her more exaggerated behaviour, because she was always a bit afraid of him, but the tragedy is that she makes herself as unhappy as she makes other people. She certainly told your parents that the baby was probably Giles's and made no secret of the fact that she intended to cause the maximum disruption for you both. But Lorna's always been extremely acquisitive and your father struck a deal with her. If she withdrew from Scotland and promised not to press any claim on Giles he would guarantee to support her and the baby and would leave her the property in France, which I gather was originally to have been shared between you, and which she coveted so much. But he also told her that if she caused any more upsets he would cut her out of his will entirely.'

'I have to admit I was secretly a bit hurt to discover that Le Colombier was left entirely to Lorna – not just for myself but because the children always adored going there so much. We all did. Giles pointed out to me that Lorna and I could never have shared it successfully – but why didn't Pa tell me any of this?' asked Isobel. 'I'd have understood if he'd explained.'

'How could he? He got a promise out of Lorna that she wouldn't name Giles as the father of her baby, but he had to give a similar promise of silence to her. Your father's whole object was to stop you being hurt. Before the child arrived I don't think your parents were convinced it really was Giles's baby either, and they didn't think Lorna was that sure herself – it could have been spite or wishful thinking. But I gather that from the moment they first saw the child there was no doubt in their minds – or Lorna's either.' Evelyn shook her head sadly. 'Your parents hoped that once she had a baby of her own – something she'd apparently always been desperate for – Lorna would become an easier, happier person.' She sighed. 'It's a tragedy it didn't happen that way. As you know, your mother went out to South Africa for the birth, but from the day he was born Lorna couldn't cope with the baby at all – could hardly bear to look at him, let alone touch him. It does happen occasionally, of course, but whether it was aggravated by the fact that he was premature and spent the first week in an incubator, whether it was triggered by post-natal depression, or whether it's just how Lorna is, we'll never know. The point is she obviously didn't bond with the baby and in the early days your mother was at her wits' end. I know it's a terrible thing to say, but I'm not sure Lorna's capable of real love. Even when she was little, I always felt there was something . . . missing.'

There was silence in the room except for the wheezing of the dog and the hissing of the fire. Then Evelyn said briskly: 'So what do you hope will happen now? Do you want to see the child again? What does Giles feel?' She thought Isobel looked anguished.

'The thing is, it's hard for Giles because he's afraid of hurting me if he shows his affection too much – afraid of underlining the contrast between Edward and Rory.' Isobel twisted her wedding ring round and round. 'When he first arrived I could hardly bear his likeness to Giles – his physical perfection, so unlike Ed. It was torture, but I told myself I must do my best for him for the sake of my mother, who'd more or less brought him up until she was too ill to cope. She always tried – not very successfully – to avoid talking about him in front of me.' Isobel pulled a face. 'Poor Mum. She was never much good at hiding her feelings.'

'That was always part of her charm and warmth,' said Evelyn. 'And you're right. She adored that child – and your father did too. But where does all this leave you?'

'Rory got under my skin – it's as simple as that. I started by being dutiful in a rather martyred, self-righteous way and I gave Giles a hard time. I'm not proud of myself. Then I started to love Rory for himself – really love him. It just sort of happened, and of course that changed things . . . and then something else happened this weekend which altered everything.' Isobel told Evelyn about Amy's reaction. 'We had no idea she knew, though I suppose we might have guessed. Children always pick up more than anyone thinks when grown-ups try to hide something from them and Amy and her music were very involved with Lorna's power struggles that summer. But it wasn't only that. She couldn't bear the idea of us sending Rory back to Lorna either – and that opens up a new set of possibilities.'

'You want to adopt him? Is that it? Even if Lorna agreed, could you really cope with that?'

'I don't know about *adopt* . . . we hadn't got that far. But yes, we'd like us to get joint custody and try to give him the security he so badly needs, a normal life. Of course we wouldn't want to cut him off from Lorna completely . . . well *I* might *want* it,' she amended, honestly, 'but I think that would be wrong. I'd like him to be *based* with us and I hope I could manage my feelings about Giles and Lorna better now. I think our marriage is stronger than it was when Lorna had a go at wrecking it five years ago. Giles promises me he doesn't feel a thing for Lorna and it gave us both a terrible fright: shook our priorities up – perhaps we even *needed* that fright; perhaps we'd got a bit complaisant – but I believe we could do this together now. Louisa said something interesting to me the other day: she pointed out that even though Rory isn't my child, he still has most of the same genes that my children have, has just as much of Pa and Mum in him as they do. I found that a very helpful new way of looking at things – but even so I wouldn't be contemplating this if he hadn't climbed inside my heart.' Isobel spoke jerkily but with great intensity and Evelyn had no doubt that she meant what she said. All the same, she thought there could be many pitfalls ahead, and she trembled for the whole family.

'The snag is,' Isobel went on, 'that I've no idea what Lorna really wants. Did she send Rory over just to upset our marriage, or did she secretly gamble that Giles would want to keep him because there's actually no place for him in her present life? One thing's certain, though. If she thinks *I* actually want him, she'll keep him out of spite. I don't know how to approach her at all.'

'Ah. Well, I might be able to help you over that. I know from your father that Lorna told her senator that Rory was the child of her ex-husband. He has the highest political ambitions and an illegitimate stepson – especially involving scandal with a sister's husband – would not be at all acceptable. I know this because Lorna wrote to your father when she got engaged to Brooke Congleton and told him so. She said it was very important any "uncertainty", as she put it, about Rory's paternity should not come out.' Evelyn looked at Isobel over the top of her glasses. 'I have that letter,' she said. 'Your father sent it to me just before he died.'

'Evie! Are you suggesting I should blackmail Lorna?'

'I'm not suggesting anything,' said Evelyn firmly. 'I'm just telling you something you might find it useful to know. What use you put the information to is entirely a matter for you and Giles. But think very carefully, Izzy. A lot depends on Giles. He needs to want this too, as much as you do and for the same reasons. And you have to accept that *if* he wants it, then you mustn't become resentful *because* he does. It won't be just one big altruistic gesture that gives you a satisfying virtue rush and then goes away. It'll be every day for all of you. That might be more difficult than you're prepared for, and if you make a mess of it Lorna will have put something over on you – and the child will be the loser.'

Isobel looked at her with troubled eyes. 'I know, I know,' she said. 'That's why I need advice. What do *you* think we should do? What do you think Pa would say?'

But Evelyn Fergusson was not to be drawn. 'God knows what Lorna may do or what her motives are, but I think your father would say that only two people can make *your* particular decision. I'm not one of them – and nor is he. I also think Hamish will be back very shortly with your group. Perhaps you'd go through to the kitchen and ask Mrs Cameron to put the kettle on so that we can have tea as soon as they come in. And could you bring me a glass of water when you come back, darling – I think I'll take one of my pills before they arrive so I can walk to the dining room without looking too much like an old crock, but I shall get you to show them round the house. I'm very much looking forward to meeting them all.'

And Isobel knew that, at any rate for the time being, she had got as much out of the old lady as Evelyn was prepared to disclose.

Chapter Twenty-three

Everyone enjoyed the garden tour. Hamish was not only extremely knowledgeable about gardening in general, but knew every plant at Tillydrum so that he seemed to be talking about intimate friends. He possessed the gift of being able to transmit his own passion for his subject to a mixed audience and make it as enjoyable and accessible to the uninitiated as to fellow enthusiasts. He had a fund of stories about the hazards and rewards of opening to the public, a store of entertaining anecdotes about the eccentricities of his forceful employer, whom he clearly adored, and a racy way with words that kept them all amused. Every plant and tree was clearly labelled, though he pointed out a few notices, beside blank spaces in various parts of the garden, which bore the sad legend: THIS RARE PLANT WAS REMOVED BY A VISITOR.

For Morwenna the afternoon was the highlight of the most enjoyable ten days she had spent in years, and when Hamish, impressed with her knowledge and obvious enjoyment of the garden, asked if she might consider doing an article on the Tillydrum gardens for a Scottish paper and said he'd like to suggest it to Miss Fergusson, she was overcome with pleasure. Somehow Catherine had managed to instil in her a new confidence about her journalistic abilities and suggest ways in which she might become a little more adventurous in her writing and give rein to her sense of humour. Perhaps she could do a series of articles on Scottish gardens? Perhaps she should try to send copy out to editors of other journals as well as her local magazine?

The Colonel watched her pleasure with quiet satisfaction. Under his conventional appearance the pilot light of a romantic nature flickered. Devotion to Queen and country, family values, loyalty, idealistic views about service, liking for order and tradition: these old-fashioned attributes were on the surface for all to see – though none the less genuine for that – but less obvious qualities including an eye for the beautiful, a dry sense of the ridiculous and a capacity for love were there for the discerning to discover. The great silver beech trees of Tillydrum, through which sunlight filtered on to moss, bluebells, wood anemones and a few remaining primroses, made a kaleidoscope of purple, green and gold which made him think of the graceful fan-vaulting and richly coloured stained glass of York Minster, where his father-in-law had been a canon, and where he'd exchanged vows with the wisp of a girl he'd adored. She'd followed him round the world, given him two children and been not only the perfect wife for a commanding officer, but his best friend. John Smithson had been devastated by her death in a car crash only a year after his retirement from the army. It had seemed very bitter that after moving house and uprooting her possessions so often, she had only been able to enjoy her first real home in thirty years of marriage for so short a time. After her death, he'd got on with his life in the only way he knew – uncomplainingly, but her absence left an aching void. Plenty of women, paid up members of the casserole army who specialise in hunting widowers, had tried to woo him with tasty dishes, but he'd never been tempted – until now. This unassuming woman with no guile or pretensions to glamour, who thought so little of her own talents but who was such an enjoyable companion, made him wonder if something unlooked for and marvellous was about to happen to them both. Even as the thought occurred to him, she glanced in his direction and they exchanged a moment of shared happiness – something that hadn't happened to either of them for a long time.

Louisa saw the look and felt like crying. It was one thing to envy Marnie the attentions of the glamorous Christopher, but that the unaccustomed feeling of isolation and bleakness which kept blowing through her like an icy wind could be triggered by such a pair of old stooges – nice old stooges, thought Louisa, but stooges all the same – as the Colonel and Morwenna left her baffled and disturbed. What is the matter with me? she wondered. Isobel had asked her much the same question the previous evening when they'd had a pre-bedtime drink in the kitchen together, and Louisa had enquired how Rory's departure had gone.

'Thanks for listening,' Isobel had said when she'd brought Louisa up to date. She felt better for pouring out all her anxieties and conflicting emotions to someone who knew the cast of characters concerned in the drama but was not immediately involved. 'I'm afraid I'm turning into a real bore on the subject,' she apologised, 'but it's so hard not to be obsessed about the whole Lorna thing at the moment. I have to ask myself awkward questions like whether a possible fight over Rory is as much about me wanting to hit back at Lorna as about his welfare. I know it's not *only* that, but I can't pretend it wouldn't give me a lot of satisfaction to have a battle with Lorna – and win.'

'You're so honest, Izzy. But anyone could see how that little boy adored you and treated you like his surrogate mum, and that has to be a two-way thing. It wouldn't have happened if you hadn't loved him too. If we only took action when our motives were entirely altruistic most of us would never take any action at all. Oh dear. Why does life have to be so bloody difficult?'

Isobel had given her a concerned look. She thought it was very unlike cheerful, optimistic Louisa to say such a thing. 'Enough about me – what about *you*?' she asked.

'Me? I'm fine.'

'I so wanted you to enjoy Glendrochatt – it's such a treat for us to have you here – but I don't feel we're making you very happy.'

'Of course you are! Everything here is wonderful,' said Louisa brightly – too brightly – not meeting Isobel's eye.

'But you came in search of something extra when you signed on for the course . . . not to do with the actual writing, I mean . . . more a change of direction . . . a new goal in life . . . some fulfilment,' persisted Isobel. 'Don't deny it because you told me so yourself. Not surprising after all you've been through and the break with Adam, but I know you haven't found whatever it is you need yet. Giles was worried about you yesterday. He says you were as brittle as a bit of broken glass and so edgy with Marnie. I know she got off to a bad start with you and me, but I thought you'd really come round to her – as I have. Don't tell me it's entirely about Christopher because I wouldn't believe you. I know we joked that he's the answer to any maiden's prayer – but I think he's more like a red herring as far as you're concerned. What's wrong, Louisa?'

But Louisa was unable to say because she wasn't entirely sure herself. All the same Isobel's words gave her a jolt – when they'd set out for Edinburgh she'd had every intention of being friendly to Marnie and she couldn't say herself what demon had prompted her to be so disagreeable. Before they set out for Tillydrum she sought her out.

'Sorry I was a bit of a cow yesterday,' she said abruptly. Marnie didn't pretend to misunderstand, but appreciated the effort it must have cost Louisa to apologise.

'Thanks,' she said simply. 'Forget it. God knows I lash out at whoever's nearest when I feel at odds with the world. Not for nothing did my younger brothers call me Miss Grump – but then I've always been prone to the black dog.' She raised an eyebrow at Louisa. 'It doesn't make it feel any better while it lasts, but at least it's recognisable – an old enemy – but I guess it's not usual for you feel like that?'

'No,' Louisa pulled a wry face. 'I'm often pig-headed and occasionally sharp-tongued – so I'm told! I've sometimes been very scared – with good cause – but I've never been given to the glooms for no reason. I've always had faith that everything would turn out all right and felt good about myself. I've never felt low and on edge the way I do at the moment. Anyway, I'm really sorry. I'll try not to be such a killjoy today.'

It's weird, she thought: it's almost as if Marnie and I have swapped roles. She's discovered the knack of being happy and I've lost it. She put on a show of being her bright and breezy self and appeared to be the life and soul of the party at lunch.

But Isobel, though grateful and relieved that the tension Giles had complained of the day before was absent, was not deceived by the glitter of false tinsel in which Louisa wrapped herself.

Tea, as Isobel had promised, was a splendid affair with tiny sandwiches and a huge fruitcake; there was ginger parkin and Mrs Cameron's special caramel shortbread, which Isobel remembered from childhood days, and plates of melting drop-scones with a choice of either crabapple jelly or the almost treacle-coloured Tillydrum honey that overpowered the taste buds with the scent of heather and was not a liking that Isobel had ever acquired. The vast, ornately carved oak refectory table in the centre of the dining room would have been much too large for a mere seven people, so Evelyn Fergusson presided at the smaller oval breakfast table in the south-facing bay window. It was covered with a white damask tablecloth, frayed at the edges with age now – like its owner, Isobel thought sadly. She noticed that Evelyn wielded the heavy Victorian silver teapot with difficulty and guessed it was painful for her hands, though she knew better than to offer assistance with this ritual.

Marnie was enchanted. As she drank tea from a Crown Derby cup and helped herself to a couple of ridged butter pats from a shell-shaped silver dish, she felt she was being given a glimpse into the sort of world that her Contessa must have inhabited as a child – the world that Luciana had brought so vividly to life to a lonely little American girl in the very different setting of a tropical island twenty years before. Christopher, half watching Marnie across the table, while he chatted politely with his hostess, thought she looked lit up with happiness and hoped desperately that he might be able to make that look the rule rather than the exception in the future. It turned out that Evelyn had visited Christopher's grandparents' garden on Mull and this led to a discussion on the notable gardens of the west coast. Evelyn was enthusiastic about Morwenna's new idea to write a series of articles about Scottish gardens and promised to give her some introductions. She and Evelyn were soon deep in rhododendron talk and, thanks to his mother's lifelong passion for gardening, Christopher managed to keep his end up in a session of horticultural name-dropping that left everyone else feeling rather inadequate.

'What on earth's a Griersonianum cross when it's at home?' laughed Marnie, mocking his display of knowledge, as they left the dining room. 'An esoteric religious symbol or some kind of Scottish mongrel dog?'

After tea, Isobel was detailed to show the visitors the Victorian paintings in the long picture gallery at the end of the house. Evelyn's great-grandfather had been a notable collector of the contemporary art of his day, though like the heather honey at tea, not all the pictures were to everyone's taste. Shivering dogs crouched mournfully beside coffins; scarlet-cheeked children – obviously about to go down with tonsillitis, suggested Louisa – wearing unrealistically clean pinafores fed ducks by village ponds or sat outside cottages in button boots, surrounded by hollyhocks; knights in armour jousted; the Lady of Shalott floated towards Camelot and lovelorn young ladies prepared to drown themselves, Ophelia-like, in lakes. There were also some charming, somewhat faded water-colours and a good many family portraits of varying dates and merit, including an exceptional one by Sargent of a dark-haired young woman in a dramatic scarlet dress, which everyone admired.

'But she looks just like you, Isobel!' exclaimed Morwenna. 'It reminds me of that stunning portrait in your drawing room – it's not only her colouring but she has the same amused look you have. It's uncanny.'

'That's Evelyn's grandmother, who was also my great-grandmother,' explained Isobel, pleased and flattered. 'Now let's go back to the library because I know Evie wants to talk to Marnie – though if anyone would rather go outside again I know that would be all right too.'

The Colonel and Morwenna said they'd love to wander round the garden if nobody minded – there were a few extra notes that Morwenna would like to jot down and the Colonel wanted to take some photographs – but the others went to the library, where Evelyn was once more ensconced in what she mockingly referred to as 'the electric chair'.

'Come and sit by me,' she said to Marnie. 'Isobel has told

me something about your search for a house up here and the reason behind it and I do have a possible idea. I've done a bit of preliminary research, but tell me more.'

So Marnie told her about the old lady's legacy and her own wish to find the childhood home of her unexpected benefactress. 'I only have my memories of what she told me when I was seven, and these,' she said, producing the two photographs from her bag and taking off the locket round her neck to show Evelyn. 'The ridiculous thing is that I don't even know what her maiden name was – though I suppose the Italian lawyers would be able to discover it easily enough. The whole thing has come as such a bombshell to me that I haven't really got my act together over lots of things. I just had this immediate compulsion to come up to Scotland and try to track the house down for myself. The initials on the locket are L.A.D.G, so perhaps her surname could begin with G?'

Evelyn studied the rather faded and dog-eared snapshots which Marnie had taken out of their silver frame and then peered through a magnifying glass at the one of the little girl and the enormous dog standing in the doorway. She turned to Isobel. 'If you look on the bottom shelf behind the piano, darling, you'll find all my father's old pre-war photo albums. Could you bring me the one for 1920 to start with?' she asked. The albums, with dates stamped on the spine in gold, were of old morocco leather, originally black, but faded now in places to a greenish brown where they'd been exposed to too much sunlight. Isobel carried one of them over and put it on the table by Evelyn's chair. Marnie watched anxiously as she turned the pages with her swollen and misshapen fingers. There were pictures of Tillydrum in which the trees were half their present height; there were shots of tennis parties taken at various different houses, the men in white flannels – no shorts to be seen then – and the women in pleated white silk tennis dresses, the hems of which came decorously to the knee; there were views of alpine scenery obviously taken on winter-sports holidays, with laughing groups holding immensely long wooden skis and huge, unwieldy-looking ski sticks pictured against cuckoo-clock type buildings, but the majority of the photographs seemed to consist of endless groups of tweed-clad men and women with guns and dogs, standing by piles of dead grouse or the occasional lolling stag with its tongue poking out. Then Evelyn picked up the magnifying glass again, scrutinised another picture and gave Marnie a look of triumph.

'Ah! I think I have it!' she said. 'I had a notion I might find what I was looking for in here. When I looked at your first photograph, I thought I recognised the house, but there are a good many castellated houses standing at the edge of water in Scotland that look very similar to this one. It's the second snapshot of the child standing in the doorway that provides the real evidence – and everything fits with my original idea. Look at the arch over the door in your picture and then take a look at this.' She handed the glass to Marnie and shoved the album towards her.

Marnie knelt beside her chair.

'You can see the same entwined initials,' went on Evelyn, 'and a date, though I can't quite make out what year it is in either picture; and then above – can you see? – carved into the stone and probably from a much earlier date, what looks like the outline of a bird – a swan possibly, or a pelican – anyway some vaguely ornithological heraldic creature. What do you make of that?'

'But it matches exactly!' Marnie's always rather pale face had gone quite pink with excitement.

On the steps of a stone building, a group of people were standing in front of a doorway, the men wearing stout plus-fours and the women dressed in suits and cloche hats. Underneath in a neat, old-fashioned hand was written: *House party at Eilean Dobhran*, 12 *August 1920*

'Oh, look,' breathed Marnie. 'There's the same dog as in my photo! It has to be the one the old lady used to tell me stories about! I can't believe it.' She ran her finger along the line of writing, almost feeling that by touching the letters she could be transported back in time. 'How do you say the name?' she asked.

'It's pronounced "ee-lan daw-ran". In Gaelic eilean means island and dobhran means otter.'

'The Island of the Otter,' repeated Marnie, entranced.

'I think your old lady was Lucy-Anne Drummond-Gray of Eilean Dobhran,' said Evelyn, looking very pleased with herself, 'and the red hair of the child in your locket confirms it for me. Most of that family had flaming hair and tempers to match it! It was their downfall.'

The others clustered round to look at the album but Marnie, choked with emotion, got up and walked over to the window. She stood gazing out on the azaleas and rhododendrons of Tillydrum but seeing in her mind's eye a different garden with very different plants; hearing a voice saying: 'Listen now while I tell you how I was once found by my dog when I got lost on the hill in the mist,' as a lonely old woman, battling to come to terms with an overwhelming loss and her own approaching death, rocked in a hammock with a frightened little girl.

Christopher walked over to her and put his hands on her shoulders. He could feel her trembling. They stood together for a moment while she collected herself, then she put her own hand to her shoulder and just touched his hand. It was an almost imperceptible, highly personal private gesture but both Isobel and Louisa saw it before Marnie turned round to face the room again.

Isobel felt a lump in her throat and had tears in her own eyes; tears partly brought on by the pathos of old photographs with their memories of times past and reminders of future mortality, but also by pleasure for Marnie at the rewards she was reaping on her self-imposed mission – until she glanced at Louisa and saw the look of sadness on her face and was reminded again that Louisa's quest, whatever it might be, was not proving so fulfilling.

'I don't know how to thank you,' said Marnie. 'You can have no idea what this means to me. There's so much more I want to ask – will you tell me all you know?'

Isobel looked at her watch. 'We mustn't be too long,' she said to Evelyn. 'We've taken up so much of your time already. Why don't Louisa and I go and gather up Morwenna and John, while you fill Marnie in with any further bits of information?'

'Excellent – you do that, darling, but don't feel you need hurry away on my account. It does me good to see people and this is such an unusual story – I want to know more myself.' Evelyn nodded encouragingly at Marnie. 'Ask me anything you like, my dear. I only hope I can tell you what you want to know.'

'Can I stay to hear it too?' asked Christopher as Isobel and Louisa went out to the gardens. He and Marnie settled down on the sofa together.

'Now then . . . what do you want to ask me first?'

'Where the house is and how to get there . . . who it belongs to now . . . perhaps most of all, did you actually know the Contessa?'

Evelyn considered. 'I certainly *met* her, because our families were old friends and my parents used to stay with her parents for shooting parties and social weekends and occasionally I was taken along with them. I have vivid recollections of what Lucy-Anne Drummond-Gray looked like. She was the sort of person you couldn't help being aware of if you were in the same house, let alone the same room, as she was. It wasn't just her marvellous hair or her beauty – and she was truly stunning to look at – but she had that other, indefinable quality which I suppose you might call "presence".'

'Charm?' suggested Christopher.

Evelyn considered this and said dubiously, 'Not exactly *charm*, though I've no doubt she could be extremely charming if she chose, but it doesn't seem quite the right word to describe her somehow. It was something harder than charm; more challenging, more exciting . . . more dangerous. A sort of devil-may-care attitude. I don't think she ever gave a hoot what anyone else thought of her.' She went on: 'But of course she was a good bit older than me and it seemed a huge gulf at the time. I was a child in the nursery and she was almost grown up and in a different world.' She laughed. 'But I was always fascinated by her and by her reputation! She cast a spell. I remember listening avidly to my mother and my governess having shocked conversations about her exploits. If they realised I was eavesdropping they would immediately stop discussing her and exchange a "not in front of the child" look, so I used to sit quiet as a mouse, lapping up the stories. All the young men in the neighbourhood were supposed to be madly in love with her and she certainly led her parents an awful dance. Had she still kept her extraordinary beauty, even in old age?'

Marnie shook her head. 'I don't know. Perhaps she had, though I certainly didn't think so at the time – but then I was seeing her through a child's eyes and to me she just seemed . . . old. But what you call "presence" – that she certainly had. Everyone was aware of her and it got up my pretty mother's nose that all the staff in the hotel paid far more attention to the Contessa's wishes than to hers.' She wrinkled her nose. 'I do remember that she smelt of violets. Children notice that sort of thing.

What about her Italian husband? Did you ever meet him?'

'Husband?' Evelyn raised her eyebrows. 'He didn't become her husband for a very long time – that was the trouble. Not, I believe, till well after the war, not till the wife he'd deserted for Lucy-Anne died. It broke her parents' hearts. "Living in sin" is what it was called then and they never forgave her. Your generation wouldn't understand what a shocking thing it was perceived to be in those days and not only by her parents but of course in Catholic Italy as well. I imagine they were ostracised by both their families. It's rather wonderful to hear that their love endured through all that. I believe there was a child too?'

'A baby boy,' said Marnie sadly. 'He died the day he was born. I know that from her diaries, but I didn't know that she and her Carlos weren't married then. How awful that her parents never forgave her – awful for her and awful for them.'

'It was all very tragic. Their only son, Lucy-Anne's older brother, joined the RAF at the outbreak of war, became a fighter pilot and was killed in the Battle of Britain. Eilean Dobhran, like so many big houses, was requisitioned by the army and was left in a bad state of disrepair after the war. The old Drummond-Grays lived on for a bit in one corner of it while everything became increasingly dilapidated, but everyone said they'd lost the heart for living, and soon after that they died within a few months of each other. I heard the estate, or part of it, was sold to pay off debts and I think the remainder went to some distant cousin who'd emigrated. I don't know what's happened to it now. I believe the house was a hotel for a time and then I think a nursing home or something like that, but whether it was let or sold I'm not sure. I'll show Isobel exactly where it is on the map so that you can make enquiries locally. I'm sorry I can't tell you any more.'

'You've been wonderful. I never expected half as much.' Marnie thought Evelyn Fergusson suddenly looked very tired and she and Christopher were getting to their feet just as Isobel reappeared with Louisa and the Colonel and Morwenna.

They all made their farewells with many expressions of appreciation. Morwenna wrote her Cornish address down for Evelyn and promised to send her a draft of a possible article about the gardens; Evelyn explained to Isobel exactly where Eilean Dobhran was to be found, north-west of Inverness, and Marnie promised to keep in touch and let her know what happened in the next stage of the search. Evelyn insisted on walking to the front door to see them off.

'I wish I could repay your Lucy-Anne, my Contessa, for all she did for me,' said Marnie. 'It's awful not being able to thank her.'

'Repay her by being happy,' said Evelyn unexpectedly.

'Oh,' said Marnie, surprised. 'I'll remember that. And thank you more than I can say. You've made her come alive for me again – and it all fits.'

As Isobel drove them down the Tillydrum drive, Flapper and Lozenge respectively hurtling and puffing their way to the bottom again, Marnie looked back and saw another gallant old lady still standing on the steps of her house, waving them goodbye.

Chapter Twenty-four

Dinner that night, at the round table in the kitchen, was like a happy, informal gathering of old friends and Giles and Isobel felt that they had succeeded in achieving the atmosphere they aimed for at Glendrochatt and were well pleased. Marnie couldn't stop thanking them both for having taken her to Tillydrum. 'I really lucked out there,' she said, shaking her head in wonder and sparkling away in a manner that would have seemed impossible when she first arrived. She and Morwenna had both been fascinated by the eclectic mix of treasures and junk, the threadbare and the opulent, in Evelyn Fergusson's house and said they'd never encountered anything like it before. Was it unusual?

Giles roared with laughter. 'Oh, it's very common in this part of the world – dealers call it "shabby chic". I have to tell you, Marnie, that most of your compatriots either think it totally incomprehensible or prize it out of all proportion. It will be interesting to see what style you adopt yourself if you become chatelaine of your own castle!' he teased. 'I await developments with interest.'

'Well I certainly don't intend to invest in piles of old newspapers by way of furnishings,' she retorted. 'I don't think anyone could assemble all that clobber on purpose.'

'You should have been up here a few years ago when there was a Stately Car Boot Sale at Dunbarnock in aid of charity. People went completely mad over the most amazing things. Poor old Neil made the mistake of announcing to the press in advance that he would sell his mother's moth-eaten old Persian lamb coat for fifty pounds to the first person to arrive. The result was that the road became completely jammed in two directions and the police had a frightful job holding the public back till the gates were opened. Two of the travelling fraternity raced each other to Neil's stall and then came to fisticuffs over who should have it and the one who lost proceeded to put a curse on the coat! It was the most successful money-raising event there'd been in the neighbourhood for years and we all had a splendid time. Isobel sold an old ARP helmet and my grandmother's honeymoon knickers for a hundred quid each.'

'How on earth did you know they were her honeymoon knickers, and what were they like?' asked Marnie.

'Oh, I found a pile of them on a shelf at the back of some old cupboard wrapped in tissue paper and still labelled *Trousseau*.' Isobel giggled. 'They were amazing concoctions in wonderful pale peach crêpe de Chine. You had to put the legs on separately and wind yourself up in satin ribbons like a gift-wrapped parcel and then there were fiddly little buttons in a rather awkward place. Tricky if one was taken short! They sold like hot cakes, but I kept one pair back for posterity.'

'A dowry for Amy?' suggested Christopher.

Everyone, including Louisa, expressed themselves delighted that the visit had proved so successful for both Marnie and Morwenna and were all full of praise for how much they'd enjoyed their day. Morwenna was overcome with pleasure at the turn things were taking in her life and as soon as they had got back to Glendrochatt had rung Joyce to tell her of the possible new developments in her writing career. Joyce had sounded very pleased, but when she'd enquired slyly how the Colonel was, Morwenna had clammed up. She didn't feel ready to expose her tentative hopes in that direction to anyone – hardly even to herself – but down in Cornwall, Joyce drew her own conclusions.

Giles, the least parsimonious of hosts, opened champagne again to celebrate the end of a successful day and mixed it with white peach juice to make Bellinis; Isobel produced a delectable Italian chicken dish with black olives and a rich tomato sauce, served with their own home-grown and freshly dug up new potatoes from the farm, which really tasted of something, followed by rhubarb meringue pie and wonderful cheese. It was all very enjoyable.

Before dinner Christopher and Marnie had gone to sit together on the white seat under the great beech tree overlooking the loch where they had started their friendship. Christopher lit a cigarette. He intended to try, not by any means for the first time, to give up smoking in the near future and thought that perhaps, if he had Marnie's support, he might actually be able to achieve it this time. He didn't want to risk making the attempt until a few imponderables in his life were sorted out.

They sat without speaking, but deeply aware of each other, watching the spinners from the previous evening's hatch of flies doing their ephemeral, but spectacular, mating dance, rising and falling as though suspended in the air like mobiles hung from invisible wires. 'All that dazzling courtship display – and then they only live for a day!' said Christopher. They listened to the rhythmic lapping of the water below them and could hear the occasional faint plop and see rings spreading out across the calm surface of the loch where a trout had risen. Curlews bubbled and a woodpecker, hammering away in some distant tree, was clearly doing overtime. Both of them felt a sense of optimism that life was at a turning point.

'Christopher,' said Marnie, breaking the silence after a

bit, tracing a pattern with her finger on the arm of the seat. 'Could I make a suggestion?'

'Of course. Anything. Just try me,' he said, looking down at her in a way that made her catch her breath.

'Well,' she said, 'on Sunday, when our week here ends, I thought I'd head straight up to Inverness in the car and go prospecting. Try to locate Eilean Dobhran and make some preliminary local enquiries. Stay in a pub or something. Today has literally been a dream come true. Would you . . . might you . . . consider coming with me? I'd just so love you to be there when I find the house. I'd love to know what you think . . .' She looked up at him and the look of consternation on his face made her heart sink. She rushed on, 'But you probably wouldn't want to . . . .'

Christopher picked her hand up and locked his fingers through hers. 'Shit,' he said. 'Oh, shit! Marnie, you must know it isn't that I wouldn't love to. There's nothing I'd like more – but I can't come then. I really, truly can't.'

She swallowed, trying not to make her disappointment too obvious. 'Oh well, not to worry,' she said brightly, giving her shoulders what was intended to be a non-chalant little shrug, a backlog of past rejections making her wish she hadn't mentioned it. 'It was just an idea. Forget it.' She tried to disengage her hand but Christopher hung on to it.

'Marnie, listen. It's the blasted parole thing . . . I'm not a free agent yet,' he said, willing her to understand. 'I'm still out on licence. My permission to come here was on the grounds that Glendrochatt might help with a future career for me – as indeed it miraculously has. Then I got an extension by telephone for one more week, but,' he pulled a wry face, 'something that's considered helpful towards so-called "rehabilitation" is one thing, an extended pleasure jaunt might be quite another. I have to go back on Sunday because I've got a date with my probation officer on Monday afternoon. I've only got a few months left to go and if I missed that I could find myself back where I started . . . in gaol . . . and that,' he said, 'would be a pity for a lot of reasons – and you're one of them. I daren't risk it.' He put his arm round her and pulled her against him. 'Don't give up on me,' he said. 'I couldn't bear it.'

A feeling of overwhelming relief flooded through her. She rubbed her cheek on his sleeve. 'Of course you mustn't risk it. I'm sorry – how dumb of me! I feel real bad I didn't pick up on that for myself.' She added wistfully, 'It would just have made it perfect, that's all.'

Christopher, deeply touched, was struck by an idea.

'How much would you mind missing the last couple of days here?'

'Well, I'm loving being here, but it's not that important. I've already got far more out of Glendrochatt than I ever expected.' She added truthfully but – for her – bravely, 'I'm loving still being here now because of you anyway. Why?'

'Well, I just wondered if we could go earlier – say on Thursday morning – and spend Thursday and Friday nights up there together, find your castle and then wend our way back south on Saturday and Sunday? I'm afraid you'd have to be my chauffeur again. What about it?'

'Awesome!' She flung her arms round his neck. When she surfaced, rather breathless, from his kiss, she said, 'Do you think Giles and Isobel would mind?'

'I'm sure they wouldn't. It wouldn't make any difference to them financially because we've already paid – and I'm sure they'd be thrilled for you to get on with your search. I think they feel thoroughly involved with it too.' He smiled down at her. 'I've had an even better idea. If I come up to Inverness chasing castles in the air with you, how would you feel about coming south with me to stay with my parents for a few days? I'd love you to meet them.'

Marnie said she couldn't imagine anything more wonderful. They sat with their arms round each other, savouring their new happiness, until it was time to wander up to the house for dinner.

Over coffee in the drawing room, they put their plan to Giles and Isobel who were full of enthusiasm and knew of an excellent small hotel in the area where they could stay. 'It's comfortable but not plush. I think you'd like it. Why don't I get Sheila to ring first thing tomorrow morning and make a booking for you?' Giles offered obligingly and received a sharp kick on the ankle from Isobel. Christopher saw it and with a twinkle in his eye said he'd be grateful to be given the telephone number but, thanks all the same, it would probably be easier if he made the booking himself. 'I can give them my credit card details and all that,' he said. He had no intension of discussing whether he and Marnie would require one room or two with Giles's secretary. Giles grinned and let the matter drop.

They discussed the programme for the next day.

'I've unexpectedly been offered a day at Islamouth tomorrow, by a godfather of mine,' said Giles. 'It's the best fishing on the Tay, so it's come at a wonderfully opportune moment and I thought Christopher and I might desert the rest of you. Now what would anyone else like to do?'

'Could John and I go to Glamis?' asked Morwenna. 'If Louisa and Marnie feel like coming with us that would be lovely, but we're quite happy to take ourselves there if not. We both very much want to see it.' She looked questioningly at Louisa. 'What about you?'

'Well, you certainly mustn't miss Glamis, but I've been there several times, so I think I won't come this time, thank you all the same. I have a great yen to go back to St Andrews and visit old haunts,' she said. She looked at Marnie. 'I suppose you wouldn't like to come with me,

339

Marnie?' she asked. 'I think you'd love it. The old town's so pretty and there's lots to see. We could have a wonderful walk along the beach too, if it's a nice day.'

Isobel held her breath, hoping Marnie would recognise that she was being offered a considerable olive branch.

Marnie hesitated for a moment. Christopher, watching her too, felt he could see her uncertainties flitting across her face like shadows. Then she gave Louisa her most brilliant smile. 'Sure,' she said. 'Why not? While the guys are off fishing, let's have a real girls' day out. I'd really like that.'

'Great,' said Louisa. 'Do you want to come too, Iz?'

'Well, if you don't mind I think I might spend the day catching up on a lot of boring chores.' Isobel thought Louisa and Marnie would get on together much better without her. 'I love St Andrews too but Ed's obsessed with the wonderful Sea Life Centre there at the moment – you know what a one-track mind he has – so I feel as if I've flogged along that road rather a lot recently.'

Louisa laughed. 'God, yes! I remember going there with you and the twins years ago. They adored it but I think perhaps Marnie and I might pass on that particular attraction this time.'

At that moment the telephone rang. Giles picked it up. 'Oh, hi there – how are you? Good to hear you,' they heard him say. 'Yes indeed he's still with us – of course you can. Hold on while I get him.' He put his hand over the receiver. 'For you, Christopher,' he said. 'It's Jonathan Mercer. Do go and take it in the kitchen if you like.'

'Thanks. I think I'll do that,' said Christopher coolly, though he felt like running across the hall. He was gone for quite a time. When he came back six expectant faces greeted him.

'Well?' said Isobel. 'Dare we ask? Good news or bad?'

'Fantastically good.' Christopher beamed at them all. 'I

can't believe it. On the strength of Jonathan's recommendation his agent has offered to see me. He wants to meet me in London as soon as possible and though of course he's not committing himself until he's read it, he thinks on Jonathan Mercer's say-so he may be able to find a publisher for *Inside Knowledge*.' He looked at Giles and Isobel. 'I don't know how to thank you both. It all started with you and Catherine and the introduction to Jonathan.'

'Nonsense,' said Giles. 'It all started with you. I've had five years of running courses like this tutored by either Catherine or Jonathan or both, and I assure you I've never known either of them react as they did over your book.' He poured out a glass of whisky and handed it to Christopher. 'Here, take this. You look as if you could do with it. You'll have to promise to come and do a talk and a signing for us at Glendrochatt when it's published.'

'You bet I will!'

'Oh, that's so exciting! We're all thrilled for you. Have you started a new book yet?' asked Isobel.

'I have actually,' he admitted, and added ruefully, 'but I started it before I came here and, post Catherine, the faults leap off the page at me.' He laughed. 'Now I keep asking myself what she would say to this and that – and whole chunks get deleted immediately!' He looked at his watch. 'It's a bit late to try her now, but I must ring her first thing tomorrow and tell her my good news.'

His eyes went to Marnie, who was sitting on the sofa, and they exchanged a long look. A fresh start, thought Christopher; a new career and a new relationship. Possibilities hung between them.

After the others had gone over to the Old Steading, and Giles had gone off to look out some fishing tackle for the morning, Isobel and Louisa stood on the steps of the house while Isobel let the dogs out for a final run.

'That was a lovely suggestion you made to Marnie,' she said.

Louisa laughed. 'Oh well, at least I've got something right for a change then.' Her tone was light-hearted, but Isobel thought she looked unhappy. 'Have you had any more news of Rory?'

Isobel sighed. 'No. I rang after we got back, but Lorna wasn't there so I had to leave a message – yet again – asking her to ring me. I don't know whether to think no news is good news or not. I keep wondering how he is and I can't get him out of my head. Let's not talk about it now or I might cry. What are you going to do next, Louisa? Where are *you* moving on to? Why don't you stay on as our guest for a few more days – for as long as you like, actually? We'd love to have you. You could be a free agent, do your own thing – give yourself a bit more space, with no pressure to contemplate the next step.'

'Oh, Izzy – you are lovely. As if you hadn't got enough going on in your life at the moment! Bless you, but no. I've decided to go home for a few days. It's ages since I had time with Ma and Pa completely on my own. They've both noticeably aged lately and I feel they might like that. Then the following week I have to be in London anyway for a long-standing appointment, and I need to make up my mind what to do about the flat. Adam very decently moved out when we split up and I have to think whether to buy him out, keep the flat on and look for a lodger, or sell it jointly with Adam and start afresh somewhere. I suppose I might even start looking for another job.'

'Isn't this a bit of a retrograde step? I thought you were in adventure mode. I thought you said you felt free to take off anywhere: go travelling; try other creative outlets. I thought the next six months was supposed to be special Louisa time – an exploration of different opportunities?'

'It was.' Louisa looked out over the garden. It was still

quite light though the colour was beginning to seep out of the flame-coloured azaleas surrounding the house and the tulips in the tubs below the steps had closed their pointed petals for the night. Swifts screamed and swooped to catch a late supper, gloriously charged with energy and speed. 'It was going to be all those things, but my sense of adventure seems to have gone AWOL. It's as though my enterprise tank has suddenly sprung a leak and all initiative is draining out of me.'

Isobel felt a frisson of unease. She gave Louisa a troubled look. 'It'll come back,' she said stoutly. 'I always think one has a slump after a crisis. Surprisingly easy to be good at the time – it's afterwards that's such a bummer. You're probably just having a reaction after taking the decision to make such big changes . . . and to ending your relationship with Adam. That can't have been easy. Come on, we must both go to bed. We've had a long day. Now where the hell's that bloody little dog of mine gone? This is the sort of moment Lozzie chooses to give me the slip and go off rabbiting.'

But at that moment a very smug-looking Lozenge came waddling up the bank, wagging her tale ingratiatingly, her stomach bulging even closer to the ground than usual.

Isobel and Louisa went back into the house. Isobel locked up for the night, and by unspoken agreement they left the question of Louisa's future hanging in the air.

Chapter Twenty-five

It was fine but overcast when Giles and Christopher set off for Islamouth on Wednesday morning.

'I told Izzy not to bother to organise a full-blown picnic for us,' Giles said to Christopher as they loaded up the car with fishing paraphernalia. 'I said a "piece" in the pocket for each of us would be fine. I hope that's all right with you?'

'Great.'

'What would you like to drink?'

'Oh, beer, lager – anything you've got. I'm not fussy.' Christopher was hugely looking forward to his day. He had been secretly relieved to discover that he would be fishing from a boat. An expert fisherman, who had fished since he was a child and caught his first salmon when he was twelve – a day of never-to-be-forgotten excitement – he would not normally have given a second thought to the prospect of being up to his waist in the middle of a powerful river, a wading stick hung round his neck, skilfully Spey-casting as long a line as might be required, but would have regarded it as part of the pleasure of the expedition. Now, however, he was uncertain how his bad leg would stand up to slippery stones and a strong current and had no wish to be either an anxiety or a nuisance to his host. Though he had no intention of giving up wading for good and felt his mobility and confidence were still improving after the latest operation, a boat, for today, seemed the perfect solution.

'Will your leg be okay?' Marnie had asked him before he left, echoing his own thought. Christopher had been touched at her solicitude. He couldn't imagine Nicola ever asking such a question.

'It'll be fine,' he said optimistically, and added, 'Will you be all right yourself? Don't let Louisa upset you, will you?' He felt extremely protective towards Marnie and had only resisted the impulse to say something sharp to Louisa during the Edinburgh trip in the knowledge that he would probably only make the situation worse for Marnie, whatever its real cause was.

'I'll be fine too. Louisa gave me a handsome apology yesterday for being so offhand and I guess today is her way of making it all okay between us. When we're on our own Louisa and I really get on very well – specially if you're not there!' she added with a grin. 'But don't let that give you any inflated ideas about yourself!'

'I'll watch it.'

'Don't worry – we'll have fun. See you this evening. Tight lines, as my father would say.'

They were both surprised to find that after only ten days in each other's company, it seemed quite odd to be spending the day apart.

Isobel waved the two fishermen off. 'Keep an eye out for an osprey,' she said to Christopher. 'I once watched one following Giles as he was fishing along that stretch of river. Oh, and you must make him point out the famous Meiklour hedge when you pass it. It's supposed to be the tallest hedge in the world – thirty metres of wonderful beeches and a local landmark. At its best at this time of year. Have a lovely time, both of you.'

Much as she liked her present set of visitors, she was looking forward to having a day without any of them around – even to being without Giles. She intended to try to get hold of her sister, even if it meant being extremely persistent. Evelyn Fergusson's information had stiffened her spine for confrontation – though what form this would take she didn't quite know.

John and Morwenna set off happily for Glamis in John's ancient but immaculate Vauxhall Sierra. Neither the interior of his car nor his light-coloured raincoat ever seemed to attract spots or stains or appear rumpled. Not for the Colonel the dog hairs, torn maps, single gloves, half-finished crossword puzzles and withered apples that seemed to breed in Isobel's car – against which Giles occasionally waged a losing battle – yet he clearly wasn't at all afraid of getting his hands dirty if required and had cheerfully volunteered to help Giles unload some logs for the house. Must be all that military discipline, thought Isobel gloomily, thinking it was time she had a blitz on the tidiness of her house, her clothes, her cupboards and her car.

Marnie and Louisa watched them drive away before setting off on their own expedition.

'Heavens – do look. John's actually wearing *driving gloves*!' exclaimed Louisa in awed tones. 'I didn't know anyone really wore those. What do you think – will those two manage to go on seeing each other after they've left Glendrochatt?'

'I guess. They'd be good company for each other, like two bits of a jigsaw fitting together.'

'They could be each other's bidie-in,' suggested Louisa.

'What on earth's that?'

'In Scotland it's the lover that lives in – something less than a marriage but more than an affair, but it sounds so much more romantic than a partner or an item or a common-law wife, don't you think?'

'A bidie-in . . .' Marnie tried it out. 'Yeah,' she said. 'I quite like the sound of that.'

'Umm. I rather thought you would,' said Louisa. She

raised an eyebrow. 'Perhaps you might be getting one of those for yourself.'

'You know what? I might, too!'

They looked at each other and suddenly they both laughed and any remaining tension between them was gone.

'If you're ready, shall we go?' asked Louisa. 'My car or yours?'

'Let's take mine. You organise our day and I'll be the driver.'

They had a brilliant time together. Each was determined to leave behind any issues between them and reach again the tentative friendship they'd several times been on the brink of achieving.

As predicted, Marnie loved St Andrews: its pleasant shops and pretty old houses; its many ancient buildings, its ruined cathedral and sense of history. Louisa, on a sentimental trip down memory lane and reminiscing about her student years at the university, was an ideal guide.

'How energetic are you feeling?' she asked when they'd parked the car and wandered up Market Street. 'Are you prepared for a climb?'

'Bring it on,' said Marnie cheerfully.

'Well, I thought I might drag you up St Rule's Tower. There's such an amazing view from the top. It'll give you an idea of the whole city and you can see for miles around, but you do have to flog up this steep spiral staircase with incredibly narrow stone steps – a hundred and fifty-one of them to be exact – and it's even more lethal coming down. I think it's worth it – if you feel up to it?'

'Of course I'm up to it,' said Marnie indignantly. 'Why shouldn't I be?'

'Probably because you have this deceptive air of

fragility and always look as if a puff of wind would blow you away,' said Louisa, laughing. 'Come on then.'

In the end it was Louisa, rather than Marnie, who got so out of breath she had to have a pause halfway up.

'Are you okay?' asked Marnie when they finally reached the top.

'I'm fine.' Louisa pulled a face. 'I'd forgotten just how puffed one got and something seems to have gone wrong with my thermostat recently – or maybe it's just the unpredictable nature of Scottish weather – and I seem to be permanently either too hot or too cold. I used to be a fitness fanatic but I've let myself go a bit lately and I'm out of training, that's all. I shall have to take more exercise when I get back – start jogging or going to the gym again. It's depressing how quickly you get unfit.'

'Well you were certainly right about the view. It's well worth the climb.' Marnie gazed down. 'It's awesome. Who was St Rule anyway?'

'Oh, some old monk who got a vision telling him to gather up St Andrew's bones from the island of Patras and take them forthwith "to the ends of the earth" for safe-keeping – or so legend has it. Imagine the inconvenience! It's after lights-out, you're tucked up in the dorm having drunk your medieval monastic equivalent of Horlicks and some bossy prefect of an angel goes and wakes you in the middle of the night to send you off on an errand like that! So poor old St Rule ups and goes to collect a kneecap, a tooth, an arm bone and a few fingers . . .'

'As you would,' said Marnie.

'Exactly, as one would . . . and off he sets with them, leaving nice warm Greece and landing up getting ship-wrecked on the bleak north-easterly shores of Scotland – and of course the bones were nicked a few centuries later anyway so he could have saved himself the trouble.'

'This must have been a great place to be at college.'

'It was. I adored it. Wish I were back here now. Which bit of your life would you most like to go back to?'

'I wouldn't,' said Marnie decisively. 'There are *places* I'd like to revisit, but I wouldn't want to go back in time. No way! That's a very threatening thought. I only want to go forward.'

'I'd like to go back to . . . oh, to many, many times.' Louisa looked wistful. 'I'd like to go back to nearly all my childhood. Everything was so *safe* then.'

'But to me, you see, everything was unsafe then. How different we are! Yet when we first met, you struck me as a devil-may-care sort of character.'

'Yes, that's right. I am really,' said Louisa, as though to remind herself. 'Come on, let's go down.'

Though not such hard going as the way up, the descent of the twisty narrow steps was certainly more hazardous, especially when they met a party coming up.

'Christopher'd have trouble getting up or down here on his gammy leg. I'm glad we haven't got him with us,' said Marnie.

'Well, that certainly makes a change!' Louisa teased, with a grin.

Marnie laughed back at her. 'Oh, Louisa,' she said, on an impulse, 'I do feel lucky. You don't know how happy I am.'

'I can guess – you've got an almost visible aura,' said Louisa, and added, 'and I'm so, so pleased for you. I really am.'

After the strenuous efforts of the tower, they pottered happily round the town, looking at the shops and visiting some of Louisa's favourite old haunts. 'I have to take you to Janetta's at some stage.' she said. 'They have ice-cream to die for, but let's have lunch first. We could pig out before we go home!'

They found an excellent pizza place and gossiped comfortably, telling each other about their respective families and homes, comparing their very different upbringings.

'How's your owl?' asked Marnie.

'All right as far as I know. I spoke to my mother the other day and she said he was fine; sleeping and eating – mostly sleeping. That's par for the course.' She looked down at her plate and suddenly pushed it away. 'I'm defeated,' she said. 'I can't finish all this. It's yummy but too much.' Marnie sent her a questioning look. Louisa said abruptly: 'Funny you should ask about Mr Brown, though. I had a terrible dream about him a couple of nights ago.'

'What was it?'

'Well, I was wandering about desperately looking for something – I've no idea what or why, you know how it is in dreams – I just knew I had to find something – and I opened a door on to a huge empty room, and Mr Brown was lying there on the floor. Dead.'

'No! How horrible! What happened next?'

'Nothing happened. That was it. I woke up feeling awful in a muck sweat.'

'Ill awful?'

'No – scared awful. Panicky.'

'It's all this rootling about in the past that we've been doing,' said Marnie, hoping to find the right words to comfort Louisa's obvious disquiet. 'I don't think it's possible to have poked around in the murky waters of childhood traumas and given them such a good old stir, as we've been doing, without some of the muck from the bottom coming up to the surface. Morwenna told me she'd been dreaming about her husband for the first time for ages. I've been obsessed with thoughts and memories about the Caribbean, but I think it's probably a good thing. I've even dared to try to remember more about Kenneth the pig-man, something I usually try to blank out. We've been living in a very intense and rarefied atmosphere lately. Everything's topsy-turvy, like in those bizarre Chagall postcards that Catherine got us to write about.'

'I suppose so.'

'Look,' said Marnie. '*Of course* you're afraid of Mr Brown dying, but you told me yourself that he must be near the end of his natural life anyway – has probably outlived the span he'd have achieved in the wild already. You said you were dreading it, but you're going to have to face it soon so perhaps your subconscious is giving you a prod – reminding you it's bound to happen sometime so you should try to lighten up about it . . . come to terms with it now before it happens?'

'That's a thought. Perhaps you're right.' Louisa gave herself a little shake. 'Yes, of course you are. That helps. Thanks, Marnie.'

They decided to head for the beach and walk along the famous West Sands which, Louisa told Marnie, were the birthplace of golf. A stiffish breeze had got up, sending white-horse waves galloping inshore, but the sun came out at the same time and turned the usually grey North Sea to an almost Mediterranean blue, and they walked for what seemed like miles, losing all idea of time. At one point Marnie was beguiled into kicking off her trainers, rolling up her jeans and paddling – but not for long.

'Jee-sus!' she wailed. 'I've lost all sensation in my feet. Are they still there?'

'You're not in the Caribbean now,' said Louisa. 'Let's run,' so they tore back across the beach, laughing and shrieking like a couple of teenagers, their hair wild, their cheeks burned by sun and wind, and felt they had earned their ginger and toffee ice creams at Janetta's before driving back to Glendrochatt.

Everyone arrived back thoroughly happy with their

varied outings. The Colonel and Morwenna had been entranced by Glamis, with its mixture of charm and history, the chilling legends and spooky stories so beloved by tourists co-existing with the feel of a loved and lived-in family home.

Christopher had caught a beautiful spring fish of twelve pounds and lost another, and Giles, fishing from the bank, had caught two, of eleven and thirteen pounds. They had enormously enjoyed each other's company and found many interests in common. Christopher felt he'd taken another important step back to normal life.

After dinner Christopher and Marnie exchanged addresses with the Colonel, Morwenna and Louisa. They made promises not to lose touch with each other – and meant it. There had been a message from Neil Dunbarnock for Marnie, suggesting that she and anyone else who might be interested should go over the following day for a drink. Marnie rang him to say how genuinely sorry she was that she couldn't come now that she was leaving Glendrochatt early. She told him about Evie Fergusson's suggestion that she should visit Eilean Dobhran and he wished her luck with her search.

'If you find your castle, then you're bound to be coming up again soon,' he said kindly, 'so do let me know when you're next in these parts and ask yourself over any time. I'd love to show you my cars.'

'You really made a hit with him,' said Isobel. 'He wouldn't say that if he didn't mean it.'

Giles and Isobel had already heard from three of the participants of the writing week, though not, to their relief, from Stanley Heslington. Win had written a charming letter to say that the week had been a turning point in her life. She had signed on for a creative writing class run by her local WEA, and sent off a couple of articles to a Yorkshire countryside magazine and one to her local paper as suggested by Catherine. She intended to do an Open University course and had already booked to go up to London in the autumn for a writing weekend-workshop run by Catherine. She was sorry, she said, that Glendrochatt had not been as beneficial for Stanley as it had been for her, but after all, she added loyally, he already had his own local literary successes and would continue with those as before. Joyce sent a colourful, jumbo-sized card of various Cornish beauty spots, to say she'd loved the course and the company but had come to the conclusion that she was better suited as a shopkeeper than an author. *I know my own limitations!* she put. She was looking forward to hearing all the latest Glendrochatt news when Morwenna got back. Bunty had sent an effusive missive, written in purple ink on pale pink, wavy-edged writing paper which she had illustrated lavishly with dancing haggises in Highland dress. She wrote that she was busy with her new project and would keep everyone posted about its progress. *Watch this space!!!!* she ended thrillingly.

If Isobel seemed a little detached and preoccupied at dinner that was because a telephone call earlier in the day had given her much to think about and there had so far been no opportunity for her to tell Giles about it or discuss it in private.

'I'm glad St Andrews was such a success. How did you and Marnie get on together?' she asked Louisa, standing at the foot of the stairs, before they went up to bed.

'We had a great time – really fun. She can be extremely good company. She's full of surprises.'

Louisa didn't tell Isobel how comforted she had been by Marnie's reaction to her owl dream. She'd been amazed to find herself confiding such a seemingly trivial, but to her disturbing, personal incident to someone she knew so little and had been grateful to Marnie, not only for taking it seriously, but for providing such a plausible explanation, and one that she had not thought of for herself. 'I almost wish I didn't like her so much,' she said jokingly. 'You'll be relieved to know, Izzy, that I think I'm giving up my bid for Christopher's attention!'

'And is that because you'd hate to hurt Marnie if he switched his attention to you, or because you know you haven't a hope anyway?' Isobel teased.

'Bit of both! Pity, though – there's just that hint of darkness about Christopher that made me think he'd be the perfect antidote to darling Adam! Shame really – I was all set for the grand passion and had cast him in the role of an irresistible force to sweep me off my feet, instead of which he and Marnie have gone and fallen for each other big time! Not what I hoped at all!'

Though her tone was light and mocking, Isobel guessed at a despondency under the banter that disturbed her because it was so uncharacteristic of Louisa. I thought she was just looking for a light flirtation, she thought. I may have got it wrong. Aloud, she said, 'Oh well, I'm glad you and Marnie aren't going to fight over him. I don't want any blood on the carpets here and I'd hate to add murder to the list of entertainments Glendrochatt can produce. We'd better order a different "irresistible force" for you – and hope he turns up soon!'

'You do that,' said Louisa cheerfully. 'After all, sticking with hope against the odds has stood me in pretty good stead in my life so far!'

'Yes, it certainly has,' said Isobel soberly, remembering how much they'd admired the younger Louisa, how gutsy and determined she had always been. 'All the same,' she said, giving Louisa an affectionate look, 'I'm relieved to know you've given up on this particular challenge.'

'I said I was *thinking* of it. Anyway we've all agreed to meet and have dinner together in London in a few weeks' time – provided Christopher's probation officer lets him off the hook, that is – but Marnie says Christopher thinks he'll almost certainly be given permission to go to London to see Jonathan Mercer's literary agent in view of the interest they've expressed in his book. We want to swap photographs of the budding authors at Glendrochatt and I want to see pictures of Eilean Dobhran, if they find it, and be brought up to speed with the latest episode in Marnie's missing-castle saga! Perhaps I should ask Adam to come too to make it a foursome?'

'Louisa, you're incorrigible! You're not to give poor Adam false hopes.'

'Poor Adam nothing!' said Louisa indignantly. 'We'll always be *friends*, for God's sake! He said he'd speak to me again soon when he rang me last week and there hasn't been a squeak out of him since.'

'Oh, *Louisa!*' said Isobel again, half-amused, but also feeling sorry for Adam Winterton, though she couldn't help wondering if Louisa's break with him was really as final as she claimed.

'Oh well.' Louisa shrugged. 'Adam knows Christopher anyway, so they could have a nice reunion and talk about tax and company law and the market and other thrilling topics of that ilk while Marnie and I talk castles. Is there any hope of you and Giles being in London next month? Then we could be six for dinner and that would make it really perfect. Do try . . . and you could see for yourself how beautifully I can behave!' she added.

'Doubtful, I'm afraid . . . you know what a pair of old stay-at-home country bumpkins we've become,' said Isobel, 'and we're always so busy up here in the summer anyway . . .'

She did not mention to Louisa that she had a pressing reason to go up to London in the very near future, but not one that would combine with social engagements.

And Louisa did not tell Isobel that she had decided to postpone rather than abandon any hopes of getting together with Christopher Piper. He was plainly in thrall to Marnie at the moment but she wondered how much they would have in common away from the hothouse atmosphere of Glendrochatt. Although her conscience would not have allowed her to make a deliberate attempt to win him away from Marnie now, she couldn't help secretly hoping that once back in the setting of the London social scene that was so familiar to both Christopher and herself, things might change of their own accord . . . and she would be there in the wings, waiting.

Louisa had not so far cast out a lure and had it spurned.

Part Three

Eilean Dobhran

Chapter Twenty-six

It was with a sense of adventure but some private apprehensions that Marnie and Christopher drove away from Glendrochatt on Thursday morning. Both felt very aware that this expedition could produce a marker in their lives at which they might look back in later years and say, 'That was our turning point.' Glendrochatt had brought them together in the first place and provided them with the chance to develop their acquaintance. Now they were on their own

Before he had telephoned the hotel recommended by Giles, Christopher had asked her: 'One room – or two? Entirely your choice . . . I know what I would like, but no pressure, I promise. I shall quite understand if it would be too soon for you,' and she had only hesitated for a moment before answering: 'Shall we go for one then?' and been rewarded by his swift look of pleasure. It had seemed to both of them, two people who had both been injured in past relationships, to express an important exchange of trust.

Evelyn Fergusson had rung Isobel the day before and left the telephone number of someone who might be of use to Marnie. She'd been making some enquiries through old acquaintances, she said, and thought that the Reverend Donald McBain, the retired minister of the now redundant kirk at Wester Finterie, might be able to help them. 'Tell Marnie that he's an old man now, but he probably knew the family, and apparently is likely to have information about what's happened to the house and whether there's anyone living there now. He might even know how to get hold of a key. Tell Marnie to give him a ring. Do mention Tillydrum and say I suggested it because I believe he once came here as part of a gardening group.'

Christopher had been relieved at this bit of information. His heart had sunk when Marnie, colourful notions floating around her head, had told him she remembered the old lady telling her how she and her brother had a secret hiding place in a wall beneath a particular window where they kept a key to a little-used door, so that they could go on expeditions at night and get in again undetected by the grown-ups. There had been forbidden rabbiting excursions, without the keeper to supervise them; they had gone trolling for trout on the loch by moonlight; they had lit a bonfire in the woods and tried to bake potatoes but had only ended up with lumps like charcoal. 'Imagine! Wouldn't it be exciting if the key was still there,' said Marnie, starry-eyed, 'and we could let ourselves into the castle without anyone knowing?'

'Too exciting by half!' said Christopher, laughing at her. He was entertained by her enthusiasm for such a far-fetched idea, while knowing that no matter how much such romantic trespassing might appeal to his companion, in the unlikely event of finding such a long-hidden key – and he had an uneasy suspicion it was just the sort of far-fetched thing that might actually happen to Marnie – he could not possibly risk being found 'breaking and entering' while still on licence. He had visions of creeping down secret tunnels, activating unseen burglar alarms, and then feeling the heavy hand of a local policeman descend on his shoulder, to be followed by an uncomfortable trip south, not in Marnie's dashing little blue Audi, but ignominiously handcuffed in the back of a police van. He hoped Marnie wouldn't have cause to write him off as a dreary old killjoy, when he would so much prefer to be her knight in shining armour.

As they set off down the mile-long drive of Glendrochatt, heading again for the A9, Marnie was glad to be doing the driving. Car journeys can provide wonderful opportunities for intimate conversation without the threat of face-to-face confrontation, and being behind the wheel gave her an extra feeling of confidence and being in command. They were both hungry to find out more about each other's lives. Marnie, in love as, she now realised, she had never been in love before, wanted to know all about Christopher's home and his family, his loves and hates and interests.

He told her about the old Tudor house in Warwickshire where he'd been brought up and where he was taking her on Sunday – a house of mellow stone and latticed windows, of ornate, twisted chimney stacks like sticks of barley-sugar and huge fireplaces; a house in which linen-fold panelling and creaky old floorboards made strange noises in the night. He told her about his mother's sunken garden where plants spilled over stone paths and roses sprawled and tumbled – *Paul's Himalayan Musk* or the wonderfully named *Rambling Rector* swarming up old apple trees and cascading down in waterfalls of pink and white; where lavender edged the flowerbeds and scented the air, and butterflies gorged themselves on buddleias; where a silver-leaved *Cytisus battandieri* spilled down a wall, its yellow flowers smelling of fresh pineapples, and an ancient globe sundial stood in the centre of the garden. He talked about the three sisters he clearly adored – the eldest, Penny, with the kind heart and congenital lack of tact, who knew what was best for everyone and was constantly bewildered when none of the family took up her suggestions. 'God, how she used to try to boss the rest of us around when we were children!' said Christopher. 'Not for nothing did we call her the Headmistress. Now she's married to a nice, dull man who likes being organised. She runs every possible local committee and is in her element as a controlling parent. But she's a real supporter in times of trouble – she used to trek down to visit me every month in prison, and that's the sort of thing that really counts.' The two younger sisters, who came after Christopher in the family line-up, were both married too, but he obviously had a special love for Jess, the sister next in age, who had been his boon companion when they were growing up. Kitty, the brilliant youngest sister, had her own travel business, wrote articles on far-flung places for glossy magazines and was a highly successful career woman, but Jess, he said, was just a lovely person with a marvellous sense of humour who was fun to be with. Marnie instantly felt a sharp, unworthy pang of jealousy.

'I think you two would really get on,' said Christopher – that rash suggestion that can be enough to put a stumbling block in the path of any possible relationship-by-marriage.

'Hmm,' said Marnie noncommittally, unfairly disliking the charming Jess, unmet.

Christopher gave her an amused look.

'Would you let me read your book?' she asked suddenly, thinking she might learn more about Christopher that way than any other.

'Of course. I'd love you to. I didn't like to suggest it,' he said, pleased. 'But you must promise not to pretend to like it, if it's not your thing.'

'I promise,' she said, hoping she'd be able to be truthful and complimentary as well, 'and I'm a great thriller reader. But now that you've got Catherine and Jonathan Mercer on side, both confirmed fans of your writing, it can't matter too much what anyone else thinks!'

'It matters to me what *you* think,' he said, 'which is not at all the same as saying we have to agree about everything. That would be very dull.'

'Oh, good. I'll be your fiercest critic, then!'

Of course they also talked about Eilean Dobhran – the catalyst for their present expedition – as they had done several times over the last few days, and he asked her again what she was expecting to do about it once she'd found it. Privately he hoped the whole thing wouldn't prove to be the most awful let-down for her.

'I don't know the answer to that myself because I daren't think about it too seriously until I see it with my own eyes,' she said. 'Until this week I didn't even know for sure that it still existed or whether it had been demolished. I still don't know if it's for sale, or to let, or what sort of money we'd be talking.'

'Don't count your castle until it's hatched?'

'Exactly.'

'Oh, come on! I know you better than that already. Don't tell me you haven't had endless wild, hypothetical ideas. Are we in charitable-foundation-for-cats'-home territory or Miss Havisham living alone among the ghosts and cobwebs?'

She giggled. 'Oh dear, is that how you see me?' She continued more seriously: 'But you're right, of course. I have had loads of daydreams – fantasies are my speciality. And yes, there's a bit of me that sees myself living there, but I also feel I need to earn this incredible good fortune that's suddenly found me, and to use it well.' She added lightly, 'I hope you'll help me come up with a brilliant idea.'

'I'll do my best.'

Then, because neither of them wanted to get too heavy, they came up with a variety of absurdly frivolous suggestions for possible uses for a derelict castle – which probably boasted dungeons and oubliettes amongst its not-so-modern conveniences – and generally sparked each other's imagination with impossible solutions and made themselves laugh. But though in one way they felt increasingly at ease together, very much on a wavelength over the absurdities of life, in another way there was a tension building between them. They were going away together after only the briefest acquaintance and both were desperately anxious that it should work.

The main road bypassed towns and villages, so they turned off it to find somewhere to eat and enjoyed a leisurely pub lunch, but later their mutual anxiety resurfaced and made them edgy with each other.

'I know this route of old. I've been coming up here off and on all my life, but as it's all new to you it seems such a waste that I can't take a turn at driving so that you could enjoy the scenery more,' said Christopher when they took to the road again. He sounded tense and it wasn't the first time he'd said something of the sort, although Marnie kept assuring him she was perfectly happy. She couldn't help wondering if it was in part a criticism of her driving skills, and this touched her on the raw.

'Is it my driving that's a problem for you or do you just hate being driven?' she asked, in a more aggressive voice than she meant to use. 'I know there are lots of men – especially ones who fancy themselves with fast cars – who loathe being a passenger and specially can't stand being driven by a woman. Are you one of those?'

'How do you know I like fast cars? We've never discussed it.' Christopher had an edge to his voice too.

'Men who are content to bumble around in old bangers when they can afford something more dashing don't usually own Aston Martins,' she retorted, and then hoped she hadn't upset him by referring, even obliquely, to his disastrous smash in his high-speed car.

'I can see you're a perfectly competent driver and I'm extremely grateful,' he replied stiffly, not willing to admit how much his present dependency irked him, and at the same time feeling put out with himself that he should have made it so obvious.

She gave him a sidelong glance. 'Only *competent*?' she queried, needled by his choice of words. 'Don't be so bloody condescending!' and she put her foot down hard and passed the two cars ahead of them extremely fast, judging the distance perfectly but cutting it much too close for the comfort of her passenger, sliding in front of them with just enough room to spare and getting flashed at by an oncoming lorry. Christopher involuntarily stamped on the floorboards with both feet, sending an electric shock of pain up his bad leg.

'Bloody hell! What do you think you're *doing*?' he demanded furiously, mortified to find himself shaking. 'There's no need to show off – d'you want to kill us both? Serve you right if there's a speed camera operating.'

'There isn't,' she said tersely. 'I've got the Road Angel on. I'm not completely stupid.'

The needle of the car's speedometer leaped up sharply and the countryside whirled past them for a couple of miles before she slowed down again.

There was silence in the car. Christopher, reliving another moment of speed and fighting panic, was tight-lipped with anger.

Then Marnie slowed right down and said in a very small voice: 'Oh, God, I'm sorry, Christopher. Truly, truly sorry. I should *never* have done that. I feel real bad – I don't know what got into me.'

'I do,' he said, after a long pause and an inward struggle. 'I was being a pompous, unappreciative ass and it got up your nose. And you're right – but it isn't that I hate being driven, so much as not being *able* to drive – and I hate myself for making such heavy weather about something so minor, so unimportant, when I think of the bloke I killed. But I shouldn't have taken my frustration out on you.' He added honestly: 'And I'm probably jealous too, because you drive so very, very well – except for that monstrous overtaking just then! There – I'm sorry too. Forgiven?'

'Yeah,' she said. 'Of course forgiven. You had every right to be mad but please don't go crazy with me again. I guess we're both pretty quick on the draw. Perhaps that's something it's as well for us both to know? Oh, look – only a few miles to Inverness. We're getting on. No more shocks now, I swear! I'll drive like a perfect lady!'

As they approached the road bridge between the Moray Firth and the Beauly Firth, Christopher said: 'I'll keep an eye out for dolphins down below. If I see any sign of them we'll stop the other side at North Kessock, so that you can have a chance to look too.'

But dolphins did not seem to be on display that day and they left the A9 at the Tore roundabout and took the Ullapool road.

They found the hotel, Finterie Lodge, a few miles off the main road, a low, gabled, whitewashed house converted from a former shooting lodge by Jeff and Cherry Barton, the present owners. It catered mostly for fishermen, walkers and honeymooners and had six bedrooms, neither too quaint nor too plush, but extremely comfortable; there was a well stocked bar downstairs – including an unbelievable selection of malt whiskies – a large cheerful sitting room, excellent drying facilities for sodden clothes, a warm welcome and, as it turned out later, excellent plain food cooked by Cherry herself – a cheery dumpling of a woman who might have stepped straight out of one of her own robust, well-flavoured casseroles. As Giles had thought, it was exactly what Christopher and Marnie wanted.

Marnie went to lean out of the bedroom window after Jeff had helped them carry their cases upstairs, to cover a sudden nervousness at the intimacy of sharing a room for the first time, very conscious that either of them might disappoint the other; that old hurts might reopen so that they could not respond to each other in the way they longed to do. She breathed in a great lungful of air. 'All my life I shall remember the scents of Scotland,' she said. 'I got drunk on it the first day at Glendrochatt and it's the same here. It's moss and gorse and heather and peaty water and the cry of curlews all rolled into one.'

'Does birdsong smell?' asked Christopher, coming to join her and putting his arm round her shoulders. 'I didn't know that.'

'It does here,' she answered firmly.

'A poet in the making! I must look to my laurels.' He took her face in his hands and kissed her and felt her quick response, but thought she still looked anxious. He wondered if she was thinking of her last disastrous love affair. 'Shall we go down and have a cup of tea and then take a look at the river?' he suggested, thinking such mundane activities might banish any awkwardness between them.

'Yes, let's,' she said, grateful for his perspicacity.

Before they had left Glendrochatt, Christopher had rung the Reverend Donald McBain to ask if he and Marnie could come and see him, only to be told that he was away. The unforthcoming female who answered the telephone had eventually admitted he would be back that evening. Perhaps they could ring later then, suggested Christopher, but he was firmly told that the Reverend would be tired when he got home and it was made very plain that a telephone call that night would not be welcome. She supposed they could try the next morning, but she really couldn't say whether he'd be up to talking to them or not. It didn't sound very promising.

'Lucky we're both so thin,' said Marnie, having resisted the offer of a full Highland tea with scones and cake. 'I must have eaten more scones in the last ten days than in my entire life! I couldn't possibly do justice to dinner if I had more than just a cup of tea now.'

Jeff directed them to a path beside the Finterie river that flowed through the grounds of the Lodge and on which the hotel owned the fishing on the near bank and they wandered happily along, Christopher eyeing the various pools and deciding how he would fish them if he had a rod with him and Marnie making castles in the air about all sorts of other things. Though she was impatient to find the particular castle of her dreams, she was so happy with the present that half of her wanted the day to go on for ever.

Over a drink before dinner they enquired if the Bartons knew anything about Eilean Dobhran and gave them a shortened version of the reason they had come.

'You mean that deserted old house up the loch?' asked Jeff. 'Rumour has it that it belongs to someone who lives abroad. We're newcomers here ourselves.' He chuckled. 'We've only lived in the area for a mere ten years – but it's been empty all the time we've been here and I should think it must be in an awful state of disrepair. Why don't you have an early dinner and then drive towards Upper Finterie, take the right hand fork where the road divides – it's little more than a track really – and go up the loch on the eastern side for a couple of miles? It doesn't get dark here at this time of year till quite late. You'll get the most stunning view of Eilean Dobhran across the water – unbelievably romantic. Of course if you actually want to get to it you'll have to go on the other road, but you can't see the castle then. There's an old lodge at the entrance to the drive but the actual house is hidden in the trees. I've never been right up to it myself because the gates are always padlocked.'

'That's a fantastic idea!' said Marnie. 'Let's do that. What time could we have dinner?'

'Whenever you like. Our fishing guests often want an early meal so that they can go on the river again after supper. Make your way to the dining room as soon as you've finished your drinks and I'll go and forewarn Cherry you'd like to eat as soon as it's ready.'

So they had an early dinner and climbed into the car again.

'Nerves feeling strong?' asked Marnie, glinting at him as she turned the ignition on.

'Rock-like,' said Christopher. 'Prepared for anything!'

After a few miles of bumping along the narrow, pot-holey track beside the river, which relied on passing places to cater for the possibility of two vehicles' meeting, they came to the fork Jeff Barton had mentioned and saw a signpost pointing left to Wester Finterie, and right to Upper Finterie. Marnie stopped the car but left the engine running.

'I imagine we'll go left here tomorrow to see the Reverend Donald – if we manage to get past the female Rottweiler, that is.' Christopher looked at the map. 'I don't think it can be very far now. I see exactly where we are and Eilean Dobhran is marked on the other side – can't be more than a mile or so.' He smiled at her. 'Excited?'

'You bet! I can't believe it!' she said. 'I want it so bad it's scary. You wouldn't believe the number of times I've imagined this moment. When I was a child I used to lie in bed at night imagining what it would be like – hearing the Contessa's voice telling me stories about it, describing it. Memory's a funny thing. It's hard to be sure how much of what I think I remember are her actual words and how much I may have unconsciously added to them in my head.'

'That had occurred to me too. Just so long as you're prepared for the fact that it might not live up to your expectations . . .' Christopher gave her rather an anxious look. 'Are you sure you're ready to risk losing your dream to cold reality?'

'I'm sure. I have to.'

'Shall we go on, then?'

To start with, birch trees more or less obscured the view to the left, but gradually these petered out and the road ran close to the edge of the loch with nothing but heather, couch grass and bog myrtle and the occasional rowan tree between the car and the water, which looked almost black in the evening light. Christopher saw the castle before she did.

'Pull off the road at that passing place that's coming up,' he instructed, 'and don't look to your left till you've got out of the car.'

Behind the hills on the far shore clouds were streaked with such vivid pink and orange light it looked as though a forest fire was blazing somewhere and the flames had got reflected in the water. Against the palest lemon sky stood the castle – stuck out into the water on a tongue of land, hills to the left and right forming a perfectly balanced backdrop. If it had been a stage set for an opera it could not have looked more unreal or more romantic. They stood gazing at it in complete silence, neither wanting to be the first to break the spell.

Then: 'What the hell's that?' asked Marnie, clutching Christopher's arm as something went shooting across the water . . . something undulating, with a long neck. 'Oh, it's gone! Don't tell me that Loch Ness Monsters live here too?' She sounded quite shaken.

'Those were red-throated divers.' Christopher felt in his pocket for his binoculars. 'I think there were about three of them. They've dived now but take a look through these when one of them pops up again. They have these extraordinary courtship displays and when several males get together and skidder through the water at great speed, with their bodies half under the surface, they look remarkably like some old plesiosaur surfacing after aeons to take a look at the twenty-first century. You're not the first person to mistake them for a monster. They'll have been having a race to impress a lady – very medieval, very in keeping with a castle!' He laughed down at her. 'If there was anyone else to race with, I'd be tempted to do the same right now!'

'You don't need to,' she said. 'You've won me already. I think you know that.'

'Happy?' he asked.

'So happy.'

Eventually they spotted one of the divers, which had resurfaced further up the loch, and Marnie was able to look at it through the glasses.

'I can't pick out any red on its throat in this light,' she said. 'Aren't there other sorts of divers? How do you know which is which if you can't see the colour?'

'Ah well, the red-throats are easy to identify because they're such snobs.'

'*Snobs*?'

He grinned. 'They always swim with their noses in the air.'

They walked a little way along the shore, arms round each other, watching the colours change and soften and begin to fade as the castle and the water seemed to get darker and darker till they became almost indistinguishable and a first faint star appeared in the sky.

'*Star light, star bright, first star I see tonight, I wish I might get the wish I wish tonight,'* chanted Marnie softly, a memory suddenly stirring of a skinny little girl being taught the old, old jingle by a fragile old lady a long time ago, and how they had both wished on a star together under a Caribbean sky.

'Let's go back now,' said Christopher. 'Tomorrow we'll come adventuring again, but I know what my wish for tonight is, darling Marnie, and there's a much more comfortable place waiting for us where I can show you just what that is . . .'

Chapter Twenty-seven

Christopher woke first the following morning. The curtains were drawn back so that early light flooded into the bedroom. After the claustrophobic incarceration in a cramped cell, usually with a cellmate and only occasionally, when he was lucky, on his own, he couldn't bear to have the curtains closed at night. Now he could hear the sound of the river – special music to his ears – and smell what Marnie had called the scents of Scotland coming through the open window – birdsong and all, he thought, amused by her mixed metaphor and delighted by her enthusiasm for a part of the world that had always meant a great deal to him. The smell of prison had been a daily endurance but something he'd made himself get used to, and more or less learned to ignore, but the confined space had been an ongoing torture. He glanced at his watch – six o'clock on a May morning – and looked down at the young woman asleep beside him.

She looked very youthful, he thought; very vulnerable – but he also knew now how passionate she could be; how responsive . . . how joyful. He remembered again his mother's question – so irritating at the time – regarding Nicola: 'If you look at her, are you moved?'

Very gently he started to trace the contours of Marnie's face with his finger: her dark eyebrows, wide forehead and high cheekbones; the outline of her jaw and the shape of her mouth.

She stirred drowsily and then opened her eyes. For a

moment she looked disorientated, not sure where she was, then slowly remembering, she smiled at him. 'Oh, hi there,' she said. 'Are we still in Scotland? Are you still around?'

'We're still here and I'm still very much around.'

'Oh good,' she said, 'how lovely,' and she turned towards him again.

After breakfast – porridge, scrambled eggs with mushrooms and wonderfully thin, crisp bacon – Marnie said she felt strong enough to try the Reverend Donald McBain's telephone number. She came back looking triumphant. 'He answered himself. He'll see us at ten.'

Cherry Barton suggested that they might like to take a packed lunch with them. 'Then it won't matter what the time is or where you end up,' she said. 'You're welcome to come back here, of course, but there isn't anywhere in Wester Finterie where you'd get anything to eat. There's a sub-post office at Finterie where you might get a packet of crisps and a tablet if you were lucky.'

'A *tablet*?' asked Marnie, mystified, wondering if secret pill-popping went on in this out-of-the-way place.

'Scottish for a particular slab of fudgy toffee,' explained Christopher, laughing. 'Very innocuous – unless you overdose! I think a packed lunch would be an excellent idea, don't you?'

'Perfect. We could picnic in the castle,' she said happily. 'Eat it in the dining room and pretend we're living there already.'

'Are we going to live there?' he enquired.

'Of course,' she said. 'It's all been pre-ordained – written in the stars or something. I know it.'

'Well, lucky you!' said Cherry. 'I've half a mind to hitch a ride and come with you both. I've always wanted to go round Eilean Dobhran.'

'We'll give you a formal invitation to dine with us when we've moved in,' joked Christopher.

'I'll hold you to that! We're doing packed lunches for the fishers anyway, so give us fifteen minutes and it'll be ready.'

Cherry also volunteered the information that the retired minister was a dear old boy – a bit forgetful about day-to-day things now and again, though very much still in possession of his marbles and a mine of information about all things local. The niece who looked after him, on the other hand, was a proper acid-drop who saw it as her role in life to prevent him from having visitors. 'Which is a shame really, because he loves to blether on about the past,' said Cherry. 'Local gossip has it that Miss McBain isn't looking to the next world for her reward for caring for her old relative – he's said to have quite a bit of money stashed away in this one, which she hopes will come her way by and by. The old chap will be thrilled to talk to you. I hope he's helpful.'

It wasn't difficult to find the Old Manse because the village only consisted of a row of cottage, a few crofts and the tiny redundant kirk. It was a typical well-proportioned old manse, harled white – though not very recently – with plain sash windows and a surprisingly elegant fanlight over the front door – a door that was badly in need of a fresh coat of paint. Whether the minister had anything tucked away or not it didn't look as if he was disposed to spend money on his house. Marnie's sporty little car looked very out of place parked outside it; an old Morris Eight or even a pony and trap would have been more in keeping. They went up the path together and were conscious of a muslin curtain in the front room being flicked back into place. There didn't seem to be a bell, so Christopher lifted the doorknocker and banged much more loudly than he'd intended. The door opened so quickly it made them both jump.

A little ferret of a woman, all twitching nose and faded blonde hair, stood there.

'Yes?' She sounded distinctly unfriendly.

'We've come to see Mr McBain. I'm Marnie Donovan – I telephoned earlier.' Marnie held out her hand.

'Well I suppose you'd best come in then.' The woman sniffed disparagingly, eyed them both for an embarrassingly long time but eventually moved aside to let them enter, ignoring Marnie's outstretched hand.

'I hope it's not an inconvenient time to come . . . ?' said Marnie apologetically.

'I'll tell him you're here.' The ferret opened a door on the right and they heard her say: 'Those folk who phoned have arrived.'

They couldn't hear what was said in reply, but: 'He'll see you,' she said, turning round and looking, they thought, disappointed. She indicated the door with a nod of her head, sniffed again and disappeared down the passage.

'Hmm. Friendly type,' murmured Christopher, winking encouragingly at Marnie. He tapped on the door and then held it open for her and rather nervously she led the way in.

The room smelled faintly musty. A stout old man with a white frill of hair round his shiny pate was sitting in a wing chair by the fire. A copy of the *Scotsman* was resting on his considerable stomach. Marnie thought he looked like an elderly Friar Tuck. Unlike his niece, he greeted them with a welcoming smile.

'Come in, come in,' said the Reverend Donald McBain. 'It's not often I get unexpected visitors nowadays. This is indeed a pleasure – you'll forgive me if I don't get up. I'm getting a wee bit slow nowadays.' He spoke in an unhurried, lilting voice, and Christopher didn't think he looked as if urgency had ever been his forte anyway. 'I'm sorry I wasn't here when you rang. It's rare for me to be away the now, but I had to go to Edinburgh for a couple of nights. You're enquiring about the castle, I believe? Miss Fergusson of Tillydrum has called this morning to ask me if I will try to be of assistance to you.'

'Oh, how very kind of her!' exclaimed Marnie, touched that Evelyn should have taken so much trouble.

'I understand you knew Contessa Martinelli – Miss Drummond that was – Lucy-Anne Drummond. Now there's a name from the past!'

'Don't tell me you knew her!' It seemed too much to hope for.

'I did indeed. My father was minister here before me, so the children from the castle or "the big hoose", as we called it then, and the children from the manse – well, we were all bairns together. I'm eighty-nine now and Lucy would have been about a year older than me, and her brother Alexander a couple of years older than that.' He laughed. 'Och! But they were demons, those two! The tales that were told of their exploits – but everyone on the estate loved them. It was a sad day when Lucy ran away to Italy and an even sadder one when Alexander was killed.' He shook his head. 'The old couple never recovered. Now, tell me how you came to know her.' So Marnie told her story yet again.

'And what is it you're wanting now?'

'First I want to visit the house she told me so much about, pay my respects . . . and then,' said Marnie simply, 'with the money she left me, if it's at all possible, I might be interested in buying it. Is it for sale?'

The old man rubbed his chin. 'Well, it is and it isn't. It's not on the market as such. It belongs to a cousin of the family, a Mr Ian Drummond, who lives in Canada. He has no family of his own so I don't know what will happen when he dies. He sold part of the estate a long time ago but he wouldn't sell the castle. I think he was sweet on Lucy when he was a lad. Well, we all were to some degree,' he said rather sadly. 'I think he felt she should have had the property when Sandy, her brother, was killed, but her parents couldn't find it in themselves to forgive her. Verra, verra sad. Ian Drummond leased the castle out twice, first as a hotel and then as a nursing home, but neither venture was a success. The company who ran the hotel wanted to buy it, and I dare say if they'd owned it they would have made a success of it, but Ian Drummond wouldn't sell so they wouldn't continue to lease it. The nursing home was never going to flourish. It's too remote here and they couldn't get the staff – or the patients either, come to that. So it's been empty for several years now.'

'What kind of state is it in?' asked Christopher.

'We-e-ll.' The old man drew the word out and shrugged his shoulders. 'It's deteriorating all the time, of course, as unoccupied buildings do, but it's no so bad when you consider that it's unheated and unlived in. Structurally it's reasonably sound. Mr Drummond pays me something to give an eye to it – there's nothing I can physically do myself, of course, but I get the local builder to take a look at the roof once a year and check it out. The biggest fear is that it might get vandalised. So far it's been fortunate to escape that.'

'It seems such a waste to leave it to crumble away,' said Marnie indignantly. 'I'm surprised it hasn't been snapped up as a private house.'

'Well, it's a listed building for one thing, so if anyone were minded to restore it – for whatever purpose – they would immediately face all sorts of complications.' He smiled his sweet slow smile. 'Ruined castles are two a penny in the Highlands . . . until, that is, you want to start doing things to them. Then they become verra, verra expensive indeed, verra verra difficult and verra time-consuming! No one would be likely to put up the kind of money it would require to put this one in order unless they owned it – but, and here's the snag, it wouldn't then be a case of doing whatever you fancied once you'd bought it, even if you had a great deal of money to spare. There are a lot of restrictions, a lot of controversial views and a lot of powerful lobbies in the conservation world. There are those who think a ruin should be preserved as a ruin, especially if it enhances a scenic and romantic view in the eyes of the public; then there are those who believe in restoration and making a house habitable . . . after all the original purpose for a house . . . but they find it hard to agree among themselves as to which period you should be looking at when you restore a building that's been through many incarnations. Are you going way back to its origins as a fortified tower house, aggressively vertical, with impenetrably thick walls and a few turrets, or to a mid-eighteenth century restoration of the original – a romantic ideal of a gentleman's country seat with fine Georgian rooms and graceful plasterwork? Or are you favouring the high Victorian love affair with all things Scottish – and the Victorians did some very fine and sympathetic renovations? Where do you start and where do you stop and who has the final say?'

'Why does Mr Drummond hang on to it if he doesn't want to cope with it himself? It seems weird. Pointless. Wasteful.'

'On the contrary, I think he feels a great responsibility for its future and he won't let it go to just anybody. I think he's hoping the right buyer will turn up sometime, and then he might – *might* – be persuaded to sell.'

Marnie and Christopher stared at him.

'Have you met him? Does he ever come over?' asked Christopher.

'I've met him once or twice, aye, and I remember him staying at the castle in the old days when we were both lads. Since he inherited Eilean Dobhran, he's been used to come over every few years, but whether he'll ever make that long journey again I don't know. He's an old man too. We're the last of our generation.' He smiled at them. 'But you're young and your lives are before you so if you want to go and look at the old place, I'm sure Mr Drummond wouldn't object. Do you want me to let you have the keys?'

'Oh, yes *please*.' Marnie was breathless with excitement and Christopher couldn't help feeling relieved that he was not going to be called on to make an illicit entry. 'What do you think it would take to get it back to its former glory, even for a different use?'

'A lot of determination, a deep purse . . . and the bottle for a fight,' said the old minister.

Christopher looked amused. 'You'd be the ideal candidate on all counts,' he told Marnie.

The Reverend Donald McBain heaved himself up from his chair with some difficulty – he really was extremely fat, so at least the sharp-faced niece must feed him well, thought Marnie, unless she was deliberately trying to hasten his demise by stuffing him with life-threatening cholesterol. He wore very ancient woolly bedroom slippers, slit open at the top to accommodate his swollen feet.

He shuffled over to a kneehole desk in the window, its top rather ink-stained and the leather coming unstuck round the edges, opened a drawer and produced a cumbersome set of keys on a chain, which he handed to Marnie.

'The smallest key is for the padlock on the main gates,' he explained. 'You may have a bit of trouble getting them opened, I'm afraid. I haven't been inside for quite a while myself, but I know they've got very rusted. The biggest key is to the outside door at the front of the house, and the next one is for the inner door. The last one is for the door at the back, overlooking the loch. You might want to let yourselves out that way and walk down to the water's edge. Take as long as you like and drop the keys back here when you've finished with them. Turn left and keep going for about half a mile. The gates are on your right. You can't miss them. Good luck.'

They thanked him warmly and, since there was no sign of the niece, let themselves out of the front door.

Marnie took a gulp of air. 'Bit stuffy in there, wasn't it?' she said. 'I'm glad to be outside again, aren't you? What did you make of him?'

'I thought he was a nice old chap,' said Christopher, 'but he didn't seem particularly surprised to see you or hear your extraordinary story. Did you think it odd that he was prepared to hand over the keys just like that?'

Marnie looked taken aback. 'I hadn't actually given it a thought,' she admitted. 'I took it for granted he'd give them to us because it all feels so right to me – like some plan unfolding. And after all, we did ring up first and he had heard from Miss Fergusson this morning, so he knew we weren't fraudsters.'

'Oh well, I suppose so – but you and the stars have clearly got it all very well organised,' said Christopher. 'Come on then. Now for the big moment . . . Eilean Dobhran itself!'

Mr McBain was right: they had a struggle to open the big gates. It wasn't the padlock that was the difficulty and they unwound the heavy chain comparatively easily, but the large rusted bolts on the huge wrought-iron gates seemed welded into the ground.

'Oh, let's forget about the car – let's try to find somewhere we can shin over the wall and then walk up.' Marnie could hardly contain her impatience to get to the house, but to Christopher's relief he managed to loosen one of the bolts with a final yank that sent him staggering backwards when it suddenly gave way, and after a bit more pushing and pulling they were able to drag the gates open and drive in.

'Thank God for that!' he said. 'I think you're determined to get me re-arrested!'

She was immediately penitent. 'Gee, I'm sorry – I keep forgetting about the prison thing,' she said. 'You should have reminded me.'

'No way,' he said, laughing at her. 'I'd hate you to keep remembering my shady past all the time. Come on then. I quite fancy being driven up to a castle by a beautiful girl in a sports car.'

Marnie put the roof of the car down so that they shouldn't miss what she called 'one whiff of anything'.

The long, wooded drive was a jungle of brambles, bracken, willow herb and fallen branches. Rabbits, astonished at being disturbed by humans, scurried about everywhere as though they were unexpectedly caught in rush hour; Christopher and Marnie could hear the distant barking of a roe deer somewhere deep in the wood and a pair of cock pheasants looked annoyed to have their jousting match interrupted.

'I guess we're likely to find the Sleeping Beauty in an upstairs bedroom when we get into the house,' said Marnie happily. 'But don't get any ideas about kissing her if we do, or I could become seriously jealous.'

'Perhaps you should watch out – it could turn out to be Bluebeard's castle,' said Christopher. 'He had some nasty little ways with pretty ladies.'

The drive opened out into parkland, studded with a few huge oaks and beeches, and as they rounded a final bend, there, facing them on the other side of a wide causeway, stood the castle.

'So it really is on an island,' breathed Marnie.

'Good, strategically, for keeping the enemy at bay!'

They drove over the wide causeway to the front of the house, where there must once have been a fine sweep of raked gravel, though grass and weeds and moss had now invaded it. From the lochside it had only been possible to see the tower, with its four small turrets at the corners, standing out against the evening sky, but from here it was apparent that there was another wing of the house on the front and what looked like a courtyard to the left – stables, perhaps? Luciana had certainly talked of riding.

Marnie stopped the car in front of balustraded stone steps, which led to the great arched doorway that was so familiar to her from the photographs. They both got out and stood gazing up at it. There was the stone plaque with the entwined initials; there was the outline of the heraldic bird – only the people from the photographs were missing, disturbingly conspicuous by their absence. Christopher saw that tears were suddenly pouring down Marnie's cheeks, all her bright excitement extinguished as if a light had been switched off. He put his arm round her and held her close.

'It looks so desolate,' she said at last in a choked voice, 'so terribly neglected and sad; so *unloved* – so full of secrets and shadows. I wasn't expecting the windows to be all shuttered like this. It makes it look . . . *blind*. And I realise my old lady's already been dead for twenty years and can't have set foot in this house after she was nineteen. Where is she now? Is there really an afterlife and if so what's she doing? Does consciousness survive or is that just our wishful thinking? Do you think all religion is really a kind of play-acting to make us feel less scared of the inevitable end?' Christopher felt her shiver.

'I don't know,' he said gently. 'I'd like answers to all those questions too, but we're not going to get them. You hoped you'd see a little red-headed girl on the steps with her great big dog. You imagined lights in the windows and the front door open and possibly a piper marching round. Empty houses do look sad – and rightly so. Houses are meant to be loved and lived in.'

'She must have been so unhappy,' said Marnie sadly. 'I feel she must have been desperately homesick to talk to me so much about this place in the way she did. She'd lost everything she ever loved when I knew her. And she never made it up with her family – they never forgave her for something that might cause temporary acrimony but would be no big deal nowadays. I can't bear it.'

'Don't cry,' he said. 'Please don't cry. You gave her something wonderful at the end of her life without having any idea at the time of what you'd done. She told you that, in her letter, and she'd never have made such an eccentric bequest if you hadn't become really important to her. Don't forget that when she told you all those stories about this place she was obviously reliving a supremely happy childhood, and she clearly had great happiness and romance with her Italian husband. It doesn't sound to me as if she'd have chosen to act any differently a second time no matter how much she paid for her decision. That's important.'

'Thanks,' she whispered. 'I'm sorry to be so stupid. After all these years of imagining it, the real thing comes as a bit of a shock.'

'Of course it does. Look, Marnie,' he said seriously, considering his words carefully, not wanting to take advantage of her moment of vulnerability; feeling there were things he wanted to say to her but afraid of saying too much too soon from both their points of view. 'I came here because I wanted to be with you, not because I shared your vision about this house. It looks depressing today, but wouldn't it be wonderful to bring it to life again? Not the *same* life, but a new one – wouldn't that be a healing thing for you to do? Wouldn't that be an exciting challenge?'

'The vision's gone a bit wobbly on me,' she said, blowing her nose violently. 'I'm not sure if I can hang on to it any more. I felt so full of confidence but now I wonder if it's all been a crazy dream.'

'All the best ideas start with a bit of craziness. You'll need some help and support – it would be daunting and depressing to take this on all alone – but taking over ailing companies has been my speciality. It's what I know about – how I've made my money – and ailing castles may not be so very different! I'd love to give you all the help and advice I can if you'd let me. What did the old man say would be needed to make a go of this place? Determination, a deep purse, and . . .?' He raised an eyebrow at her.

She gave him a watery smile, '. . . and the bottle for a fight,' she finished for him.

'Exactly. Let's put all these imponderables on one side for the moment,' he said. 'Let's just go exploring and see what we find. We'll fling back the shutters and let some light in on the situation. How are the cold feet feeling now?'

'Getting a bit warmer again, thanks,' she said. 'That's a fantastic suggestion. I'd love your help. I suppose it would be a bit cowardly to walk away at this stage wouldn't it?'

'Definitely. Come on then.'

It seemed so dark when they first entered that Christopher had to grope his way to the window to let the daylight in. One surprise was that the castle still had some furniture in it. A beautiful but battered drum library table stood in the middle of the hall. Someone had left an ordinary kitchen type mug on it, which had left a ring. Over the carved stone fireplace hung a huge still life of dead birds and a ham on a pewter platter, with fruit and flowers and insects, in a wide, crumbling gilt frame – a cobweb hanging from the top of the frame might have been part of the picture. Incongruously there was a modern metal bedstead propped against one wall, a legacy from the castle's incarnation as a nursing home no doubt, as was a wheelchair in which mice had nested. Christopher and Marnie wandered from room to room, flinging open shutters as they went and discovering unlikely things – a set of bound copies of *Punch* from the nineteen twenties lying on the floor beside a clinical pack of grey cardboard bedpans, still wrapped in polythene. 'Very useful if you're trying to furnish a house from scratch,' Christopher grinned. They found a Victorian musical box with an inlaid rosewood case on a window seat. Christopher raised the inner glass lid and pulled the handle at the side and the spiked brass cylinder rolled into action, filling the room with a bell-like, nostalgic rendering of 'The Bluebells of Scotland' that seemed to epitomise the mood of the place.

A studded door on the right opened on to a spiral staircase, the stone steps carpeted in tartan, which led them up to a charming long, low room with a barrel ceiling, beautiful plasterwork and a stunning view over the loch. It looked as if it might once have been the main drawing room, and at one end of it Marnie was enchanted to discover a portrait, a conversation piece, showing a man and a woman sitting on a garden seat with two teenage children, a boy and a girl, lounging on a rug on the grass, forever enjoying a sunny afternoon. They both had red hair.

She looked at it for a long time, recognising clearly an

older version of the little girl in her locket, and searching for traces of the old woman she had known. Then she walked over to the other end of the room to inspect the picture over the fireplace, and suddenly gave a cry of distress.

'Look.' She was gazing with horror at something at her feet. Christopher looked. Lying on the hearth was a dead bird. He went over and picked it up. 'It's a tawny owl,' he said. 'Poor thing, it must have fallen down the chimney and been unable to get out again. Lucky there weren't any ornaments to get broken. We had an awful mess at my home a few years ago when a jackdaw came down the chimney while my parents were away. It came out in the drawing room and smashed a Famille Rose vase – not to mention bringing down bags of sticky soot. The mess was indescribable! And I'll never forget my astonishment as a child on waking up once to find an owl sitting on the top of the wardrobe in my bedroom looking down at me. I wanted to keep it as a pet and was awfully cross when my mother let it out of the window. I don't think this one can have been dead more than day or two. Look how beautifully its feathers are marked . . .' He broke off, suddenly aware that Marnie was looking distraught. 'Oh, Marnie, come on. It's sad, but I'm afraid this happens occasionally with these big old fireplaces – don't take it to heart.'

'No, no – you don't understand. It's because it's an *owl*,' she said, as if he were being extraordinarily dense.

'What difference does that make? I've always loved owls. You're not superstitious about them, are you?'

'Not for myself,' she said, looking agonised. 'This isn't about me or this house. Don't you see? This is *Louisa's* owl.'

'Don't be ridiculous! How could it possibly be her owl? Her family live in Yorkshire for God's sake!'

'I don't mean the actual one . . . but Louisa lives in dread of her owl dying and she told me she'd had a nightmare about it the other night. Now it's happened . . . just like in her dream.'

'Of course that isn't what's happened! Owls die all the time, all over the country. They get killed on roads, they get sick, they die of old age . . . and they fall down chimneys. You're letting your imagination get away with you. You wouldn't have thought twice about it if she hadn't happened to tell you about it.'

'But that's the whole point – she did tell me,' said Marnie obstinately.

'Look,' he said, trying not to sound impatient, but disturbed by her intensity. 'We've all been rootling around in our past, and owls are clearly important to Louisa – it's what she wrote about in the same way you wrote about the Caribbean. It's been on her mind as your strange childhood has been on yours.'

'Yes, I know. That's exactly what I told her too . . . it's what I thought myself at the time . . . but now this has happened it changes things. You must admit it's a very strange coincidence.'

'I don't admit anything of the sort . . . you're reading a significance into this that's not there. You're getting yourself in a state about something that isn't really your issue because you've got so much genuinely difficult emotional stuff to cope with yourself. I believe it's called displacement.'

'Oh, spare me the psycho-babble,' she flashed. They glared at each other, their tempers rising dangerously, and then they both said 'Sorry' at exactly the same moment.

'Damn, damn, damn! I didn't mean to sound so pompous and unsympathetic,' said Christopher, cursing himself for a fool. 'It's just that I can't bear to see you so upset, when I really don't think you need to be. Let's finish our tour of the house first, then when we go outside I'll find somewhere to give the bird a decent burial, and this evening we'll ring up Glendrochatt to tell them all about finding your castle and you can check up on Louisa. I'll bet you anything you'll find she and her owl will both be fine, but it will put your mind at rest and you needn't tell her about this one if you think it might upset her. How's that?'

'Okay,' she said, making a conscious effort to calm down, feeling rather foolish to have been so dramatic. 'Yeah . . . I'd like to do that. I promised Isobel I'd let her know how we got on anyway. I see why you think I'm over-reacting, but it really freaked me out. Let's go on up to the top of the house now. I remember being told that the children's nurseries were on the top floor of the tower and that the Contessa and her brother used to get out on to the battlements, which was strictly forbidden, and frightened their mother into fits.'

'Good idea. And I know what else I think we ought to do pretty soon.'

'What?'

'Eat! I don't know about you but I feel distinctly peckish. How about having our picnic after that?'

'Goodness, yes. I'm starving too!' She determined to put the owl out of her mind. 'We could have it by the loch.'

They spent a fascinating hour exploring the tower. The view from the battlements was breathtaking, worth every moment of the steep climb up another spiral staircase. They found the sinister oubliette and the various chutes for pouring boiling oil that had so captured the imagination of a small Marnie – one of them in what Marnie said was the nursery bathroom. Christopher marvelled that she had remembered so much detail of what she'd been told so long ago.

'This view has got everything – fields and woods, the loch . . . the hills . . . and you can see the river from here too,' he said, when they'd climbed through a trapdoor and were looking down on the surrounding countryside from a dizzying height. 'What a fantastic place for a child to grow up . . . can you imagine the fun? No wonder your Contessa had such vivid memories, though judging by the way my sisters fuss over their respective broods I doubt if her mother ever had an easy moment! I quite see why those attic windows have bars on them. You're right – those rooms must have been the nurseries.'

'What a difference light makes,' said Marnie. 'Now that the shutters are open the feeling of gloom has quite gone.' Walking round the battlements they got a bird's eye view of the gardens. To the south, there had obviously once been a parterre, and straggly bits of box hedge remained here and there, while the pattern of formal beds could be seen from above, imprinted in ghostly outline on the grass that had seeded itself everywhere.

'My old mum would go wild with ideas if she could see this,' said Christopher. 'The garden is crying out for rescue.'

'Could we try and get her here? Do you think she might help me too?'

'What a lovely idea. Let's suggest it to her on Sunday. I think she'd jump at it. You could ask Morwenna too.'

They fetched the picnic from the car and found a sheltered spot by the edge of the loch. Christopher scooped a hollow grave out of the shingle and covered the body of the owl with stones.

It was late afternoon before they could bring themselves to leave, by which time they had walked miles round the grounds and ventured into every corner of the building. Since Marnie said she was hopeless with a camera, Christopher took endless photographs both inside and out. With every moment they became more enchanted with the place – and more enamoured of each other. By the time they ate their lunch, sitting at the edge of the loch, neither of them had any doubt that Marnie should try to make a bid for the castle. The idea that they might become partners in a joint venture was ticking away in Christopher's head like a time bomb, but he was determined, for both their sakes, to resist suggesting it till they'd returned to England and left the whole fairy-tale idyll behind. He knew he needed a new business project to throw himself into, one that could be fitted in with his writing – he was clear about that – but one that would use his proven flair for negotiating and considerable organisational skills.

Neither of them made reference to the possibility of a different, deeper kind of collaboration, though the thought hovered between them, unvoiced. Christopher remembered how envious he'd felt of the way the Grants seemed to achieve such a harmonious dovetailing of marriage and business partnerships.

Back in the house, they carefully shut all the doors and shutters again and locked up. Christopher's leg had started to play up and Marnie felt suddenly exhausted, completely drained by the emotions of the day. They walked back to the car and took a last look at the castle.

'It's got its eyes shut again,' said Marnie, 'but, oh, Christopher, what a place!'

'It's just sleeping till we come back again.' He took her in his arms and kissed her. 'Thank you for letting me share today with you,' he said. 'I shall never forget it. I wish I'd met your old lady too.'

They handed the keys back to Mr McBain and in exchange got the name and address of the Canadian owner before driving back to Finterie Lodge.

After dinner they rang Glendrochatt. Giles answered. He sounded delighted at Marnie's news. He said Isobel had unexpectedly had to go up to London and wouldn't be back till the following evening. 'Do ring her tomorrow,' he said. 'She'll want to know every detail.'

'How's everyone else?' asked Marnie.

'In great form,' said Giles. 'I took John and Morwenna and Louisa for an expedition today. We went up the Tilt and had a splendid day out.'

'Oh, good. We sure want to hear news about the Colonel and Morwenna! You must keep us posted about developments there. And is Louisa okay too?'

'Louisa's absolutely fine, very well – did you want to speak to her? I think she's only gone to make a call to her parents about going home on her way south. Shall I ask her to ring you back?'

'No, don't worry. Give her my love and say we'll see her in London as we planned, when we all get back. I've got her number. And I'll give Isobel a ring over the weekend.'

'Yes, you do that. We're all missing you very much. Good luck with everything.'

'Well?' asked Christopher, as Marnie put the telephone down, looking very relieved. 'Everything all right?'

'Fine,' said Marnie. She came and sat on the arm of his chair. 'You were right, of course . . . I was over-reacting this morning. Please forget I was so stupid.'

'I could never think you stupid,' said Christopher. 'But I'm glad all's well with Louisa. Now let's think of us and plan our day tomorrow.'

Chapter Twenty-eight

Isobel sat back in her seat on the train to London on Friday morning and closed her eyes, thankful that she would have several uninterrupted hours in which to try to order her thoughts. She knew that the evening ahead of her would be testing and that important issues for the whole family depended on what she managed to achieve.

Running Glendrochatt as an arts centre was always busy, often challenging and occasionally taxing, but for the most part Isobel adored her life, revelled in the variety of people who came on the courses and got great satisfaction from encouraging their differing interests and talents; she loved the fun and challenge of running a joint venture with Giles, took great pleasure in the concerts which had become such popular events locally and felt proud that they had succeeded in transforming Giles's ancestral home into a flourishing concern, which enabled them to keep it as a home for their children. The downside was that it wasn't always easy to find time for private life.

After they'd gone to bed on Wednesday night, she and Giles had lain awake for hours discussing the unexpected turn events had taken, trying to look at possibilities for the future from every conceivable angle, discussing the problems they might face if they were successful in their bid to have Rory living with them on a semi-permanent footing, even considering his possible adoption; anticipating the difficulties she might be faced with when she met Lorna.

Giles had very much wanted to come to London with her, but though in some ways it would have been lovely to have his company and support, Isobel felt strongly that she would cope with Lorna better on her own.

'You dealt with her after the drama with Ed,' she insisted. 'You had all the unpleasantness of banishing her from Glendrochatt. I feel I need to deal with her this time. If you come too, she'll think it's only you that wants Rory to be part of our family, but if I go alone she'll know it's my decision too. That's important.' Giles had reluctantly agreed, but only on the understanding that if Lorna became impossible, Isobel would ring him and he'd fly down to join her.

Earlier that day, after she'd seen everyone off on their various expeditions, Isobel had gone into the drawing room, where she was least likely to be disturbed, intending to keep on ringing Lorna until she eventually got hold of her. She had been disconcerted, on being put through to the Congletons' suite at the Ritz, when Brooke Congleton, to whom she had never previously spoken, answered the telephone himself. Lorna, he informed her was out. She had gone to her hairdresser before going to a lecture on the great plantation homes of Virginia, followed by a ladies' luncheon, given by the American ambassador's wife in aid of charity – which it was naturally, he said, very important that Lorna should attend and be seen to attend. Very important.

'But I will tell her you called,' he said graciously. 'She'll be sorry to have missed you. I know that will be a matter of regret for her.'

'So when can I speak to her?' Isobel remembered Sheena's description of Senator Congleton and envisaged him smoothing his silver hair with his free hand. 'I keep trying to get hold of her, but she hasn't rung me back. I want to know how Rory is.'

'Ah . . .' said the senator. 'Yes indeed. The little boy.'

'So?' asked Isobel. 'How is he?'

'Well, I'm glad of this opportunity to thank you personally for coming to our rescue over the child,' said the senator. 'It was, and indeed still is, greatly appreciated, but I guess – indeed I am perfectly certain – that Lorna will already have thanked you most warmly for your sisterly generosity in that direction, and let me just say this to you, Isobel . . .' He paused. 'May I call you Isobel?' he asked.

'Yes, of course . . . please do,' said Isobel, wondering how long and repetitive Brooke Congleton's political speeches might be if he could make such heavy weather of an ordinary telephone call. She waited, but the senator appeared to have lost his thread and didn't seem to know what it was that he wanted to say. 'So how *is* Rory?' she asked, trying not to sound impatient. 'Has he settled in? Is he all right?'

'Well,' said the senator, grasping at the thread again, 'I was coming to that. I won't pretend to you that there aren't problems; serious problems. In fact it would be fair to say the situation is far from easy. Not easy at all. We are experiencing certain difficulties with the child. Knowing him as you do, I imagine this will come as no surprise to you.'

'What sort of difficulties?' asked Isobel with a sinking heart.

'I dare say his behavioural problems are nothing a good therapist will not be able to sort out, given time . . . and we do have a very, very good therapist back home who will advise us . . . but what we don't have is time. Time is of the essence in our lives. We are very, very busy people.' He paused impressively and Isobel longed to say *If you're so busy why don't you get a move on?* but managed to restrain herself. 'I have been suggesting to Lorna,' Brooke Congleton went on, 'that perhaps it would be better if the boy's father played some part in his upbringing. It seems to me that he has not shouldered his responsibilities at all so far.'

'What do you mean?' asked Isobel. This was not what Evelyn Fergusson had led her to expect. Did he know about Giles after all?

'I have put it to Lorna – for her consideration, you understand; naturally it must be her decision – that she should send the child back to South Africa to be raised by his father until he is more mature. Naturally Lorna would keep a watching brief.'

'Goodness! And what does Lorna think?' Isobel wanted to scream that Rory was not some parcel to be packed up and re-addressed every time it suited his stepfather to get rid of him, but at the same time a solution to everyone's problems started to seem possible.

'It's fair to say that Lorna has not yet come round to my way of thinking over this,' admitted the senator ponderously. 'No doubt she will do so in due course – she is a very, very reasonable person – but at this moment in time she is unwilling to get in touch with her ex-husband and reopen old wounds. My own inclination is to have my attorney call him and suggest he should come to an accommodation with us. I find it reprehensible that he has played no part so far in rearing the boy. Lorna has never claimed a dollar from him for maintenance of the child.'

No, thought Isobel, I'll bet she hasn't! Her mind was racing. Aloud she said: 'This is very upsetting news. It's possible,' she went on, groping her way, conscious of gaping pitfalls if she said the wrong thing, 'that because I've brought up a family myself and have got to know Rory so well in the last two months I might be able to offer some helpful suggestions. We really didn't have any problems with him once he'd settled in with us. But I need to see Lorna and talk it over with her in person.'

'Quite,' said the senator. 'Quite. But may I say to you . . .'

'What exactly is the problem with Rory's behaviour?' interrupted Isobel. 'I can see he must be very unsettled after all the changes he's been through, but surely he can't have been that bad. He's only *five*, for goodness' sake and he's only been back with his mum for a week. And children always punish their mums for leaving them, even for a short time. It's standard.'

The senator said gravely that that was a very, very interesting observation, but he did not, at this stage, and on the telephone, feel at liberty to go into details over a possible clinical condition that had not, as yet, been properly assessed. He impressed on Isobel what a vital year this was for him politically, how he needed Lorna's support full time and how the nurse they'd hired to look after the child didn't seem able to manage him any better than his mother could. Not once was any question of Rory's welfare mentioned. He then informed Isobel that he was waiting for a highly significant call to come through from the States, and, much as he'd enjoyed talking to her, he felt he really must bring their call to a close.

'That's fine by me,' said Isobel, 'I'm pretty busy myself. Perhaps you'd tell Lorna that I could come up to London on Friday for one night to talk things over, but if she wants my help over Rory she'll need to ring me as soon as she gets in so that I can arrange things this end. It's over to her,' and she rang off.

Regaling Giles with this conversation that night, she said: 'Do you know, I suddenly felt sorry for Lorna! He sounds such a bogus old windbag. I'll bet he's good at dodging awkward political questions and waffling on about nothing, using ten words when two would do, but no amount of money and glamour and moving in high circles could compensate for having to listen to someone like that pontificating all day. But oh, Giles . . . poor Rory! He must be wretched. So bewildered. No wonder he's being a perfect pain.'

Lorna had indeed rung back . . . an unusually subdued-sounding Lorna . . . and Isobel had agreed to go up to London to meet her. 'Just the two of us,' she said firmly, though having spoken to Lorna's husband she did not think for a moment that Lorna would be at all keen to discuss Rory's paternity in front of him anyway. They arranged to meet at a little restaurant off the Pimlico Road where Giles and Isobel often dined if they were in London together. It was simple and spacious and had good straightforward Italian food. Isobel declined Lorna's invitation to dine at the Ritz, even though Brooke Congleton would be attending a dinner elsewhere.

'Think very carefully, Iz,' Giles had said as they lay side by side in their big bed at Glendrochatt, both of them exhausted by weighing up hypothetical pros and cons. 'Even if Lorna agrees – even if, as we suspect, it's what she really wants from us, it's a major, major step we're contemplating. If we were to take Rory on, the caring is bound to fall more on you than on me, but you'll have to be sure you won't resent it when I get involved too. Comparisons with how Ed might have been, if things were otherwise, will be really hard to cope with, no matter how good and generous your intentions are, and resentment of his relationship to me is bound to crop up occasionally. Our marriage is more important to me than anything else. I put it seriously at risk once – if this were to come between us now, I don't think I could cope.'

'I know,' she whispered. 'I can't promise never to be resentful or stroppy – I know myself too well for that – and I know this has to be something we work at together, but out of all our agonies and disappointments and struggles and triumphs with Ed, I think his greatest gift to us is that we've learned some tough lessons about loving – real loving . . . at any rate the theory,' she added with an ironic shrug. 'I'm not so unrealistic as to feel certain we'll get this *right* but I do believe we're strong enough to *try*. And it wasn't just you, darling. I know I put our marriage at risk five years ago too. I think this might be a chance for us to make something good out of that whole nightmare of a summer when we were all thrown off balance. Of course Amy's views tipped the scales, didn't they?'

Going over this conversation now, as she sat in the train, she thought that she would be able to cope with the reality of Giles's relationship with Rory, provided that the long shadow of Lorna did not fall across their marriage again. That would be another matter altogether.

Isobel arrived at the restaurant first. She had booked a table in the corner and could see the door from where she sat, so when a large chauffeur-driven limousine drew up outside she guessed who would step out of it.

It was five years since they had seen each other and Lorna's elegance and good looks had been notable then. Isobel wondered how the years would have marked her since her attempt to commandeer her brother-in-law; whether motherhood – though clearly not a satisfactory relationship for her – would have mellowed her rather chilly beauty.

Lorna was wearing a simple black linen shift dress that left no doubt that tucked discreetly out of sight would be the label of an exclusive designer; the length of her elegant legs – always the envy of Isobel, whose own legs were of the sturdy variety – was enhanced by the impossibly high heels of her Christian Louboutin shoes. Her pale blonde hair, which had been long last time Isobel had seen her, was much shorter now and expertly cut to look casual while remaining perfectly groomed; it immediately made Isobel aware that her own curly mop was badly in need of a trim. Lorna wore a choker of pearls so large that Isobel would normally have assumed them to be fake, but which, she now thought, might very possibly be real. The heads of the other diners swivelled to look as Lorna made her entrance. Across the room, the sisters surveyed each other.

Isobel thought, if I was a stranger and had no idea who she was I'd long to know more about her. You can't see such physical perfection, such polish, and not feel impelled to gaze at it . . . but oh, how blank her face is. Has she already had one tweak and tuck too many? Has she lost any capacity for spontaneous fun and affection or is her skin just too tight to express emotion? Behind that marble façade, can she be happy?

Her immediate reaction to the dreaded reunion with her sister was one of sadness for an unfulfilled woman who had once been full of promise but had somehow managed to miss out on all the things that bring real happiness – and a consciousness of her own blessings in comparison. It was not at all what she had expected to feel. Damn, thought Isobel . . . damn, damn, damn. I mustn't start feeling too sorry for her.

Lorna was well aware of having caught the interest of everyone in the restaurant, but it came as no surprise. She would have noticed even more had the interest been missing. She knew it was her ability to attract instant admiration and attention that was her chief hold over her husband: should there be any sign of its waning, then Lorna would be a worried woman. It had not always been so; she looked at her younger sister and thought of the occasions in their childhood when it seemed that no matter how hard Lorna tried, Isobel eventually stole her limelight – not because she deliberately made a bid for it, not because she was as pretty or as clever as her older sister and certainly not because she was as competitive, but simply because everyone warmed to her. Isobel made people laugh and forget their troubles; her own unself-conscious enjoyment of life was so infectious that, in her company, others enjoyed themselves too. Isobel had been the thorn deeply embedded in Lorna's flesh for a very, very long time.

When Lorna's marriage to John Cartwright, the success-ful South African eye surgeon whom she'd married on the rebound, finally failed, she had returned to Scotland intent on reclaiming Giles Grant for herself, but her carefully planned campaign had backfired miserably. Six years later, released from restraint by the death of her father, she decided to settle an old score. She did not intend, this time, to make an attempt to win Giles back, but thought that by inserting Rory – so ridiculously like Giles – into the Grants' life for a short time she could cause an interesting upheaval in the marriage she still resented so much, with-out having to be present herself. She had not, however, bargained for the effect her son's return might have on her own marriage. In her mind's eye she had envisaged a reunion with Rory that would charm her husband, but this touching tableau had not turned out as planned and her always precarious relationship with her son had rapidly gone from bad to worse. Brooke Congleton had made it abundantly plain that he did not at all care to see his elegant ice-goddess turn into a rumpled harridan unable to cope with the passions of one small boy. It had not taken Rory long to discover that throwing a tantrum was the only sure way to get his alarming parent's full attention and at the same time, once he'd got carried away in a really good scream, temporarily override his own long-standing fear of her. There had been a highly embarrassing scene in the reception area of the Ritz, in view of several fellow Americans and a good many other shocked onlookers, when Lorna had completely lost her temper with Rory. It was as though the Mona Lisa had suddenly jumped out of her frame and thrown a very public wobbly in the hushed atmosphere of the Louvre. Brooke had been extremely angry afterwards in a cold way that Lorna found deeply menacing and, as the third wife of a rich and ambitious man who provided her with the sort of lifestyle she had always coveted, she was suddenly very afraid. She remembered with horror her similar loss of control with Edward at Glendrochatt five years before – and its near disastrous consequences.

Isobel got to her feet when Lorna came in but for a moment neither sister knew how to greet the other. Then Lorna swooped towards Isobel and presented her, at a safe distance of several inches, with an immaculately made-up cheek.

'Iz! What an age it's been! How are you?'

'I'm fine,' said Isobel. 'You look quite dazzling, Lorna. I don't know how you do it.'

'Thank you . . . with a lot of hard work and self-discipline, I'm afraid,' said Lorna, taking in the untrimmed hair and the grey strands at Isobel's temples.

'No wonder I can't achieve it then,' said Isobel wryly. 'I couldn't in a million years be bothered . . . but you obviously can and the result is sensational. Lorna . . . we have a lot to talk about and some of it's going to be testing for us both. Shall we have a drink and order before we get down to the hard bits?'

Lorna looked disconcerted for a moment at this direct approach. Then she nodded and shrugged. 'All right,' she said. 'Whatever you say. This meeting is your idea.'

They made conversation in such a stilted manner that Isobel later told Giles it felt like pushing a car uphill. They talked about their parents and about Le Colombier, the house in France which Lorna had inherited and intended, she said, to keep as a holiday retreat; they talked about Lorna's new life in Washington, about Brooke's political aspirations and the possibility of his running for higher office. Eventually, in a tight voice, Lorna managed to enquire about Glendrochatt, about Giles and Amy . . . and then in an even tighter voice about Edward. Isobel tried to reply as normally as possible but the constraint between them was almost unbearable. When the waiter brought the menu, they ordered a bottle of house red and fettucine al Gorgonzola with a green salad for them both. When the food finally arrived, Isobel took a good swig of wine and decided to get down to the issues that had brought them face to face after so long.

'Lorna,' she said, 'I'd like you to tell me the truth about Rory.'

'He's being impossibly difficult. I don't think Brooke is prepared to put up with his scenes for much longer and I'm in a very tricky position. I gather Brooke said something to you about it on the phone?'

'He did, but that's not what I meant. I want you to tell me who Rory's father is.'

Lorna hesitated. Then she said: 'Did Brooke tell you that he wants me to send Rory back to South Africa?'

'Yes. That would be a bit awkward for you, wouldn't it, Lorna? You've let your husband think John Cartwright is Rory's father, haven't you?'

'It seemed . . . simpler. And it could have been true.' Lorna looked defiant.

'Then why did you send Rory to me and hint that he could be Giles's son – even though you'd denied it when he was born? You certainly waited till Pa had died before making any such suggestion, and you must have known that one glance would be enough to tell Giles and me what you wanted us to know.'

Lorna crumbled her bread roll and looked uneasy. 'You both knew it was a possibility already.'

'Perhaps,' said Isobel. 'But it's not just a possibility now. Giles and I both know it's the truth and so do you, but just for the record, Lorna, I do have the scientific proof in case it should ever be needed legally in the future, for whatever reason. But how would you feel about Brooke's seeing Rory and Giles together?'

Lorna's large eyes widened suddenly. Isobel thought she looked like a Stubbs painting of a twitchy horse. 'Iz! That mustn't happen. Ever. You wouldn't?'

'Oh, but I would . . . if I had to. Why shouldn't I?'

The sisters eyed each other, testing old strengths and weaknesses.

Isobel said: 'You started this, Lorna, but now that we know Giles is Rory's father, we both think he should have a say in Rory's future too. How do you feel about that?'

'Glad!' Lorna spat the word out. 'Glad that there's a bit of Giles that is still mine and always will be and there's nothing you can do about it.'

Isobel felt her stomach lurch. Don't lose your temper, she told herself; don't get sidetracked into old recriminations. They had been picking at their food without tasting it. Now Isobel gave up the pretence and put her fork down. A vision came into her head of Rory's piteous face as he'd clung to her and begged her not to send him away. She remembered again the surprise of Amy's impassioned plea: 'You *can't* send him back to Aunt Lorna, Mum. He's terrified of her. Think of the effect she had on Ed. Have you forgotten how she practically killed him – how she literally frightened him into one of his fits and he nearly died? How can you be so cruel?' Amy had said: "Aunt Lorna is a wrecker and she always will be. She'd ruin his life.'

Making an effort to sound calmer than she felt, but

conscious that her voice was choked with emotion, she said: 'So what do you really want me to do, Lorna? If it gives you satisfaction I'll admit that I find it very painful that Rory is yours and not mine. If you wanted to underline the difference between my son and yours, then you've succeeded. But I've grown to love Rory for himself and of course Giles loves him too. We've talked it over endlessly and I came to offer that we should have Rory at Glendrochatt on a more or less permanent basis – to bring him up for you as Mum was practically doing until she got too ill.'

Lorna said nothing.

Isobel went on, trying to be generous and offer Lorna a face-saving escape route at the same time. 'We lead a more child-friendly existence than you do so it's easier for us. Giles has talked to our lawyer about it and we're both agreed that we could give Rory a secure base – a real home. I'd never try to cut him off completely from you, and it could only be with your full agreement – but there'd need to be several conditions from our point of view, and they would have to be legally binding. You couldn't suddenly demand him back on a whim. I'm not sure of the legal jargon, but something like Giles as his father having care and control and you having access.'

She could see that Lorna was struggling with herself. Isobel waited, afraid of saying too much, afraid of saying too little. Then Lorna said in a low, passionate voice: 'I've always been useless with children, you know that. They never like me, though I'll never understand why. God knows I've tried. I so envied you yours – even Edward in a funny way. Well, not perhaps Edward himself,' she amended, 'but what you seemed able to feel for him in spite of everything.' Isobel winced but Lorna rushed on, unaware of her sister's reaction. 'I'd always thought I wanted a baby for myself – someone to love *me* best – but from the moment Rory was born it was a disaster. He screamed every time he saw me and was only happy with Mum or the nanny, and I knew that the whole miserable thing of always being second best had started up again. I almost hated him – and he certainly didn't love me and still doesn't. These last days since he came back have been a disaster. Now I'm terrified he'll cause me to lose Brooke – and that I couldn't bear.'

Isobel looked at her beautiful, talented, tormented sister with pity and thought this was one of the most revealing conversations they'd ever had together – and one of the saddest.

'But Lorna,' she said tentatively, 'are you happy with Brooke? Do you love each other? Is it a good enough relationship to be worth so much?'

'Oh, *love, happiness* . . .' said Lorna bitterly. 'You sound like Mum. She was always asking me that sort of thing. You of all people should know I've only ever loved one man – so what chance have I had to experience a good relationship? I only know I couldn't bear to lose Brooke now and I certainly don't intend to. We're good together – he needs me and the life suits me perfectly. I'd do almost anything to keep my marriage.'

'Even if it means parting with your child?'

Lorna hesitated for a long moment, and Isobel wondered if she was going to change her mind. Then: 'Yes,' said Lorna. 'Even if it means that.' She suddenly leaned across the table and almost hissed at Isobel. 'But Brooke mustn't know who Rory's father is,' she said. 'None of this "father having custody" business . . . it's *you* as my *sister* who must have custody, however the lawyers arrange it. After all, there are plenty of precedents in past generations of aunts and uncles taking on a brother or sister's child for whatever reason. You must never tell Brooke about Giles. Let him go on believing John's his father and once Rory isn't under his feet all the time, upsetting me and causing trouble, he'll lose interest in the subject, I assure you. He has more important things to think about! But you must take Rory back with you tomorrow. I can't cope with him any more and we fly back to the States next week. I wish you joy of his tantrums.'

'I'll come and pick him up tomorrow morning,' said Isobel. 'We can sort the legal stuff out later. What you decide to tell your husband is your affair. I certainly won't volunteer any information to him and I don't see him wanting to be in touch with us – interest in child welfare doesn't seem to be his forte,' she said ironically. She added quietly: 'But I'm not lying for you either, Lorna, and one day – perhaps a long time in the future – Rory will be entitled to the truth.'

Lorna eyed her sister for a long moment, weighing her words and her resolution; making her choice. Then she got her mobile out of her bag and spoke briefly into it. Almost immediately the car in which she'd arrived drew up outside the restaurant and Lorna was gone – leaving Isobel with a victory and an aching sense of sadness.

When Isobel arrived at the Ritz the next morning she was directed to the Congletons' suite. She wondered if the senator would be there, and was half-relieved, half-disappointed to find only Lorna, a uniformed nanny – and Rory, with his legs stuck straight out in front of him, looking very small on a very large sofa. He also looked unnaturally tidy with slicked down hair, pulled up socks and neatly tied shoelaces. When he saw Isobel he hurled himself across the room like a rocket, nearly knocking her over with the force of his onslaught.

'Aunt Iz! Aunt Iz! I knew you'd come! I knew it!' he cried, clutching her round the waist and burrowing into her as though he wanted to climb inside.

Over the top of his dark head, the sisters' eyes met. Isobel's were filled with tears but Lorna's looked as expressionless as marbles.

'Well, Izzy,' she said. 'I see you've managed to get the love of my son as well as the love of Giles. I hope you're not going to want anything else of mine. Goodbye for now, then, Rory. I hope you'll behave better for Aunt Isobel than you have for me. I'll see you sometime,' and she turned and walked out of the room without a backward glance.

Chapter Twenty-nine

Christopher and Marnie arrived at Christopher's home, Nether Pacey, in time for dinner on Sunday evening.

They had gone back to Eilean Dobhran again on Saturday morning and explored the stables. In what had obviously once been the tack room, Marnie had discovered a pony's bridle with a snaffle bit and a red brow band, hanging beneath an enamelled plaque marked *Merrylegs*, and felt that the ghost of the elusive little red-haired girl had come closer. Christopher thought the stable block would lend itself marvellously well to conversion in much the same way that Giles and Isobel had used the Old Steading at Glendrochatt as accommodation for staff and course participants. It depended what sort of use Marnie had in mind for the castle – always supposing she managed to purchase it. She sent a long e-mail to her father – who, as her trustee, needed to be consulted – describing everything they'd discovered and asking him to make enquiries about Ian Drummond in Canada.

'We always tease Dad about being like the Mafia if we want to find out about anything or anyone,' she said. 'He has contacts everywhere.'

'Do you think he'll approve of your wild venture?' asked Christopher.

'I don't know, but I hope so. He very much encouraged me to come searching. I was quite surprised – but all those years ago, when he met her, he fell under the Contessa's spell too,' she said. 'And he loves crazy ventures – the crazier the better, especially if everyone else says it's not got a cat in hell's chance of succeeding!'

Christopher laughed. 'I rather like the sound of your father. I know the feeling. That's why I got hooked on the rescue of failing companies, I suppose. It's one of the reasons I'm getting such a kick from all this encouragement about my book when some people had been saying I didn't have a chance of getting it published.'

'I thought you said it was your mother's idea that you should come on the Glendrochatt course and that she'd always encouraged you to write?'

'It was and she did – but it wasn't my mother I was thinking of.'

Marnie guessed he was thinking of Nicola, the ex-girlfriend about whom she felt extremely curious and somewhat uneasy. Once Nicola discovered that Christopher might possibly become the successful author of page-turning thrillers, would she make a play for him again, and if she did would he withstand her?

Though in one way Marnie could hardly bear to say goodbye to the castle, there was suddenly so much to look forward to in the future for both of them that they felt ready to go south. Before they left Glendrochatt, Christopher had e-mailed the novel to Jonathan Mercer's agent, Barry Forster at Barnes & Peterson. 'The magic of technology,' he said. 'It took me eighteen months to write in longhand and about two minutes to send all thirty chapters to London. Fingers crossed he'll like it.' He was very much looking forward to meeting Barry Forster.

Christopher was adamant that it was too far for Marnie to drive from north of Inverness to Warwickshire in one day, so at the suggestion of Jeff and Cherry Barton they booked into a Wolsey Lodge run by some friends of theirs only a few miles off the M6 near Carlisle.

They had a hilarious evening, much entertained by

Marge and Dahlia, the joint owners. The contrast in style with Finterie Lodge could not have been greater. Here all was glitz and glitter, as though a thieving magpie had been responsible for the decor. Jelly moulds and warming pans, old horse brasses and kettles – there was hardly an inch of wall surface that wasn't covered with gleaming copper and brass; gold-sprayed bulrushes stood to attention in fireplaces and wallpapers had a metallic sheen. Venetian glass ornaments, at their garish worst, competed for position with multi-coloured art deco lamps and there were several eye-catching examples of the work of a local artist who specialised in collages made from milk-bottle tops. Glass baubles, dangling dangerously from light fittings in the low-ceilinged rooms, made Christopher complain that he needed a tin hat to avoid concussion every time he got to his feet. Wind chimes tinkled in the garden.

'Oh brother! Wouldn't I love to see this place at Christmas,' exclaimed Marnie, awed by such an Aladdin's cave of collectively terrible taste. 'What do you suppose they get up to then?'

'Imagination boggles.'

But their two hostesses were kindness itself, the food at dinner was good if rather elaborate and the bed in the frilled and flounced bedroom was large and comfortable. They both relished this extra night together before they had to expose their developing relationship to the scrutiny of relations and friends.

'Hold me,' whispered Marnie, turning to Christopher in the small hours of the morning. 'Please hold me very tight.'

Godfrey and Elspeth Piper were sitting under an old cedar tree in the garden doing the crossword and listening for the sound of the car when Christopher and Marnie drove up to the front of the house. Juno, the stoutest and deafest of the pair of ancient Labradors who were dozing at their feet, had alerted them a few minutes earlier to an imminent arrival. She had suddenly raised her head, though no sound was detectable to human ears, and struggled to her feet – arched back sagging like a favourite armchair – before pottering off round the side of the house to station herself by the front door. Juno always knew when a member of the family was about to appear. Her timing was infallible and Elspeth swore she could have greeted her family with perfectly soft-boiled four-minute eggs at the ready by relying on Juno's inner clock. The Pipers heard the scrunch of wheels on gravel and then – after what seemed rather a long pause – the slamming of a car door and voices.

'Well, that sounds like them – pity we shan't be able to finish the crossword now,' said Godfrey, who would never have admitted that he was just as anxious as his wife to see Christopher. 'Wonder what this American he's picked up will be like?'

Marnie turned off the ignition and surveyed the house that Christopher had so lovingly described to her, with its wisteria-covered walls of mottled stone that seemed to have soaked up centuries of both sunlight and shadow. She knew that the house, and even more its occupants, were extremely important to him and felt her own dysfunctional home life had not equipped her for being thrust into the middle of what was obviously a close and happy family. Christopher read the anxiety in her eyes and leaned over to kiss her – a loving, lingering kiss.

'Courage,' he said, when they finally got out of the car. 'Don't run away! Here's Juno come to greet us – now I know I'm home.' The old dog circled round them doing a geriatric impression of a frolic, as if a very old rocking horse had been gently set in motion. Christopher fondled her ears. 'Hello, old faithful,' he said. 'I see you haven't got any thinner in the last fortnight! Meet someone very special in my life. We've got to make her feel at home – d'you know that?' Juno wagged her rudder of a tail as Marnie bent down to pat her.

'See?' said Christopher. 'You're approved of already! Come on,' and he took her hand and led her into the house.

The evening had gone better than Marnie had dared to hope, her usual awkward constraint with new people rapidly wearing off under the warmth of Elspeth Piper's welcome and the relaxed atmosphere that she created round her. Godfrey Piper was more reserved, with a formal, old-fashioned courtesy, but she thought she detected a twinkle in his eye and Christopher had told her that behind a poker-player's straight face a tremendous sense of humour lurked.

'Oh, by the way, darling,' Marnie overheard Elspeth say to Christopher as they were going in to dinner, 'Nicola rang twice. She said she couldn't get you on your mobile but I didn't think you'd want me to give her the Glendrochatt number. She wants you to ring her so I promised I'd tell you. She's in London.' Christopher looked noncommittal, but Marnie's heart lurched and she wondered what his mother thought of the ex-girlfriend about whom he talked so little.

In fact, after Nicola's brassy self-confidence, Marnie's initial shyness did her no disservice in her hostess's eyes, and Elspeth, unobtrusively studying her son and deeply grateful that he seemed so miraculously restored to something like his former self, went out of her way to put her guest at ease. The current that flowed between Christopher and this diminutive young American with the pre-Raphaelite face was unmistakable, but, thought his mother, there was more than mere sexual attraction at work – though that was clearly present too – and the thought crossed her mind like a warning wisp of grey cloud on a sunny day that either one of them could be seriously hurt if anything went wrong between them. Goodness knows, she felt Christopher had been hurt enough, but she sensed something so vulnerable about Marnie that she found her curiously moving. She sent up a prayer for them both.

Christopher was relieved to see that Marnie – used to her own high-powered tycoon of a parent – knew just how to flirt gently with his equally successful and sometimes formidable father, and Godfrey Piper was soon regaling her with all his best jokes and stories, delivered deadpan, and making her laugh. Christopher and his mother exchanged an amused look.

There was so much news to share and Godfrey and Elspeth proved such interested listeners that they all lingered over dinner without noticing that it was quite dark before anyone thought of putting the lights on. They drank to Christopher's future as a writer, and to the success of Marnie's efforts to buy Eilean Dobhran.

'What a romantic story! It's not often we entertain someone who's about to purchase a castle in the air,' said Christopher's father, raising his glass to Marnie and smiling at her. 'May all your dreams come true, my dear.'

'I can see Dad's rather taken with your new friend,' said Elspeth, as she and Christopher carried the plates out to the kitchen.

'Good,' said Christopher. 'I very much want you both to like her.'

Christopher had warned Marnie that his mother would be unlikely to put them together on this visit and they had agreed in advance to forgo any corridor creeping – at any rate for tonight. Elspeth escorted Marnie up the wide, creaky staircase to the main spare room, a comfortably shabby room, overlooking the garden, with faded chintz curtains, piles of books and a vase of polyanthus on the dressing table.

'Oh, what a wonderful smell!' said Marnie in delight. 'What is it?'

'It's mostly the wisteria,' said Elspeth, 'but there's also a bed of lily of the valley below this room. One of my favourite flowers.'

'Mine too. Will you show me round your garden tomorrow? I want to pick your brains about the castle's garden. Did Christopher tell you?'

'He did, actually. I can't think of anything I'd enjoy more – but you mustn't let me bore you.' They stood by the open window together, inhaling the scent of an English summer garden, different from the wilder, mossy smells of Scotland, but equally delicious in its own way, Marnie thought.

'You must be so excited about Christopher's book,' she said. 'I gather it was all your idea that he should go to Glendrochatt. He was the star of the writing week.'

'I'm thrilled about it. Not altogether surprised, because it's what I always felt he could do. He had a tremendous imagination as a little boy, and when he was at school he won all sorts of essay prizes, but after university he took a different route. This has come at the perfect time. It's just the sort of lucky break he needs after . . .' She paused. 'Did he tell you he's had rather a rough patch recently?' she asked cautiously, not sure how much Marnie knew and not wanting to be the one to tell her anything about Christopher that he might not have chosen to share with her already.

Marnie nodded. 'Yes, he did . . . about the accident and

the prison sentence and everything. It must have been awful for you and your husband too. Christopher said you'd been a complete rock for him all through his worst times.'

'Thank you,' said Elspeth, touched. 'The last two years have been hell, not only the horror of seeing him in prison but seeing how much he blamed and tortured himself over what happened. Rightly so, no doubt, but it was painful for us to witness. I can't tell you how wonderful it is to see him looking so much better. I wouldn't have believed two weeks could have done him so much good. He's transformed. Now, do you think you've got all you want? You must be exhausted after all that driving.'

'I'm sure I've got everything anyone could possibly want, thank you. It's so lovely here.'

'Well, don't hurry in the morning. Potter down to the kitchen whenever you feel like breakfast – in your dressing gown if you like. I'll be around,' and Elspeth kissed her visitor goodnight and went down to let the dogs out.

With no Christopher to occupy her in other ways, Marnie intended to start reading his book that night. She was still glued to it at two o'clock in the morning.

'Well, darling,' Elspeth said to her husband after they'd got to bed. 'What do you think of the new girlfriend?'

'Big improvement on Nicola anyway,' said Godfrey. 'Much more interesting. I should think there might be fireworks, though. I think she's got her head in the clouds, a mind of her own and a lot of hang-ups – a difficult mix. And we know how hot-headed Christopher can be. Still, sparks are better than a dead fire.'

She said: 'What an old fraud you are, darling! You pretend you're not the least bit interested in people and then after one evening you can sum someone up better than I can.'

'Oh, surely not,' he teased, taking her hand as he always did before they fell asleep. 'Anyway, let's hope it lasts long enough for him to have a bit of fun and recover his self-respect.'

'I hope so. Oh, I do hope so.'

'Well, if anyone ever makes Christopher half as happy as you've always made me, he'll be a very lucky man,' said Godfrey.

'Or drives him half as mad?' she asked.

'That too,' he said. 'Goodnight, my love.'

Chapter Thirty

Christopher and Marnie stayed at Nether Pacey for a week. Resolutions about corridor creeping did not last.

To his relief, Christopher had little trouble in getting permission from his probation officer to go to London and made a date to have lunch with Barry Forster, who was extremely encouraging on the telephone about *Inside Knowledge*. He said he had already sent it to commissioning editors at two publishing firms, one of which was Jonathan Mercer's publisher. Now that she had read it, Marnie was even more enthusiastic about Christopher's writing and had been able to tell him truthfully that she could hardly put the book down.

She made a couple of critical suggestions about the plot, which impressed Christopher with their pertinence, and though his initial reaction had been to disagree he eventually conceded that she had a point and made some minor alterations. She was fascinated to know which of the characters were based directly on his prison experiences.

'Well the background is certainly authentic,' he said. 'Horribly so. No one could have researched that better, but I've discovered that writing fiction is a very odd process and I don't really know myself where all the characters come from. I suppose inevitably you draw on your own experience – not necessarily first-hand experience, though, so it's not as autobiographical as everyone thinks. Some of it's what you've gathered from other people. Then you add some purely imaginary ideas. It's a bit like watching my mother making soup. She chucks a whole lot of ingredients in the blender plus some stock she's brewed up out of leftovers, perhaps adds some fresh vegetables, seasons it liberally with this and that, churns the whole thing up – and what comes out is quite different from what went in.'

'And does she make good soup?' asked Marnie.

'She does actually. Perhaps it's her soup-making gene, transmuted a bit, that I've inherited. When we were children and we asked what she was concocting, she'd always say, "Oh, it's just bits and pieces," and "bitty soup" was always what we asked for when we came home from school. It was ages before I discovered it wasn't a proper culinary term.'

'I can't imagine having a soup-making mother,' said Marnie. 'I guess it's kind of symbolic. Steaming bowls of soup for comfort and nourishment . . . not my experience!' Then she laughed. 'Your book's quite steamy in places too,' she said, raising an eyebrow at him.

Christopher grinned. 'Just authentic research.'

It was a source of enormous pleasure to Christopher that she got on so well with both his parents, challenging his father at Scrabble and playing duets with him in the drawing room after dinner – rather badly, but with a lot of laughter – and gardening and chatting endlessly with his mother. But when his sisters made a great effort to come over to see him (and to inspect the new girlfriend, thought Marnie suspiciously) her prickles immediately sprouted again and everybody got scratched.

It was perhaps unfortunate that they all managed to arrive from different destinations within minutes of each other and the sound of the shrieks of greeting and laughter, the babble of reunion, the wild exchange of hugs had left Marnie standing halfway down the stairs in a state of actual physical paralysis.

From then on the day had been a disaster. She had been chippy and touchy, argued needlessly with bossy Penny, clashed with confident, dashing Kitty and been unnecessarily offhand with Jess, the favourite sister, whose efforts to be specially friendly had shamed her and made her feel infinitely worse about her own gaucherie and lack of grace.

The obvious family affection they felt for each other beneath the teasing and the banter, all the in-jokes and childhood reminiscences which they shared with Christopher, brought out the very worst in her. She felt a complete outsider, and because she minded too much endeavoured to give the impression that she didn't care at all. To make matters worse, Christopher, acutely disappointed by her apparently unfriendly reaction to his beloved family – and, as the day wore on, theirs to her – had shot her a look of extreme annoyance across the lunch table, which had not been lost on her. After tea, when they were preparing to leave, she could bear it no more and had suddenly disappeared, taking the two portly old dogs with her, and fled up the fields at the back of the house without saying goodbye.

It had not made a good impression and Christopher had made excuses for her that sounded lame even in his own ears.

After they'd gone, he went in search of her and found her sitting on an old tree stump, looking her worst.

'Well, that was a bloody failure, wasn't it?' he snapped. Then he saw how red her eyes were, how blotched with crying her face, and his exasperation melted away. 'Oh, shit, shit!' he said. 'I'm sorry. It was all too much, wasn't it?' He came and sat beside her and tried to put an arm round her, but she shrugged him off and they sat in silence.

'I told you I didn't have any social graces,' she muttered at last. 'Now perhaps you'll believe me.'

'I don't give a damn about social graces. You were just plain bloody rude!'

'And you wanted your sisters to like me?'

'Of *course* I did,' he said, not even trying to pretend that they'd warmed to her. 'I wanted them to like you and you to like them – and they would have done if you'd given them half a chance. Having one's nose bitten off is painful, especially if it's unprovoked. But I ought to have managed to make it easier for you. You've got perfectly good social graces when you choose to use them but you're like a dog that's so terrified of not being the one to get the first bite in that it starts snarling even if tails are being wagged at it . . . and it's become the most God-awful habit. But shall I tell you something else? Of course I'd very much rather you *didn't* snarl at my family – but it doesn't change how I feel about you one jot. It's *you* I want. I knew that this afternoon with absolute certainty, even when I wanted to shake you for being so spiky and aggressive. I suppose that's why I felt so furious. I do love you, Marnie.'

It was the first time he'd said it.

'Warts and all?' she whispered, miserably ashamed of herself.

'Warts and all,' he said, 'and I've got plenty of those myself.' This time when he took her in his arms she didn't pull away. He looked down at her woebegone face and felt overcome by tenderness. Then he laughed. 'But you sure as hell produced a bumper crop of warts today – back to that first evening at Glendrochatt when you glared so dauntingly at all of us, daring us to like you! Kitty certainly got her comeuppance when she started broadcasting to you about the West Indies!' He grinned at the memory. 'She chose the wrong target there. Serves her right! But my mama always says we're an impossibly daunting gang when we get together and it was stupid of me not to have realised it would be so threatening for you.

Bad luck that you had to meet all the sisters together for the first time . . . but I'm a stupid oaf not to have helped you more. Am I forgiven?'

'I don't know why I do it,' she said tragically. 'I don't want to. It's like whenever I specially long to make a good impression on anyone, I have to go kick them in the teeth first. I feel real bad, especially when your parents have been so lovely to me. Then I couldn't bear myself for being so horrible, so I ran away and made it even worse. You've got every right to be mad. I am so, so sorry. I'll try to be nicer next time – if there is a next time – but you'll have to help me and I don't come with any reassuring five-year guarantees.'

'Cheer up, prickly-pear,' he said. 'Try trusting people for a change. Now let's persuade these fat old ladies to take a bit more exercise and give your face time to recover. I want my beautiful goose girl back. Remind me to find the book and show you the picture of yourself. We'll go back through the wood and you can see some of Shakespeare's England after all that wild, Scottish scenery you're so hooked on.'

Later that evening, when she was helping Elspeth lay the table in the kitchen for supper for the four of them, Marnie apologised profusely for her ungraciousness.

'I don't know what you must have thought of me,' she said repentantly. 'Christopher was very cross with me, and I can't begin to tell you how ashamed I am to have been so rude when you've been nothing but kind to me.' For answer Elspeth gave her a big hug and told her to forget it, but privately she felt troubled and thought that Marnie's exceptionally thin skin might prove more difficult to deal with than she had first supposed. She had found herself defending Marnie to two of her daughters.

'Well! Out of the frying pan into the fire,' Penny had said

disapprovingly. 'Hope this one doesn't last long – she's even worse than Nicola.'

Kitty had petulantly pronounced her an absolute disaster. 'Don't you go and be too nice to her, Mum,' she instructed her mother. 'You're such a soft touch. We don't want her clinging on to Christopher just because she thinks this might be a cushy weekend pad. Think how long we all had to put up with noxious Nicola.'

'Oh, *Kitty*,' said Elspeth crossly, thinking of all the tiresome young men her youngest daughter had inflicted on them over the years. 'You really can be very thoughtless and insensitive.' Kitty tossed her head and went off to raid her parents' garden for flowers and vegetables to take back to London. Her father always said the garden looked as if it had been stripped bare by locusts after a visit from his youngest daughter.

Jess had just looked bothered and asked, 'I'm not sure what to make of Chris's new bird. Is she always so terribly *fierce*? Do you like her, Mum?'

'Yes,' said her mother decidedly. 'Pa and I both like her very much, and think she might be just what Christopher needs at the moment . . . unlike Nicola, she brings out the best in him. They certainly seem very happy when they're together – and goodness he can do with some happiness – but it's early days and they can't know each other very well yet. But she was certainly rather tiresome today and she does seem terribly insecure. Let's all give her another chance before we make any judgements.'

One of the probation officer's conditions for Christopher was that he must reside in his own flat in Battersea and stay at the same address if he was in London. The flat had been let while he was in prison but luckily the tenants had recently moved out, so it seemed the perfect solution that Marnie should stay with him too. She had never been so happy in her whole life. Christopher worked at his new book every day while she went to work at her father's London office. She'd had an SOS from the UK managing director, whom she had worked for when she was living in England, to ask if she could help out on a temporary basis as his long-standing PA was having emergency surgery and had gone off sick in the middle of sensitive negotiations for a crucial deal. As Marnie was so familiar with the way things were done and he'd heard she was back in England, he thought she could be extremely helpful. She had jumped at the offer, glad to have a job to keep her busy while Christopher wrote.

For the rest of the time they happily explored each other – body and mind.

One day she had a long telephone call from her father, who had managed to get in touch with Ian Drummond. 'But you'll have to see him personally,' he said. 'How would you like me to come to Canada with you and help with the negotiations?'

'Oh, Dad, that would be just so great. Would you really do that for me?'

'I might be able to fix some business in Toronto. You'll have to be prepared to fly over at fairly short notice to fit in with my schedule. I'll call you.'

Christopher could see that Marnie was over the moon at her father's suggestion, and felt relieved that she was going to have some serious support on her mission-impractical to buy a castle.

'I do wish you could come with me too,' she said wistfully. He longed to be able to go with her himself but suddenly foresaw a potentially serious difficulty in their relationship which clearly hadn't occurred to her.

'You do realise that there's a likelihood of my *never* being able to go to the States with my criminal record, don't you?' he asked.

Marnie looked horrified. 'Oh, surely, when your parole is over . . .? It will all be different then . . . won't it?' she said.

'As things are at the moment, I wouldn't have a hope in hell of getting a visa,' he insisted. 'I think you should break it to your father that you're going out with a gaol-bird.'

'That's horrible,' said Marnie indignantly. 'I *never* think of you as a gaol-bird!'

'Well let me be thankful for that,' he said lightly, but his heart sank. He'd been counting the days to the end of his parole in a few months' time, thinking that he would soon be able to put the whole wretched three years, if not exactly behind him, then certainly to one side, and move forward. There was a very important question he was longing to put to Marnie, but he was determined to wait till he felt it would be right to do so.

Now he wondered if it might become more complicated than either of them had bargained for.

They had several times rung the Grants to catch up with Glendrochatt news and been delighted to hear from Giles and Isobel – their first joint friends, as Marnie proudly pointed out – the news about Rory. 'There's lots of agreements still to be ironed out,' Isobel told Marnie, 'but Rory is so thrilled to be here we feel we're doing the right thing, and my sister's returned to the States with her verbose husband. Amy and Ed seem genuinely delighted that Rory's back, which is a comfort. Keep us posted about any developments over Eilean Dobhran, won't you?'

'Do you know one of the uses I might like to put the castle to if I get it?' Marnie had asked Christopher one night.

'No, tell me.'

'Well,' she said, 'I talked to Isobel a lot about Edward one day and she told me how desperate she'd often felt when he was little with so much anxiety and pressure –

not only with the times when he was rushed to hospital and they were fighting for his life, but also when they were trying to get the right schooling for him and to help him become more socially acceptable, let alone to come to terms with the fact that he will always be different and dependent. She said that it puts huge strains on a marriage and told me how fortunate she felt to have had so much support from family and friends; to have had enough money to get help when the twins were little so that Amy didn't get neglected. She said so many families she'd met through Edward struggled with much worse problems and didn't have half as much respite. And I thought wouldn't it be wonderful to turn Eilean Dobhran into somewhere offering peace and comfort for people who need a break – for whatever reason. It could be a proper hotel too and some people would pay the full rates, but if I could set up some sort of foundation or bursary scheme, it could provide a respite for those who couldn't otherwise afford it. I thought Isobel and Giles would be perfect to have on a management committee to advise and help. What do you think?'

'I think it's a great idea,' said Christopher. 'A worthy use for the Contessa's money.'

'Will you help me with it?'

'You know I will,' he said, yearning to say more.

Nicola arrived on the doorstep unannounced one evening when Christopher had gone to have a drink with his father at his club to discuss some family business. The two young women looked each other over. Nicola introduced herself. 'Do you know what time Christopher will be back?' she asked.

'About half past eight, I think,' said Marnie politely, hackles on end but consciously trying not to snarl.

'So . . . are you living here with Christopher now then?'

'Yes.'

'Oh well, tell him I called, will you – just to pass the time of day? I used to live here with him too. I might have known he wouldn't last long without finding himself a replacement. He always needs a woman around. I should watch your back if I were you,' and having shot this inspired poisoned dart at her Nicola walked off, not at all dissatisfied with the expression on Marnie's face.

Christopher was furious when he heard that Nicola had turned up, knowing she would have had trouble in mind, but Marnie did not tell him what she had said.

Louisa rang Marnie to confirm their plan to meet. She sounded in bubbly form and said the two weeks at Glendrochatt had recharged her batteries and given her lots of ideas about her life, though not writing ones, and not the ones she'd thought she was looking for. She was going to keep her flat and get another job in London after all. They made a date for a fortnight's time. Marnie suggested a restaurant, but Louisa insisted that she'd like to produce supper for them at home.

'I thought I'd ask Adam too,' she said, 'so that we can be a foursome. I know he likes Christopher.'

'Great,' said Marnie, secretly relieved that there would be someone else there too, and curious to meet Adam. 'Christopher took some fantastic pictures of Eilean Dobhran. I'm longing to show them to you.'

As it turned out Marnie was unable to keep the engagement because she was in America. Her father rang – in typical whirlwind fashion, she told Christopher – three days before Louisa's supper party, to say he'd booked her on a flight to New York and they could fly together to Toronto the following day in his private plane. He had a lot to tell her.

She rang Louisa to try to alter the date for dinner. 'Oh, it's very sad you won't be there, but couldn't Christopher still come?' asked Louisa. 'You and I can have girls' lunch together when you get back. I'll need to know all the stop-press news about Eilean Dobhran. Will you trust me with Christopher while you're away?' she'd added teasingly.

'Of course I trust you,' Marnie answered untruthfully.

'Ring her back and say we'd rather go together on another night. She can have a tête-à-tête with Adam,' suggested Christopher when she told him about Louisa's request, but Marnie, intent on practising trust, and unwilling to backtrack to Louisa, protested that she didn't want to do that.

'I really don't want to go without you,' said Christopher, but Marnie perversely insisted he should. I have to be grown up about this, she told herself. It seemed like a test of her own faith in Christopher, an attempt to overcome her jealousies and suspicions.

Christopher went to Heathrow with Marnie to see her off, wishing he could have driven her there, counting the weeks till he would get his licence back. The flat seemed intolerably empty without her. He had never felt this sense that a vital part of him was missing on the numerous occasions when he and Nicola had been apart. He telephoned Jess and asked himself round to supper with her and her GP husband, promising to get there early enough to see the children.

Marnie sounded full of excitement when she rang from New York to say she'd arrived safely. She was having a brilliant time with her father, and they were off to Canada tomorrow. She wasn't sure whether they'd stay the night at a hotel in Toronto or fly back the same day. It depended on her father's business.

'I wish you were here,' she said. 'I miss you so much.'

'I wish I was too. By the way, I still love you. When did I last tell you?'

'Not for *ages* – not since yesterday. I love you too.'

Chapter Thirty-one

The invitation from Louisa had originally been for 'oh, half past eightish, but turn up any old time that suits'. Christopher arrived at her little house in Wandsworth to find Adam Winterton had got there first. Louisa, looking pretty and casual in a clingy top and a floral skirt made of some floaty material, led the way through the kitchen to a little paved garden at the back. Her long legs were bare and very brown and she had on a pair of kitten-heeled mules that click-clacked sexily on the tiled floor as she walked.

Adam was sitting on a swing seat, a tall glass in his hand, but got to his feet as they came through the kitchen door.

'Christopher – how very good to see you again. Louisa's been telling me you're about to abandon City life to become a best-selling author! That's wonderful.'

He was a thick-set man of medium height, and Christopher thought that if he hadn't known what a formidable intellect lay behind his pleasant open face and slightly ruddy complexion, he would have put him down as an outdoor type, a farmer perhaps or a soldier.

'I don't know about a best-seller – I haven't even got accepted by a publisher yet!' Christopher protested. He smiled rather wryly. 'I used my enforced idleness at Her Majesty's pleasure to try my hand at writing. Good to see you again too, Adam.'

'We decided it was warm enough to have drinks out

here,' said Louisa, 'and I thought Pimm's would be nice and summery. That's what Adam and I are drinking, anyway – or would you rather go straight on to wine?'

'Pimm's would be fine.' He could see there was a big jug, ready mixed, full of ice and cucumber and fruit. Louisa poured him a very large glassful. 'Here – steady on,' he said.

'It's so exciting that Marnie's found her famous castle,' said Louisa. 'I'm longing to hear all about it. I've been telling Adam the whole riveting saga.'

They chatted away easily and Christopher remembered again how much he'd always liked the other man. He couldn't help noticing how often his eyes rested on Louisa with love and amusement and thought what a pity it was that they'd split up. After about half an hour Adam looked at his watch and stood up. 'Well, I'm afraid I really must be off now or I'll be late for this client I've got to see tonight,' he said. 'We must get together again soon, Christopher. I'll be in touch. Let's have that dinner that unforeseen circumstances prevented us from having three years ago and I'll look forward to meeting Marnie. Louisa's told me lots about her. I'm so very sorry I couldn't stay to meet her this evening.' He kissed Louisa. 'I'll see myself out and I'll give you a ring tomorrow,' he said, and was gone.

Christopher glanced questioningly at Louisa.

Louisa gave him an unfathomable look. There were spots of high colour on her cheeks.

'Didn't I tell you Adam couldn't stay?' she said. 'Such a pity. Some tycoon who has to fly off somewhere early tomorrow or something and seems unable to cut his toenails without seeking Adam's advice.'

'No, you didn't tell me,' said Christopher, 'but I'm sure the toenails will be exceptionally well trimmed.' After a moment, he asked casually, 'As a matter of interest, did you tell Adam that Marnie couldn't come tonight either, Louisa?'

'No,' she said, looking him straight in the eye. 'As a matter of interest, I don't think I did.' She added lightly, 'Anyway, it's lovely that you're here now . . . so we'd better have something to eat, don't you think? It's all ready in the kitchen.'

'Something to eat would be great,' he said, 'just so long as we both know that I have to go home after dinner.'

'Of course,' she said. 'If that's what you want. I hope you've brought some photographs to show me?'

Christopher said he had. 'I thought Marnie might have wanted to show them to you herself when you have lunch together next week but she insisted that I should bring them tonight. I'm really very pleased with them – it'll give you an idea of what a mysterious, romantic spot Eilean Dobhran really is.'

'Oh, good – and I must show you the pictures I took at Glendrochatt. Some of them are hilarious. There's a terribly funny one of Bunty dancing reels.'

It was easy to chat away about Glendrochatt and all their new mutual friends but there was something about Louisa that disturbed him though he couldn't quite define what it was. She was always sassy and amusing – but this was different. There was a sort of hectic gaiety about her, a reckless glint in her eyes that made him wonder if she'd already had too much to drink. He was surprised he hadn't noticed before how very thin she was, but in her figure-hugging top and flimsy skirt she looked as slender as a willow wand.

They had delicious cold tomato soup, curried chicken and a strawberry tart, sitting in Louisa's pretty kitchen-cum-living room, with the French windows to the garden open.

'What a delicious dinner – really up to Glendrochatt standards, and that's saying something!'

'We've got a brilliant local deli,' said Louisa with a grin. 'Don't delude yourself that I've been slaving over a hot stove. That's not my style at all.'

'I'm relieved to hear it,' he said, laughing at her.

They talked about all sorts of subjects and an unperceptive fly on the wall might have thought they were both having a thoroughly pleasant evening. Louisa was particularly good company, sharp and funny and out to please, and Christopher did his best to be entertaining and appreciative without sending out the wrong messages – a difficult balancing act to achieve. But all the time a tension lay beneath the surface. How odd love is, thought Christopher. Here is this very attractive woman issuing an unmistakable invitation to me that any man would envy, but which I'm not going to take up because my heart is firmly on the other side of the Atlantic.

'Coffee?' asked Louisa.

Christopher looked at his watch. 'No thank you, not for me. You've given me a wonderful evening, Louisa, I've really enjoyed it, but now I must be getting back.' He got to his feet.

'Don't go,' she said, and there was a pleading urgency about her that made him deeply uneasy. 'Stay for the night, Christopher – just this once. Please don't go.'

'I must,' he said gently. 'You know that. I've enjoyed being with you very much and I think you're lovely, Louisa. I'm incredibly flattered you should want me to stay, but I couldn't do that to Marnie . . . and I don't really think you could either. We would both regret it.'

'Don't say that!' she said passionately. 'I *know* I'm behaving badly. I know I shouldn't be doing this but I can't help it.' She looked as if she might cry. Then she whispered, so quietly that he could hardly hear her: 'It may be my last chance.'

At that moment the telephone rang. Louisa hesitated for a moment and then answered it.

'Oh, hello,' he heard her say. 'No, of course it's not too late for me. It's very kind of you to ring at this time, though. Oh, I see. Yes. Please tell me then . . .' There was a long pause while she listened intently to whoever was speaking the other end. Christopher saw her put a hand on the back of a chair as though to steady herself. All the colour had drained out of her face. She almost seemed to shrink and wither before his eyes like a winter apple.

'Yes, I see,' she said finally. 'I understand . . . I'll see you tomorrow then. Ten o'clock. I'll be there. No, I'm not alone – there is someone here with me. Thanks for telling me.'

When she put the telephone down she sank on to a chair at the table and buried her head in her hands.

'Louisa . . . whatever is it? Tell me what's happened.' He was appalled by the look on her face.

She looked up at him, face ashen, eyes enormous. She was shaking.

'It's happened,' she said. 'What I've always dreaded. It's got me at last. That was my oncologist, the dear, lovely man who's seen me through so much, ringing me with the result of a scan. My cancer has metastasised. It's gone to my liver. It's gone everywhere.'

Christopher knelt beside her and held her for a long time while she suddenly wept, great racking sobs that felt to him as if they would wrench her fragile frame apart.

'I am *so* frightened,' she whispered at last. 'So terribly frightened. I don't feel ready to die.'

'Did he say that?'

'Not in so many words . . . but I know too much after living under the shadow of this thing for ten years. He said "not good news this time, I'm afraid" and that he'd like to see me again tomorrow and discuss what he calls "any possible options". I went for a routine check-up last week and they weren't happy – shadows on the X-ray, they said, might have to check the bloods again, just to be safe, probably nothing to worry about . . . all that guff . . . and so they did more blood tests and a full scan. Now he's rung me with the results.'

'Would you like a drink? Can I get you anything?'

She gave a watery smile. 'I'd love a cup of tea – just good strong builder's variety. It might help pull me together. I'm so sorry to do this to you, Christopher.'

'For God's sake! I'm glad to be here with you.'

He made two mugs of tea and they went and sat on the sofa together and he listened while she told him how the cancer had returned three years ago after a long remission; it hadn't been directly related to the original Hodgkinson's, though they'd always warned her that that put her at greater risk of getting other types of cancer. This time it had been breast cancer. She'd had a partial mastectomy, a reconstruction and radiotherapy and thought she'd beaten it again. All the signs had been good. 'There have been one or two niggles just lately – not symptoms exactly, nothing I could pin down, but I told myself I was fine. Now I suddenly feel so very tired of being brave,' she said wearily.

He remembered Marnie finding the dead owl and telling him about Louisa's dream, and it made him go cold.

'Do your parents know?' he asked.

She shook her head. 'Not yet. It's only happened in the last week. I'll have to tell them now, of course, but they've been through so much with me that I didn't want to worry them unless I needed to.'

'Don't shut them out,' he said. 'Their help will be in trying to help you.'

'I know,' she said. 'I'm well aware of that, but it doesn't make it any easier. I'll ring them in the morning.'

'What about Adam?' he asked tentatively. 'He obviously still loves you. He'll want to support you over this.'

'I know that too,' she said. 'Darling, faithful Adam . . . who I've relied on and taken for granted for years. This will be terrible for him too. I will tell him, of course – but I don't want anyone else to know just yet. I couldn't cope with other people's reactions and emotions at the moment – you've no idea how difficult that is. It'd just be too much. I've got to get sorted in my own head first. Promise me you won't tell anyone.'

'What can I do?' he asked. 'Would you like me to ring Adam now to see if he could come back and be with you?'

'We wouldn't get him. He won't have his mobile switched on and I don't want to leave a message tonight. Talk to me, Christopher,' she said. 'Just talk to me about something, anything . . . anything except cancer.'

So he told her about childhood holidays, about long-ago, gap year travels and later university escapades, and she listened and laughed and asked questions until suddenly he realised she'd fallen asleep, in the way a small child can fall asleep, literally between one word and the next. He found a coat hanging in the hall and covered her with it. She looked absurdly young and desperately vulnerable and his heart turned over with sadness as he looked at her . . . but not, he thought, with love. Whatever the mysterious alchemy is that ignites a fuse between a particular man and woman, it had not sparked that special fire between him and Louisa – or not as far as he was concerned. He wondered what he ought to do. Clearly she could not be left to wake – perhaps hours later – only to find herself alone when she would have to face again, after temporary oblivion, the frightening reality of what was happening to her.

He stacked the plates and put them in the dishwasher, making as little clatter as he could, but she slept on, so he fetched the paper intending to read it, but found he could neither concentrate nor see properly in the dimmed lighting. As he didn't want to put the overhead light on for fear of waking her, he sat in the semi-darkness and pondered about the future, for himself, for Marnie, and for gallant, wayward Louisa, sleeping beside him.

He heard a clock strike midnight, so he reckoned it would be seven o'clock in the evening for Marnie, whether she was in New York or Toronto. She would be expecting a call. He had told her he would ring her as soon as he got back to the flat after dinner and report on the evening, but this was no moment to be asked for explanations. His mobile was switched off, and when he turned it on he saw that he had one missed call. He pressed 121 and listened to Marnie's voice, teasing but a little anxious too, he thought. 'Hi there – what a very long supper you're having! Ring me soon. Have lots to tell you. Love you.' His heart sank. He decided to text Marnie and try to forestall any conversation with her until the morning. He punched in a brief message saying that something unavoidable and unexpected had cropped up and he would call her tomorrow. He thought she would find it extremely bothering and imagined all her defence mechanisms springing into action as she read it. *Thinking of you. Don't forget I love you*, he added, and hoped she would believe him.

Louisa woke in the small hours, and, as Christopher had guessed, the misery of remembering what had happened was almost worse than being told for the first time. But she was touchingly grateful to find him still there.

'You should go to bed properly now,' he said.

'Will you stay with me?' she asked. 'I know I ought not to ask it of you but I promise I won't cause any trouble now.' She gave him a wobbly little smile. 'I just don't think I could bear to be alone tonight and I think Marnie would understand though I promise not to tell her if you'd rather not. Please?'

'Of course I'll stay with you,' he said. 'Marnie certainly wouldn't want me to leave you like this. Of course she'll understand.' He hoped this was true.

'You could sleep on the spare room bed,' she said. 'I'm afraid it's not properly made up but there's a duvet on it.' She looked at him sadly, knowing he would never now give her the one thing she had thought she wanted from him, but deeply grateful for his presence and support. He followed her up the stairs and she came and kissed him goodnight, and thanked him and clung to him. He held her to him for a minute, fighting an urge to respond to her more fully.

'Don't give up, Louisa,' he said urgently. 'You've beaten this thing before . . . you can do it again. People do make extraordinary recoveries from cancer against all the odds. I know that from my doctor brother-in-law. *Anything* can happen.'

'Even dying,' she said, with a bleak attempt at humour. 'We're always telling each other "Don't worry, it may never happen" and most of the things that secretly scare us witless won't . . . but dying *will* happen one day to all of us. It's just that I don't feel nearly ready for it yet.'

'Perhaps one never does,' he said, aching for her, feeling helplessly inadequate to bring reassurance. 'Have you got anything you can take . . . a sleeping pill or something?'

She nodded. 'Yes. I will do that . . . but will you wake me in the morning in case I oversleep? I have to get up to go to the hospital.'

'I will.'

He watched her go into her room, knowing that, pill or no pill, she would probably cry herself to sleep.

In the morning, as promised, Christopher went to check on Louisa. He had in fact looked in on her twice during what had been left of the night, and listened – but there had been no sound and she appeared to be sleeping.

Now he tapped at her half-open door twice, and then put his head round it. 'Louisa?' She was curled up in a tight little ball and didn't move. For an awful moment he wondered how many sleeping pills she might have taken.

'Louisa . . .' he said again, louder, and was mightily relieved when she moaned softly and stirred. 'It's just after seven. I promised I'd wake you. You have to go to the hospital.' He hated reminding her.

'Adam?' she asked sleepily.

'No,' he said. 'No, it's Christopher. I'm still here.'

She sat up suddenly, blonde hair tousled. She had nothing on and he couldn't help noticing again how thin she was – painfully, scarily thin. He looked away quickly. She pulled the duvet up to her chin.

'Christopher? Oh, of course . . . I . . . I remember now.' He could see from her face that recollection was flooding painfully back.

'I'll get you a mug of tea,' he said.

When he went back upstairs with it, she was sitting on the edge of her bed with a dressing gown on and had brushed her hair. He felt very rumpled, scruffy and unshaven.

'Did you sleep?'

'I took a pill as you suggested – went out like a light. Christopher?'

'Yes?'

'Thanks,' she said. 'Thanks for everything.'

'It was nothing. Wish I could have done more. Is there anything else I can do?'

'No, I'll be fine . . . but perhaps you could just hang on while I have a shower and answer the phone if it goes? It might be the hospital and I wouldn't want to miss the call. Dr Allandale said he'd get someone to ring early if the appointment had to be changed.'

'Yes, of course,' he said. 'I'll go and wait downstairs.'

When he got down to the kitchen, he hesitated for a moment, then picked up the telephone and rang Adam.

There were no more messages on his mobile but he wondered what there would be on the answering machine in the flat. Not that there was anything he could do yet anyway, he thought. It would be two thirty in the morning for Marnie.

He could hear the sound of water running upstairs when the telephone in the kitchen did ring. He picked it up. 'Hello?' he said. 'Hello?' But there was a click and the line went dead.

'Who was that?' asked Louisa, coming down a few minutes later.

'I don't know. I dialled 1471 but it was one of those "we do not have the number" calls.'

'Oh well, thanks anyway. I'll ring the hospital to check just in case.'

'Darling Louisa,' he said. 'I hope you don't mind, but I've rung Adam. He's on his way. I'll just wait till he comes.'

At that moment the doorbell rang. Louisa ran to answer it and flung herself into Adam's arms. Christopher quietly slipped away.

He walked to the bus stop at the end of the road with a very heavy heart; wondering what the future had in store for Louisa.

When he got back to his flat he went straight to the answering machine. It showed three missed calls, but no messages had been left. He knew with a deadly inner certainty who the early morning caller had been . . . and why she would have been ringing Louisa's house first thing in the morning, UK time.

Chapter Thirty-two

The trip to Toronto had been an unqualified success on many different levels. Marnie had thoroughly enjoyed the companionship of her father – she didn't think she could remember a time when she'd ever before had him all to herself for twenty-four hours, or felt so close to him.

She'd spent the first night with him and her stepmother, Toni, in their New York apartment and enjoyed seeing her three half-brothers, only the youngest of whom was also Toni's child. She was fond of them all in a semi-detached way, very different from the Piper family's full-on commitment to each other, and got on reasonably well with all of them – so long as they didn't have to be together for too long.

'Dad,' she'd said suddenly, soon after they'd taken off for Toronto, 'in all your adventurous life, have you ever had a feeling of certainty that you've met your soulmate?'

Her father gave her a quizzical look and rubbed his chin. 'Soulmate? I guess I could be a bit of a late developer in the soul department.' He chuckled. 'I've been a bit more of a body man myself,' he said cheerfully. 'I think Toni and I rub along pretty well – ten years together coming up, would you believe? Never would have thought I'd last that long with one woman, but soulmates? I dunno about that. I take it you think you've met such a rare creature, young lady?'

'I think I have.'

'Better put some salt on his tail then,' he said, drily.

She looked at him sideways, gauging his mood. 'He's done time,' she said.

Her father threw back his head and roared with laughter. 'Oh, Marnie-Jane,' he said. 'You never cease to astonish me. Here I am chasing rainbows with you on one of the most unlikely, crazy, romantic enterprises that's ever come my way, and you choose this moment to tell me you've taken up with a criminal!'

'I didn't say he was a *criminal*,' said Marnie indignantly, but greatly relieved that her volatile parent had reacted with such good humour. 'I said he'd been to prison.'

'What did he do then? You don't usually get put inside without some reason.'

So she told him all – or nearly all – she could about Christopher Piper: about how they had met and where, on the first stage of her search for the house that had lived in her head for twenty years; about Christopher's death by dangerous driving charge and his spell in gaol; about his past career and his intended new one and about the fact that he'd been with her when she'd found Eilean Dobhran – and that she loved him. 'Six months ago I still couldn't have imagined I'd be feeling like this about anyone,' she said, 'only I know now that this time it is quite, quite different. This is real.'

'One does tend to think that every time,' said her father.

Marnie shook her head impatiently. 'No, I'm serious, Dad. This *is* different.'

'Is that so?'

Jerry Donovan looked at his feisty, interesting first-born child, who not so long ago he'd nearly lost and who had caused him much anxiety over the years; his only daughter, for whom he'd always had a sneaking admiration even when she was an awkward, obstinate, plain little girl. He guessed she could still be awkward – not his daughter for nothing, he thought – but looking at her now he thought the plain little girl had grown into a very attractive woman and something – or more likely someone, by the sound of it – had certainly caused her to bloom since he'd last seen her a couple of months ago. That mad old contessa who'd given him such a drubbing had seen some special quality in her all those years ago that wasn't obvious to anyone else at the time – and she'd been right. 'One day I think your daughter will surprise you,' she'd said. '*I* shan't be there to see it, but *you* will. Mind you look after her. This is what I propose to do,' and she'd unfolded her weird scheme to him.

'I don't approve of dangerous drivers,' said Jerry Donovan severely, now. 'A car is a lethal weapon and should be treated accordingly. I've always taught you and your brothers how to handle them with that in mind. On the other hand . . .' He looked at Marnie's anxious face. 'On the other hand,' he said, 'I do have a weakness for a really good thriller and I've always wanted to meet a successful author.' He watched her face light up with relief and amusement. 'Maybe this soulmate and I'd better meet sometime soon,' he went on. 'See if our souls sync with each other, or whatever souls do, only it'll have to wait till I come over to London. He certainly won't be allowed over here. Did you figure that out?'

'Yes,' she said. 'He warned me,' and she sent out a grateful thought to Christopher. Lucky he'd told her.

'Now,' said her father. 'I want to give you a letter. Prepare yourself for a shock.'

He fished in his pocket and took out a square envelope of thick ivory-coloured paper addressed in blue-black ink. Marnie recognised immediately the elegant, spiky hand-writing she knew so well.

'Dad?' She looked at him uncertainly.

'Read it,' he said. 'I've kept it for you for over twenty years.'

She held it for a long moment before she tore the envelope open with shaky hands.

Dear Marnie-Jane,

You will know by now about my legacy to you, but if you get this letter, it will be the end of a treasure hunt, which you will only have embarked on if the short time we spent together meant as much to you as it did to me. You will have found Eilean Dobhran, my 'Island of the Otter'. If you want it, it can be yours. Your father will explain. He may be an unsatisfactory father, but I think he is an honourable man who will carry out my wishes. I did not want you to be burdened with the house unless you really wanted it. You still have a choice. There are no binding conditions. If you decide to become the new owner of such an old and probably crumbling place, I ask three things: use it well and love it well and enjoy it. Do you remember me teaching you to recite a poem by Christina Rossetti? Those are still my sentiments exactly. I may or may not know what your choice will be, but I hope one day you find a great love, as I did, to share your life with, and if consciousness survives, as far as I am able, I will send you my blessing and my love.

    Luciana

She couldn't speak. Tears poured down her face. She handed the letter to her father. He read it too.

'Unsatisfactory father indeed! She had a bloody nerve. What's all this about a poem then?' he asked, his own voice suspiciously husky.

She quoted:

> *'For if the darkness and corruption leave*
> *A vestige of the thoughts that once I had,*
> *Better by far you should forget and smile*
> *Than that you should remember and be sad.'*

444

They had met Ian Drummond for lunch in the Sutton Place Hotel, a tall courtly old man in his late eighties. He confirmed what the Reverend Donald McBain had told her. After the death of the Contessa's parents, despite having begged them to leave the castle to their daughter, as he felt was proper, and not to him, he had inherited Eilean Dobhran. He had never felt comfortable about it, had not welcomed the responsibility or needed the money he could get from the sale of it, and had always kept in contact with his cousin. After the death of her husband, and hearing she was ill, he'd gone over to Italy to discover what she would like him to do with the property and received the extraordinary reply that she hoped he would hold it available, for a twenty-five-year period, for Marnie-Jane Donovan, should she wish to purchase it out of the money she would inherit from the Contessa's will. He was on no account to get in touch with the young woman himself – it was to be up to her to approach him.

'It sounded a very bizarre request,' he said, 'but my cousin always led her life by her own rules. It was part of her charm and also the thing that made her so impossible to deal with.' He smiled at Marnie. 'You either did what Lucy wanted you to do or you fell out with her,' he said. 'There had been too much falling out already, and it didn't matter to me. I didn't want to live there myself and I have no children . . . and besides,' he added with a gleam, 'I'm an old romantic at heart and I rather liked this idea of a treasure hunt. I met your father and we agreed to follow Lucy's wishes – but I never really thought I'd meet you.'

'You mean you two have met before?' she asked, looking from him to her father in astonishment. They nodded. She thought they were both enjoying themselves.

Her father had gone off to his business meeting then, and left her to talk to Ian Drummond. They had sat companionably in the comfort of the hotel and drunk iced tea.

He was a charming, gentle old man and she found it easy to tell him something of her dreams and ideals for Eileen Dobhran, then listened entranced as he shared his childhood reminiscences of the castle and its pre-war lifestyle and painted a picture of Marnie's old lady as a vivid, unforgettable girl – the glamorous older cousin whom he'd always admired and been half in love with. He told her that he had no wish to profit from the house – she could have it for a nominal sum to cover any legal costs that might ensue. 'Use all the money that Lucy left you for a good purpose,' he said. She asked him if he would come on the board of the foundation she hoped to start, and he replied that so long as he still had his health and his wits he would be delighted. They agreed that the legal details could be left to him to sort out later with her father and their lawyers – and she hoped with Christopher too. She kissed him goodbye and promised to come out and see him again soon. She felt that through him she still had a living link with the person who'd made such an impact on her life.

When her father returned, there seemed no point in staying on in Toronto so they decided to fly straight back to New York that evening, which would give Marnie extra time at home. She could hardly wait to tell Christopher her news but had no intention of speaking to him while he was still with Louisa. She watched the time impatiently. She reckoned he might have left Louisa's dinner party by eleven thirty, English time, but was disappointed to find his mobile still switched off, and left a message. When, much later, there had still been no call but she got his text, every suspicion was aroused. Unavoidable? Unexpected? Who did he think she was? She battled to keep hold of her embryonic experiment in trusting . . . and felt it slipping rapidly out of her grasp.

*

She went to bed but not to sleep. She tossed and turned, tried to read a book and gave up, turned the light on and off . . . and on and off . . . and tried unsuccessfully to switch her angry imagination off too; she padded along to the kitchen and made herself a hot drink. Then she picked up the phone.

At six o'clock in the morning she was just falling at last into an exhausted sleep when her mobile rang.

'Marnie? Thank God I've got you at last.'

'You've been trying so hard, of course. Where were you?' she asked furiously.

'Didn't you get my text?'

'I certainly did, though what the hell it meant I really don't know. Your story sure better be good, Christopher.'

'It is,' he said tersely. 'Look, darling Marnie . . .'

'Don't you darling me,' she said unpleasantly. 'Answer me one question. Did you spend the night with Louisa?'

'You already know that I did.' Christopher, in London, who had held out as long as he could bear in order not to disturb her in the middle of the night, felt his own temper starting to rise. 'You rang to check up on me this morning, didn't you? And you hadn't even got the guts to speak when I answered.' He struggled to calm down. 'Look,' he said, 'it's not at all what you think. Let's not get into a confrontation. Yes, I spent the night at Louisa's house, but for a very good reason which I'll tell you all about when you come home.'

'Why should I believe you?'

'Because,' he said disastrously, 'I'm afraid you'll just have to trust me for the moment.'

'Trust?' screamed Marnie, beside herself with hurt, misery and mortification. 'Don't you dare to talk to me about trust any more! Very convenient – play on my insecurities, read me pious lectures about trusting people more, then sleep with someone else the minute my back's turned! Obviously you wondered if you'd backed the wrong one between Louisa and me. I didn't come up to expectations so you thought you'd try the other option! You two-timing bastard! I thought you were different and you know what? I even told my father I thought I'd found my soulmate!' She laughed hysterically. 'Go to hell, Christopher Piper,' she said. 'I never want to see you or hear from you again . . .'

Christopher, white with anger, slammed the telephone down.

Later, he contemplated ringing Louisa to ask if he could e-mail Marnie with an account of what had really happened, but a genuine conviction that Louisa had more than enough to cope with without being embroiled in lovers' quarrels – particularly this one – plus a less worthy sense of fury at Marnie for not giving him the benefit of her very obvious and unflattering doubt, stopped him from doing so.

On the other side of the Atlantic, Marnie seethed and bubbled with resentment, not only with Christopher, which was so painful she felt physically ill, but also against Louisa – Louisa, to whom she had offered her friendship; Louisa who knew very well the depth of her feelings for Christopher but to whom, in Marnie's view in her present wrought-up state, cock-teasing was just a light-hearted parlour game.

Her father had left early on another business trip without seeing her, though he would be back the next morning. Her stepmother Toni watched her uneasily, made excuses to check on her, and wondered if she should alert her husband to the fact that Marnie seemed alarmingly disturbed about something.

It was twenty-four hours before Marnie rang Louisa – at which point she felt that if she didn't give vent to her sense of outrage and betrayal she thought she might, literally, burst.

Louisa was sitting in the garden with Adam. The blackbird still sang from the roof of the next-door house; the laburnum cascaded with yellow streamers as it always did at the beginning of June; the background hum of London's rush hour traffic sounded the same as ever, but for Louisa everything had changed. When her mobile rang, she answered it automatically.

'Oh, hi there, Marnie,' she said, and thought with surprise that Christopher must have told Marnie about her even though she'd asked him not to mention it to anyone, but that it really didn't matter. What difference could it make now? Everyone would know soon enough. 'Christopher told you then?' she queried.

'No,' said Marnie scornfully. 'He didn't need to. But I know all the same. How could you, Louisa?'

'What are you talking about?'

'Don't give me that! You know very well. How *could* you, Louisa? How could either of you do that to me? You *knew* how I would feel. I know Christopher spent the night with you.'

There was a drumming in Louisa's ears. She heard her own voice speaking as though from very far away, as though she were under water. She felt very tired.

'Yes,' she said. 'He did. He spent the night here – and do you know why he stayed? He stayed to look after me . . . not to go to bed with me. I might have liked to sleep with Christopher, but there was never any question of it for him. He stayed to hold my hand – if you like to put it like that – because I'd just been told my cancer has returned and I'm dying, that's why. Christopher slept in the spare room.'

'Oh my God,' said Marnie, some three thousand miles away. 'Oh my God.' An image of a dead owl came into her

449

head. She was appalled. 'Oh, Louisa . . . I don't know what to say . . .' But for the second time in twenty-four hours the line went dead because someone had hung up on her.

Marnie went to find her stepmother, looking quite distraught. 'Toni – please help me. I've messed up big time. I've done something awful and made a terrible, terrible mistake about someone – about two people actually. I have to get back to London as soon as it's humanly possible. Can you help me get on a flight?'

'Sure,' said Toni, breathing a huge sigh of relief that whatever black misery had been bearing down on Marnie, it had at least been acknowledged so that some action could be taken. 'I'll get straight on to your dad's office,' she said. 'No worries.'

Later Marnie had poured out the story to her stepmother, and wept tears of real anguish for Louisa and bitterly remorseful ones over her own misplaced mistrust of Christopher.

'Is he worth it, this superman?' asked Toni, remembering the last, disastrous man in Marnie's life.

'Oh yes – he's worth it,' said Marnie, 'and I'm sure going to have to try to make amends for my awful, habitual jealousy. It may be too late.'

Marnie's text to Christopher consisted of just two words. *Coming home*, it read.

Christopher heard the key turn in the lock at two o'clock in the morning. He'd had no idea when to expect her, but he was standing in the hallway when she came through the front door.

'I've come back – if you'll still have me,' said Marnie.

Christopher opened his arms and she walked straight into them.

Chapter Thirty-three

Isobel and Giles were the first to arrive at Carafini, the restaurant in Lower Sloane Street that was a favourite haunt of theirs when they stayed at the Sloane Club opposite.

The Grants had come down to London for a meeting with lawyers to discuss legal arrangements for Rory's future, and it had been Giles's idea to have a mini reunion with some of the participants from the writing week in May. They always tried to have a week away from Glendrochatt after the season had finished and before they settled in to the Scottish winter and the psychological adjustment of having their house to themselves again. Giles had already planned most of the events for the following year and October was a month to which they both looked forward with pleasure and relief.

The day before, Isobel, needled by the sartorial humiliation she had endured at the hands of Lorna on her last visit to London, had treated herself to a London haircut and paid a satisfying but expensive visit to Pantalon Chameleon in Duke of York Square where she had bought a pair of purple suede trousers, this purchase then necessitating another little trip to Brora, further down the King's Road, to find a trendy cardigan to go with them. Giles had been very enthusiastic about the result of this spending spree and Isobel was feeling uncharacteristically groomed and chic.

'Who do you think will arrive next?' asked Giles. 'The Newly-Weds or the Still Walking Outs?'

'Well, here comes someone,' said Isobel, peering out on to the street through the big plate glass windows. 'Oh, good – it's Christopher and Marnie. Oh, Giles, isn't it lovely to see them like this – laughing together and looking so happy? Wonderful to think they met under our roof. Cupid was busy at Glendrochatt this summer, wasn't he?'

A good deal of noisy greeting and much hugging and kissing ensued as Christopher and Marnie came in through the door.

'Oh, wow, Isobel! Don't you just look a million dollars,' said Marnie, standing back and looking at her admiringly.

'Well don't sound so surprised – it's my new cool image. You don't look too bad yourself. Being the chatelaine of a castle must suit you,' said Isobel, laughing.

'And here comes the bride,' announced Giles. 'Morwenna . . . John . . . great to see you both. How are you? But I don't need to ask!'

It had been a cause for general rejoicing when the marriage had taken place in early September ('quietly' so the announcement in the paper read) between Lt. Col. John Smithson and Mrs Morwenna Gilbert. The ceremony had taken place in a little church in Cornwall, within sound of the sea, near the village where Morwenna lived, and all those dining at Carafini had been present. Giles had given the bride away and toothy Joyce, resplendent in shimmering turquoise eye-shadow and a matching hat, had been matron of honour. Amy had provided the music, accompanying the small congregation as they sang the hymns chosen by the Colonel, 'I Vow to Thee My Country' and 'Praise My Soul the King of Heaven', and later playing an arrangement of 'Jesu, Joy of Man's Desiring' at Morwenna's special request. The newly married couple had walked out of the church to the rather unlikely Strathspey strains of 'The Glasgow Highlanders' – not something usually played at Cornish weddings, but chosen to honour the country where they had met. The bride and groom had radiated happiness and the honeymoon had been spent on a gardening tour round the west of Scotland.

There was much catching up to do and everyone talked at once.

'Guess what today is?' announced Marnie. 'It's the last day of Christopher's parole. Isn't that great? We're going to be able to stay up at Eilean Dobhran together for the rest of the autumn now the renovations are due to start. He's a free man at last!'

Everyone congratulated him.

'We're hugely looking forward to inspecting Eilean Dobhran for ourselves when we come up for the first meeting of the Trust in November,' said Giles. He and Isobel had been touched to be invited to join Christopher and Marnie, Marnie's father, old Ian Drummond and Lord Dunbarnock as founder members of the new charitable foundation, to be called the Luciana Trust. In answer to her tentative suggestion to Neil Dunbarnock asking if he might consider joining them too, Marnie had received a charming letter from him saying he would be delighted to do all he could to help. 'You couldn't have thought of anyone better,' Giles had told her. 'Neil may be eccentric but he's very shrewd and extremely generous – a huge asset on any committee. Glendrochatt owes a lot of its success to him.'

'We've decided to ask Jeff and Cherry Barton if they can put us all up at Finterie Lodge,' said Christopher. 'Sleeping in the castle in its present state might not be everyone's idea of a jolly weekend! Marnie thought it might make the newly appointed trustees resign very quickly.'

Everyone knew that the forthcoming publication of

Christopher's book *Inside Knowledge* was causing considerable interest in literary circles as there had been a good deal of media hype about it – entirely due, Christopher modestly claimed, to his criminal record – the publicist's gift – rather than his writing talents; it had already earned its author a two-book deal with a well-known publishing firm.

'How's the new book coming along, Christopher?' enquired John. 'I've always heard that second novels are much harder to write than first ones. Is that true?'

Christopher groaned. 'Bloody terrifying!' he said. 'That's what second novels are.'

'I take it you're not using the same setting for this one?' Isobel teased.

'No chance! This one's set in the world of high finance – still lots of scope for dirty dealings, though.' Christopher grinned.

'What's the latest on Louisa?' asked Morwenna. 'John and I were so touched to get a card from her the other day.'

'I'm hoping to visit her tomorrow if she's up to it,' said Isobel. 'How did you find her this morning, Marnie?'

'Fantastic as usual – unbelievably brave.' But Marnie shook her head sadly. 'She's been allowed home from hospital for a few days, though she has to go back soon because they're going to try out some new drug on her. Did you hear about the baby owl Adam's found for her? Wasn't that brilliant of him? It's given her a tremendous boost – she's absolutely mad about it.' Marnie laughed. 'I don't think the hospital were quite so thrilled when they discovered Adam had smuggled it in to visit her. Don't think they'd ever had an owl in the oncology unit before. It's the cutest thing – absolutely hideous, but dead cute.'

'Adam's opening a bottle of champagne with her tonight, and they're going to drink to Glendrochatt and all of us here because Louisa's so disappointed they can't be with us too.'

There was a lot more news to exchange. Giles and Isobel had just heard that Amy had been awarded a major music scholarship and were also celebrating the end of a happy summer during which Edward and Rory had cemented their bond with each other; Rory's growth in confidence since Isobel had returned home with a troubled, anxious little boy a few months earlier had been a joy to witness. He had ceased to be 'difficult', Isobel told them, and was now often delightfully naughty instead: not at all the same thing, as she proudly pointed out. Morwenna's first 'new-look' gardening column had been voted a great success and she and John promised to come up to Eilean Dobhran so that she could advise Marnie about the garden.

They unanimously agreed to try to make the reunion dinner an annual event and keep alive the close friendship they had formed in such a short space of time. Several toasts to the future were drunk, including a special one to Giles and Isobel, because, as Christopher, who proposed it, said, without that week at Glendrochatt, so many marvellous things would not have happened, so many secret hopes would not have been realised – and his eyes met Marnie's across the table. There was a spontaneous murmur of approval, but when he proposed a toast to 'absent friends' there was a long silence afterwards, because nobody could trust themselves to speak.

Christopher and Marnie drove back to the flat in her little blue Audi.

'Do you remember what you called me this evening?' asked Christopher.

'Not particularly – what did I call you?'

'You said I was a free man at last,' said Christopher. 'So I feel free to ask you the question I've been longing to ask you for months, but swore I wouldn't till today.' He looked down at her with a laugh in his eyes. 'I think I've lost my taste for being completely free,' he said. 'Will you marry me, Marnie?'

'Yes,' she said, giving him a look of dazzling happiness. 'Yes . . . oh yes!'